DEPEND ON ME

A BOOK BY AMARIS I. MANNING

Also by Amaris I. Manning

We, pEOPLE

THIS STORY contains content that may be sensitive to some readers, including, but not limited to, depictions of and references to suicide, graphic violence, racism, prejudice, substance abuse, sexual harassment, sexual assault, eating disorder, and PTSD. Please be mindful of these and other possible triggers, and seek assistance if needed before, during, and after reading.

February.

Week 2, Monday.

Today, I woke up—tired. I thought about going back to sleep, maybe ditching, say I'm sick or something, but my folks wouldn't buy it. So the universe wins. Guess I have to endure another day of school. I tell myself that it won't be all too bad. I mean, it's only school.

Before I know it, I'll be outta here. Can't say I'm sad at the thought...because I'm not. Thank friggin' God, I'll be outta here, away from this shithole. But at the same time, I know things ain't gonna get any easier the more I sit here, complaining. The only reason I'm writing this all out anyway is that Counselor Malik thought it'd be a good idea than holding stuff in, which I don't. I'm as open and honest as they come, you know? I'll think of something else to say later, maybe. I gotta go.-- D.G.

I let out a sharp breath as the warm air blasting through the vents of my car hits my face. I rest my head back against the headrest, and my lashes flutter shut. I can hardly find the energy to unbuckle my seat and bolt inside the building since I know what to expect. It's been this way for weeks now. I go in, people stare, teachers ask how I'm doing—it's routine at this point.

This morning I practically gripped onto my bed, not wanting to get up since I knew what would happen once I arrived at school. When my phone buzzed on my dresser, I turned off the alarm, but it was only six-something in the morning. It usually takes me about twenty to thirty minutes to get dressed and head off to school. Traffic is never an issue in the morning when I leave, so I wouldn't be late regardless.

But this morning, I wanted to miss out. Even though my parents bolted into my room, screaming for me to get out the bed this morning, I didn't want to listen.

I can still hear my mom's voice as I sit in the car. *"Donald! You have to get to school! If you don't, Lord knows you may not walk at graduation!"*

I should've felt sick at the thought of not being able to walk at graduation, but I didn't. Instead, I just remained in bed, sheets pulled over my body while feigning sleep to hide the fact that I was purposely trying to shut my folks out.

Yet, here I am.

In my car, parked in the parking lot outside the ten-story building, my eyes now glued to the time on my wristwatch that I was bold enough to wear. I remember the day my dad had given me the watch. It was last year for my seventeenth birthday. I know dad focused on my gift while mom focused on Morris-Lina's gift. Dad didn't have to say that the watch was from him alone. I could just tell.

I mean, it doesn't matter. I still liked it. I just never really wore it. I remember the first time I wore it, abuelo had died. We had to attend his funeral on a rainy Thursday afternoon, and Morris-Lina was a mess. A crying mess. Mom had packed a box of tissues in her bag for when Morris-Lina had to cry. I was sitting next to dad the entire time as he held a stoic gaze during the whole service. I looked down at one point to glance at the silver watch, and I grazed the dial with my thumb.

Dad had nudged me, telling me to pay attention to the service rather than checking the time. But I wasn't checking the time. I was just suppressing the thought of abuelo being gone for good. I had to look somewhere else. But dad wouldn't have believed me at the time. Even if I tried to tell him, he probably wouldn't have listened to me since he spoke so coldly, and his scowl made me feel uneasy. His cold gaze always set me on edge, ever since I was little.

I wouldn't cry from it, but I'd feel less human. Less of a son, at least. He never gave Morris-Lina that scowl. If anything, he'd always give her the kind of gaze that made her feel safe and at home. The corners of dad's lips would always curl up whenever he'd look at her, and he'd press a kiss to her head, making her feel like his child while reassuring her of his love.

Then there was me.

It's a pretty funny thing, though, now that I think about it.

Mom will often do the same thing to me that dad does to Morris-Lina, but not as much. Maybe once in a while, but not every time she sees me. Perhaps because she felt sorry for me since dad would invest so much into Morris-Lina, but I didn't blame him.

I didn't mind.

I'd rather him be honest and show me how he really feels rather than just feign his liking for me.

I jump up when I hear a sudden tap against the glass window of my car. I look over, blinking to adjust my vision as the bright, gray sunlight gleams through the window. I squint and start to recognize the tall figure standing outside of my car. His dark brown hair is tousled, forest green eyes, fair skin, a puffy gray jacket over his maroon uniform shirt neatly tucked into his fitted brown slacks, which were secured around his waist by his brown belt.

Just Christopher. I softly breathe.

I roll down the window with the knob on the side of the front door, and I can feel Christopher's warm breath as he leans in to meet my eye level.

"We got fifteen minutes 'til homeroom, mate," he says through his thick Irish accent. "You in a daze or what?" His accent was always thick—some people could hardly understand him. But it's not as strong compared to when we first met during freshman year. Back then, it'd take me a few seconds to know what he was saying.

I look down at the watch latched around my wrist to check the time. *7:45 AM.*

I sigh, throwing my head back against the headrest.

I thought about rolling into school around the time homeroom officially started, which was eight in the morning, but Christopher was standing outside of my car. He keeps knocking on my car door, wanting me to get out so I can head inside with him. Not because he didn't want to go in alone—probably because he doesn't want *me* to go in alone.

I guess the thought of taking on another day of hearing people remind me that the school now only has one Gonzalez kid to deal with doesn't settle with him as much as it does with me. I mean, I'm not settled with it. But I'm numb to it at this point, I guess.

I remember the day I returned to school after everything that happened. Mom told Principal Vickins that I'd be out of school for a few days because of the funeral arrangements. Principal Vickins was understanding about everything, which didn't surprise me at all since Principal Vickins knew us very well and knew the severity of the situation.

Of course, it was severe—my sister died.

Duh.

You can't penalize someone because someone died, right?

Even if you could, Principal Vickins wouldn't. She wasn't that type of lady. But of course, I had to come back to school. My time had run out, and I had to catch up on things, or I wouldn't be able to walk for graduation. I'd graduate, nonetheless, but being able to walk down the aisle and receive my diploma in hand was necessary— at least to my parents.

Christopher taps against my car door once more, and finally, I lunge forward and press my palm into the front of the steering wheel, sounding off the horn. Christopher flinches, turning away and tucking his head down with his arms covering his ears to shield the unbearable sound.

I remove my hands from the wheel, and everything is silent. I paid no attention to the few random students walking by, eyeing us as I remained in the car while Christopher stood up straight. He glares at me, folding his arms over his chest.

"Was that necessary?" he hisses, nostrils flaring.

I snort. "Was you knocking on my car necessary?" I roll up the window, not giving him a chance to speak up, even though his mouth was already open to say something.

I reach for my bookbag and slip my arm through one of the straps before turning off the car engine. As I get out of the car, Christopher shuffles his way over to me, barely giving me space. I can feel the warmth from his body as he stands close to me, and I let out a sharp breath as I shut the car door.

Christopher shoves his hands in the pockets of his jacket as we start walking up to the school's front doors. "Well, aren't you a sight for sore eyes, eh?"

I snort. "Quit being funny." I bump my arm into him, nudging him a little, and he rocks to the side, chuckling. I sigh. "But seriously, you didn't have to wait for me, Chris. I got this."

He knows that, I think.

"I know that," I hear him mutter. I notice his eyes trail downward as his sturdy boots crunch against the chunks of snow on the sidewalk. "I just don't think you should have to deal with this alone, you know?"

A strange feeling tugs in my throat, and I bury my face into the collar of my black jacket. The bushy faux fur along the collar tickles against my cheeks as I pull the collar in closer to my face. I think about possibly changing the subject since I know Christopher has a habit of bringing this up.

He's no better than Counselor Malik.

Constantly having to find some way to bring up Morris-Lina—what happened to her. I know it's something people often talk about. It's normal. Death, I mean.

Not so normal when you find your sister lying in bed with leftover pills in the palm of her hand, even though she had already swallowed more than the doctor prescribed.

In my head, I can still see her eyes shut, her lips slightly parted as if she was still breathing somewhat. She was so still when I lowered the blanket from over her face. Mom had told me to get her up since it was almost time for dinner. Morris-Lina always struggled with sleeping, so I figured it wouldn't have been so hard to get her up. But when I knocked on the door, she was still tuckered out. I went to lift the blanket off her face, and that's when I noticed the pills in her hand. I must've rocked her about three times before going downstairs to tell mom that Morris-Lina wasn't waking up. I told mom about the pills. Dad soon came home. Mom was standing in the living room, holding her head while letting out hysterical cries. Dad was holding her as a few police officers walked in to speak with them.

I remember the room growing smaller—the house shrinking. My stomach was churning. I counted backward from twenty while gripping onto my wrist. I could feel the flesh sinking into my nails as I was getting to ten.....everything spinning.....and spinning...

"DON!"

The ice swipes under the heel of my boot, and I nearly lose my balance. My hand clutches tightly to Christopher's shoulder as his arm loops around me to hold me up.

"Shit!" I pant, my heart thumping loudly in my ear.

Christopher practically shoves me forward while keeping his hand on my back to make sure I can stand upright.

"You good?" Christopher asks, throwing his arm around my shoulder.

I clear my throat. "Yeah," I chuckle. "Just thinking about stuff."

"Mmm." Christopher sniffs. "Well, as I said, I know how people get with you, so just know that—"

"*—you're here for me.* Yeah, I know." I roll my eyes, unhooking his arm from around me. He stops in his tracks as I step in front of him and turn on my heels so I can stare him in the eyes. The way Christopher arches his eyebrow and lowers his eyelids makes it seem like no matter what I say, it's just going in one ear and out the other.

I snort, shaking my head. "Do you have to look so disgusted?"

"Do you have to sound like such an ass?" But the way he said, "*ass*" sounded more like "*arse.*"

I sigh. "You, Pete, Car, Ben, and Meagan. You're all such softies."

He lightly jabs me in the hip. "Be grateful you have the people you have, eh?" He stuffs his hands back into his jacket pockets. "Such a donkey."

I snap my head back up and glare at him. Christopher cocks his head to the side, arching his eyebrow.

The more I gaze into his eyes, the more I feel my stomach twisting in knots. As much as I want to flip him off for thinking that I'm acting like a douche, I don't. Not because I'm scared of him—Lord knows how often I've flipped Christopher off since we've met.

Probably more times than I can count on my fingers and toes combined. I just hate the thought of me finally nodding and telling him he's right and has a good point.

I'm not saying that he doesn't. He does, but if I told him that he was right, I wouldn't hear the end of it. I already know that once I enter the school building, I'll listen to all sorts of things.

I see the way the other students lock their eyes on me as I walk down the halls, getting to my classes. I can hear their comments, even though they try to whisper and mutter, so I don't hear anything, but somehow, I can still make out what they are saying.

One less Gonzalez we have to deal with, they say.

Such a shame, they'll say.

Sucks to be him.

Wonder if he knew she'd go out like this.

You hear about Donald Gonzalez? His sister? That wacko?

Never anything new. Honestly, some of the things said I've heard since freshman year before everything that happened had happened. Morris-Lina would listen to it for herself too. Always. They'd never cut her a break.

Christopher just wanted to take some of that off of me, I guess. Constantly reminding me that he's going to be by my side through it all, even though I already know he means every word he says. He's such a golden boy. He doesn't even realize how much I know him by now. How much I do trust him. How much I know that he's a real one.

I feel my lips become dry, and I press them tightly together while burying my face into the collar of my jacket again. Christopher reaches into his pocket to retrieve his phone. His eyebrow arches when he glances at the screen.

I hear him mumble Peter's name before pressing down on the keys of his phone. I check my watch. *7:50 AM.*

Usually, Peter is waiting for us right by the front door, but he's all of a sudden a no-show. Peter is the kind of guy who rolls out of bed fifteen minutes after his alarm goes off but can get to places five minutes before he has to be there. So for him to not be at school by now was a little strange since he's usually waiting for Christopher and me by the front door. He'll always sit outside on the top step of the front entrance, either eating a breakfast wrap his aunt made him before she'd head off to work or playing some game on his phone.

Christopher huffs as he dials Peter's phone number and presses the button to call him. He put the phone on speaker, so I could hear the call.

I tell Christopher that Peter is probably on his way, but Christopher shrugs.

"It's almost eight," Christopher sighs. "He should've texted if he wasn't going to show."

"Please," I huff. "Peter ain't missing school. His aunt will kill him before that happens."

Christopher just shrugs, letting out a low whistle.

It was true. Peter's aunt was strict when it came to him staying in school. The only thing that would keep him from school is if he had one foot in the grave and the other on a banana peel. Stuffy nose? She'd give him some tissues. Fever? Gave him some cold medicine and sent him to school with a thermos of chicken noodle soup.

No excuses.

It's not like Peter could fight his aunt anyway. She was technically his legal guardian after his mother was deemed *"unfit"* to raise him, but Peter still spent time with his mom. As long as his aunt allowed him to.

Like the other day, Peter was able to spend time with his mom after school. Christopher also went over since he promised to help them pull weeds from Peter's mom's garden, but that's all. They probably stayed a little longer after, catching up on things since it's been so long since Christopher's been over Peter's mom's place. I haven't been over her place either since Peter's aunt gained custody of him.

It's been five, maybe six years now.

Anyway, after four rings on the phone, Peter answers but it's not his voice. Instead, Christopher and I hear rustling as if the phone is being tossed around. Then there is panting. I inch closer to Christopher as he holds the phone, pulling it up to his ear, trying to make out what is going on.

"Pete?" Christopher questions, practically raising his voice. "Peter?!"

The rustling on Peter's end of the phone call seems to get louder until we finally hear Peter screech out, "GUYS!"

Christopher flinches, the phone nearly slipping from his grasp before he clutches it into his chest. I feel myself jump from the thought of Christopher's phone hitting the ground, and I let out a relieved sigh when he catches it.

Christopher holds the phone out for us both to hear Peter on the other end. "Where are you, Pete? We gotta—!"

Peter grunts and sounds as though he is nearly out of breath. "I'm by...way!"

Either the connection sucks, or something is up.

We then hear a grunt followed by shouting. But the shouting isn't from Peter. Christopher's grip tightens on the phone, and he snaps. "Where are you, Peter?!"

Panting, Peter gasps, "By...market...spring...GAH!"

His voice is washed over by rustling and a loud thud. The call drops.

Christopher furrows his brows, and then I realize what Peter was trying to say.

"He's by Salad Market on Spring Garden!"

Christopher nods, and without a second thought, we dart up the street. We didn't care about the ice, snow, or how much time we had until the bell sounded, signaling the start of homeroom. Christopher and I already knew that we were screwed initially, but it wasn't like we had a choice.

I mean, yes, we did—but we'd be horrible if we chose wrong.

Cars come to a sharp halt and honk at us as we run across the street against the light. Christopher calls out to the drivers, telling them he is sorry, but I tug on his arm, pulling him forward.

"You wanna give them the motive to run us over anyway?!"

Christopher huffs, "At least I won't be known as a douche!"

I snort, and we run up the block, soon reaching the corner to Salad Market. Immediately, I hear a loud mixture of voices saying all types of things, and a yelp pipes up amid the voices.

It's coming from the alleyway outside of Salad Market. There aren't any windows or doors on the side of the building. So it's not like anyone inside would've noticed what was going on unless they walked outside. But no one was going to do that. Everyone was all about minding their own business and keeping to themselves. A random person walking by wouldn't have dared to step in and stop the three guys pounding on the boy on the ground. The boy, being Peter, is curled up in a ball, blocking their fists, hitting on him while keeping his arms over his head.

I waste no time yanking one of the guys off of Peter. I snuck up behind the guy. He is taller with broad shoulders, but I manage to grip him by the collar. In the spur of the moment, my fist crashes into the guy's face, busting his lip. The guy stumbles back, holding his face while groaning.

I notice the logo on his polo shirt. It's a mascot of an eagle with the letters **LFHS**, stitched in gold underneath the eagle.

Friggin' Lincoln Freedman High School!

I realize that all three of the guys are wearing polos with the Lincoln Freedman logo.

One of the guys turns back and spots me after I knocked his buddy on the ground, but Christopher lunges at him before the other guy has a chance to do anything to me. The guy Christopher takes on is lanky, but they're both around the same height. That left one guy for Peter to take on himself. A stocky-built douche with buzzcut hair.

I turn around, ready to take on the tall guy again, when I'm suddenly up against the wall. His fist plunges into my stomach. He roughly throws me on the ground, and I feel a heavy kick thrust against my hip. Then another. And another.

I am ready for the next one this time, and I get a hold of his ankle as he lifts his leg, ready to plunge his foot into my chest once I roll on my back. But I don't let him. I manage to get him. He hops on one foot as I hold onto his ankle.

Using my strength, I yank the guy's ankle to the side, making him roughly collapse on his back against the concrete. My bones are practically shaking as I push myself up on my feet, and I find myself leaning against the brick wall for support as I stand up. I dot my eyes over to Christopher as he gives the lanky one a good, hard punch to the mouth, causing blood spray from the slender guy's mouth. Then I see Peter, finally standing tall over the stocky-built one, kicking the guy against the wall. Peter presses his hands against the wall for balance, making sure he gets the guy good.

I notice the guy I'm dealing with starting to roll over to stand up.

Nah, you like ganging up and fighting unfairly. See how you like it.

I grab the guy's shoulder and turn him over to face me. My fist plunges into his face, and I hear the *CRACK* loud and clear. I grip the back of the guy's jacket and throw him into the street, but he doesn't roll far into the middle of the road. He is almost rocking off the sidewalk, holding his face while taking quick glimpses at the blood in his palm as blood drips from his nose.

The guy stands up while covering his nose.

"You broke my nose, you motherfu—!"

He doesn't get the chance to finish that sentence when Christopher tosses the lanky dude into the prick I just decked, knocking them both down onto their backs. The two of them rock against the ground while lying down on the pavement, holding their backs.

I hear a loud grunt from behind. I turn around to see Peter up against the wall as the stocky-built guy plunges his meaty fist into Peter's gut.

I rush over to pry the guy away from Peter. I grip onto the collar of the asshole's jacket to hold him in place before forcefully bashing the top of my head into his face. He lets out a painful groan and loses his balance. His feet scrape against the ground as I haul him over to the other two douchebags. They finally stand up, using each other as a crutch to stand.

They immediately reach for the stocky-built one as I hurl him into them. Without a second thought, all of them take off, running into the street, dodging the cars that drive up the road. They aren't even halfway down the end of the block when Peter spontaneously calls out, "Suck on that, turkeys!"

Christopher reaches over and smacks his hand upside Peter's head, making Peter wince.

"Zip it," Christopher scolds. His voice is stern, and Peter's eyes slowly drift downward. Without thinking, Christopher starts going off, accusing Peter of causing the ruckus. "How'd you even get mixed up with them? You know to get off at Spring Garden when taking the train."

I butt in. "Cut it out, Chris! It ain't his fault. You know them Freedman douchebags started it. They've been harassing us since the start of the school year." And I am right.

I remember back in September when Principal Vickins arranged an assembly to inform all of us about an incident between a couple of students from our school and a few students from Lincoln Freedman. Apparently, someone from Lincoln Freedman posted a comment on social media about someone from our school, and then the student from our school responded to their comment, and then shit hit the fan. Some students from our school have been jumped by Lincoln Freedman, a high school in South Philly.

Meanwhile, our high school, Gabe-Day, is in Center City, far from Lincoln Freedman. So for students from Lincoln Freedman to bump into students from our school, they would have to catch the train Northbound to jump us, which is excessive.

Peter, for instance, catches the Southbound train at Fairmount Station and gets off at Spring Garden to get to school. The odds of him running into students from Lincoln Freedman would've been slim to none since Lincoln Freedman is nowhere near our school. But a couple of douchebags from Lincoln Freedman thought it'd be a good idea to take a trip to Center City and thought Peter would've been the perfect victim.

Luckily, Peter could answer Christopher's phone call just in the nick of time, and Christopher and I were able to intervene before further harm could come to Peter.

Christopher finally realizes that I have a good point—which I did—and he rests his hand on the back of Peter's neck. He sighs.

Peter slowly lifts his gaze to glance at Christopher, even though he is slightly unsure of himself. Christopher is the tallest out of all of us, standing at 6-foot-something. Peter comes in second, being 5'11", and then there is me. Five feet and seven inches. It is never fair when any of us have to look each other in the eyes.

Christopher feels too tall while Peter and I feel too short. But the thing about Christopher is that he never looks down on us. He will never try to make it seem like a big deal that he is a bit taller. Probably because it makes him uncomfortable himself.

I put my hand to Peter's back, patting him lightly.

Christopher finally goes, "They weren't too rough on you, were they?"

Peter shakes his head, his jaw tightening.

"Well," I huff out, "that's all that matters, right?" I sling my arm around Peter, pulling him in close to me. "Bet they'll think twice before messing with any one of us again, huh?"

Peter snorts, nudging me lightly on my side with his elbow. "Oooh, my hero." He dramatically fans himself like a damsel in distress. When I roll my eyes, he snickers.

I look back at Christopher, and an irritated look washes over his face. He suggests that we get going since we are now fifteen minutes late for homeroom. Christopher tries not to sound agitated at the thought of rolling into school fifteen minutes late, but the aggression is still present in his voice. On the way back, I could tell Peter sort of felt responsible, even though nothing was his fault.

There's a moment where we finally reach the building, and just before we are about to enter the school, Peter reaches out to touch Christopher's shoulder, but then he draws his hand back and closes his lips.

He probably had the urge to apologize, even though he shouldn't have been sorry.

I sigh.

After we scan our ID tags to check-in to school, Christopher practically drags Peter and me up the steps while muttering under his breath. He let Peter go when we reached the second floor so Peter could get to his homeroom class. I watch Peter bolt down the hall until he comes to his homeroom class.

"Don!"

I whip my head around and see Christopher standing at the top of the steps to get to the next floor. He cocks his head to the side, motioning for me to get a move on.

I roll my eyes, sprinting up the steps to meet him at the double doors on the third floor. Christopher scratches his eyebrow as he swings open one of the doors, and I catch it before the door swings into the wall, alerting the whole floor that we had just arrived.

I can tell by the way Christopher tightens his grip on the straps of his book bag that he is over everything. He always takes attendance very seriously, mainly because his dad is always on his case about every little thing he does. I can wholeheartedly admit that I do understand, considering that my parents are no different.

Although, Christopher's dad does all he can to keep Christopher out of the house. My parents will sometimes be a little less harsh about attendance. It's always been that way. Probably because I always had the grades to back things up whenever I had to. I would never come home with anything lower than a 95 or a 90.

Neither would Morris-Lina. Sometimes.

The one time she came home with 67, mom lost it on her. Sophomore year. I remember everything clearly.

....

I ran my fingers one last time through my hair before cutting off the shower water. I could feel goosebumps forming on my arms as a cool breeze entered through the bathroom since I had the door propped open to let out some of the steam from the shower. Mom would always fuss about the mirrors being fogged up since everyone in this house loves to take hot showers like it's nothing. So, we'd leave the bathroom door propped open a bit to let some of the steam out. But once we're finished, we close the door completely to cover ourselves, which I did.

I reached from behind the curtain to shut the door before getting out of the shower, and I patted myself dry with my towel. I then heard a loud voice coming from the other side of the door, calling out, "Morris-Lina! Get back here!"

I groaned as I stood up straight and wrapped the towel around my waist.

I settled my hands on the edge of the sink and let out a sigh, looking down at the sink.

I could only imagine what possible things could've set my mom off with Morris-Lina this time. It's becoming a daily routine with them. Mom calls out Morris-Lina for something, no matter how small, Morris-Lina fusses back at mom, and then dad has to come in to separate them.

This time, dad wasn't home. He had to work the late shift, so he probably wouldn't get back home until around dinner time. Maybe a bit later. I know he had to get up earlier than the chickens this morning to get to work.

I sighed, looking up at my reflection.

"You're not even giving me a chance to talk!" This was Morris-Lina. "You never give me a chance to talk! You always think you're right!"

I dared myself to open the bathroom door, but I didn't dare to step out of the bathroom. At least, not yet.

The two of them were standing right outside of Morris-Lina's bedroom, going back and forth.

"It's just one test! It's not a big deal!"

Mom scoffed. "It is a big deal!" Mom held up the paper, pointing to the corner of the page. "Sixty-seven?! What happened to your tutoring sessions, huh?!"

"I go to tutoring, but it was just one little fluke, is all."

"It's not a fluke! Stop talking like that!"

"Like what?"

"Like this doesn't mean anything!"

"Mom, I never said that." Morris-Lina's tone suddenly changed in her voice, as if she was suddenly regretting everything in her life at the moment.

She's right. She never said that it didn't mean anything, mom.

I felt my chest suddenly tighten, and the side of my head started to ache. I wanted to wham my head into the wall, possibly end the bickering altogether since I would've caused a more enormous ruckus. I'm pretty sure I'd be doing the neighbors a favor since they're much older and don't have lives. They don't go anywhere and probably have to listen to the effed-up show that is the funhouse of the Gonzalez residence.

The center for neighborhood entertainment.

I sighed.

Suddenly, I heard mom go, "If Donald can get a hundred on his test, why don't you?"

Knots twisted in my stomach, and I felt my throat become dry.

I did get a hundred on my test for biology. Morris-Lina had to take an anatomy class, which is very different. If Morris-Lina had biology, she probably would've gotten a 90 or at least an 85. She's never really taken a liking for science, to be honest. Her thing was history and geography.

I knew that. Mom and dad, sure enough, knew it too.

So why would mom have to make a blunt statement like that?

Then I heard Morris-Lina, "Don't know what to tell you. I'll do better next time."

Mom went, "You better. Until then, you're grounded." Then I heard heavy footsteps stomp their way down the steps.

I could hardly catch my breath. I put my hand to my chest, taking slow breaths until I felt my heart rate finally go down back to normal. I wanted to swing open the door and rush out, maybe tell mom that she was just overreacting. But who was I to determine whether or not my parent was unreasonable? All they would think is that I don't know any better, especially mom.

She'd probably tell me to just go in my room before she grounded me next or something.

What good would that do?

I cleared my throat and peeked my head through the door. I could see Morris-Lina, still standing outside of her bedroom while eyeing her test in her hand.

Her cheeks looked flushed, and her arms were practically shaking. My heart sank.

I started to step out of the bathroom, and I opened my mouth, wanting to tell her that everything was okay, but I froze. I suddenly lost the ability to even think of words altogether.

Instead, I watched her turn away and bolt into her room, slamming the door shut behind her.

· · · · · · · · · ·

I lift my head when I notice Christopher snapping his fingers in front of my face. I flinch back and immediately smack Christopher's hand away from my face, earning a chuckle from him.

"You are quite dazed today, aren't ya, Don?"

I realize that he was probably trying to talk to me just now, and I didn't pick up on a word he had said. Or perhaps I just think he was, and he didn't say anything at all. But then again, why else would he have snapped his fingers in my face?

Clearly, to get my attention about something.

I clear my throat, adjusting the collar of my jacket. "You're a bit something today, aren't ya, *Chrissy?*"

Christopher immediately looks at me as if I am his biggest foe on the planet, and his cheeks flush while his jaw tightens. His nostrils suddenly flare, and I notice that he clenches his fists as they remain by his side.

For a second, I thought he was going to hit me for calling him that again. *Chrissy.* At first, calling him *"Chrissy"* was harmless, totally fine. But then, by the end of our freshman year, calling Christopher *"Chrissy"* became a death sentence since people would go around mocking him.

Not any of us—myself and Nathan (at the time). Not even Peter, even though it was before we knew him.

But one tall, lanky guy who was a senior had whistled at Christopher, calling him *"Chrissy,"* and then tossed Christopher a bra. He even said to Christopher, "Fits the name better, doesn't it?"

I remember Christopher marching right up to that guy and socking the daylights out of him. It was the first time I'd ever seen Christopher *that* heated. Heck, it was the first time I've ever seen him sock anyone, let alone be pissed off about something. I always thought he had thick skin, but it just goes to show that even a collected guy like him can get rough sometimes too.

But what's funny is that whenever Peter and I call him *"Chrissy,"* he'll get mad, but he'll never want to murder us or knock us into a coma. He might punch us or smack us on the head or something, but that's nothing compared to what he'll do to other people who call him that name.

Still, I always find it amusing for some reason whenever I see him get all flustered and huffy-puffy. It's not a typical sight, I guess. As I said, he's often calm and collected. So well behaved. A golden boy.

I bite down on my bottom lip to prevent the chuckle from escaping my lips as I take in the pissed-off look on Christopher's face.

When we enter our homeroom classroom, our teacher, Mr. Hua, looks up from the papers on his desk and stares us down. I feel my body freeze from his intense gaze.

Mr. Hua always had a charm about him. From his dark brown eyes that were close to looking black, his short black hair that is always combed nicely, to his sharp jawline, defined features, and dapper suits that fitted his lean build perfectly— there's no denying that he was a nice guy to look at sometimes. Most females in this school have probably fallen for him at least once or twice, and most guys probably aspired to have good looks like him someday.

But my God, his glares always send shivers down my spine.

It doesn't help whenever his thin lips lift into a halfhearted smile, either. When he does that, it feels as though he is trying to mock me. Not intentionally, I hope.

Christopher nudges me, clearing his throat. I immediately straighten my posture, tightening my grip on my bookbag strap. Mr. Hua adjusts the glasses on his face while remaining in his seat at his expansive desk.

"Mister Gonzalez. Mister Duncan. Here proud *and* punctual." Sarcasm rang through his words. His eyes drift to the clock above our heads to check the time. "Twenty-five minutes late. I'm sure you have a good reason, no doubt."

A giant ball forms in my throat, and I feel my heart thumping so hard in my chest, I think it is going to pierce right out of me. I wonder if Christopher can hear my heartbeat since he is standing so close to me. He just gives me a side-eye glance before turning his attention back to Mr. Hua.

"Well," Christopher begins, "we do. What happened was—"

"—My car broke down on the way here, so we had to take the train, and there was a delay, sooo. Now we're here." I pulled that right out of my ass. I don't even know where that came from. *Why did I do that?*

Judging from the side-eye glance Christopher was giving me, I could tell he was probably thinking the same thing as I was. *Why would you do that, Donald?*

I mean, to be fair, it did save our asses.

Mr. Hua marks us late and tells us to have a seat. Christopher and I usually sit next to each other near the back of the classroom. A couple of other students are near us, but they don't pay us any attention, which I am grateful for because I am not in the mood for eavesdroppers.

The second Christopher and I sit ourselves down in our seats, he leans over and whispers to me in a hiss, "Why would you say that Don?!" I open my mouth to speak, but he cuts me off before I can even get a word out. He adds, "We could've just told him the truth. Hua would've understood."

I snort, shaking my head. *Yeah, sure,* I wanted to tell him.

I try to imagine the two of us going to Mr. Hua, explaining to him that the real reason we were late was that we decided to play heroes and save our friend from a couple of cowards from Lincoln Freedman. We were able to save the day, which explains why we're late.

Yeah, let's tell him that, genius.

Mr. Hua would think we're such *great* boys.

I almost laugh at the thought because no one actually gets off the hook for playing the hero. It's bullshit, come to think of it. I mean, even if Mr. Hua did believe us and would understand, would it even matter in the end?

After all, it's not like there's any proof of what we did. No one's stopping to record or take pictures of a couple of high school delinquents handling business that shouldn't have even started in the first place. It's because no one cares.

And I remind Christopher of that. I tell him that even if we were honest with Mr. Hua, what were the chances he'd care? I'm not saying that Mr. Hua wouldn't give a damn about us, but the situation itself? He'd probably find it either hard to believe or, just think, *whatever.*

An unsure look crosses Christopher's face as he sits back in his seat, hands folded on his desk while letting out a quiet sigh. For the first time in a while, I've never seen him look so unsteady—so uncertain with himself. It is pretty ridiculous, to be honest.

I mean, maybe it is because he feels on edge about something like this happening again. Or perhaps it has something to do with the fact that he hates lying.

Christopher was never a good liar. His folks didn't bring him up that way. Well, at least his mom didn't before she had passed. His dad would sometimes have no issues with lying, which was funny since he hated being lied to.

Anyway, before the bell sounds, signaling the end of homeroom, I reach for Christopher's wrist as he starts to rise from his seat. He looks at me with his eyes suddenly big like a puppy's.

I clear my throat as I let go of his wrist. I want him to know that he can take things at ease for once since everything will be alright. He always has this bad habit of taking things too seriously, though I don't blame him. Ever since his mom died, Christopher has been so serious. He does have his moments when he's able to lose his mask and loosen up a while. Peter will always tell him that he's so uptight, and Christopher will just ignore him. But Peter is right. I know it. The rest of our crew knows it, and deep down, Christopher probably wants to correct that about himself.

But with everything going on with him right now—dealing with his dad, then school, and applying for college—the chances of Christopher cutting himself a break are slim to none.

Christopher slips himself free from my grasp and clears his throat, rocking on his heels.

"I'll see you at lunch, yeah?" he asks, then pressing his lips together tightly.

I hold my gaze on him, letting out a silent sigh. I open my mouth to tell him that he will, but I also want to say everything I am thinking. I want to say to him that he does not need to be so serious. I also don't need him to worry about me either.

But instead of telling him all those things, I just let out a quiet sigh, forcing a faint smirk on my face.

I nod. "Sure thing, man." I wink, clicking my tongue.

He rolls his eyes, snorting to himself. Then, he is out the door, heading to his first-period class, P.E., with Mr. Aziz. Meanwhile, I gather my things to head to my first-period class, which is Honors Algebra II with Mr. Enrique. It isn't a difficult class, to be honest. When people hear that a class is an Honors class, they immediately think the worst and believe the course is probably impossible to get through, but in reality, it's not. It requires more work, yes, but it's not impossible if you apply yourself.

To be frank, I was surprised that I was assigned to Honors classes in the first place. I mean, I probably shouldn't have been surprised since I always ace my tests and work real hard—not to brag. But usually, Honors students are model students.

Perfect attendance. Civil. Able to do what they're told without asking questions. Diligent. Ambitious but not difficult. Everything that everyone wants to be.

Like Christopher. But surprisingly, he's not an Honors student.

When I was assigned to my first Honors class sophomore year, I remember asking him if he had any Honors classes, and he scoffed. He didn't seem insulted that I was able to be put in an Honors class. He thought it would've been silly for him to even be considered. I never understood why.

It's not like Christopher gets C's or D's. He gets A's and B's. But he had told me, *"You're such a donkey. You don't even realize how big of a brain you got in that noggin of yours. You're meant to shine brighter."*

Back then, I didn't understand what he meant by that. Or if he meant it at all. I figured he was probably just a decent friend and was spewing nonsense that meant nothing but somehow fit the moment. But now, I sort of get it. I think.

As I pass through the mob of students who are also heading to their first-period classes, I think maybe Christopher believes I am meant to be more ambitious than I set myself to be. I don't mind being ambitious.

I'm Donald Gonzalez.

My name alone screams ambition—everyone knows that. Well, ambition, among a bunch of other things that people aren't afraid to share aloud. Most of those names not being things I should be proud of, but I always let them roll off my back because I know they're meaningless. Plus, it does give me a good laugh, here-and-there.

When I get to my Honors Algebra II class, Mr. Enrique is already writing equations on the white erase board at the front of the classroom. I sigh and head to my seat.

As I sit down, I look up and see Meagan rush into the classroom, speed-walking to her desk, which is next to mine. Her dark brown hair is in box braids and is pulled up in an updo, and she wears a long black cardigan over her uniform shirt, which is tucked into her black slacks. When she slides into her seat, she takes a breath with her eyes closed. I can tell she's wearing light makeup.

I don't know why, though. She's already beautiful without it. And I've seen Meagan without makeup before. Recently, actually. It was during the weekend. I had stopped by her house without giving her a heads up that I was coming over. I knocked on the door, and she answered. I remember the look on her face when she saw me standing at her doorstep. Her eyes were wide as if she had seen a ghost, and she was utterly lost for words.

Not gonna lie. I was too.

I wasn't expecting her to answer the door, to be honest. But she did. And it was honestly a pretty lovely sight, seeing her without makeup. She doesn't look bad with it on. She's stunning. Heck, she was beautiful the first day I met her on the first day of school this year.

She was a fresh face, and I honestly didn't expect her to even talk to me. But she did. It was all by chance. We just happened to be assigned to the same class.

And now, six months later, she's a great friend of mine. She's my favorite person to be around, to be quite honest.

It's kind of funny but pitiful since she's a sophomore, and I'm about to graduate in a few months and move on with my life.

Anyway, Meagan looks over to me and presses her lips together in a faint smile. The corners of my lips curve upwards instantly, and I wink at her. I can tell from the way she gently places her pencil and notebook down onto her desk that she's nervous. She's always nervous on test days.

Honestly, I don't get why.

It's math. Math isn't hard. It's like a puzzle, and all you have to do is find the missing piece to fit the equation and solve the problem. Kind of like a scavenger hunt. But that's probably just me.

I get that not everyone gets math, but someone bright like Meagan should have nothing to worry about. The last time we had a test for Mr. Enrique, she passed with an 87.

I told her that she did great, but she rolled her eyes and reminded me of my grade. 100.

I told her, *"So what? It's just a number. Doesn't mean much."*

She scoffed. *"Funny coming from the guy who sets himself with such high standards."*

That kind of stung. *"Ouch. Way to break my heart, kid."*

She laughed, insisting that she was just joking around. She didn't mean for me to sound like such a snobby, stuck-up guy who only aimed to be the best and leave everyone in the dust. But I knew that. I knew she didn't think of me that way. If she had, she'd be a fool to stick around me then.

But even though I'm not that guy, I'll admit, I didn't expect her to stick around me this long. Maybe for a few weeks or so once I gave her a chance to see some layers of me. I figured it'd be a good idea to show her the good parts of me and see how comfortable she'd get.

But to be honest, I didn't know what the good parts were.

Me making witty remarks every time she had something corny to say? Giving her rides home in my car? Letting her come over to my place to study and prep for our math tests together? Or me just calling her *"kid"* to make her believe that's all I could see her as?

I just didn't want to overwhelm her. Guess I didn't if she tolerates me.

Anyway, Mr. Enrique finishes writing the equations on the erase board for us to use as references during our test. He instructs us to clear our desks as he passes out the bulky calculators to use during our tests and a piece of scrap paper. I glance at Meagan when she receives her calculator and scrap paper. She starts biting her nails, then her lips, then her nails again. It takes everything in me to not flick a small piece of my eraser at her head to get her attention.

I wanted to lean over and whisper something calming to her, but Mr. Enrique would've been on my case in a hot minute if he caught me talking. So, real quick, I keep my phone under my desk and on my lap, and I send her a short text message.

Still willing to bet my car on you for sure kid ;)

Send.

I look up, stuffing my phone back into my pants pocket. Meagan reaches into her pocket and takes out her phone but keeps it on her lap and out of sight. I watch as she unlocks it and reads the message. She puts her phone away in the side pouch of her book bag and shifts her gaze to me.

I constantly remind her of my Golden Rule when it comes to my car. *No eating or drinking in the car, and you never mess with my car.* I mean it too. Not a single piece of food or drip of a drink, including water, is allowed in my car. And nobody is allowed to mess with it. It was passed down from generation to generation, so I had to treasure that car with my life. And yet, I still told Meagan that I'd bet my car on her with anything she did.

Whether it was her writings or a test. I'd bet my car on her achieving it all, and I knew she would.

Plus, it meant a lot more telling her I would do such a thing if it earned me a smile from her. That giggly smile where there'd be crinkles by her eyes and her teeth would show. If she was about to crack up, she'd snort a little but would tuck her head away so I—or anyone—wouldn't notice, but I could still hear her anyway.

I'd tell her a million times that I'd bet my car on her if it earned me that smile and laugh from her every time.

After Mr. Enrique finishes handing out the tests, he sets his timer and tells us to begin. And just like that, I'm locked in on my test, and the answers come to me.

. . . .

Lunch rolls around, and I sit at our usual table with Peter, Meagan, Christopher, Carmen, and Benton.

I still find it funny how Meagan and Benton are sophomores, yet they decided to roll with us. I mean, to be fair, Peter is the only junior in the group, but Meagan and Benton could've dipped if they wanted to and found people who were at least going to be here a little longer.

But I guess in both of their heads, they were thinking: *Oh, well, I'll just settle for these guys. They'll be outta here soon anyway, but we can learn from them.* Yeah, that's probably it.

Meagan sits next to me during lunch, which isn't anything new, but I figured she'd probably want to sit next to Benton since the two of them were talking as they walked into the cafeteria and came over to our table. They were laughing, looking at something on Meagan's phone before she put it away once she finally took a seat at the table. Benton was then wiping his eyes, still chuckling at whatever he and Meagan were talking about.

Benton sits down in the space between Peter and Christopher, and Peter has a look of confusion frozen on his face as he slowly chews his food with his mouth closed.

I snort, a smirk suddenly begins to form on my face. "Look, Pete, we all know Benton's gorgeous but stop staring, alright? You'll scare him."

I'm not lying either. Benton is a looker. Sharp, defined features, smooth-looking lips, wavy silky dark hair that is cropped shoulder length, and judging by how good he looked—even with his uniform being a bit baggy on him—he's got some muscle on him.

I wouldn't be surprised if Meagan had a crush on him. Most people did. Benton Son was fresh meat and eye candy to a lot of people. It didn't matter that he was a sophomore either.

Peter turns his attention to me, and he gives me a look that reflects his lack of tolerance for my jokes at that moment. "Oh, you're *sooo* funny, Don," he drawls. Peter then dots his attention back to Benton as he pops open his small bag of mini cookies. "What's got you laughing all teary-eyed, Son?"

Benton shakes his head, a faint grin still curved on his lips. As he takes out his lunch from his bookbag, he keeps his head down, chuckling a bit to himself. I notice Meagan pressing her lips together in a tight grin as she takes little glances at him.

She finally admits, "It's my fault he's on a giggle streak. I showed him a video, and it's just...oh God, it's great."

Benton snickers. "It's fantastic!"

Peter rocks into Benton, playfully bumping his shoulder. "Well, well. Anyone who can make a dude laugh that much must've won his heart." His gaze shifts directly to Meagan, and a smirk comes across his face. "Wouldn't you say so, Meagan?" Wink, wink.

To no one's surprise, Christopher reaches over and plucks Peter on the back of his head. Peter whips his attention over to Christopher and attempts to do the same thing to Christopher, but Christopher smacks Peter's hand away. Carmen stands up from her spot next to Christopher and grabs both of them by their wrists. She glares at them, unlike anything I had ever seen. Christopher has to look away, but I doubt he felt any type of shame. Peter looks away, fearing that he'd probably turn to stone if he stared at Carmen any longer.

Carmen is such a doll-face, very pretty and very sweet-looking. So for her to give them such a stern look, it doesn't settle too well since she looks like she will bring hellfire on them if they keep acting like putzes.

Carmen holds her scowl while shaking her head as she mutters, "Tan infantil."

When she finally lets go of their wrists, Peter whips his head around and frowns. "*Oye!* You take that back!" Peter then snaps his attention to Christopher. "If anyone's childish, it's him. His fault anyway."

Carmen just rolls her eyes and sits back down in her spot next to Christopher. She rests her head on his shoulder and massages his arm. "He is a bit foolish, ain't he?" She kisses his shoulder.

I feel myself wanting to hurl, but at the same time, my lips curl into a smirk.

I remember when Christopher grew the balls to take Carmen out on a date. I was home, chilling in my room, listening to Javi Ray— one of the best Latin male artists –and I got a text message from Christopher, reading: **The deed is done. Got a date tonight.**

I called him and asked, *"What you mean, you got a date tonight?"*

He replied, *"With Carmen. I'm taking her to Lela's Soul Cafe in Germantown."*

I remember smiling like an idiot while clapping my hands as if we had won the Superbowl. It was about damn time he grew some balls and asked her out! He's been crushing on her hard since sophomore year when they first met. Not to seem dramatic, but it has been painful watching him fall for her. Carmen's a doll, no question, and a couple of guys liked her. At one point, I thought she was pretty cute, and I had some interest, but then I realized Christopher had feelings for her. He didn't have to tell me. I just knew. I could tell. It was obvious.

I wasn't going to be that guy who was selfish. Christopher deserved someone like her. Plus, I was unsure of my feelings, anyway. Christopher's feelings were definitely certain.

But Christopher was on edge about taking Carmen out on a date. She knew it was a date too. It wasn't them just hanging out like friends. They were still friends, but it was still a date.

Regardless, things went well because the next day, Christopher called and told me that they were going out again the following week.

Now, here they are. Sitting at the lunch table, holding hands under the table with Carmen's head resting on Christopher's shoulder. None of us cringe at their small display of affection. Meagan is the only one out of all of us who is smiling like a full-blown dork. She tries to hide it by covering her mouth as she eats her lunch, but her smile widens whenever she looks at Christopher and Carmen.

I rock against her, nudging my shoulder into her lightly. Meagan's big brown eyes immediately look up at me, and she keeps her mouth covered with her hand as she continues to chew her food. Her eyes sort of glisten from the sunlight piercing through the barred window, making her eyes look hazel. I even notice some glitter from the highlights on her face from her makeup.

The gold highlight looks good with her complexion. Dark brown and smooth. Her lashes seem longer too. I mean, Meagan naturally has long eyelashes, but she probably uses mascara to make them look longer than usual. But her eyes stand out the most, though. When I look at her, I feel trapped in them.

I never realized how pretty her eyes were, I guess.

That's when I realize that I've been staring longer than I should have, so I clear my throat while holding the grin on my face. Meagan presses her lips together and continues to look at me with her lips slightly curved upward.

She asks me, "You good?"

I tell her, "Of course I am, kid." I throw my arm around her, attempting to convince her with a wink.

But as expected, she doesn't believe me.

She hits me with, "Donny, I know you. What gives?" and arches her eyebrow.

Donny. Hearing her call me that always made me want to laugh on the inside. I just wasn't used to someone calling me a name that wasn't *prick, douchebag,* or *asshole.* People would call me those things all the time. I actually considered changing my name a few times for some sick amusement.

But not Meagan, though. She decided to call me *"Donny"* right off the bat, and I let it stick. I never minded. It was like a perfect trade-off. I get to call her *"kid,"* and she calls me *"Donny."* It's fair—a thing between us.

Anyway, I assure Meagan that I'm fine, and she just looks at me. I look right back at her. I'm not annoyed with her. I just don't want her to think I'm dodging the question, giving her something to worry about. She has nothing to worry about.

Meagan lets out a sigh. "You can always trust me, you know?"

I shake my head, a faint chuckle escaping my lips. "Yeah, I know." My eyes are on her. "Stop worrying so much."

"Well, you're my friend, so."

I dramatically gasp, putting my hand to my chest. *"Moi?!* Why I never would've guessed."

Meagan rolls her eyes, annoyed.

I chuckle. "You chose to stick around. This is what you get."

Taking the straw of her apple juice into her mouth, Meagan shakes her head, rolling her eyes. "Yeah, yeah."

I laugh, pulling Meagan closer into me as we listen to Peter and Christopher go back-and-forth with each other about God knows what while the rest of us watch it all unfold.

Week 2, Tuesday.

Honestly, I don't have much to say as of right now. Just like yesterday, I woke up tired. I wanted to skip school today but my folks would've been on my case, maybe. Mom and dad were going back and forth when I came out of the shower, so, I had to get to school. Take my mind off things for a bit. I'm sure things will get better, eventually. I don't know.--D.G.

I hear mom call me downstairs as I am tying the laces to my black snow boots. I can't help but let out a low groan as I sit up and sigh out. I could only imagine what she could possibly want from me. It's cutting close to seven in the morning, and even though it doesn't take me long to get to school, I like being there. Beats being here and dealing with screaming matches between mama and papa at the crack of dawn.

I can guarantee that the neighbors probably set their clocks in the morning to catch the show that goes on in the Gonzalez household every day. It never ends, not once. Not a day of peace. Even if there's silence, it's never a peaceful silence—there's still some sort of tension in the air.

So many times, I would want to open my mouth and say something about it. Maybe suggest that we talk about it, but that's some therapy shit that I'm not good at doing anyway. If I were as good of a talker as Counselor Malik then maybe, but right now—nah, no way. If anything, my parents would probably look at me up and down as if I had hit my head on a pile bricks, ridding some of my brain cells.

Who am I to say anything, to be honest?

Even if I was good at talking with my parents, what are the chances they'd even listen? Using words of aggression seems to be the only thing that works in this household, anyway. Been like that for as long as I can remember. But things weren't always like this. There'd be days where we could all talk to each other like ordinary folks. Sometimes we were like those ridiculously happy and settled white families we'd watch on TV when Morris-Lina and I were little. Unlike them, though, mama and papa were still strict and would sometimes whoop Morris-Lina and me if we were out of line, talking back, or doing something stupid.

Things suddenly changed as Morris-Lina and I got older. I'm a hundred percent positive it hardly had anything to do with us since Morris-Lina and I grew out of our childish ways. However, Morris-Lina had setbacks whenever she decided to stop taking her medication and lied about it. I'll never say it aloud, but I blame myself for that. I know it is ideal to blame the parents, but I was her twin brother. I should've stuck up for her more whenever mom or dad would get on her case about certain things. School. Her health. Boys. Anything.

I thought that I made things up with Morris-Lina when I decided to help her take care of her pregnancy. She didn't want it to happen, and she didn't want to go with the option she had in handling things, but she had no other choice. If our parents had found out about it, they would've probably thrown her out of the house. Well, maybe not that, but I'm sure they would've been done with her. Dad probably would've tracked down the guy she was dating at the time and would've killed him. Literally. So, we had to keep it on the down-low. I thought maybe things would've slowly gotten better for her afterward. Slowly.

But I guess I don't have the best judgment.

Yeah, I could quickly point fingers at mom and dad for this, but what good would that do?

Counselor Malik likes when I talk about this sort of stuff, but every time I do— even when I think about it—I get sick to my stomach. I feel nauseous as I snatch my heavy black jacket from the back of my chair at my desk, and I head downstairs.

When I reach the bottom of the stairs, I am met with my mother's stern eyes as she stands by the front door, slipping her arms through the fur coat dad had gifted her three Christmases ago. The brown fur was like satin—the kind of fur that glows in the sunlight—but I hated the texture. It was kind of rough, but mom was still very fond of it. It's not like dad hasn't gotten mom nice things before, but she at least showed great appreciation for that coat. Maybe it made her feel complete since she was able to walk into her workplace with her face well-done, hair pressed nicely, and wearing her heels with the fur coat to top it all off.

But it was just a facade.

I don't know how people at her job perceive my mother, but she's not the luxurious type. She's far from it. But she's not a simple person either. She's in the middle. Maybe it's 60/40? I don't know. She's hard to describe.

Anyway, mom shifts her gaze to her cellphone as it vibrates in her hand. Her eyes nearly pop out of her head, and she picks up the pace, snatching up her work bag off the hook in the closet. She practically slams the closet door shut before looking back at me as she starts to head out the door.

"Donald." She pauses, probably forgetting why she had called me downstairs. It's not the first time that's happened either. Her stern gaze lightens up, and she lets out a soft breath. "Te amo, mi hijito."

Mi hijito. That's something I haven't been called in years. It's almost foreign to me.

My throat feels dry but I still manage to tell her, "Yo también te amo, mamá." Then she is out the door.

I feel knots suddenly twist in my stomach, and I check my phone time—seven on the dot.

I honestly have no clue what all of that was about, and I probably shouldn't waste my time trying to figure it out. Maybe mom felt terrible about how much she and dad were fighting earlier while dad was getting ready to leave for work. Perhaps she just wanted to actually take the time to tell me that she loved me.

I mean, I know she loves me. She's my mom.

Let it go, Don. It's nothing. Just get something to eat.

I trust the voice in my head. It's nothing. Absolutely nothing. I know better than to take things too seriously or overthink. Morris-Lina would always get on my case about that, saying that I need to learn how to stop thinking so much and just let things go. I always thought that statement was funny coming from her. Especially when we were kids.

She always took things to heart. But I can't say I blame her, though. It's hard to not take things seriously when everyone is constantly on your case after a certain point. Well...the same goes for me, too, I guess.

But Morris-Lina always had a target on her back. I tried blocking that target as much as possible, but every time I tried, she'd just get pissed about it. Well, not pissed, but she didn't want me to take things off her back.

Regardless, I can't say I noticed the target on her back right from the start. I'm stupid for that too.

I'm her damn twin brother. Shouldn't I have done better? I should've at least assumed—

The familiar ringtone coming from my phone pulls me from my thoughts. I retrieve my phone from the depths of my pants pocket and check out the name on the lock screen. **Pete.**

My eyebrows wrinkle. It's not like I'm late leaving to get to school or anything. In fact, Peter is the last person to call me if I was late.

I clear my throat before answering the phone just in time before it went to voicemail.

"Yo," I manage to get out as I let out a soft sigh.

"Hey, I know you're on your way probably, but quick question..." Peter suddenly pauses, and I can hear him clearing his throat. He usually does this when he's nervous about something, and that's a rarity in his case. *Something must really be up.*

I ask him, "Pete, what is it?" He lets out a sharp sigh as I lean against the fridge. I think back to yesterday, hoping to God that he didn't run into any other punks from Lincoln Freedman on his way to school. He's gotta be on the train by now. I ask him again, "Peter, what is it?"

Finally, he asks me, "Are flowers still a thing? You know for a promposal?"

I snort as I keep the phone against my ear. *This guy, are you kidding me?*

I hear Peter add on, "I was thinking about roses, but that seems like overkill, doesn't it? No one likes roses anymore, right?" and I pull open the refrigerator door and take out the carton of my milk.

"Cálmate, Peter. Hold up a second," I finally manage to say as I sit the carton of milk on the kitchen counter. The guy was like a runaway freight train, asking all sorts of questions about flowers and promposals.

I'm not saying that this stuff usually doesn't matter to Peter. Still, I would expect Christopher, of all people, to be panicking about promposals and flowers...given that he is dating Carmen. Peter, however, has no reason to worry about that stuff. He's not obligated to go to prom. In fact, he's hardly ever mentioned being interested in attending prom.

Maybe once. But it was just once, and then it became forgotten. Now all of a sudden, he's panicking about asking someone to prom? Strange.

Besides, Peter is the spontaneous type. Not saying that he's not a smooth guy, but he'll just wing it half the time when walking up to people and asking them ridiculous or pressing questions. He doesn't need a big sign or some flowers to pull things off.

Plus, Peter's a nice-looking guy. With his pearly white smile, dark brown skin that is smoother than chocolate, honey brown eyes, and dark brown hair that he usually keeps in a small afro, Peter could charm anyone to go to prom with him. But I can't imagine who he'd ask. He'll often joke about asking Meagan or Benton out, but there's no way it would be either one of them. Especially not Meagan. She's not even interested in going to prom—she made that obvious multiple times whenever Morris-Lina or Carmen would bring it up, trying to convince her to go.

And Benton...

Well, I doubt Peter actually has a thing for Benton. We often make jokes about Benton's natural good looks, but Peter likes to poke the most fun at him. Sometimes Benton will ignore Peter's comments, but most of the time, he'll get shy and turn his head away to hide his face. Christopher, of course, will either pluck or pinch Peter to get him to leave Benton alone, but Benton always steps in and tells Christopher that everything is good.

But like I said, I doubt Peter actually has a thing for Benton. I don't know who Peter could have a thing for.

At one point, I was sure he had a thing for Morris-Lina, but then he got over it. I'm glad too. The last time Morris-Lina dated one of my best friends, it didn't end well. I hate thinking about it—when Morris-Lina went out with Nathan Hendricks. Back when Nathan was actually a decent, trustworthy human being. Long before he let Diana Clovis slither into his pants and became her little puppet.

Anyway, when I finally ask Peter who's the lucky victim he's planning to ask to prom, he laughs nervously. "Go to hell, Gonzalez."

I snicker. "Only if you go with me." I snatch myself an apple from the fruit bowl near the kitchen sink and take a bite. "Seriously, why not ask Chrissy about this? I'm no expert in that department."

"Chris wouldn't stop asking me who I'm gonna ask."

True. "Fair enough."

I glance at the clock one last time before telling Peter that I would talk to him more about this at school, and he sighs. Before I end the call, he begs me to not say a word about this to anyone—especially not Christopher. I actually thought it was pretty funny with how desperate Peter sounded.

Either this guy is in love, or he was just embarrassed. Perhaps both—he was so in love that it was embarrassing. I've never heard him sound like this, ever. Regardless, I kept my word, telling him, "I gotchu."

Then I end the call.

It doesn't take me too long to get to school. I arrive a couple minutes before the first bell sounds, signaling everyone to head to homeroom. I practically sprinted up the steps to get to the third floor, even though I was still on time. Still, I imagined receiving another scolding by Mr. Hua, even if I walked into homeroom a few seconds after the second bell.

It's not that I'm scared of Mr. Hua. I just didn't like how I felt yesterday after Chris and I walked in late. *Helpless.*

God, I hate that feeling.

Luckily, I manage to get to homeroom before the second bell goes off. I slide into my usual seat as the bell sounds, and I let out a sigh—*Alabado sea el Señor.*

I settle my bookbag on the floor against my chair when I get a text message from Peter, asking me if I could possibly meet him in the bathroom after first period. I wrinkle my eyebrows.

This guy is whipped.

I press my lips together to prevent myself from cracking up. I try to think of possible people that could've captured Peter's interest, but no one comes to mind. Like I said, I know he'll tease Benton, but there's no guarantee that he has a thing for Benton. Even if he did, who cares? I know that his aunt is super traditional, but

I doubt she'd kick him out if he did happen to like guys since she's the only family he really has left. Legally, he can't stay with his mom, so. By law, until he's eighteen, his aunt is all he has.

Anyway, I look up from my phone, which I keep on my lap under my desk as Mr. Hua starts to take attendance in alphabetical order by last name. He goes down the list while I keep my hands stuffed in the pockets of my jacket until he is done since I can't text. Mr. Hua is probably one of the few teachers who hardly allow texting during homeroom. Friggin' homeroom. It's not an actual class. All we do is just sit and twirl our fingers until it's time for first period.

But sometimes, he isn't so strict about it, and he'll allow us to be on our phones. But that's a rarity. When he does allow us to use our phones, we have to keep our phones silent. Otherwise, we can't use them. But he mainly doesn't like us being on our phones while he is taking attendance since some students hardly pay attention, and he gets agitated.

Mr. Hua calls out Christopher's last name hastily, and everyone looks in the direction where Christopher sits. Right next to me.

He looks dead. Deader than dead. His skin is pale, dark circles under his eyes, eyelids heavy, hair tousled in every direction. Still, Christopher manages to respond, "Here!"

I can tell that took a lot out of him.

I can't believe I didn't notice him like this when I came in. Probably because I had my mind on Peter and his situation. But seeing Christopher in this state was appalling.

Well, not shocking— concerning, I should say.

Christopher is usually so put together and…not dead.

I open my mouth to whisper his name, but he settles his head back down on the desk, using his arms as a pillow to muffle out any sort of sound around him. My lips suddenly feel dry, and I gulp.

I sit back in my seat and let out a sharp breath.

What is today? Tuesday? Tuesday what?

Quickly, I press the home button on my phone to show the lock screen. I look at the date. *02/08/2013.*

It's February 8th. His mom died on the 10th.

Ah, shiiiit.

It's no wonder Christopher is in a bit of a slump. Whenever it's the week of his mom's death, he's always off his game. It's been two years, but it feels like it literally just happened, so I know it's impossible to know how Christopher feels.

Usually, after school, Morris-Lina and I would take Christopher out to get his mind off things, but it's not easy trying to make someone forget their parent's death. Especially when it's so sudden. I wasn't there when it happened, but from what Christopher told me, he could hear his mom singing in the kitchen from his bedroom, and then it was suddenly quiet. When he came downstairs to check on her after a couple of minutes had gone by, she was on the ground—mouth agape, eyes open, the body still, not breathing.

They said it was a heart attack, but his mom was healthier than an ox—no one could believe it. Not even him.

I sigh. I suddenly start to think of when I found Morris-Lina in her bed, wrapped up in her bedsheets, laying in her bed. Unlike Christopher's mom, Morris-Lina at least had her eyes closed. It could've fooled anyone to believe she was actually sleeping. Just sleeping before I realized—

"Gonzalez!" Mr. Hua's voice booms through the room, and my heart nearly leaps from my throat. *Oh, right. Attendance.*

I sit up in my seat and clear my throat. "Here! I'm here!"

It suddenly becomes difficult to keep my voice straight as the words escape my lips, quivering. And it doesn't help that Mr. Hua takes a long pause, giving me a glance, before finally going back to the attendance sheet and calling the next name after mine.

I sit back in my seat, my shoulders suddenly sinking as my throat becomes unbelievably dry. I don't even think a drink of water could help me out. I hear the murmurs around me as a few students take quick glances at me before whipping their heads back around once I catch them.

I suddenly feel a vibration on my leg, and I nearly jump, and Mr. Hua cuts his gaze to me. I run my fingers through my hair as I lean into my desk, propping my elbows up on the surface while resting my head on my hand. I shift my eyes to Christopher, who finally lifts his head into the daylight. He doesn't say anything to me—he just buries the side of his face into his arms that remain folded flat on the surface of his desk while keeping his soft gaze on me.

I press my lips together in a smile, hoping that he'd at least smile back. He does. Thank God.

The bell eventually sounds off, signaling the end of homeroom. I unlock my phone screen as I gather my things and head out the door. Two messages. One from Meagan and one from Peter. The one from Peter was expected, though. He just wanted me to confirm that I would meet up with him after first period to help him out with his sudden promposal crisis, which is the dumbest thing ever—but it's Peter. When I opened Meagan's message, I couldn't prevent the corners of my mouth from pulling upwards, nor could I stop the chuckle that followed. It was only a GIF of a dancing panda bear—no follow-up message for context.

I was walking to the stairway when I responded back: **Why?**

She responds: **Why not?**

I snort.

Me: Careful! Starting to sound like me ;)

Meg: …

Me: Actual words, chica

Meg: Never…

Me: u just did lol

Meg: …

Me: ;)

A heaviness is suddenly thrown against my shoulder, and I am rocked into the wall as I reach the second floor. The roughness of the wall scrapes against my palm as I try to catch myself from falling to the ground. When I look up, I see the douchebag looking right at me—eyelids drooped and a mocking smirk twisted on his ghostly face.

"Watch where you're going, amigo," he huffs, but the way he says *amigo* sounds more like "ah-mee-gew".

I stand upright, fixing the collar of my jacket. The stench of weed follows him as he proceeds to walk through the double doors. Guys like him I could take on any day, but it couldn't be today.

I briskly made my way to Mr. Enrique's class, clenching my fist to calm myself down. Mr. Enrique is sitting at his desk, looking through a folder that contains God knows what in it.

The bell goes off. Everyone was settled into their seats as Mr. Enrique finally stood up to close the classroom door. I take a deep breath and loosen my fist as Mr. Enrique writes today's date on the whiteboard in green marker.

Another deep breath.

I look over and spot Meagan hastily pulling her braids back into a ponytail while remaining seated and keeping her eyes on Mr. Enrique. Once she's done, she looks over at me while opening her notebook. A smile forms on her face before turning her attention back to Mr. Enrique.

I finally relaxed.

Just chill out, Don. Chill out, I remind myself.

Week 2, Wednesday.

"I know you can do better than that, Gonzalez!" Mr. Aziz's voice echoes throughout the entire gym, causing my ears to ring. I can feel him standing over me as I lower my body back down and use my strength to push myself back up. I can feel the unbearable tightness within my arms expand to my chest. I let out a sharp breath and fight against the sensation. Mr. Aziz's voice starts to fade as I look forward and lower myself back down, keeping only an inch of space between me and the ground. I rise back up.

I hate drills. These damn drills.

Me and everyone else in the class.

Mr. Aziz stands over other students, keeping his hands behind his back, and he glares everyone down, just waiting for one person to collapse. In my head, I pray to dear God that no one collapses. If someone does, that poor soul has to do at least six laps around the track—or at least until it pleases Mr. Aziz.

FWEET!

Heavy breathing escapes from practically everyone's mouth, and everyone stands upright in unison. I can feel my heart pounding heavily in my chest as I finally stand up off the ground, settling my hands on my hips while trying to catch my breath. It's not the fact that Mr. Aziz had us do push-ups that has me a bit winded—it's the amount we had to do.

Honest to God, it was more than twenty. Twenty is nothing to me. I'll admit that I have a lot of strength, and it does show when I have to carry certain things or do drills. But at the same time, I'm not the kind of guy who will do push-ups in my bedroom every five or twenty minutes before going to bed. I'll only work out when I'm bored out of my mind, usually on the weekends.

My attention remains locked on Mr. Aziz as he glares us all down, standing straight while keeping his hands behind his back. He's like a drill sergeant, and the slightest eff-up from us will be our deathbed.

He checks the time on his watch. "Alright, hit the showers."

Sighs of relief practically echo throughout the gym as the other students waste no time heading to the showers. I walk over to my bookbag on the bleachers and unzip the front pouch, pulling out my water bottle. As I sit down on the bottom bench, Mr. Aziz makes his way over to me.

"I dismissed you to the showers, Gonzalez." He crosses his arms over his chest and glowers at me.

I nod. "Yeah, I know. I'll be in the back shortly." I lightly shake my water bottle. "Just want to get a few sips in, is all."

This time, he just presses his lips together and gives me this look that makes me question myself. He nods his head before walking away, leaving me alone to sit in the quiet.

Usually, I'd be the first one hitting the showers after doing drills, but I had to sit out for a few minutes for my sake. I already knew that the second I stepped into the locker room, the other guys would have something to say. I expected them to have something to say. Not that I cared, but today, I didn't want to hear any of it. I knew what the outcome would become, and I didn't feel like having to deal with it either.

Besides, before I left for school this morning, my mom was lying in bed, still tucked in—hacking horrendously into tissues. She called me into the bedroom she and dad shared and asked me to help her sit up in the bed. Before I left, she made me promise to have a good day. Her literal words: *"Be a good boy today, mi hijito."*

She was half-asleep, slurring her words. But I kissed her forehead as she finally dozed off.

So, I had to refrain from decking those douchebags in their fat mouths. It's bad enough that I can't do anything in the classrooms because I'm sure the teachers would immediately label me as the aggressor. So I just have to sit in class, listening to the other students as they whisper ridiculous things to each other while looking at me. Sometimes, I'll hear Morris-Lina's name slip out of their mouths, and something in my head suddenly shuts them out. I'll shift my attention back to the teacher and focus on the lesson. Sometimes I'll just stare at the clock as time *ticks* away.

I sigh.

I check the time on my phone. The buzzer will sound off in about ten minutes, signaling the end of third period. Thank God I have lunch after this—nothing to worry about being late or on time anyway. Still, I feel my skin starting to crawl from the dried sweat on my body, and that's when I finally decide to take a shower. I leave my bookbag on the bench and head to the men's locker room.

It doesn't surprise me when I hear loud conversations and laughter as I enter the locker room. Even though it continues as I head to my locker, I suddenly feel eyes glued to me. I shake it off.

I open my locker and grab my towel and washcloth. As I strip myself down to my underwear, I hear a couple of guys muttering to each other with smirks on their faces as they watch me. One of them happens to be Austin Brown. Of course, he's taller than me with his broad shoulders and incredibly muscular build. But I guess all that thickness also went to his head since he's a little dense.

I pay them no mind as I fold up my clothes and stuff them into the plastic bag for me to take them home and wash them. I suddenly feel Austin's presence hovering over me like a gray crowd, or maybe a horrifying creature—like the Slim Man that lurks in the woods at night. He leans against the locker beside me with his arms crossed and a dimwitted smirk on his face like he's about to do something cunning.

"What took you so long, Gonzalez? We were starting to think you were too good to be around us or something," he snickers.

I tighten my jaw and close my locker shut.

In my head, I flip him off, telling him, *"Vete a la mierda!"*

In reality, I grab my towel and washcloth and walk away from him. I can hear him and a couple other idiots snickering as I make my way to one of the empty showers. I take off my underwear and wash under the steaming hot water. When the water hits my skin, I feel my muscles relax, and my chest opens up. The fragrance from the soap reminds me of the lilac candles mom would always light up in the living room whenever I would come home from baseball practice after school during my sophomore year. Morris-Lina would be sitting in the dining room, doing homework since mom would want to keep an eye on her for no reason.

It annoyed the hell out of Morris-Lina, but she'd never complained. At least not when mom was around. The memory continues to burn in my mind as I rinse the soap off my body, and I feel my eyes suddenly start to burn.

I pinch them closed shut. *Shit, shit.* I hiss.

The burning begins to lighten up as I blink. I turn off the water and reach for my towel, wasting no time to dab my face. I blink again, and my vision clears.

I wrap the towel around my waist and wring out the washcloth before tossing it in the disposable bin. I slip on my underwear, still keeping the towel around my waist. I let out a sigh, running my fingers through my damp hair. As I walk back to my locker, I feel eyes on me again, but I try to ignore them as I remain quiet.

When I finally make it to my locker, I dry off and moisturize my skin. I hear a chuckle from behind, and I roll my eyes when I realize it's Austin Brown. He is fully dressed in his uniform, and the front of his hair is slicked back almost perfectly, showing off his clean undercut. It really pisses me off when people go out of their way to mess with someone. He'd be better off just leaving and not saying a word to me. Otherwise, he'd be walking out of here choking on blood and his teeth.

"You must really think you're too good to be around us, huh?" he snickers, creeping closer to me with a smug look on his face. "We're all men here. Relax, unless you got something you're trying to hide."

He swiftly snatches the towel from around my waist, and my body jerks. Faint chuckles surround me, and I tighten my jaw. I shift my gaze to Austin and he just snickers, mocking me. He inches closer to me until he is practically hovering over me, resting his arm against my locker, trying to intimidate me. As if.

He looks down at me, still holding that smug look on his face, which starts to piss me off. I clench my hand into a tight fist as I keep my eyes locked on him.

"What are you gonna do about it, wetback?" The words roll off his tongue effortlessly as he speaks lowly, looking me right in the eyes.

Nathan Hendricks steps in between us before I can even make a move or open my mouth to tell him to screw off. He came literally out of nowhere, pressing his arms against our chests as he wiggled himself in between us. It took me a minute to even realize that it was Nathan. His blonde hair styled neatly, his familiar blue eyes staring at me desperately. My chest tightened.

Austin shoved Nathan away from him, causing Nathan to practically stumble into me. Luckily, Nathan could catch himself to prevent himself from falling any further. He then whipped his head around to Austin, and the two of them had an intense staring contest that only lasted a few seconds since Austin finally decided to walk away. And like magic, everyone else chose to mind their own business.

I notice Nathan's shoulders relax as he stands upright and turns his attention over to me. He asks me, "You good?"

I just nod, hardly looking him in the eye.

He opens his mouth like he's about to say something, but he closes it shut, and his eyes soften. He lets out a sharp breath and finally walks away. I feel my stomach twist in knots as he leaves. What was that even about, anyway? Him intervening?

It's not like he could gain anything from it, anyway.

I tried to forget about it as I changed into my regular school uniform. As I fasten my pants and slip on my shoes, I suddenly start to think about Meagan and when she told me that Nathan had suddenly turned a "new leaf." I decided to take Meagan to the lakeside that dad used to take Morris-Lina and me when we were kids. It was one of my favorite places.

While I was driving, Meagan told me that Nathan was now part of the theater program and how he was her informant during her absence from school because of her heart surgery. It's not that I think of Meagan as naïve because she's not. If anything, I'll take Meagan's word for anything.

But at the same time…it's Nathan.

The same Nathan Hendricks, who had no problem taking my name and running it through the mud. The same Nathan Hendricks, who went after my sister and broke her. The same Nathan Hendricks, who belittled us like a sick joke. And yeah, I'll admit, once upon a time, it was the three of us—me, Nathan, and Christopher. But being friends with Nathan will probably be the worst part of my life and my biggest regret.

Yet, Meagan swears up and down that he's turned around.

Christopher feels the same as well. When I meet him by the stairway to head to lunch, I tell him what happened in the locker room, and Christopher just tilts his head and raises his eyebrows.

I know that look. That's the *"I told you so"* look.

I scoff. "You can't be serious, Chris. Really?"

"What? I didn't say anything."

"Your face did."

He snorts. "What do you me—?"

"You think Nathan's turned around, don't you?"

Christopher shrugs, pressing his lips tightly together to form a straight line. That's basically his way of saying, *"Yes,"* but he'll just deny it if I even say anything. I roll my eyes.

We get to the cafeteria, and Christopher wastes no time sitting next to Carmen at our table. I snort, the one side of my mouth pulling upward. Peter sits across from them and rolls his eyes while chewing on a straw. I sit next to him. Christopher looks up at us while Carmen keeps her head rested on Christopher's shoulder.

"What?" Christopher asks, seeming bothered by us.

Carmen leans forward, pecking him on the jaw.

Peter groans. "Get a room. Jesus Christ."

"I think it's sweet," a familiar voice follows. I look over as Meagan sits next to me. She whips her attention to me, and a smirk spreads on her face.

Almost uncontrollably, a smirk plasters on mine, and I feel my face start to warm up. I snap out of it. I clear my throat and turn my attention to Peter. He continues to chew on the plastic straw that was meant for his small carton of chocolate milk, and he keeps his gaze downward.

I throw my arm around him. He turns his head away from me, still holding his gaze low. I sigh. Christopher lets out a soft sigh, keeping his eyes on Peter. We both figure that he's probably still bummed over how things went yesterday after Peter mustered the courage to ask Jen Li to prom.

Of all people, none of us would've expected Peter to take an interest in Jen Li. She's cute, yes, but he's never talked about her. Not once. I mean, we all knew they had environmental science together, but that was about it. Plus, I swore I heard a rumor that she was going out with some guy on the robotics team. Then again, it might've been just a rumor since Jen Li has never walked the halls locking arms with anyone.

Still, I met up with Peter yesterday after my Honors Algebra and gave him a quick pep-talk before he finally made his move. I watched from behind the hallway corner, and I was surprised when I saw him approach Jen Li as she was switching out her books. He was hiding a single red rose behind his back, and when she finally looked at him after closing her locker, he gave her the rose. I could tell he was nervous, but he just kept smiling, and she started smiling.

Then out of nowhere, she kissed him on the cheek and left. When Peter turned around, that pearly-white smile of success was plastered on his face. He was practically on cloud nine.

But after school, Peter looked as if he had seen the most depressing pet adoption campaign ad on television. I was about to ask him if everything was alright, but he just shrugged it off, saying that he was fine. That's when I saw Jen Li leaving with some guy's arm draped around her shoulder, pulling her closer as they talked and laughed.

It was terrible. Christopher sort of put two-and-two together on his own and suggested that we all go to Chinatown for some fried ice cream. And we did just that.

Now, Peter's sitting at the lunch table, sulking.

He really liked this girl, huh?

I sigh.

"Where's Benton?" Peter suddenly asks.

Meagan shrugs. "I think he's at home."

Peter presses his lips together, and a look of disappointment washes over his face. He was already disappointed, but he looked more disappointed now that Benton wasn't coming to lunch. He's the type of person who likes when everyone's together. That's just him. Probably because of how he was raised. His family was never really together for anything, so he sort of relies on us to always be together for things like this—lunch, after-school hangouts, and regular squad hangs.

But after Morris-Lina…I don't know what Peter's idea of all of us being together looks like now.

After school, I offer to take Meagan home, but she says that she has to stay behind for a bit to help with some "theater stuff." As she said that, I noticed two people standing by the auditorium doors, looking at us. Meagan must've realized I was looking over her shoulder because she turned around and waved at them.

The one guy was dressed in an oversized hoodie with his arms folded as if he was annoyed. He looked familiar.

Wait—is that—?

"Just start without me, Preston!" Meagan calls out to them.

Oh, right! Preston Highmore.

I forgot he and Meagan were friends and did theater together. He just waves her off and goes back inside the auditorium. Meanwhile, the other guy just stands there with his hands stuffed in his pockets. He finally moves off the doors and approaches us. As he comes closer, I realize it's *him.*

Nathan.

The knots in my stomach start to come back once he finally comes up to us, standing beside Meagan. I keep my eyes on her, and she clears her throat. I can tell from the look on her face, she feels just as uneasy as I do. I didn't tell her about what happened in the locker room, nor do I plan to—she'd just rub it in my face, saying that he's changed and all that bullshit.

It's all bullshit.

"Hey, Nate," she says, turning her attention to Nathan while giving him a faint smile.

Nate? So it's "Nate" now?

He smiles back at her. "Hey." His attention turns to me.

I could tell that he wanted to say something, but I don't want to hear anything from his mouth. I didn't care what Meagan or Christopher thought of him. I knew who he really was, anyway.

"See you tomorrow, chica."

I feel Meagan reach out for me, but I don't give her the chance to keep me there. It's not that I didn't want to. I just couldn't. If I stayed any longer, I would've decked him. I'd feel good about it, but for Meagan's sake, I couldn't do it. So, I just get into my car and head home.

Week 2, Saturday.

I wanted to sleep in today since it was just that type of day. It was drizzling outside, the neighborhood was quiet (which hardly happens), and my parents are out and about doing God knows what. I know mom works today, and dad will probably visit my tía Yoselin and sit with her for a while. Lord knows when he'll get back home. It's been a while since I've even talked to my tía Yoselin. The last time I saw her was at the funeral. For Morris, I mean. Of course, none of us wanted to reunite under that circumstance, but it just happens all the time, I guess.

Ha, it's kinda funny too, you know? This so-called "family" ain't much of a family 'til something terrible happens. That's just how it is. I don't wanna continue with this. I gotta do something since I can't sleep-in anymore.—D.G.

My phone starts buzzing like crazy as I flip the pancake over to cook on the other side. It sizzles, and the smell of cinnamon hits through my nostrils, and it reminds me of why I love cinnamon pancakes so damn much. I didn't want to stay in bed all day, so I figured I might as well eat something. Mom usually orders us breakfast on Saturday mornings, but since she had to work today, I was on my own, which I didn't mind. Saves her money.

Anyway, I reach for my phone from off the countertop behind me. I furrowed my eyebrows when I realized it was Christopher calling. He's been in such a slump this week. I figured he'd use today as his advantage to sleep in and keep to himself— especially since yesterday marked the day his mom died. I was surprised that he even had the will to come to school yesterday. I thought it was even bolder that he tried to keep a happy face whenever Meagan and Benton were around.

I know it's hard for him to talk about his mom's death, but he was still off, even when trying to feign being okay. So it was no surprise that when Christopher had left the lunch table, Meagan quickly asked us if he was alright.

"He was acting weird," she said, and she was right. Christopher is a terrible actor, so he never considered joining the theater.

But finally, Carmen was the one to tell Meagan and Benton about Christopher's mom dying. She said, *"Today marks the day she died. It wasn't that long ago either, so it's still hard. Even if it was years ago, it'd be hard. He doesn't like to talk about it, and we don't like bringing it up, so just act normal. For him. Please."*

They didn't fail in upholding that task. As soon as Christopher returned, everything was back to how it was—us talking about anything, laughing, joking. We all did it for him. But still, it takes him a couple of days to really come out of that dark place. We'll take him out somewhere after school to help cheer him up, but it still takes time for it all to settle in. We usually give him a day or two to keep to himself, which is why I was a little surprised to see that he was calling me.

Still, I answer the phone.

"Yo," I say as I go back to making my pancakes.

"Hey," he says through his thick Irish accent. "Got any plans?"

I shrug. "Not really. Just making pancakes."

He snorts. "Making pancakes is a plan?"

"Anything involving food is a plan." I grab a plate from the cabinet above my head and place my finished pancakes on it. "Seriously, what's up? Tired of being cooped up on a dreary day?"

Christopher huffs, and I hear him plop down somewhere. Probably on his bed because he let out a sharp sigh afterward like he was comfortable. "Funny. Don't you like weather like this, weirdo?"

"Oi! Look who's talking, *cabrón*." I cut off the stove and tossed the spatula into the sink. I let the pan sit on the stovetop to cool down before rinsing it out.

As I rip off a corner piece from one of the three pancakes I've made, Christopher asks me if I'd be down to go with him to the sandlot a couple blocks up from my house. Just the two of us.

"You still got that pitching machine I gave to you, right?"

I finished chewing the smooth piece of pancake that was in my mouth before telling him, "Of course I do."

We both agree to meet at the sandlot in half an hour, which is fine with me. To be honest, I wasn't expecting Christopher to reach out to me and ask to hang out. Like I said, he usually takes a day or two to himself after getting through the day of his mom's death. So for him to want to ask to hang out so suddenly is unlike him.

Still, I ate my pancakes, washed the dishes, and got dressed. Before I knew it, I put on my heavy black jacket, and I was out the door. Getting the pitching machine into the backseat was no trouble at all either. Sure, it was a bit heavy, but I managed to fit it in there.

When I finally get into the car, I throw my head back against the headrest and let out a sharp breath. My hands suddenly feel sore from lifting the pitching machine into the car. My palms are red, and there are marks on them from where I picked up the pitching machine. I rub my hands together, closing my eyes. I remember when Christopher gave me the pitching machine as a surprise. It was actually him, Carmen, and Peter. They were all in on it.

We all decided to go over Chris's after school to hang out. But I should have known something was up when Carmen came up from behind me with a smirk on her face. It was the kind of smirk that reminded me of a sneaky villain who thinks they can outsmart the hero when really they can't—but Carmen sure enough fooled me.

The next thing I knew, Christopher and Peter wheeled out a giant…something…that was covered with a blanket. Christopher snatched off the blanket and revealed the pitching machine. It wasn't giant. It was the perfect size for transportation, and it looked new, although it wasn't. I knew it belonged to his dad, but I would hardly see them use it. Suddenly, Christopher had told me that it "was" his dad's, implying that it was no longer in their possession.

I remember the smile on his face when I realized that he was giving the machine to me. I practically knocked us both down to the ground when I wrapped my arms around him. I've received many gifts that I consider to be great. But this felt like the greatest gift of all time. At that moment, I realized that I actually had some great friends.

Well, I already knew I had great friends, but that moment was definite confirmation of it.

I finally pull myself out of my thoughts, and I check the time on my phone. I have to get going. Knowing Christopher, he is probably already waiting for me at the sandlot.

The rain continues to drizzle down faintly, but it is still a bit chilly outside. I don't bother clicking on the radio to make up for the silence—there's no need. It won't take me long to get to the sandlot anyway. Besides, Christopher was right. I am a bit of a weirdo for liking weather like this.

Dad thinks I'm a bit like my abuelo since he enjoyed dreary weather. As much as I enjoyed spending time with abuelo, I don't remember little things like that about him. But I remember dad crying when he was alone with mom in their bedroom. The door had been cracked open, but not by much. Dad's head was in his hands, elbows rested atop his thighs, and sharp breaths escaped his lips. Mom just sat with him, holding him close. She said all types of things in Spanish, but she spoke softly. I remember thinking that she was praying, but I didn't know for sure.

All I know is that was the first and only time I've ever seen my dad cry. Even after what happened to Morris-Lina—he didn't cry. All I kept thinking was—why? I mean, I didn't either, but I didn't know what to believe at that moment. I was just all over the place. My mind was practically mush, and I didn't know what emotions to feel. I was so many things. Angry. Confused. Sad. Shocked.

But I did feel things at least, unlike him.

The sound of a car horn blaring behind me snaps me back into reality, and I realize that the traffic light has turned green. I raise my hand to apologize to the person behind me as I pull off and turn the corner.

It doesn't surprise me at all that Christopher is already there at the sandlot, waiting for me. He stands outside of his car while looking down at his phone. I park right beside his car, and Christopher finally looks up as I get out of the car.

"Took yeh long enough," he says, looking right at me.

I roll my eyes. I notice the twisted smirk on his face, and I look away. "Help me get this out of here." The words slip through my lips like a demand, but Christopher still makes his way over to the backseat and helps me lift the pitching machine out of the car without leaving a scratch.

The drizzling finally stops as we carry the machine center field. Christopher loudly huffs, resting his hands on his hips. "I forgot how heavy this thing is," he breathes.

"It's not that heavy," I smirk.

Christopher arches an eyebrow, his lips remaining slightly parted. I do my best to not laugh. I could tell that he wanted to smack me upside my head or pinch me, but he restrained himself. He just mutters, "Jesus."

I watch as he walks back to his car and pops open the trunk. He comes back over to me, carrying a baseball bat in one hand and a bag full of baseballs in the other. He wastes no time giving me the bat as he fills the machine with baseballs.

I unzip my jacket and walk up to the base. It's not like I haven't played ball in a long time. We're not even playing ball—we're just taking a couple of swings, that's all. But the feeling is still strange since I told myself I would let those days stay behind me. It wasn't that I was bored or sick of baseball. I still enjoy it, but everyone swore up and down that the only reason I'd make it through college was if I received a baseball scholarship.

In a way, the arrogance I had to put up with made me leave the baseball team my junior year. I knew I was good, but people used that to be condensing, and I wasn't putting up with that shit anymore. I didn't want baseball to be the only I was known for being suitable for. Plus, family always comes first.

Morris-Lina wasn't in the best place during our junior year. Mom would yell at her. Dad would hardly know what to do with her. I knew it was because of her medication. Ever since she was diagnosed, everything just spiraled. So, I had to be there for her. I owed her that much.

Anyway, Christopher finishes loading up the baseballs, and he asks me if I'm ready. I slip off my jacket and tie it around my waist tightly to not fall off. I get into position as Christopher starts up the machine. The first ball comes flying towards me. I swing. I hear the crack come from the bat when it taps swiftly against the ball. Christopher looks up with his mouth open in awe as the ball goes flying back to the far end of the field.

Christopher looks back at me, one side of his mouth pulled upward in a smirk. He calls out, "Show off!" and another ball fires out. I smack it with the bat, and it flies over Christopher's head. It doesn't go as far, but he considers it far enough. He even calls out, "And it's outta here!", trying to pull off a southern accent, which he does terribly.

I snort. "Quit being such a dad already and keep 'em coming." And Christopher does just that.

The baseballs continue to come my way, and I manage to hit them each time. Some go farther than others, but feeling them hit against the bat is what really matters. It's not like I'm reliving the "glory days," as some folks say. I'm just able to clear my head for some reason. Hearing the crack when the ball connects to the ball, a part of me can focus more.

It's refreshing.

I signal for a time-out, and Christopher turns off the machine. I jog over to him and hand him the bat.

"Looks like you still got it, huh?" Christopher snickers, looking back at all the baseballs spread out far behind him on the field.

I stretch my arms out, and I hear my elbows pop. It feels good. I let out a relaxed sigh. "Surprised I never lost it," I joke. "Wanna take a crack at it?"

Christopher practically wheezes, shaking his head. "C'mon mate, you know damn well I ain't got it."

"Bullshit," I huff, throwing my arm on his shoulder. "Anyone can play ball, Chrissy. Let's set that straight."

The grin on his face fades away, and an unamused look takes over. He lightly shoves me off him, and I can't help but chuckle. "Quit being a twit and help me get these balls up," he demands.

As we're collecting the balls one-by-one, Christopher suddenly asks me, "Your birthday's coming up. Any plans?"

I feel my throat tighten. A shiver runs down my spine as I think about his words. I know my birthday is in a few days, but I've done all I can to not think about it. After all, it's not just my birthday people will be celebrating. It's something I really don't want to think about. Not now, not ever.

I clear my throat. "I haven't given it much thought," I reply.

"Really?" Christopher stands up straight, tossing the balls in his hands into the bag. "Eighteen is a pretty big deal."

I snort. "Not as big as people make it out to be."

I toss the two baseballs in my hands into the bag and look up at Christopher. He stands there with his arms folded across his chest, swaying a bit. I can tell he wants to say something as he keeps staring at me. But whatever he wants to say or is thinking of saying, I don't want to hear it. At least not right now. Especially if it has to do with my birthday.

"I just, uh, don't want to think about my birthday right now, you know?" I tell him, clearing my throat. "It's not something that's usually on my list of things to think about it daily since it's just not really a priority."

Don't be an ass, don't be an ass.

Christopher sighs. I pray to God that he's not going to say anything, but he does anyway. I feel my chest tighten, and the air suddenly becomes heavy, almost humid—but it's 50-something degrees out.

The words escape from Christopher's mouth effortlessly as he asks me, "Is it your birthday you don't wanna talk about, or is it her?"

A sharp breath. *He just had to say it. Seriously?*

I turn on my heels to look away from him, but he doesn't get the message. Instead, he continues, insisting that it's alright for us to address what's really going on here. That it's okay for me to admit that I don't want to celebrate my birthday because of Morris-Lina and us not celebrating our birthday together.

Christopher then goes, "We have to talk about her. At least sometimes we can."

I press my lips together in a straight line and turn back so I can face him. I keep my eyes on him as my chest becomes unbearably tight. The thought of her burns in my mind, and it's like a hammer to a nail. Without thinking, I open my mouth and basically tell him to drop it. I don't yell at him. It just comes out.

I even reminded him that if he didn't like us talking about his mom, why should we bother talking about Morris-Lina? It seemed pretty fair, but judging from the look Christopher gave me, it was also unfair. Maybe it was a bit unfair. His mom died two years ago and from natural causes. Morris-Lina—

It was literally a couple months ago, and she had just taken too many of her pills. She probably didn't even realize how much she took, which is why there was some leftover in her hand. That's what I think. I don't care what others want to call it.

But maybe that's why Christopher feels the way he is—because it was so sudden. What happened to his mom was sudden too, but it was two years ago. So, he was kind of able to wrap his head around it more.

I sigh.

"Sorry." I can hardly look him in the eye now.

He just nods. "Yeah." He sniffs, but he isn't crying. "Me too."

I watch as he walks away to get the rest of the baseballs. My heart plummets down to my stomach, and I suddenly feel sick. If I could strangle myself to death, I would. Instead, I continue picking up whatever baseballs I can find, and I put them back into the bag.

We don't pack up and leave right away after we pick up all the baseballs. Christopher helps me load the machine back into my car, and he puts the bag of baseballs and the bat into the trunk of his car. We then sit on the grass, looking out into the empty field.

There aren't any cars driving by, so it's quiet. It's nice. It kind of reminds me of the lake dad used to take Morris-Lina and me to when we were kids. It was always quiet up there. If it was nighttime and the stars were out, I'd be in Heaven.

Christopher groans as he lays down in the grass, facing the sky with his hands behind his head. I look back at him as he sighs.

"It's been a hell of a couple months," he sighs.

I lean back until my back finally touches the ground. I look up at the gray sky as the clouds clump together, leaving no possible hope for sunshine. The breeze picks up a bit, and I look over to Christopher. He suddenly asks me, "You don't have to tell me, but what would be your birthday wish? Just asking?"

I think about it.

"Some friggin' peace and quiet."

He snorts, thinking I was joking, but I actually meant it.

Week 3, Sunday.

I felt sick to my stomach this morning. It wasn't a stomach bug or from something I ate—I just can't explain it. Ever since Chris brought up wanting to talk about Morris-Lina, I've been on edge. Why the hell did he even have to bring her up like that? Then I'm the bad guy when I say something about his mom...

Shit. I know Counselor Malik thinks writing this stuff out is good, but it's starting to become a real pain in the ass. I don't like it at all.

Oh well. Mom and dad want me to spend time with mi tía Yoselin since she asked about me yesterday when dad was over there yesterday. I think they're just trying to get rid of me. I heard them fighting over something again this morning. They weren't as loud as before, but I could still listen to them. It really pisses me off at times, but I can't say jack shit about it.— D.G.

I hear my aunt Yoselin call my name from inside the house, and I look up. I watch as my little cousin Yago chases after his little brother, Gabriel, while wielding a small branch. The laughter that comes from Yago reminds me of a psychopathic clown that I would expect to go from a horror film. His eyes are wide with thrill as he chases Gabriel like a madman. It also doesn't help that Gabriel's screams become more and more desperate as he pleads for his big brother to stop chasing him.

I call out to them, *"Oye! Oye!"* as I stand up from the red patterned tiles leading to the grass in the backyard.

Before I can approach them, Gabriel swiftly runs up behind me, and I feel his little fingers grip onto my pants leg. He practically buries his face into his hands as he whimpers. I whip my attention to Yago as he runs up to me and nearly stumbles when he meets my gaze. I grab onto his arm as he trips forward, and I yank the branch out of his hand. I toss it off to the side, far from Yago's reach, as I pull him up 'til he's standing upright.

I practically crouch down to level with him as his big brown eyes practically peer into my soul as if he's pleading innocence. Meanwhile, Gabriel suddenly grips onto the back of my jacket and shifts away from Yago. I can feel Gabriel's head resting against my back, and I sigh.

"It was just a joke," I heard Yago mumble under his breath as his gaze shifted away from me.

"Well, it wasn't all funny, was it?" I keep a straight face.

Yago practically yanks himself free from my grasp and crosses his arms over his chest, keeping his eyes away from me. He goes, "Hmph!" and I can't help the chuckle that slips through my lips.

For a second, I think about Morris-Lina and how she would always cross her arms and pout whenever mom or dad would scold her for her excessive teasing when we were kids. She would always try to jump up from behind me and scare me, and sometimes I would get so scared that I would hyperventilate. Mom and dad would always get so pissed at her, and I would feel bad. I would try to tell them that it was no big deal, and only sometimes would they let her off the hook. We were little kids, after all.

I chuckle to myself. I look back up at Yago as he kicks the ground while standing in the spot. He's muttering all sorts of things to himself while huffing and puffing. I suddenly feel tiny, slim arms wrap around my neck and thick hair tickle against the side of my face. I glance at Gabriel from the corner of my eye, and his big doe-brown eyes glisten from the sunlight.

They get their innocent charm from their father because there's no way in hell they would've picked up from my tía Yoselin.

I look back at Yago, and he finally gives me his attention. I reach out and ruffle the curly mop of hair on his head. Of course, he groans and stomps his foot, whining for me to stop.

I snort—*this kid.*

I tickle my fingers against his throat and all along his neck, sending him into a fit of giggles. He can hardly speak as he tries to beg for me to stop, but I ignore him. Before Yago gets the chance to run away from me to escape my tickling, I scoop him up and pull him close to me. His giggles start to soften as he wraps his arms around my neck, leaning against me a bit.

I shift my attention to Gabriel and wrap my arm around him, bringing him forward and out of hiding from behind me. Gabriel throws himself at me, latching his tiny arms around me while burying his face into my chest.

I look to Yago. "What do you say?"

He sighs. "I'm sorry."

"Don't tell me." I nudge my head to Gabriel, who is now looking up at Yago with big eyes.

Yago fiddles with his fingers. "Sorry, Gabriel."

Gabriel just nods his head and buries his head even more into my chest. I sigh. I don't recall being this clingy when I was four.

I could feel someone standing behind me, and I noticed Yago's attention shift upwards, looking behind me. I turn around and see my tía Yoselin standing there with her hands on her hips and a grin twisted on her face. Her open-toed heels make her seem taller than she actually is, but I know to the kids she's like a goddess. A scary, intimidating goddess who uses makeup and her sense of fashion to hide the wrath within.

"Boys." She arches an eyebrow as her grin gets a bit wider like a creepy clown. "Looks like you two are really enjoying your primo Donald's company." She doesn't sound irritated when she says my name either.

She crouches down to look at them, and I feel Yago come a bit closer to me. It's not like Yoselin is hard on the boys like my parents were hard on Morris-Lina and me when we were kids. If they do act up, she'll give them the occasional pop to the mouth or pinch their ears, but she's never spanked them. Even so, she is still scary, I'll admit.

Yoselin reaches out to both of them, and they immediately go up to her, freeing me from their grasps. Gabriel practically tries to sit on her lap, although Yoselin pushes him off her lap a bit since there is no way she was staying crouched down that long while in her heels. Meanwhile, Yago has his arms folded over his chest and lips in a straight line. It's not like he knows he's in trouble, but I can tell that whatever she has to say to them, he's hardly intrigued. That is until she finally tells them.

"Mamá has to go run some errands. But I thought it's such a nice day, how about you boys go spend it with su primo Donald? Say…at the park?"

Broad smiles and eager eyes immediately take over both boys' faces. Yago leaps to me, jumping up and down while clenching onto my arm. He asks me, "Donald is that okay? Please! *Pleeeease!*"

I suddenly realize why I'm still in a dilemma on figuring out whether or not I'd want to have kids in the future. On the one hand, kids wouldn't be so bad to deal with. They'd keep me busy, and they'd be mine—something I'd be proud of. On the other hand, they're manipulative devils—using their innocence to charm and con people into doing what they want.

This right here is a perfect example of that. Then again, I don't really have a choice anyway.

I sigh as a faint smile crosses my lips. "Get your boots on."

Both boys jump around each other, chanting, "Yay! Yay! Yay!" before finally running into the house. Yoselin chuckles to herself as she finally stands upright and looks down at me. She thanks me for taking the boys and just for coming over, period.

"They missed you," she says.

I stand up from my crouched position and somewhat meet her eye level. Her heels make her taller than expected. "I missed them too," I tell her as I stuff my hands in the pockets of my jacket. The cool breeze erupts goosebumps on my arms, and I shiver.

"Let's talk inside." Yoselin makes way for me to enter the house and follows me inside.

I look back as she slides the door shut behind us. When she looks back at me, her lips are twisted, and that's when I realize something is up. So, I ask her, "Everything alright?"

Yoselin nods, pushing the front strand of her hair out of her face. "Of course." She pauses. "Can I ask the same to mi sobrino favorito?"

I snort under my breath, looking away from her. "I'm your only nephew," I remind her.

She shrugs. "Doesn't matter. Still my favorite." She comes up to me and settles her hands on both sides of my face. My skin crawls from her icy touch, which is ironic since she gives me the warmest smile. "Are you sure you're okay?" This time her voice is serious but softer.

I wrap my fingers around her wrists and remove her hands from my face. I nodded, telling her that I was okay. She just smiles, telling me, "Okay," as if she believes me. In her eyes, I can tell she doesn't buy it. But I really was okay. I didn't have to get a lecture from her either. It's bad enough that Christopher and Counselor Malik are on my ass.

Before Yoselin has the chance to say another word, little, heavy footsteps come stomping down the steps in a hurry. I watch as Yago and Gabriel run up to me— boots on, laces tied tightly, and their coats all zipped up.

Gabriel reaches his arms out for me to pick him, and I cave. I scoop him up as his little arms wrap around my neck. A big giggly smile is plastered on his face, revealing the gap between his two front teeth. Yago tugs at the hem of my jacket, and I look down at him.

He asks me, "Can we go now, Cousin Don-O? Estoy listo!"

I chuckle. "What about your hat and gloves?"

"I got them," Yoselin says, walking to the closet. She comes back over with Yago and Gabriel's hat and gloves. She hands Yago the blue pair to match his navy blue coat, and she slips the red pair on Gabriel to match his dark red coat.

She then tells them, "Remember to stay close to su primo Donald. Do not go off and stay away—"

"—*stay away from the back gate of the park*," Yago completes her words for her in a groan.

Yoselin smirks, looking down at him. "Sí, mi pequeño."

I wrinkle my eyebrows. The only park around here isn't really much of a park, to be honest. It's a playground that's right up the street, and I'm sure the boys always go there—especially after school. Most of the neighborhood kids do. It's always been that way, and it's never been an issue for anyone before. So I don't understand why she wouldn't want them to run around, even if it's near the back gate. Nothing is near there, and the gate is always locked so they can't run out into the street.

I ask Yoselin, "What's wrong with the back gate?"

The way she looks at me, it's as if I am supposed to know something, but I am still a bit lost. She sighs. "A couple of dealers occupy back there now. They've been taking up most of the area now. It's ridiculous."

"Mom calls them *'drogadictos tontos',*" Yago blurts out.

Yoselin gives him a look that makes him shut up right away. She looks back at me, and I remember that I am still holding Gabriel in my arms. I put him down and told the boys to wait for me by the door. They run off, and I turn my attention back to Yoselin.

"When did this all start?" I cross my arms over my chest.

"Since gentrification." She doesn't bat an eyelash when the words slip out of her mouth. "At first, it was just outside some corner stores. Now, they're on the playgrounds, even outside some department stores. The other day when I was on my way to work, I saw some of them sitting outside the boys' school. Not even around the back or the side. Right in the front." The frustration from her voice shows on her face. She crosses her arms over her chest and looks towards the boys.

I take a sharp breath. I would expect someone to call the police to possibly have the area monitored since the neighborhood is supposed *"family-friendly,"* which is total BS because shit does happen there. But *occasionally.* There were like a few break-ins, but that was about it. Never any drug dealing or shootings. She didn't mention any shootings, but that's what usually ends up happening once drugs start taking place.

And like she said, it's all thanks to gentrification.

Even though I don't visit Yoselin and the boys often, I remember how the area used to be. It's still lovely where they live. It's not like Chestnut Hill or the suburbs, but it is a nice, quiet area. Everyone takes care of their property, kids will usually play outside and in the street without worries, and some old people will be doing their morning or afternoon walks. The houses are nice too, and the roads. I can only imagine how much they pay in taxes.

And now, they're hit with this shit. It's still a nice area, but I don't know how long ago the dealers moved up are where they live. Yoselin said it's been a couple of weeks or so, but I doubt it. It's probably been more than just *a couple of weeks or so.*

I ask her, "Did you tell my dad about this?"

Yoselin whips her head around with her eyebrows furrowed. She looks at me as if I have two heads. I don't understand why, though. My dad works for the city. I don't know precisely what he does, but I know that he's damn good at it since he moved up from being a secretary. Fifteen years later, he's now carrying a briefcase, dressed in affordable but stylish suits, earning good pay.

I don't see why Yoselin just wouldn't come to him about it. She had the chance to tell him when he swung by the other day. I know she doesn't really like that he works for the city since she feels they don't do shit, but I mean, it's something—her telling him. At least he'd relay the message to someone so they could come up with a possible solution.

"He works for the city," I remind her. "He could put this in someone's ear and possibly bring some attention to it."

She quickly responds, "There's nothing your father can do. For all we know, he knew this was going to happen." There is fire and venom in her words. I can tell it's the frustration of the situation gnawing at her more so than my father and his capability.

My throat becomes dry and itchy. I cough, hoping it helps get rid of the feeling. It hardly helps at all. I just give Yoselin my word that I'll keep an eye on the boys. When Yago sees me head for the door, he wastes no time to jump up from the bottom of the steps and head towards me. Gabriel follows him and grabs my other hand.

Before we're entirely out the door, Yoselin walks up to me and rests her hand on my shoulder. I look at her. She moves her hand to my cheek, and her eyes have a sudden honey glow due to the natural light coming through the screen door.

She sighs. "Confío en ti, mi sobrino favorito."

"Gracias, tía."

She finally lets us head out the door. The boys and I just walk up to the park—well, the playground—and I think about Yoselin's words the whole way there. What she said about my dad. He does work for the city. So…did he have any idea this would happen?

For so long, their neighborhood has been at ease. Everyone pays their taxes, everyone owns lovely homes and nice cars. Why screw it all up now? I can understand why she'd be frustrated.

I would be too. I just imagine one of these days, God forbid, a kid is playing out in the street, and something happens.

But dad wouldn't let that happen. He'd speak up if she'd tell him.

What do you know, Donald? You don't even know what your dad does.

So? You can still bring it to his attention.

But you're gonna make it worse since it's not your place.

I'd kick myself in the balls right now if I could. I just tell myself to forget about it, and I watch as Yago runs straight for the swing set once we get to the park. I look down at Gabriel, and he points to the curvy slide that's part of the jungle gym.

"Think you're tough enough for that one, huh?" I ask him.

Gabriel gives me a giggly smile, and I can't help but snicker when I see the gap between his teeth again. I bend down and have him climb up on my back. As I walk up the steps of the jungle gym, I look over and notice a group of guys huddled at the back gate. It's about four of them, and they're all just looking out in different directions—smoking, drinking.

Stay in your lane, Don. I tell myself this constantly as I reach the top of the steps and let Gabriel climb off my back so I can go down the slide with him.

Week 3, Wednesday.

I haven't told my folks what tía Yoselin told me the other day. About the dealers hanging around the school and the playground and even around the department stores. I know there's not much I can really do about it, and I want to tell my dad about it, but what are the chances he'll listen to me? If anything, he'll just ask why Yoselin didn't tell me for herself. Then I'm looking like an invasive clown. And I don't wanna put mi tía in a lousy position either because then, mom'll think that she's endangering the boys, which isn't the case at all.

Mom is always quick to overstep and judge. She did that with Morris-Lina. She occasionally does it with me too. God, I can only imagine what it was like growing up with her. Before abuela died, she would tell me that mom was always so difficult. Ha, abuela told me she once called mom "pequeño demonio loco" whenever mom would drive her up a wall.

God, I miss abuela. I miss a lot of things, to be honest.—D.G.

I tell myself to stop biting my lips as I watch as Counselor Malik flips through the pages of my journal. I always get on Meagan about whenever she bites her nails slim. Meanwhile, I can already taste the blood from where I peeled a small part of the skin from my lip. The taste is somehow calming, though.

At least at the moment, maybe.

I shift my gaze to the other side of the room, looking out the window. All I see is smoke emerging from the top of a building, fogging up the glass window. The window is cracked open, welcoming in a cool breeze, and I can hear police sirens and cars driving up and down the street. I somehow manage to get lost in it all until I hear Counselor Malik's voice interrupt my daydream.

"Would you like the foam ball I have set aside for you?" he asks. I suddenly notice his eyes narrow downward. "You're tapping again." He says it so nonchalantly with a faint grin on his face.

I look down at my leg and realize he was right. I stop moving and stuff my hands in my black leather jacket pockets. I'm not nervous if that's what he thinks. There's no reason for me to be.

This isn't our first rodeo. Every week, he has me scheduled to come in, and he reads whatever I wrote to see if there's any *"progress."* Some people think it's effective.

I say bullshit. At least for me, it's bullshit. But I get that Counselor Malik is just trying to do his job, so I try to make an effort.

Plus, I'm almost one-hundred percent certain that if he had it his way, he wouldn't schedule to meet with me as much. After what happened to Morris-Lina, Principal Vickins and my parents had me scheduled for a weekly session with Counselor Malik at least three times a week. Depending on circumstances, I used to go to him at least once or twice bi-weekly—sometimes once every other two weeks.

Counselor Malik finally closes the journal and places it down on the small table beside his chair. He sits with his legs crossed and sits back in the chair as if he is the ruler of the room. He probably is given that this was his office, but still. I thought it was a bit mocking, but I just sat in my chair, looking at him.

"Well, I'm glad I can confirm that you do your homework." A faint smile plays on his lips. "But I can also tell that you're hardly giving your all with this project I gave you."

I wrinkle my eyebrows. *What the hell does that mean?*

I shake my head. "What are you talking about? I'm writing just like you told me."

"Yes. You are. But all you're doing is writing. You're not open as you write. You're ignoring the underlying purpose of this whole process."

The fact that Counselor Malik sounds so confident of himself, it almost makes me laugh.

I lean back further in my seat and look out the window. I try to figure out what more this guy could want from me. For the past couple of weeks, he's been bugging me about writing literally anything that comes to mind. It's not like I don't want to write.

I'm just not as passionate about it as someone like Meagan would be. She could write her out heart out for days and do something beautiful with it. That's her purpose. That's what I admire about her.

Not me. I don't have desires like she does. Well, I have desires, but they're not like hers. Her desires are creative.

A scoff slips through my lips, and I turn my attention back to Counselor Malik. He looks at me as if I owe him some sort of explanation. Even though I've made it clear to him that I've done all I can, wrote all that I could write, he still looks unconvinced. The knot in my stomach tightens, and I feel goosebumps start to rise on my arms.

I tell him, "You said to write what I was thinking, and that was it. What more could you want me to do? Unless I just bullshit the rest?"

A snicker comes from him. A friggin' *snicker.*

He then reaches over, picks the journal back up from the table, and flips through the pages. He stops and reads one of my journal entries aloud. I feel my chest tighten as he recites the words to me as if I don't remember what I had written. It makes my skin crawl in a way, but not to the point where I feel disgusted with my own being.

It's more so a feeling of wanting to get up and storm out the room before I did or said something I'd regret. But I can't move. It's like my body is glued to the chair, and the only way for me to get out is when he's ready for me to leave. So, I sit there and listen to him read the journal entry aloud.

I close my eyes as I take in every word he says, every word I have written. The memory burns in my mind, and my throat goes dry.

Today it felt like the end of time. Sounds dramatic but true. Mom and dad were yelling as usual, and it didn't help that it was so early in the morning. Morris-Lina always considered us the freak show, and she certainly was right. The only words I could make out from their argument was Morris-Lina's name. It was stupid. All of it was stupid. I tried going back to sleep, but it was pointless. Dad had left, and mom was about to wake me eventually. If things had panned out differently, I'm sure we would all be happy about it.

He rereads the last line, his voice sounding calm. *"If things had panned out differently, I'm sure we would all be happy about it."*

Hearing the words come out of his mouth causes a burning sensation to burst in my chest. My throat feels as though someone has their hands clenched around my windpipe, and I am left breathing through only my nostrils. I honestly don't know why I wrote that nonsense. I was probably writing to have something written and called it a day.

It was meaningless, but of course, Counselor Malik has to make it seem like something it isn't. As expected, he asks me, "What do you mean by that?" He places the journal back on the small table and sits with his hands folded as he waits for my response.

My lips feel dry, and the burning sensation in my chest tightens. It's as if someone is sitting right on my chest with all their weight on me. I clear my throat and pull my jaw as I think about what to say. Because I have to say something. If I don't say anything, he'll think I'm avoiding whatever he's hoping to get out of me. He'll think I'm purposely trying to get one over him, and that's the case at all.

I just don't know what to say.

If I'm honest, that last line doesn't mean anything. I don't even know what I meant when I wrote it down. I don't even know why I wrote it in the first place. Like I said, I was just writing to have something written. But what are the chances he'd actually believe me?

I let out a sigh and have the sudden urge to crack my knuckles. The cracking sound that comes from the bones in my knuckles and my fingers brings me sweet relief. I feel calm all of a sudden.

I finally respond to Counselor Malik, "At the time, I thought it was a smart thing to say. I don't know. It was a spur in the moment kind of thing. It was just a few words that came to mind."

Counselor Malik shifts around his chair. "Donald, words don't just come to the mind for no reason. Usually, it's because of something we feel deep down but don't want to admit since it makes us feel uncertain."

My eyebrow arches. "Uncertain?"

He sighs, sitting up in his seat. "Like...weak or incapable of realizing certain feelings we have. A sense of incompetence within ourselves. That's why in the heat of passion, some people will say things they don't mean to hurt the people they love because they're actually at battle with themselves." He sounds confident in himself again. But I can tell he's trying not to make me seem like the one at fault. He tightens his jaw and clears his throat before looking back down at his notepad that sits on his thigh.

I know he has a good point, but I don't think of myself as *"weak"* or *"incapable of realizing certain feelings."* I know when I'm feeling something, and I make my feelings known. That's why some people can't stand me. Do I let that bother me, though?

No, not at all. Besides, I have bigger things to worry about than knowing whether or not a couple of putzes and douchebags give a crap about me. The only people I really need are the people who have been there for me already.

Chris. Car. Pete. Benton. Meagan.

That's just fine with me, and if Counselor Malik thinks I need more than that—he's mistaken. But I know the guy is just trying to do his job. So, I don't fight him when he suggests that I continue writing in the journal, and he schedules me for another appointment next week. I just take the journal from him and stuff it back into my bookbag. The bell sounds off, signaling the end of lunch and the counseling session. Relief flows through me as I finally stand up from the chair—*gracias, Dios.*

As I stepped out of Counselor Malik's office, about to close the door, I heard him call out to me one last time. I look back at him, and he stands to get a better look at me. When he steps further into the natural light coming in from the outdoors, I realize just how sharp he looks.

The sunlight really shows off the smoothness of his tan face, his luscious dark hair falls in waves over his shoulders, his charcoal-colored suit fits him like a glove, and he wears matching black dress shoes that have a shine to them when he stands in the light. He looks like a million bucks. He probably gets that every day too. He probably could've done something else with his life, but Counselor Adriel Malik does fit him.

I watch as he stuffs his hands into his dress pants' pockets and lets out a sigh. His eyes remain locked on me as if he's trying to see me sweat. Not a chance. He finally tells me with focused eyes, "Recuerde contar hasta tres." He then gives me a half-but-meaningful smile.

Count to three. Right.

He tells me this all the time, insisting that it'll help with whatever stresses come my way. And it does help at times. I can hold myself back more often from decking clowns like Austin Brown. But I never count aloud. I keep it all in my head. I don't need people thinking I'm losing my mind or something.

I just nod, giving Counselor Malik a faint smile before closing the door behind me as I continue to leave.

I sigh.

It still baffles me at times whenever Counselor Malik speaks Spanish. He's one of the few faculty members of the school who speaks another language so casually, which is ironic since Gabe-Day is a pretty diverse school, and most of the teachers speak more than one language—usually English and Spanish. Then, teachers like Mr. Hua and Mrs. Castello speak three or four languages. I think Counselor Malik knows five languages, including American Sign Language.

He once brought his son to the school with him. Everyone was gushing over how cute the kid looked, and he was a cute kid. He was a mini version of Counselor Malik, only with green eyes instead of brown. But turns out his son was deaf. He had a hearing aid, but Counselor Malik would still use sign language to communicate and interpret for him. Counselor Malik once said that his son knew how to speak, but he preferred using sign language.

It reminded me of Gabriel. Even though Gabriel doesn't know sign language, he would make gestures—like nodding and pointing to things—to indicate whatever he's trying to say...without actually saying it. I don't know why Gabriel's like that. He's not deaf. He just refuses to speak.

But he'll laugh. I like hearing him laugh. It's a bit quiet, but I know he's breathing at least. He laughs a lot too, so I know it gives tía Yoselin some relief.

When I get to my locker, I snort when I see Peter leaning back with his head against the locker beside me. His arms are folded over his chest, and his face screams misery and defeat.

I figure he's still bummed about Jen Li since his next class is with her. It also turns out that they sit next to each other. That sucks.

I open my locker to switch out my books. "The cafeteria had burnt mac-n-cheese again or something?" I try to make a joke, but Peter looks at me as if I am the worst comedic alive. I snort. "Oh, come on, you're acting as though it's the Last Days. You still haven't gotten over her?"

"It's not like that, Don." The look on his face softens, and he shifts his body around wholly to face me. He sighs. "She wants to talk to me. After school."

I shrug. "So? Isn't that a good thing?"

Peter's eyes become the biggest part of his face. "She was locking arms with some other guy after accepting my promposal to her! What if this is like a set-up, and he's the competition? What if she just tells me that I wasn't good enough to take her? What if—?"

"*Oye!*" I rest my hand on his insanely tense shoulder. "If you want, we'll stay close by in case something like that does go down. We'll take you out, beat the guy up if he tries anything, call it a day." I try to sound optimistic, but the way Peter's eyes wander gives away his doubt.

He hardly looks me in the eye when he nods. I sigh.

I open my mouth to speak, but then I hear someone from behind me go, "Hey, Donald!"

I roll my eyes. When I turn around, I see Carmen arm-locked with Christopher and a big smile plastered on her face. With them, it's Meagan and Benton. Even though Benton chopped his hair short, the waves still perfectly shaped his face, showing his sharp cheekbones and chiseled chin. I'll admit, when I first met him, I was envious.

Seeing him and Meagan standing together, side-by-side, whether they're laughing or just talking like friends do, I always picture them being together. Not that it matters—they're just friends. And they're neighbors. So they were bound to be close anyway. Plus, he's never expressed any interest in her. It wouldn't surprise me if she did either—lots of girls like staring at Benton. But unlike them, she gets the pleasure of spending most of her days with him. And he gets the joy of spending most of his days with her. Not that it matters.

I shake myself out of my thoughts when I notice Carmen suddenly cling to my arm and rest her head against my shoulder. She practically yanks me towards her, and I groan, pulling myself free.

"Chill." I then look to Christopher. "C'mon, man, get your girl."

Christopher just snickers, and Carmen just rolls her eyes. She goes, "Stop being such a baby. I just have a proposition for you."

I snort. "Oh yeah? I'm *thrilled*." I'm sarcastic.

As I lean back against my locker, throwing my arm on Meagan's shoulder as she stands near me, Carmen's lips curve upward in a sinister grin. "You will be. You're gonna take Meagan to prom."

My body freezes, and I can feel Meagan's body become tense. I don't even have to look over at her to see the look on her face. I just know that she probably looks just as baffled as I do. I don't make it obvious. At least, I try not to. The sudden lump in my throat becomes unbearable, and I clear my throat, hoping it goes away.

Only Carmen would think this was funny.

Luckily for her, Christopher swoops in and throws his arm around her, backing her away from me a bit. "She's only saying that because she's desperate," he says, giving her a side-eye glance.

Carmen groans. "Well, I need someone to go dress shopping with me, and you keep insisting, but I can't let you see me in my dress."

"It's prom, not a damn wedding," I blurt, trying to hide the frustration in my voice. I look over at Meagan as she finally starts to relax. She leans back against the locker a bit, keeping her arms crossed over her chest. The way she looks at me, I can tell she's still a bit embarrassed by Carmen's dumb joke. I pull her closer to me. "Don't sweat it, kid. She was just joking around." I chuckle.

I'll get Carmen back for this one.

Meagan shrugs. "I know." She then looks at Carmen. "Look, I'll help you find a dress, but that doesn't mean I'm going to prom. So don't bother trying to—"

"—*find you a date*. I knoooow. But I don't get why you're so against it." Carmen then leans into Christopher. "I'm sure after the whole Mary Walsh failure, Don would sure be open to the option." A twisted smile.

I tighten my jaw and shoot my eyes at Christopher. "Control her." I can't hide the irritation in my words as Carmen starts to chuckle.

She had no right to bring *that one* up.

Yes, I did ask Mary Walsh to prom, but it was only because I gave Meagan my word. If I asked Mary Walsh to prom, Meagan would submit one of her writings into the Annual Writing Competition hosted by the School District, which, come to find out, she was one of the finalists for. She said that the banquet would be some time during the summer, but I knew she would end up being one of the final candidates. No doubt about it. So, the wager we had paid off. Even though things went wholly left on my end. Still, it was worth it. Meagan got the opportunity of a lifetime and was now victorious.

Besides, I knew I would be humiliated one way or another. Mary Walsh never really liked me much anyway. She made that obvious multiple times. So by asking her to prom, I only made a bigger fool of myself since I knew the rejection would be inevitable. I could've spared myself the embarrassment, but I had to show Meagan that I was a man of my word.

It's all over and done with now.

Meagan sucks her teeth, rolling her eyes. She gives Carmen a look, hinting at her annoyance.

Carmen groans. "Alright. Fine. No date for you. But can you at least come to help me pick out a dress?" She pouts, quivering her bottom lip as she slowly waddles over to Meagan like a penguin.

A faint chuckle escapes Meagan's lips, and she nods, caving into Carmen's ridiculous pouty-face. "Only if you promise to drop your attempts at getting me to go," Meagan adds, arching an eyebrow.

Carmen places her right hand over her heart and raises her left hand. "I swear on the graves of mi abuela Celeste and mi abuelo Julio." She's serious this time. She then latches onto Meagan's arm with a big smile on her face. "This is perfect. Just the two of us. We'll go right after school."

Meagan opens her mouth to say something—probably object to the idea of going after school since her mom is so serious about her curfew—but Carmen interrupts her. "And don't worry, I'll drop you off home once we're done. I promise you'll be home before it gets super late."

Meagan doesn't even get the chance to say anything since Carmen walks off, heading to class before the bell goes off a second time. Everyone else starts to get the same idea, too, heading off to their classes. Meagan sighs, rubbing her forehead with her fingers. Obviously, she regrets everything that just happened, but I don't rub it in her face. I just nudge her in her arm a bit to get attention, and I flash a smile.

"You got this, kid. Like I always say." I wink, clicking my tongue. Then, I head straight to my fifth-period class on the fourth floor.

……..

As soon as the sixth period ends, I meet up with Peter at the front entrance as promised. To my surprise, Christopher and Benton were already there with him. Although Christopher being there shouldn't have surprised me compared to Benton being there since Benton always dips out right away once school lets out.

Then again, Peter probably found some way to convince Benton to stay behind. After all, if things with Jen Li go downhill, Peter's going to need all the support he can get. No matter how many times I tell him that he has nothing to worry about—which he doesn't—Peter gets flustered and assumes the next catastrophe is around the corner.

Peter peeks outside through the window to get a look at Jen Li. He takes a sharp breath, biting his lips. If I could shake some sense into him, I would, but I know that's the last thing he needs right now. Honestly, I can't say that I blame him for being nervous since there is a chance he could face the same embarrassment I did when I asked Mary Walsh to prom like an idiot. Jen Li could turn around and just blow up at him unexpectedly, making Peter feel like a real doofus.

But if that were the case—why would she kiss him on the cheek?

Maybe it was just a spontaneous move that meant nothing to her, but still. It's pretty bold coming from someone who is probably taken and doubts Peter could stand a chance.

I throw my arm around Peter's neck, pulling him closer to me a bit. All I'm able to say is his name, "Peter," before he abruptly cuts me off.

"Don't. Say it," he says lowly. "I know what you're gonna say. Please don't jinx me here, alright?"

I back off him, raising my hands defensively.

Peter swiftly heads for the double doors and takes a deep breath. Christopher looks at me with his eyebrows furrowed. I can tell he's worried about how this will go down just as much as I am. It's not that we don't have confidence in Peter. I wouldn't doubt him for a second. Out of all of us, Peter's the best when talking to people. He has this vibe about him that just makes him seem more approachable and easier to talk to, even though he's sometimes way in over his head.

Benton, Christopher, and I watch Peter through the window as he approaches Jen Li outside and talks to her. I already know that as people continue to leave the building, they're probably watching us. I can hear some people muttering under their breaths, and a few will often stop and stare as we remain clumped together like three nosy idiots.

Christopher is the one who finally speaks up at a point and goes, "Oi! Got an eye problem? Lose something? Keep moving!"

I shake my head. I can tell that Benton feels somewhat uneasy with the possibility of people staring at the three of us as we watch Peter and Jen Li. So, he backs away a bit and just sits at the bottom hallway step. I could quickly tell him that it was not a big deal, but then I remembered that he's not like me. Benton is the type of guy to receive glances of admiration, not glares. Even if he doesn't intend for people to stare at him, they do because they like him.

It's not like he's walking around, and people think the worst possible things about him. Instead of looking at him and thinking, *Good riddance*, they think, *Woah, look at him*.

I know for sure the rest of the guys get looks like that. Peter with his charming smile and cute face. Then, Christopher with his green eyes, naturally curly hair, and sharp jawline. I receive a few compliments on my looks, but the idea people already have of me makes it easy for people to overlook my appearance.

"Is he done yet?" I hear Christopher ask all of a sudden.

I turn around and realize that he's sitting next to Benton. I must have been lost in my own thoughts. I didn't even see him move away from me. I look back out the window and see Peter and Jen Li waving to each other as she leaves with a smile on her face.

I assume that things went well. And as soon as Peter gives waves for us to come outside, he tells us just how well things went between the two of them. Turns out the guy Jen Li left with the other day after school was her brother, and he was recovering from a surgery he had a while ago. So, she had to help support him as he walked down the steps.

Peter also told us that Jen Li had wanted to ask Peter to prom for a while herself, which was no surprise. Like I said, he has a cute face and a charming smile. Plus, Peter is a good guy.

Peter sighs. "I feel like an idiot."

"For worrying yourself to death over nothing and then realizing that I was right all along?" I snort.

Peter flips me off.

"So," Christopher chimes in, throwing his arm on Peter's shoulder. "Where to? The girls are out doing their shopping. I say we should treat ourselves after this ridiculous holdup." He tries to ruffle Peter's hair, and Peter immediately shoves him away.

"Lay off, will you?" Peter grumbles.

Christopher just chuckles. "How about some milkshakes from the ice cream shop?" He looks over at Benton, who just stands there with his hands on the straps of his bookbag like the Golden Boy he is. "Benton? You in?"

Before Benton can open his mouth to say anything, Peter snaps his fingers and turns to Christopher as if he just had an epiphany. "Not the one in University City? That's closed 'til further notice."

I furrowed my eyebrows. "What?"

Peter nods. "It was on the news. The place was shot up last night, and the cops are still on the move, looking for suspects. I think five people were shot in the store, including the owner."

I feel my chest tighten at the thought. I don't watch the news, especially not first in the morning. When Morris-Lina and I were kids, we would come downstairs for breakfast, and mom would always have it on. But over time, mom grew tired of the news, and dad worked for the city. So, I guess there was no need for us to watch it every morning.

When Peter mentions that one of the victims was a thirteen-year-old kid, I tighten my jaw, and my throat becomes dry.

A kid. A damn kid. You shoot a kid?

I think about the boys—Yago and Gabriel—and what Yoselin told me about the dealers when I was over her place. I remember seeing them chilling near the back gate of the playground, watching the kids and their surroundings. It didn't use to be like that, just like it was rare to hear about a kid getting shot at University City in an ice cream shop. Well, five people getting shot at an ice cream shop in University City.

And the shop usually closes around six, so it wasn't even super late at night. People were still out and about.

I hear Benton say something in Korean, pushing his hair back with his hand. He sighs. "I hope the kid is okay."

Christopher, Peter, and I nod in agreement.

Thirteen.

Christopher rocks on his heels. "I suppose we should get going home, then." He then looks at Peter. "I'll take you home before your aunt starts throwing a fit, yeah?"

Peter nods, sighing. "Yeah, it is about that time anyway. I promised I'd make dinner too since she gets back late." He turns to me and reaches his hand out for me to grab. "See you later, man."

I latch my hand with his and pull him in for a quick hug. "See you."

I do the same with Christopher, but Christopher rests his other hand on my shoulder afterward and looks me in the eyes. He asks me, "You okay? You seem down."

I shake my head. "Nah. I'm good. I just have some things to get done when I get home. So." *No, you don't. What things?*

Honestly, nothing was wrong, and the only thing on my mind was getting home. I don't know why Christopher probably thought otherwise. But he doesn't ask any follow-up questions. He just nods, giving me a faint smile with his lips pressed together, and then he walks off with Peter.

I look at Benton. "I'll take you home," I tell him.

He nods and thanks me.

Week 3, Thursday.

I woke up this morning thinking about the kid who was shot at the ice cream shop. I didn't want to write about it in my journal because I knew it would be something Counselor Malik would probably nag me about, and I wasn't for it. Instead, I just got out of bed, got dressed, and went straight to school.

Now, I'm sitting in homeroom, soft music playing through my earbuds as I look down at the book I have opened on my desk. It's a novel by Jace Gregg, which I started reading not that long ago—about a month or two ago. I brought it from the bookstore and started reading it a couple days later. I usually don't get into young-adult romantic fiction stories, but after reading a couple of chapters, I now understand why Meagan likes reading Jace Gregg's books so damn much.

The characters seem pretty realistic, and the story isn't so bad. It's just the concept of love that I can't seem to grasp. The main character—Hank?—is in love with his best friend, but he doesn't want to be, so he goes out of his way to hide his feelings for her, but that only makes things more complicated once she gets a boyfriend? In a way, it sort of makes sense, but what I can't understand is why didn't he take the chance when he had it?

And his best friend—Aubrey—is a bit ridiculous herself. She flirts with Hank occasionally but still remains with her boyfriend, who's an absolute piece of shit. Paul is his name, so it makes sense. Then again, the story itself does live up to the title.

I flip the book over to get a quick glance at the title.

CHASING AUBREY HUNTER.

He's chasing alright. I snort to myself.

My phone suddenly vibrates in my pants pocket, but the music continues to play softly in my ears. I bookmark the page before checking my phone. I keep the phone in my lap and glance up as Mr. Hua remains seated at his desk, marking papers for one of the many classes he teaches. He keeps his focus on the paper he holds in his hand, and he pushes his glasses up against the bridge of his nose with the other hand.

I look back down at my phone and double-tap the screen.

I can't help but wrinkle my eyebrows when I realize it's a text message from Benton. *Benton?*

I unlock my phone to read the text message. I quickly glance up to make sure that Mr. Hua isn't looking at me. Instead, he's still focused on the papers he's grading. So, I look back down at my phone and read Benton's message.

Benton: thnx again for the ride last night :) my mom liked meeting u too.

Oh. Right. The guys and I were supposed to go out somewhere after school yesterday, but Peter told us about the ice cream shop being shot up. We decided to call it a day and head home. I took Benton home, and the car ride was quiet for the most part. I shouldn't have been surprised and expected a conversation to carry through the whole ride since Benton hardly speaks to anyone except for Meagan.

Plus, I couldn't stop thinking about the kid who was shot at the ice cream shop. I mean, four other people were shot as well, and my heart goes out to their families as well—but *thirteen years old.*

Anyway, it wasn't until I got closer to his place that a conversation started between Benton and me.

He asked me, *"What do you think of Meagan? As a person?"*

I remember feeling my heart thump heavily in my chest, and I cleared my throat to get my thoughts together. I told him, *"She's great. She's...her. Smart, ambitious, a bit shy but not too shy."* I cleared my throat again. *"Why-uh-why, you ask?"*

Benton shook his head. *"It's just...she's a great friend, but my mom doesn't get that that's all I see Meagan as. She thinks I should pursue her, but I don't think so. I don't know."*

I asked him, *"Well. Do you have some type of feeling for her? Maybe?"*

Benton shrugged. *"I don't know what I like."*

I chuckled a snort. *"C'mon, chico. Everyone has some type of idea of what they like. Think about it."*

He sighed. *"Maybe, someone bold, someone simple but also out there a bit, someone with a great smile and always laughing."*

I furrowed my eyebrows. It took me a second to put the pieces together as he continued speaking. He definitely wasn't talking about Meagan as he went on.

He added, *"Someone who really pushes boundaries and is not sorry about it."* That's when it clicked.

"Someone like Morris-Lina?" I asked.

I came to a red light, and I looked at his face. His cheeks were flushed, and his lips were parted as if he wanted to say something, but he was stuck. My eyes widened. Never in a million years would I have thought that the timid, bright, Golden Boy Benton Son had a thing for my sister.

My twin sister! Morris-Lina Gonzalez! Of all people!

I admitted to him that I thought he was scared of her all this time. He would always get quieter and timid whenever she was around, messing with him and cracking jokes. He would often look away, even. Those aren't really signs of crushing on someone. But, he did confess that he was scared of her at one point. Well, *"terrified,"* actually.

But that terror soon became admiration, he said.

He thought of Morris-Lina as someone he would want to be with and someone who could also keep him grounded. He didn't love her, but he liked her. But then he said, *"I know the rule on not dating a friend's sibling, so you would've had no worries."* He said it so nonchalantly that it was kind of relieving. I could've brought up the last time a friend of mine dated my sister, but that was a story for another day.

Plus, Nathan Hendricks was the last person I wanted to talk about. But Benton seemed like an okay guy. Although, I couldn't see him and Morris-Lina lasting for a long time. He'd probably think she was too much, or she'd think he just wasn't enough. I don't know. I didn't say anything about it at the time.

I remember pulling up to his place, and he groaned. It was apparent that he was overthinking the situation. I told him to relax and that all he had to do was say to his folks that he didn't want to pursue Meagan if he only liked her as a friend. I mean, it's not surprising that they'd want him to be with Meagan since she'd be great to be with—as a partner.

Benton shrugged. *"I have no chance with this, though."*

I rolled my eyes, resting my head back. *"Keep thinking like that, and no girl will come your way."*

"That'll be fine."

I looked at him. He looked at me.

We laughed a bit before he finally got out of the car. Before I could pull off, his mom came outside, and I met her. We talked for a bit. I think her name was Robin or something like that, but she said it was spelled with a "Y," not an "I."

So, "Robyn"? I doubt I'll see her again. Or maybe not for a while.

Someone taps my shoulder, and I look over to see Christopher. He turns his body around while remaining in his seat so I can get his full attention. I pause the music playing from my phone and take off my earbuds.

"You okay?" he asks me.

I nod. "Why wouldn't I be?" I'm not trying to be an asshole.

"You didn't respond to my text last night. I wanted to know if you'd be down for a movie night at my place tonight."

I arch my eyebrow and reach for my phone. He probably messaged me late last night, and I missed it. I didn't go to bed super early, but my notifications are usually silenced after a specific time. When I scroll down the lists of text messages, I find unread messages in the group texts. I read the text messages.

Chris: Squad movie night at my place tomorrow night?

Pete: i'm down XD

Car: okie!!

Meg: I'm in!

Benton: Sure!

Chris: Don???

I respond to the group text: **hell yea!**

Christopher's phone vibrates in the side pouch of his bookbag, and I smirk. He rolls his eyes.

"Won't your dad be pissed with all of us coming over, though?" I ask him as I stuff my phone back into my pants pocket. "Or he's not gonna be around for the next few days?" The words come out as a joke, but that's honestly the only way we're ever allowed to have squad hangouts at Christopher's place.

His dad makes it clear that he doesn't like any of us. Especially me. Whenever I come over, even if it's to study, Chris's dad will give me this look that makes me feel smaller than I actually am. But I never say anything about it. He'll just deny it, calling me "Champ," or whatever—even though there's always some form of spite in his words. He's like that even with Carmen and Peter. Sometimes towards Meagan and Benton, but he hardly ever sees them.

And Christopher's not dumb. He knows how his dad really feels about us. It didn't even surprise him when his dad suggested that Christopher date someone else and not Carmen.

"When I asked him 'why?', he just kept beating around the bush, thinking I could do better," I remember Christopher telling me a couple days after he and Carmen made their relationship official.

But Christopher will never tell Carmen about that, and I don't blame him. But she's not dumb either. She's always known why his dad never liked her. She's intelligent, beautiful, talented, and not white. And yet, whenever it comes to getting things done around their house, his dad somehow doesn't mind us being around all of a sudden. I wish I could deck the guy, and Chris knows how much I'd want to, but I only hold myself back since it's *his* dad.

Christopher sits back in his seat, stuffing his hands into the pocket of his gray sweatshirt, which has the school logo patched on the front on the upper-right side. The bell sounds off, and the silence is disrupted by moving chairs and students chit-chatting as they leave homeroom. Christopher hauls up his bookbag from off the ground before lightly smacking my shoulder to get my attention.

"I'll see you later, alright?" he asks.

I nod. "For sure."

We bump our fists together before he dips out of the room to get to his first class period. I close up my book and slip it into my bookbag.

As I get ready to leave, Mr. Hua calls my name as I inch closer to the door. I stop in my tracks, and my heart nearly pounces out of my chest. It's not that I'm scared of Mr. Hua. He just caught me off guard.

I take a breath and turn on my heels to face him. "Yes, Mr. Hua?" I try to keep my voice straight as I approach him at his desk.

He takes off his glasses and looks up at me with a faint smirk playing on his lips. I always forget just how perfect he looks, even without his glasses. His eyes practically peer into my soul while the smirk remains on his face. It's like a twisted mind game, but I don't melt like butter. I just gave him my attention with no issue at all. Mr. Hua clears his throat and leans forward, propping both of his elbows upon his desk while intertwining his fingers together.

He tells me, "I always thought you were clever, Mister Gonzalez, but I never knew you could be so obvious when it comes to texting in my class."

Shit. He did see me. Crap.

I want to smack myself in the head. Although, I don't get what's the big deal. It's homeroom, for crying out loud. It's not even an actual class. We just sit here and do nothing until it's time for our actual courses to start. That's what I want to tell him. But I know he'll scold me for it, and I'm not in the mood for that right now.

"Mister Hua, it was—"

"You don't have to explain," he cuts me, holding up his hand. He then sits back in his chair, crossing his arms over his chest. "I know it's not fair for you all to sit here for about an hour, twirling your fingers."

I chuckle. So, even Mr. Hua thinks it's irrational too.

But then, he adds, "But I have rules for a reason." This time his smirk fades a bit. "Next time, I'll have to confiscate your phone. Understood?"

Shocker. "Yes, Mister Hua." I nod.

His charming smirk reappears. "I also wanted to know how you are doing. Usually, you're always so lively, asking my permission to leave so you can visit Missus Rojas. Is she no longer your biggest fan?"

It's true. Sometimes Mr. Hua will allow me to leave to visit Mrs. Rojas's class. But I would only go to sit with Meagan and Benton. The three of us would talk about *Allegiance Society* and all sorts of stuff. But *Allegiance Society* was our main thing. It's the best manga-turned-anime series in the world right now, and I remember when Meagan and I took the official Alliance Aptitude quiz to determine our Circles.

It was on the first day of school. She admired the tattoo on my forearm of the Hunter's Mark, a crescent arrow. She was amazed at how similar it looked to Jaxton Chyde's, one of the main characters and part of the Hunter Circle. It was the first time I saw Meagan so excited about something. So, I thought it was pretty funny when she was annoyed that I was aligned with the Hunter Circle after taking the Alliance Aptitude quiz during our lunch period that day.

I don't exactly know her Circle Affiliation. She'd probably be a hybrid like Renei—half-werewolf, half-hunter. Like Renei, Meagan is fierce but sometimes timid, quick on her feet, passionate, bright, and downright beautiful. I definitely can't see her being aligned solely with Werewolf, even though she's a die-hard Agron Melhart fan, which I don't understand because Agron is not that bright of a guy. To me, Renei had the best character development in the manga. Although, the writers for the anime series did her character dirty a couple of times, especially for the second season finale.

Meagan, Benton, and I would talk about *Allegiance Society* as if it was all we knew. Especially Meagan and me. It would sometimes make me laugh whenever she gets so passionate about it while comparing the manga to the anime and then hearing her voice get high-pitched a bit.

It was kind of cute.

"Mister Gonzalez!" Mr. Hua's voice brings me back to reality. "Is everything okay?"

I shake my head, a flustered chuckle slipping from my lips recklessly.

"Sorry, I was just thinking," I tell him. I get myself together. "I am fine, though. Thanks for asking, Mister Hua."

He just looks at me and nods. I can tell he probably doesn't buy it, but he still lets me go so I can get to class before the second bell goes off. As students start to take their seats for his class, I look behind me, and I head out.

When I make it to Honors Algebra, Mr. Enrique is writing the date on the whiteboard, and most of the class is already in their seats. I spot Meagan as she sits back in her seat at her desk while looking down at her lap. It's obvious she's at it again—reading. Her long box braids fall over her shoulders and down her back. She also wears a patterned headband to keep the hair out of her face. Her lips are twisted, and her eyes remain glued to the book in her lap as she flips to the next page. I press my lips tightly together to hold in the chuckle wanting to escape from my mouth.

When I slide into my seat, I look at her. I notice the highlights on her cheeks and at the tip of her nose. I can tell that her lip gloss is fresh on her lips, even though she presses her lips tightly together to concentrate on the book she keeps hidden on her lap while she reads.

I snicker.

"Do you have to be such a creep?" Meagan suddenly asks me, still holding her attention to her book as she flips to the next page.

Damn, she's a fast reader.

I mean, I've always known she was a fast reader, but never that fast. She just turned the page a few seconds ago.

I sit back in my seat and snort a chuckle, shaking my head. It's funny how she thinks no one notices her reading whenever she hides her book under her desk. It's not like Mr. Enrique has a policy against reading whatever sappy book she enjoys. Although Jace Gregg isn't so bad, but just too corny at times. But I can't let Meagan know that I just started reading one of his books. She'd never let me live it down.

I finally tell her, "I've never seen someone so committed to such sappy writing. Especially someone who can knock 'em out the park on her own." I wink when she glances at me.

Meagan presses her lips tightly together to hide the smile curling on her lips, but a chuckle slips out instead. She turns her attention back to her book and marks the page.

"Actually," she says, closing the book. "I started venturing into something a little less sappy."

She holds up the book, making sure I can see the cover clearly. It's an illustration of a dark-skinned woman with a scar on the right side of her face and tribal tattoos across her shoulders. Her right eye is golden brown, while the left is a gorgeous dark blue. Behind her, it is a mountain and a silhouette of a wolf's head, howling.

Meagan reaches out and hands me the cover to get a better look at it. I read the title.

THE NIGHT'S RECKONING.

The surface practically shines from the classroom lights, and the pages are thick as I skim through. I don't even bother reading the back description since the cover alone gives me _Allegiance Society_ vibes. Although, _Allegiance Society_ is probably the only franchise that can perfectly blend science-fiction with the supernatural.

I suddenly hear Meagan go, "Trying to find something to hold me over 'til the new season of Allegiance Society is released."

I snort. "Well, this seems right up your alley then." I pass the book back to her. "Looks intense too."

Her eyes go wide. "Oh, it is." I watch as Meagan slips the book into her bookbag and pulls out her notebook and a pen. She sits back in her seat and lets out a sigh. "But it's a good kind of intense, you know? A real game-changer."

"Sooo....pretty much you?" I smirk.

She snorts. "Yeah, sure. Hashtag, Black Girl Magic."

I chuckle, earning a smile from her. Her gaze shifts to the front of the classroom once Mr. Enrique shuts the classroom door and proceeds to start the class.

I try to stay focused as Mr. Enrique reviews questions and breaks down new equations. I look over at Meagan and notice the frustration in her eyes as she copies down some of the equations Mr. Enrique writes down on the board. I can tell she's trying to understand it, and I know she does, but she has a habit of overthinking. Still, the way her eyebrows wrinkle and the intense glare in her eyes—it's hard for me to not stare at times.

But I'm not staring. I'm not a creep.

I turn my attention back to my notebook, writing down random equations to distract myself since Mr. Enrique is just on repeat at the moment—

"Donald," I hear Mr. Enrique say my name, and I snap my head up from my notebook. I can hear people turning in their chairs, and I know a few of them are looking at me, but I block them out.

Mr. Enrique makes a bold choice, asking me to come up to the board to solve the problem he wrote out. "Why don't you give this one a try?" He steps aside while holding out the marker in his hand for me to take.

I look at the problem on the board. I realize what it is I have to do. Find the roots of the polynomial function by factoring. I sigh and take a quick glance at Meagan. She tightly presses her lips together in a straight line and sucks in her cheeks.

I look back up at Mr. Enrique and sigh. I can feel my heart pounding in my chest as I get up out of my seat and approach him. I can feel everyone's eyes remain on me as I take the marker from Mr. Enrique and proceed to the board.

They're probably thinking, *Gonzalez? Really?*

I bet they're wondering, *What does he know?*

He's just lucky.

"Put a sock in it," I whisper to myself as I face the board.

I glance over at Mr. Enrique as he stands off to the side, watching me with his arms crossed over his chest. I notice the faint grin on his face, but it's not like he's mocking me. He actually seems interested. Like, he's confident in me for some reason.

I mean, I should know why he'd be confident in me.

I know math. It just comes easy to me. So solving this will be a breeze. As I examine the problem, the solution jumps out at me instantly. It's hardly a hassle. I just do it, just like that.

Once I'm done, I hand Mr. Enrique back the marker, and he nods his head, telling me, "Awesome." He pats my shoulder.

As I sit back down in my seat, I can hear a couple of guys behind me muttering to each other. I don't bother turning around since it'll only be a waste of time. Plus, the last thing I need is to prove these suckers right, falling for their trap.

So, I just keep my eyes forward, feigning interest in Mr. Enrique's lecture until the bell finally rings.

.....

Once classes are over, I meet up with Christopher, Carmen, Benton, and Peter by the school's front entrance. When I get to them, Peter wastes no time making my presence known, going, "It's about damn time!"

I roll my eyes and hiss, "*Silencio.*" I look around. "Where's Meagan?"

"She's on her way," Benton says, looking down at his phone. "She just messaged me. She had to do something."

I nod.

I suddenly feel someone roughly bump into me from behind, and I practically stumble forward. I manage to catch myself by gripping onto the wall, and I look over. Austin Brown and a couple of his lapdogs look back at me, smirking and chuckling.

"Watch it next time." There's pure venom in Austin's words, even when a smile plays on his face.

I tighten my jaw.

Suddenly, Peter blurts out, "Choke on a dick, assholes!" and they immediately stop in their tracks.

There's a wild mix of emotions plastered on Peter's face. I can't tell whether he regrets what he said or regrets getting their attention because of what he said. Regardless, it doesn't change anything. It's four of them. Minus Carmen, it's four of us too.

So it'll be a fair fight.

Austin and his lapdogs waste no time turning their attention back to us. Austin's eyes are dark, and a twisted smirk plays on his lips as he glares right at Peter. He knows damn well that Peter's the one who said it.

He snorts. "You say something, pup?"

I notice Peter tighten his fist as it remains by his side.

Pup. He *hates* being called that. It makes him feel incompetent, worthless as if he can't do anything for himself. That's what it means anyway. At least, whenever someone like Austin Brown uses it. It sounds cute, but it's actually demeaning.

Before Austin even gets the chance to take a step forward towards Peter, Christopher moves up, blocking Peter from Austin's view. Christopher is only a couple inches shorter than Austin, but he hardly has to look up at him. They're practically eye-to-eye, but Austin's broad shoulder and build still make him bigger.

But that doesn't matter to Christopher. It never has.

He stares Austin dead in his eyes, hands on his hips, jaw clenched. He's not intimidated one bit. Austin knows it too.

That's why instead of taking a swing, Austin just scoffs and looks Christopher up and down.

"Wanker," he hisses, mockingly feigning an Irish accent.

Before he gets the chance to leave, a girl calls out to him from behind us. She walks past us to get to Austin, and she locks her arm with his. I roll my eyes—Diana Clovis, of all people.

It shouldn't have surprised me when they got together after she ditched Nathan a couple months ago. She and Austin were more perfect for each other anyway. They're both twisted in the head. Ironically, everyone swore up and down that she would've married Nathan, or they would've just made it through college or some dumb shit like that. The thought makes me sick. It makes me even more ill thinking about how she slithered her way to Nathan and ruined Morris-Lina.

Puta de mierda.

I go over to Peter once Austin leaves with his wench and lapdogs.

Peter is practically shaking, but not in fear. His fist is clenched so tight by his side that I know his nails are going to leave marks in his palm. I put my hand to his shoulder, drawing his attention away from Austin and to me instead. Before I can say anything, Christopher makes his way over to us, and my heart sinks. It doesn't help that Christopher is taller than us, but I know it's not his intention to look down at us.

Especially Peter. Not right now.

Peter feels bad enough. He can hardly look Christopher in the eyes as he lets out a shaky breath. His voice quivers as he mutters, "Sorry," as if he's ashamed.

I practically glare at Christopher while keeping my hand on Peter's shoulder. Christopher opens his mouth to speak, but he notices me looking at him. So, he closes his mouth and just lets out a sigh.

Carmen comes up to Christopher's side and holds his hand. When Christopher looks down at her, she's practically giving him a look similar to mine, but it's not as intense. She looks like an angel when she glares at him. She then looks at Peter with soft eyes, even though Peter can hardly look at anyone at the moment.

Peter probably doesn't even know what came over him.

If anything, it was expected for me to have the balls to say something like that to Austin. I mean, I do have the balls to say something to that piece of shit anyway.

Peter is good in a fight. But Austin is the type of person who will fight to do some real damage without mercy. Peter doesn't need that. God forbid Austin goes wild on him. I can only imagine what Peter's aunt will think of him then.

I bet that's what Christopher is thinking too. That's probably why he's trying to find the right words to say to Peter. But he can't. Not with all the different people walking past us and looking after what just happened.

Benton suddenly clears his throat and says, "You made it."

We look over as Meagan finally comes up to us with a tired look on her face, but she still manages to force a smile.

"Of course," she pants, settling her hands on her hips. "Sorry. I had to help Nate—I mean, Nathan, with theater stuff." She lets out a breath.

Nate.

It still gets me when I hear her call him that. It wasn't that long ago the very thought of him repulsed her a bit. At least, that's what I thought. She didn't seem too thrilled when he popped up out of nowhere on the first day and made a fool of himself, hitting on her like a jackass. Turns out that was just a prank, nonetheless.

Although, according to him, it was actually *"a dare."*

"You okay?"

Meagan stares at me with her big brown eyes and slightly parted lips. I think about her question, and I quickly glance at Peter. He nods his head, and the corners of his mouth slightly curved upward.

I nod. "Yeah." I look back at Meagan. I throw my arm around her, pulling her close to me. "We were getting restless, no thanks to you." One side of my mouth curves upward into a grin.

Meagan rolls her eyes. "I said I was sorry."

"Alright, enough, you two," Peter groans. "Bad enough, we gotta deal with these love birds." He gestures to Carmen and Christopher, who remain holding hands. "Give Benton and me some hope that singles still matter too, alright?"

Meagan scratches her arm and looks up at me. I expected her to find some smooth way to slip away from me when Peter made his joke about us being together, but she just turned away again. Thankfully, Christopher uses this opportunity to smack Peter's arm.

Peter winces, flipping Christopher off. Carmen nudges Christopher, telling him to leave Peter alone as if Peter's innocent. Christopher just rolls his eyes.

"You get the backseat," he tells Peter.

Peter just shrugs. "I had no doubt."

We finally decide to get going, and Meagan lets out a sigh.

I look at her as I keep my arm around her. "You good, kid?"

She nods. "You?"

I pretend to give it some thought.

Meagan snorts. "You are something else. For real."

I chuckle. "We discussed this," I remind her. "I'm your something else. So take it or leave."

She just smiles up at me, and I can't resist the urge to smile back.

March.

Week 1, Tuesday.

For the first time in a long time, I woke up feeling optimistic. Nothing has changed between my parents, although they have been quieter towards each other since the last time they argued. But even when there's quiet, it feels like chaos. Last night, dinner was God awful.

They were acting like complete strangers to each other, sitting in silence and hardly acknowledging each other. They've had arguments before, but never something this bad. Although, they wasted no time nagging me about what I wanted to do for college. I already submitted my college applications, even to the schools that were overseas. I honestly didn't think it was a bright idea to apply somewhere overseas, especially since I didn't know what Morris-Lina would do without me for so long. But it was actually her idea for me to study abroad. I bet mom and dad took it as a joke, the thought of me going to school overseas. It wouldn't surprise me if they did. God, the only one who actually had some kind of faith in me, is now the person I no longer have. This sucks balls. I'd shoot myself if I could.-- D.G.

The steam from the shower water fills my lungs as I run my fingers through my hair to wash out the soap. I keep my eyes closed and let out a sharp breath. I can't ignore the slight soreness in my shoulders, thanks to the excessive drills we had to do for Mr. Aziz during gym. Followed by a game of badminton.

I friggin' *hate* badminton.

It's not that I'm bad at it. I'm actually pretty good. But I just never really enjoyed it. Some people like it, but I don't. Plus, Mr. Aziz usually has us play in pairs, and of all people, I had to get paired with Nathan.

When Mr. Aziz called my name, telling me that I would be with Nathan, I felt chills go down my spine. I remember looking at Nathan, and even he thought it was ridiculous. But we also knew it was predictable. It's just like in the movies. Two people who can't stand each other always get paired with each other.

But unlike those fluff fest of films, Nathan and I aren't going to end being "an item" or friends or something dumb like that. It doesn't matter that he's on good terms with Meagan, all of a sudden, which I still can't understand.

Nathan...and Meagan? Friends?

I don't mind it, but it's not something I can easily get used to. Then again, Meagan has always been the accepting type. Maybe it's because she goes to church. It's easier for her to forgive and move on. Or perhaps it's just because she's built that way. Regardless, it's not something I would want her to change.

It's what makes her good. Too good.

There's definitely nothing wrong with that either.

Sigh.

Tough it out for her, then.

That's all I gotta do. Just tough it for her.

So I did. Even though Nathan and I didn't talk to each other, we were civil while playing badminton against each other. We took turns serving, had a good game, and before we knew it, it was time to hit the showers. I thought about maybe waiting things out like I did last time, but Mr. Aziz didn't give me a choice.

As I sat down on the bench, waiting for everyone else to finish up in the showers, Mr. Aziz walked over to me and gave me a stern look.

He told me, *"You heard me, Gonzalez. Showers. Now."*

I open my mouth to protest, but he settles his hands on his hips and arches his eyebrows. I notice his nostrils flare a bit as he continues to glare down at me. I don't know his problem, but there is no fighting him this time. I just keep my mouth shut and reluctantly go to the showers.

As usual, the locker room roared with laughter and conversations. I didn't pay anyone any mind as I stripped myself down to my underwear and wrapped a towel around my waist. I noticed a few guys staring at me from the mirror attached to the inside of my locker door. There was a burning sensation in my chest, but I bit down on my lip.

I kept telling myself to count to three.

Now, I'm standing under the showerhead as warm water trickles down my back. I feel my shoulders starting to relax, and the smell of vanilla from the soap swims through my nostrils.

Once I'm fully clean, I turn off the water and let out a sharp breath as I rub my eyes. I lean back against the wall, and a shiver erupts down my spine from the sudden contact. I tell myself to get a grip, knowing that I'll have to face everyone out there in the locker room. The worst-case scenario is that I actually have to end up decking someone.

Restraint, I tell myself. *Have some restraint.*

I groan, running my hands down my face.

I dry myself off with the towel and slip on my boxer briefs before wrapping the towel around my waist. I walk back to my locker to change into my clothes. As expected, there are still a couple of guys lingering around, talking. The bell hasn't gone off yet, so it shouldn't have been a surprise.

As I moisturize my skin, I notice someone walk up to me from the corner of my eye. I look over as Nathan—wearing only his boxers with a towel wrapped around his neck—unlocks the locker next to mine. He gives me a quick glance and presses his lips together in a half-smile, nodding his head.

I raise my eyebrows and turn away from him.

There's no need to talk. I hardly have anything to say to him, and I don't mean that out of malice. Even if Nathan and I did have something to talk about, I doubt the conversation would last. It would probably just be small talk. The last time we spoke to each other, we ended up fighting after exchanging a few words with each other. Who can say the same thing won't happen if we tried talking now?

I slip into my pants and fasten them. As I put on my belt to hold them in place since my pants are a bit loose around my waist, Nathan clears his throat and turns his body towards me.

"Nice work today," he says, moisturizing his arms. "You do badminton in your free time?" He's making small talk. That's what this is. Fan-friggin-tastic.

I don't bother looking him in the eye as I fasten the buckle to my belt, but I don't ignore him. I shake my head. "I hate badminton." I make sure I don't sound hostile.

Nathan tilts his head. "I didn't know that." He reaches for his uniform shirt.

I shrug. "That's a bit of a surprise since we used to tell each other everything." I don't even try to check my tone at this point. It's not like I'm trying to start a fight. I'm just making a statement.

The silence that comes from Nathan says otherwise. I look up at him as I sit on the bench to put on my sneakers. Regret washes over his face, but he tries to hide it as he slips on his pants, giving him the chance to look away from me. For a brief second, I actually feel a sense of regret myself. Like I'm the prick in this situation, and I probably am, but I should have a right to be.

Keyword being *should*. That doesn't mean I have to be.

I then think about Meagan. I think about the fact that she's at least trying to give him a chance. I think about her calling him *"Nate"* instead of *"Nathan."* I should hate it, but I don't. I can't. Even Christopher thinks Nathan's turned around, and he hasn't even talked to him yet. At least, not that I know of.

I guess it's just me who's slacking then.

I sigh.

"Thanks, though," I finally tell him. "You were good too." And I left it at that.

Nathan looks at me with shock in his eyes, but he tries to play it cool. He just nods his head and goes back to getting changed.

I rub my forehead as the bell sounds, signaling the end of the third class period. I know that if either Meagan or Christopher found out about this, they wouldn't let it go. There's no guarantee that Nathan wouldn't say anything to Meagan about it, but I'm pretty sure that he's like me and wouldn't make it a big deal.

Sure, he was a bit surprised when I complimented him, but based on what I know about Nathan, he's not the dramatic type. He'll take things by surprise, and then he'll just let it go after it sinks in. That's one of the things that I liked about him. He was always chill before Diana came crashing into the picture.

Damn.

I shut my locker, gathered my things, and headed straight to the cafeteria for lunch. As I'm walking up the steps, I get a text message from mi tía Yoselin, asking me if I could babysit the boys this weekend since she has to attend a conference for her job. She doesn't really owe me an explanation since I don't mind watching the boys. Even though Yago gets on my nerves sometimes, he's not that bad of a kid. And even though he's four, Gabriel isn't really high maintenance.

I text her back that it would be no problem, and she responds with a heart emoji and a smiley face. I stuff my phone back into the pocket of my leather jacket as I pull open one of the heavy doubled doors.

As soon as I enter the cafeteria, I hear a familiar voice call my name. I whip my head around and see Peter emerge from the long line for the vending machine, and he darts to me like a child eager to see their parent after school. He throws himself at me, wrapping his arm around my neck, pulling me close to him.

"About time you showed up," he chuckles. "Listen, we gotta know what you think about doing next weekend."

We finally get to our table, and everyone is already seated, eating. My eyebrows wrinkle in confusion, and I try to think about what Peter's talking about. We didn't make plans for next weekend. Not that I know of anyway.

I ask Peter, "What's next weekend?"

His eyes go wide, and his jaw hangs open. I notice Christopher shaking his head, and Carmen gives me a look that makes me feel like a buffoon.

Did I miss something?

"Uh, hellooo!" Carmen twirls her finger, making the coo-coo sign. "You only turn eighteen once! You lose your mind?"

Oh. Right. My birthday.

Goddammit.

I sit next to Meagan as she takes a sip of her orange juice. She starts snapping her fingers as if she just had the craziest epiphany, and she takes a huge gulp.

"That's right!" Her eyes practically light up when she remembers my birthday. I never told her about my birthday, but I'm pretty sure Morris-Lina had told her at some point. "C'mon, we gotta do something for you." She rests her hand on my arm, and I feel the hairs on the back of my neck spike up.

I chuckle. "Stop being such saps," I tell them. "It's not that big of a deal. Seriously."

Meagan snorts, shaking her head.

I quirk an eyebrow. "What?"

"This coming from the same guy who went all out for my birthday? Oh, please." She wiggles her wrist, making the charms on her bracelet lightly jingle.

It's the same bracelet I gifted her for her birthday in October. I babysat the boys two weeks prior and took them to get ice cream in Chestnut Hill. While we were walking, I noticed the bracelet on display at the front window of the jewelry store. It was something about it that just made me think Meagan would like it, so I got it. I also purchased a few additional charms—a Holy Cross, a book, a pencil, and a car.

As the woman rang everything up, I remember her asking me, *"Is she your soulmate?"*

I nearly choked and furrowed my eyebrows. *"I'm sorry?"*

"This bracelet is part of our Lovers Collection." A smile played across her face as she placed the bracelet in an elegant box and wrapped it up. *"I'm sure she's a lucky one."*

I wanted to explain that it wasn't anything like that, but it wasn't her business. She was just a nice old woman who liked to ask ridiculous questions that had nothing to do with her.

But her assumption did mess with my head a bit. I thought about possibly returning the bracelet once it was Meagan's birthday. It would've been a shitty thing to do, but I would've probably just taken her out somewhere instead. But then, Morris-Lina turned me around and basically told me to get a grip and insisted that I give Meagan the bracelet.

"The worse thing a Gonzalez can be is a backer-downer. That's not us, and it sure as hell ain't you. She'll like it, and when she does, you owe me ten bucks."

She was right about Meagan liking the bracelet, but I sure as hell didn't give Morris-Lina ten bucks because of it.

Seeing Meagan smile the way she did when she opened the box...it was something else. Really, it was—which was great. Better than great, actually.

I chuckle at the memory.

Meagan arches her eyebrow. "What? I'm serious."

I shake my head. "I know you are, kid. I'm just saying that I'm good. Besides, you deserve something special." I wink.

I hear Peter snort under his breath and mumble, "Talk about a hopeless romantic." I cut my eyes to him, and the smile on his face melts away, and he starts stuffing his face with chocolate pudding.

Benton lets out a huff and stretches his arms up and out, making his shoulders crack. It's like music to my ears, and Meagan's eyes widen in shock. She whistles and gazes at him as if she's in love.

"That was *nice*," she gasps.

"Yeah, man. Goddamn," Peter chimes in with a mouthful of pudding. "That seemed like it felt nice.

Benton's cheeks flush, and he chuckles, crinkles forming by his dark eyes. "Thanks." He quickly turns away and goes back to eating the rest of his lunch.

I pat Benton on the back and thank him for saving my ass, getting the attention off of me, and about my birthday. If the conversation carried on much longer, I'd probably end up more pissed off than I should've been. It's not that I don't appreciate them all wanting to do something for my birthday. I do, really.

But that's not something I like to think about.

Not today, not tomorrow.

Instead, I look forward to getting home right after school, getting my homework done, and then trying to finish the rest of *Chasing of Aubrey Hunter* just for the heck of it.

Week 1, Thursday

I took a deep breath as I stood at the home plate. I felt a strange tug in my throat, and my stomach bubbled with acid. The cool hair hit the back of my neck, sending a new sensation of chills down my spine like it was nothing. I thought I would get frostbite, but there was no way.

It's only seventy-something degrees out here anyway.

Focus, I thought to myself as I planted my feet firmly on the dirt.

I bent my knees a bit as I kept my eyes glued on my dad as he stood at the pitcher's mound. His red-and-black patterned flannel hung loosely on him, and his white tee-shirt was tucked into his blue jeans. His eyes were fixated on me as if he was trying to shrink me with his mind. He tightly gripped the baseball in his hand, lightly revealing the veins in his arm. He wore his ball mitt and tossed the ball into the glove on his other hand.

He twisted around as if he was cracking his back and shrugged his shoulders once he faced me. "Alright, get ready, son." His deep voice rattled me a bit as I tightened my grip on the bat. "Remember." Dad then held up the ball, so I could see it in his hand. "Focus. Everything else around you is just a distraction, son. You gotta block 'em out. Focus."

Son.

I suddenly felt nauseous after hearing him call me that. I shouldn't be, but I was. But the severe tone of his voice made me realize that he wasn't calling me "son" to be playful or lighthearted. He was dead serious.

I huffed as I got into position, holding up the bat behind me as I kept my gaze locked on the ball.

I watched as dad tucked the ball into his glove, and he let out a huge breath. He shrugged his shoulders and lifted up his head. As I blinked, he released the ball, and it came charging towards me. I felt my heart leap into my throat as the knots suddenly loosened in my stomach.

I made sure my grip was tight, and I could feel the skin of my palms sink into the glossy wood of the bat as I took a swing. The loud CRACK from the ball echoed once it bashed into the front of the bat.

"Holy!" I heard my dad shout.

The ball flew to the far end of the field, but it was out of our sight.

I chuckled out a sharp breath.

Dad whipped his attention back to me, and a smile suddenly appeared across his face. It wasn't a broad smile, but it was the first time it made me realize that he was actually proud.

"Well, would you look at that," he said as he approached me. "Seems like someone's going pro."

I looked at my shoes, tapping the bat on the ground. I felt my nerves starting to settle down the closer dad approached me. For a second, I could relax with him around. He suddenly placed his hand on my shoulder, and I looked up at him. I could see his closed-mouth smile below his mustache that he always kept neat and trimmed. I always thought it was funny how he looked older when he smiled but looked younger when he kept a straight face with me—which was most of the time.

Maybe because I wasn't so used to seeing him smile at me the way he does with my sister—all warm and reassuring. Sometimes he would if I came home with my report card or the first time I mentioned that I was interested in playing baseball. But that was about it.

I had to take it all in as he ruffled my hair.

I knew he hated my hair sometimes too. He and mom would always debate on me getting it cut, but mom liked that it was a mop of curls. She thought it brought out my "boyish charm" and made me look my age.

Whatever.

Dad sighed. "Looks like you'll be locked in for that team at your new school."

I nodded. "Hope so."

"Hey," he said firmly. He leaned down a bit to meet my eye level and pressed his lips together. I could see the hesitation in his eyes as he lifted his hand and touched the side of my face as I looked at him. He blinked, but I could tell he meant business. He added, "What do I always tell you and your sister? It's okay to hope, but it's not okay to doubt. You got this, Donald. You hear me? Don't be like that. Ever."

I took a deep breath and pressed my lips together in a tight smile. I had to blink to prevent the water from escaping my eyes. I had to keep it together. But I knew that dad meant what he said. He really did.

So, I nodded. "Yeah." Another sigh. "Thanks, dad."

"Yeah." He patted my shoulder. "I got you, son."

. . . .

The sudden knock on my car door window makes me practically jump out of my skin. My heart instantly lodges into my throat, and I feel every bone in my body tighten. When I look out the window, I see Christopher as he looks in, waving his hand to get my attention.

My nostrils flare as I relax my head back into the headrest. I feel my heart slowly start to ease its rhythm.

I could kill him if I wanted to.

I check the time on my wristwatch. *7:50 AM.*

I roll my eyes. It's about that time, I guess.

I turn off the car engine and grab my bookbag as I get out of the car.

I shut the door behind me and slipped the keys into the front pouch of my bookbag. I can feel Christopher's eyes on me as he stands there in silence with his hands stuffed in his coat pockets, rocking side to side like a sad penguin.

I sigh. "You don't have to wait for me." I tighten the straps to my bookbag and stuff my hands into my pants pockets.

Christopher shrugs, looking off to the side. "Maybe." A long pause. He turns his gaze to me, squinting his eyes a bit due to the bright sun. "You've been in your car for about an hour, though."

I arch my eyebrow. "You were watching me?"

"No," he snorts. "I got here earlier, but then I decided to grab a bite at the donut place up the street. I talked with Carmen on the phone for a bit since she won't be here. When I came back, you were still in your car, so." He shrugs, tilting his head to the side. "Yep. About an hour."

I try to think on what to say as he looks at me as if I'm supposed to be okay with him still watching me from a distance—kinda. I've never heard of something so weird or ridiculous from him before. Christopher is usually less weird than this.

But I now guess why.

"Why isn't Carmen coming today?" *That's what it is.*

He shrugs. "She told me not to say."

I purse my lips, arching my eyebrow as I give him an unconvinced look. He rolls his eyes as a defeated sigh slips out his mouth. He tells me that she's out of town, visiting her dad's side of the family for the day since her uncle is sick and in the hospital. It wasn't out of the kindness of her heart to visit her dad's side of the family since they're a bunch of heathens that get off to drama and bigotry. He says that the only reason why Carmen agreed to go was that her mom didn't give her a choice.

"She tried reminding her mom that they're terrible people, but her mom basically said kick rocks." The hurt on Christopher's face was evident. He tries to hide it by pressing his lips together and rocking on his heels, but he can't fool me.

They are terrible people. Her dad cheated and put Carmen and her mom through so much hell as if it was fun and games. It was a miracle that Carmen didn't fall off the rails during her junior year when all of it was going on. Carmen would come to school looking a hot mess as beautiful as she is. Morris-Lina would bring Carmen into the bathroom almost every morning before homeroom to do her makeup to help her look nice so she wouldn't have to deal with everyone ganging up on her.

Still, Christopher was there for her through it all. No matter how many times she overlooked him liking her and tried to show that she wasn't interested in him at the time, Christopher would hold her hand and make sure that she knew everything was going to be okay.

We don't talk about any of this stuff or bring up her dad's side of the family because Carmen still feels triggered by it. She has a right to feel that way.

I sigh.

"Tell her that I'm sorry about that." I mean it too. I am sorry.

Christopher nods. "Yeah. She knows. We all are." He sniffs from the chilly breeze that hits us suddenly. "But back to you. What's got you sitting in your car with such deep thought?"

I tighten my jaw.

I don't know why I was even thinking about my dad—him helping me practice for my tryout for the school's baseball team. It's silly to think about. I don't even know why I thought about it. It's not like I was a little kid, remembering the good days. It was almost four years ago. Morris-Lina and I were getting ready to enter Gabe-Day, make names for ourselves.

And we sure enough did, but not in the way we imagined.

I shake my head.

"It was nothing." I push the front of my hair back, and Christopher just gives me a look. "What? A guy can't get some privacy in his own car?" I snort and approach him.

I throw my arm around his neck, pulling him in close to me as we start to head to the school's entrance. I tell him that he worries too much, and Christopher just rolls his eyes, snorting a chuckle.

"Is it too much be decent, then?" he asks, tilting his head to me. "Or were you really just jacking off for about an hour?"

I roll my eyes, and the cold air hits my throat, making me shiver a bit. "Ha-ha, you got jokes," I drawl. "Seriously, I'm fine."

Christopher opens his mouth to say something, but he changes his mind and closes his mouth. I already have an idea of what he'd probably say.

Be lucky that you have friends that care, mate.

I know I'm lucky. I'm damn lucky. But that doesn't mean that everyone has to be on my case, thinking that's something is always wrong with me. Some days, I'm just not in my usual mood—if that makes sense.

I wish they'd get that. Especially Chris.

He, of all people, should know how that feels, to be honest.

We head straight to homeroom and make it just in the nick of time as the bell sounds off. Mr. Hua shoots his attention at us, and my legs suddenly freeze as I stand in the doorway. I expect him to call us out since we're just showing up at the sound of the bell, but instead, Mr. Hua flashes us a grin and resumes writing on the board.

He's so blinding.

Christopher nudges my arm and tilts his head toward where we usually sit. I'm right behind him as we head to our usual seats. The two guys sitting in front of me have their own conversation, but it's hard for me to block them out since they suck at whispering—especially the dark-haired guy.

I can't block them out by listening to music since Mr. Hua has already warned me once that he'd confiscate my phone if he noticed me using it during homeroom. And I already finished reading *Chasing Aubrey Hunter*, which was absolutely ridiculous the way it ended. Hank ends up with Aubrey—as expected—but then he dumps her because he didn't feel good enough for her, and then she dies out of nowhere.

I shouldn't have been surprised, though.

It's Jace Gregg.

I don't see how Meagan loves his stuff. It's not bad, but it's not great either. The writing style is good, but his stories are either trippy or predictable. If I had the knack for writing like Meagan, I'd probably come up with something better. But that's her territory.

Plus, she's a natural.

I sigh and slouch as I sink into my seat. I look around the room, and everyone either has their head down asleep, talking to someone next to them, or is studying.

I could do that—study.

Mr. Enrique didn't give us any new material for Honors Algebra II yet, which was weird since he's constantly throwing stuff at us almost every day. He's probably running low on new things to throw, I suppose.

Although quite frankly, that's how things are for my other classes, except for Physical Education. I'm all caught up for A.P. English with Mr. Acosta. We do a new experiment every other day for my A.P. Chemistry class with Mr. Throne and refer to the textbooks when completing our worksheets. Also, all of our tests are open-note since they're based on our experiments.

Then, Economics with Ms. Phan is basically bullshit. She's one of those teachers who believes that "experience is the best teaching method" and doesn't believe in tests. Instead, we write reflection essays on whatever topics she assigns for our assigned groups. It's a sweet deal, but not when most of the class bullshits everything and hardly gives a damn. And then, I'm the one having to fill in the gaps left by everyone else since Ms. Phan looks at the whole group rather than an individual's efforts.

I sigh and finally decide to rest my head down on my desk. I would ask Mr. Hua if I could bounce and waltz right into Meagan and Benton's homeroom class, but it's pointless. I don't know why, but it just feels pointless to do it today.

Maybe I'll swing by tomorrow.

Besides, knowing Meagan and how studious she always is, she's probably reviewing her worksheet for Mr. Enrique, even though our next test is two weeks from now. He's been surprisingly cutting back on the quizzes since he now just puts everything on the tests and does an excessive amount of reviewing during class time.

Not that I'm complaining.

It sure brought a sense of relief to the rest of the class.

As I nuzzle my head into my arms that I use as a pillow between me and the desk surface, I can't help but listen to the conversation between the two guys sitting in front of me. I'm hardly listening, but one of them says something about the corner store on their block having to close down because the owner was robbed at gunpoint. The owner then moved the next day, which was crazy because it takes time for someone to move out.

He was probably saving up to get out of there.

The other boy then talks about one of his neighbor's being jumped by a group of guys while walking home after his late-night shift. A couple of people had heard the commotion and could help his neighbor out, but he had to get rushed to the hospital since he was banged up really badly.

"And the weird thing is that they ain't take anything from him," he practically gasped. "They just beat him up real bad, probably for nothing. The guy was seventy."

Shit.

"That's messed up, bro," the other guy sighs.

Really messed up.

"He's alright, though," the boy adds. He sounds younger than the other guy. It's probably the dark-haired one. "His son is a cop too. Nice guy, I met him. But after this, Lord knows what's gonna go down."

"That's crazy."

"I know." The boy scoffs. "We're planning on moving by the end of my junior year, but if things get worse and we end up like North Philly, it may be sooner."

The other guy lets out a long sigh. "Do what you gotta do, man. Tell you the truth, people are being moved out left and right around here, and all this shit is going down. I gotta walk my brother straight to school before I get here now to make sure he alright."

Dread suddenly settles at the pit of my stomach. I think back to what mi tía Yoselin was telling me a couple weeks ago about the drug dealers that would occupy the back gate of the playground in their area. She said they would even hang out at the boys' school, which really made my stomach twist in knots.

"*Since gentrification,*" she had said.

I think about the kid who was shot at the ice cream shop in University City. I went home the day Peter told us about it and looked it up. There were tons of local reports about it, and the kid was in critical condition but ended up dying a few hours later. All the news reports and articles said that he was shot in the stomach.

13-YEAR-OLD NORTH PHILADELPHIA SHOOTING VICTIM IDENTIFIED AS DREVON HARRIS.

GUN VIOLENCE KILLS YOUNG HONORS STUDENT.

ASPIRING ATHLETE DREVON HARRIS SHOT AND KILLED, SUSPECT REMAINS UNKNOWN.

BUZZZ!!!

I let out a sharp breath at the sound of the bell, and the sound of students starting to disperse to their classes follows. I feel a light tap on my back, and I lift up my head. Christopher looks down at me, and I can see the immediate concern in his eyes as I stretch out my arms before standing up from my seat.

Before he had the chance to ask me his usual question, I beat him to the punch by answering for him.

"I'm fine." I somehow manage to keep my voice straight, even though it feels like a giant ball is stuck in my throat after the conversation I had just heard.

I pat Christopher on the shoulder before hooking my arm around his neck, guiding him out of the classroom with me.

I suddenly hear Mr. Hua's voice as we step out. "Have a good day, boys."

Neither one of us could tell if he's being sarcastic or genuinely wants us to have a good day. Still, we both acknowledge him as we leave the room.

"You too, Mister Hua," we both say, ideally in sync that it's close to being creepy.

Christopher and I make it to the double doors, ready to part ways for the day since his class is down the hall from the stairs, but he grabs my wrist to stop me from leaving.

I arch my eyebrow and snort a chuckle. "I don't think Carmen would be too thrilled with you coming onto me so strong, Chris." He rolls his eyes and lets go of my wrist. Even though I'm laughing, he's clearly trying to be serious about something. I can see it all over his face. I know what it is. He doesn't even have to waste his breath to ask me if I'm actually okay like he usually does. I beat him to the punch again when he opened his mouth, letting him know that he was worried about nothing.

Christopher snorts as if I'm trying to be funny.

"You don't seem fine to me. Not a minute ago, and definitely not almost two hours ago when I saw you this morning."

I have to look away from him this time because I know that I'll feel worst if I continue to look at him. It's not even like I feel sorry about something—I don't think I do. I sure as hell have nothing to feel sorry about other than this unnecessary conversation he's trying to stir up.

I have to take a breath, and I quickly count to three in my head before looking him in the eyes again. He's not going to let this go. I can see it in his face. He'll probably walk away and just say, "Okay," if I tell him nothing's wrong again.

But Christopher's meaning of "okay" is actually: *I don't believe a word you say, and I won't stop.*

I have to think of something. Even if it's ridiculous.

I let out a defeated sigh, and I just tell him, "I didn't get a lot of sleep." *Typical.*

He gives me a look like he's expecting more.

So, like an idiot, I give him more. I keep pulling out of my ass. "There was some stuff going on at my place. My parents were arguing about some bullshit, and it kept me up last night. I don't know. It's all fine now, and I'm used to it. They've been like that for some time, and you know that. It was just...I don't know."

I press my lips tightly together as Christopher parts his lips slightly open, trying to find the right words to say. I feel like a colossal asshole, making this shit up, but he's the one who kept pressuring me for some reason why I'm acting however he thinks I'm acting—even though I'm fine. I should feel bad—but I'm not completely lying.

I am a bit tired, but it's not from lack of sleep.

I don't know why I'm a bit tired. I just am.

I reach out and touch Christopher's shoulder, telling him to relax. I let him know that everything was fine and that I'd be fine.

He doesn't fight me this time. I guess it's probably because I gave him some sort of believable explanation this time. I didn't just leave him hanging like I usually do. I want him to relax and let it go, but then I remember—it's Christopher. That's never going to happen. He's my best friend. Getting him to back off of me is like a fish drowning.

Christopher grabs my hand and removes it from his shoulder.

"You can always sleep at my place when it gets rough, mate," he says, his accent thick.

I chuckle. "With your dad?" Another chuckle. "Yeah, okay."

Christopher snorts, a grin on his face. "Have a little faith in me. I'll keep him out of your way. You'll have one of the spare rooms. Each one has its own bathroom. I'll bring you food."

I nod. "Thanks, manservant," I joke, feigning an English accent, which makes Christopher raspberry before walking away.

I can't help but laugh as I watch him walk down the hallway to get to his first class period. I know Christopher was hardly kidding about me staying over at his place since he's no stranger to my parents' bickering. Sometimes, they would argue in a different area of the house, hoping that the two of us couldn't hear if Christopher would come over—but it wouldn't work. Christopher would try to play things off and find something else for us to do to get our minds off of it, which helped. But I knew part of it was guilt. He felt guilty that I had to deal with that almost every night.

Although, his home life is no better either. After his mom died, his dad hardly said two words to him or swung at him over something stupid. If not that, his dad barely acknowledges that he even exist.

If not that, his dad barely acknowledges that he even exist.

If anything, I should be the one offering him to stay at my place, and I have, but Christopher knows that it will drive his father wild. Christopher once told me that when he thought about moving to Ireland after graduation, his dad lost it and threatened to kill himself. Christopher called his bluff, but that same night, he found his dad unconscious in the bathtub under the water, attempting to drown himself.

He was able to revive his dad alone, but it made him sick having to do it. He told me, *"I wanted to just walk away after I got him out. I wanted to get far away enough before calling the paramedics, but he's bloody mad. I couldn't risk anything."*

Meanwhile, I'm using Christopher's guilt for my situation with my parents to my advantage to get him off my back.

You're the asshole, I tell myself as I walk through the double doors and head up the steps to get to my first period class.

Week 1, Friday

It's been a hard night, trying to sleep. I couldn't stop thinking about that kid that was shot a couple days ago. I spent the night reading a few articles about the shooting last night, and I know I shouldn't have, but I couldn't help it. Then I thought about what those two guys in my homeroom were talking about—someone being jumped and a store owner being robbed at gunpoint. It was sickening, but stuff like this happens all the time around here. Just not in certain parts of Philly. Now they're happening in those parts, all thanks to the effed-up system of things.

Maybe I should talk to my dad about it. But what are the chances that he actually knows a damn thing about any of it.--D.G.

I wait for Meagan by the front entrance once classes end for the day. Christopher had plans to take Carmen out tonight to cheer up after dealing with her dad's side of the family. Meanwhile, Peter offered to take Benton home since it was on the way to his mom's place.

I was a bit surprised that Peter was making a bold move by visiting his mom without his aunt's supervision, but he swore that he would be fine. But the thing he didn't understand was that his aunt wouldn't know he was visiting her, and I reminded him that.

He just shrugs. "I'll be alright. I promise. I just have to drop off some supplies she needs, and that's all."

I ask him, "What supplies?"

He sighs. "Some toilet paper and a few...women stuff." It didn't really bother him that he had to get that stuff for his mom. And Peter swore that if he needed anything else, he would text me since Christopher would be uptight if he found out that Peter visited his mom alone.

It's not that Christopher doesn't trust Peter's judgment. Chris just knows how Peter gets when he's with his mom. He gets too hopeful and is let down more times than anyone can count. It really pisses us off, but there's nothing we can really say about it since it's Peter's mom.

As horrible as she is—no one insults someone else's mom.

That's our oath to each other.

I sigh.

I check the time on my watch as a couple more students walk past me, leaving the school. It's inching close to four o'clock, and there's no sight of Meagan.

I pull out my phone from my back pants pocket, debating whether or not I should send her a text message. When I scroll through my text messages and click on her name, my fingers freeze when the keyboard pops up on the screen.

Just ask her where she is. It's not a big deal.

I know it's not a big deal, but at the same time, I wonder if it'll just be a waste of time. Besides, it was no rush waiting for her. Depending on her mood, we would either hang out at my place, or I'd take her home. I always let her decide.

I stuff my phone back into my pants pocket and decide to wait for her in the auditorium. I realize that I'm probably in the way as people continue to walk out of the building. Even though I'm standing off to the side, away from the door, someone would find a reason to pick a fight and accuse me of being in the way.

The second I open one of the wooden doors to the auditorium, I spot Meagan standing center stage while talking to some guy. He looks familiar. I take a few small steps forward to get a better look at him. He's fair-skinned, and his face looks close to perfection with his strong jawline, sharp cheekbones, and big brown eyes that were close to black. He keeps his hair styled neat, having the front pushed back and off to the side. He wears a gray, oversized hoodie that makes him smaller than he probably is, and his black slacks are tucked into his matching black boots.

I don't even realize just how close I am to the stage until Meagan looks over at me, and a smile crosses on her face. She waves for me to come up, and the guy just shoots me a glare, keeping his arms crossed over his chest as he rocks on his heels. It isn't until he entirely turns his body to face me that I realize it's Preston Highmore.

What's his deal?

I clear my throat before walking up onto the stage and approaching Meagan.

"Sorry for the hold-up. I was just wrapping things up," she explains as if she's pleading for my forgiveness.

A small chuckle escapes my mouth as I shake my head. "Kid, it's no worries." I look around and notice a few tables and chairs set up all over the stage in no specific order. "What's all this?"

Meagan opens her mouth to speak, but Preston cuts her right off, answering for her. "For our next show, which is in a few weeks, but we're a little low on a crew, as you can see." His eyes remain locked on Meagan as he speaks with annoyance, but he's so monotoned, it's hard to tell the level of his annoyance.

Meagan rolls her eyes. "We're making progress."

Preston snorts. "Barely." He then looks at me with an unsatisfied look on his face. He looks at me up and down while keeping his arms folded over his chest. "You seem like a heavy-lifting guy. No need to take that shirt off to prove it. I have a good eye."

I nearly choke, and Meagan sucks her teeth.

"Preston," she groans.

He just shrugs his shoulders as if he could care less. "Just putting it out there." He's not ashamed.

I know Preston from just seeing him every once in a while in the hallway. We never had classes together. If we did, I bet he'd try to avoid me. I know he's the type of guy who is hardly interested in attention and tries not to associate himself with attention-seeking people. I also know that he got his ass kicked a few times by a couple of douchebags after he was caught making out with some guy under the bleachers last year. Luckily, the guys were suspended, but it still wasn't enough, in my opinion.

I shake my head and shift my gaze up to Preston as he gives me a deadpan look. "I'm flattered but, I don't think I'd be the best option."

He tilts his head, unsatisfied.

Before he opens his mouth to say something, someone calls out to Preston from a distance. We all look over as a tall boy with ash-blond hair and a dimpled smile approaches us. He wears a jean jacket over his solid black tank top, and I notice a lacrosse jersey in his right hand. When he comes up onto the stage, I can see the name on the shirt as he drapes it over his forearm.

PETROV.

Erik Petrov.

He wastes no time making his way to Preston, plants a quick kiss on his lips, and wraps his arm around Preston.

When I look over at Meagan, my eyes widen, and she tries to hide the smile creeping on her face by looking down at her shoes. Despite earning a kiss from Erik, Preston keeps a deadpan face and shifts his gaze to Meagan. He snaps his fingers at her to get her attention, and she slowly looks up at him while trying to hide the smile on her face.

"Eh," he goes, stuffing his hands in the pocket of his hoodie. "Get over yourself. What's so funny?"

Meagan rocks on her heels, shaking her head. "Nothing."

Preston nudges Erik. "Erik, this is Meagan. She's one of our actresses for the show, and she's also working with me on promotions."

Erik nods with a smile. "Preston's told me about you."

Meagan shrinks back, dramatically putting her hand to her chest as if she's baffled. "Oh? He has now?" She cuts her eyes to Preston while keeping an opened-mouth smile on her face.

Preston's eyes widen with regret, and he quickly pats Erik's hand to stop Erik from rambling on. He tells Erik to meet him outside, and Erik kisses Preston again before leaving. Meagan nearly squeals but quickly buries the sound by biting down her lip. Preston shoots a deadly glare at her and puts his middle finger to his lips as if he's telling her to shut up.

In this case: *Shut the fuck up.*

An inevitable need to laugh stirs up inside of me, but I do my best to hold it in as I look down at my shoes. Yet, the laugh still manages to come out as a snort, and Meagan gently hits my arm with the back of her hand.

"Sorry, kid," I tell her through chuckles.

Meagan folds her arms over her chest as we walk off the stage. "Oh, please. Your apology is *sooo* convincing." She picks up her bookbag from one of the seats in the front row and slips it on her back, tightening the straps. "So, what's the plan? Am I going over your place or naw?" She pushes her headband back to keep the braids out of her face.

I shrug. "I was kinda leaving that up to you. It's the only gentleman thing to do, you know." I rest my arm on her shoulder, slightly curling the one side of my mouth upward.

Meagan twists her mouth and averts her eyes away from me. She rubs her arm as if she's on edge about being left with the decision-making. I remind her that it's not a big deal, and I fully wrap my arm around her, pulling her in closer to me as we head out of the auditorium. She rests her hand on my chest to brace herself from how quickly I pulled her in, and she looks up at me for a brief second.

She isn't shocked—just thought it was unexpected. I guess?

But then Meagan lets out a snicker and slightly rests her head back against my shoulder as we walk to my car. She asks if it's okay to come over to my place since she's not in the mood to go home just yet.

Plus, she knows I'll get her home before the street lights come on. I always do since her mom is super strict about Meagan's whereabouts and just doesn't like me.

No matter how many times Meagan swears otherwise, I know damn well her mom does not like me. Not even by a small percentage. She just tolerates me being friends with Meagan, that's all. And I get it. What parent would want their child to be associated with the infamous Donald Gonzalez?

Still, Meagan insists on hanging out and coming over to my place when she doesn't want to be bothered with going home. The second I pull my car into the garage that was once our hangout spot—having a couch, a cooler, and a nice set-up—but is now a regular garage full of storage and some empty space, Meagan digs into her bookbag and pulls out her phone.

I can hear her typing away as I turn off the engine. I look over at her as the signature *SWOOSH* sound pings from her phone once she sends the text message. I figure she's probably texting her mother, letting her mom know that she's hanging out with me, so her mom doesn't file a missing person report.

I sigh.

As we get out of the car, I get a text message from my mom, asking me if I could make dinner tonight since she's coming home late tonight. I text her back that it's no problem, but at the same time, I want to bash my head into the door as Meagan and I enter the house.

It's not that I hate cooking, it's no problem for me. I was always asked to cook between Morris-Lina and me if our parents came home late since I would always be in the kitchen with abuelo when I was younger. Plus, abuelo once told me that women love a man who can cook with passion.

He would tell me stories about how he taught my dad how to cook, and dad would always get frustrated when abuelo would share those stories with me. Dad wouldn't throw a fit about any of it, but he would get annoyed and try to shut down the conversations. I never understood why. It wasn't like abuelo was making dad seem less of a man. After all, he was able to swoon mamá.

But I always wanted to believe that the reason dad would get so upset was that abuelo lost his ability to cook after my dad's mother left them when he was only two. Abuelo always kept her picture in his wallet, but he never told me or Morris-Lina her name. He just called her, *"Mi corazón."*

Abuelo said he's never loved another woman other than her, and he's never tried pursuing anyone else. I often try to picture him being reunited with her—the woman he loved—in the afterlife. I doubt dad does it, so I try to think about it and pray for the best. I never know if God hears me loud enough, but I believe abuelo at least deserves that. Something hopeful.

I take Meagan's coat and hang it up in the closet by the front door for her. I do the same with my jacket and pull out the hem of the uniform shirt from my pants, allowing the bottom of my shirt to flow freely past my waist.

I watch as Meagan sits on the brown faux leather couch in the living room across from our TV, and she pulls out a textbook for one of her classes. I press my lips together in a tight smile as I quietly approach her from behind the couch. She lets out a huff, keeping her focus glued on the textbook as she flips through the pages like a woman on a mission. She reaches back into her bookbag and pulls out her binder and a small pouch full of different colored pens.

I remain quiet, standing behind her, admiring her determination as she tucks one of the pens behind her ear and holds a red highlighter in her teeth while flipping through her binder. This isn't a surprising sight for me—seeing Meagan like this. Whenever she comes over to study, she always lays her stuff out and starts color-coding her notes and rewriting different critical points for her to remember. When we review our math worksheets, I offer her my notes, and she'll take a picture of it on her phone but then rewrite everything in a way she'll understand.

She'll twist her mouth and furrow her eyebrows as she writes. Sometimes she'll purse her lips and tap the end of the pen to her lips when she gets in deep thought. I'll even notice her fiddle with her hair, twirling her ends whenever she gets stuck on a question and overthinks a solution.

But when Meagan is really into her studies and is on a roll, she'll start marking up her notebook with highlighters and making bullet points with different colored pens. Like right now.

I lean down and settle my arms on the back of the coach, making sure that I don't make a sound as Meagan reads the page of her textbook, guiding her finger across the words as she mouths the words to herself.

When she leans back, I inch my head closer to her ear, looking down at the masterpiece of colors she's made from her note-taking.

"What you got there, Picasso?"

Meagan practically leaps out of her skin and swiftly leans forward, covering her face while sitting on the couch. The fit of laughter that blurts out of my mouth as I stand up straight starts to soften as she slowly turns her attention over to me, looking over her shoulder with a stern scowl on her face. Her nostrils flare, and she bites down on her lip.

"Oh, c'mon, kid," I say, as I take a step back, trying to settle down. "I didn't know I was gonna scare ya. If I did, then I would've given you a warning."

Meagan slaps her hand down on her textbook as it remains open on her thighs. "I wasn't scared." Pause. "You just got me off guard a bit, alright?" She sits up with her back straight and leans back, trying to get herself together.

I snort a chuckle. *Oh, please.*

I head upstairs to my room, change out of my uniform, and try to find something more comfortable for cooking while also keeping in mind that Meagan is still a guest in my home. Usually, I just walk around in an oversized tank and my boxer shorts, but that's not going to work for today.

I throw on a pair of gray sweatpants and pull the drawstring so it fits around my waist. I go through my drawers to find a shirt to wear, and I glance up at the baseball sitting at the top of my dresser next to the framed picture of Morris-Lina and me back when we were kids. It was taken back when I was in the minor league, and my team lost our first game. I remember feeling disappointed in myself, but then Morris-Lina ran up to me after the game. She said something to me that made me feel less upset with myself and put me in a headlock.

Mom wanted a picture of us, so dad told us to get ourselves together and knock it off.

I remember Morris-Lina whining, *"Daaad, we're just playing."*

Then, mom retorted, *"But playing becomes fighting. Also, girls don't act like that, niña."*

So, I wrapped my arm around Morris-Lina's shoulder, and she tightly hugged me while laughing. It was as if she was trying to squeeze my guts out. So, I tried tickling the back of her neck, laughing. We just couldn't stop, but we remained facing the camera, and dad just gave up and took the picture.

I remember mom being annoyed by Morris-Lina and me, but she didn't make a fuss after the picture was taken. She just shook her head and told us to come on so we could head home. It was hot that day, so we had to get home.

I take a sharp breath as my chest tightens and my windpipe starts to close. I clear my throat and manage to find a black tee-shirt for me to throw on.

When I head back downstairs, Meagan remains seated on the couch, flipping through her textbook and muttering to herself. I bite down on my lip, so I don't laugh aloud.

"I feel you staring at me." She shifts her attention to me, arching an eyebrow. "Is something up?"

Way to go, Gonzalez.

"Nah." I head into the kitchen. "Want anything?"

"I'm good!" she calls out.

I lean back on my elbows onto the countertop and think about what to make for dinner. Usually, mom is particular if she asks me to cook something since she's picky as hell. Unlike me, dad, and Moe, she doesn't like her food too spicy. Not because the taste bothers her. She used to tell me that when she was growing up, abuela always cooked spicy foods. Mom eventually grew tired of it and swore she would never eat spicy foods ever again once she could live independently.

I sigh.

Based on the ingredients we have already, my best option is to make ropa vieja— pulled stewed beef with mixed vegetables. I also think of making some rice as a base, so I check the cabinet to see if we have any white rice.

We do.

So, that's what I cook. Ropa vieja and white rice.

As I start cooking, I hear footsteps behind me, and I look over my shoulder as I stand at the counter. Meagan leans on the wall to the kitchen entrance with her arms crossed over her stomach, watching me. I could easily pretend not to notice her as I stirred the onions and peppers in the skillet. The steam from the skillet presses on my face, and I crack open the kitchen window above the sink, letting the cool air come in.

I go back to the stove and sauté the onions. "Still creeping?" I look over my shoulder, curling the corners of my mouth upward, winking at Meagan.

She fidgets her fingers as she approaches me, but she's a bit hesitant with each step she takes. When she stands beside me, her arm brushes against mine, and I look at her. She presses her lips tightly together as she eyes the steaming vegetables.

"I didn't know you could cook." A faint smile forms on her lips, and then she shifts her gaze to me.

I snort a chuckle. "Yeah, well. If you don't know, now you know." I wink, clicking my tongue.

Meagan shakes her head, chuckling. "I can't with you sometimes."

I bump my shoulder into hers. "You know you love me."

She rolls her eyes.

I carefully pick up a small piece of bell pepper and hold it up to Meagan's lips for her to taste. She furrows her eyebrows and looks at me as if she's ready to make a run for it. I tilt my head and press my lips together in the form of a pathetic pout, making whimpering sounds as if I'm a sad puppy.

"I don't like spicy foods," she says, looking at the piece of pepper in my hand.

I roll my eyes. "It's not that spicy."

"It's a bell pepper, Donny."

"Yeah, so?"

She opens her mouth to protest, but I arch my eyebrow, smirking. She knows well enough that bell peppers are not really hot or spicy. So, there's no reason for her to be so worried. Plus, I've seen Meagan eat spicy food before. She never complained.

What's the big deal?

Is it because she's never tasted my food before?

I'm not a bad cook.

Meagan closes her eyes as she bites the pepper from my fingers and chews. She opens her eyes and settles her hands on her hips.

I snicker as she finally swallows.

"Not bad," she says, rocking on her heels.

"All I did was saute it. I didn't even add the extra stuff yet."

"What are you even making?" She stands on her tip-toes to rest her chin on my shoulder, even though we're practically the same height. Although, I'm only taller by four or five inches.

I add in the garlic and sprinkle some salt. "Ropa vieja."

"Oh." Meagan lifts her chin off my shoulder and takes a small step back. "I'm in the way."

I arch my eyebrow. "No such thing." I turn back to the skillet. "Besides, the meat is already prepped, so I don't gotta be over this for that much longer."

Dad had made a dish earlier in the week that had pulled beef. I don't remember what it was called, but it tasted great, and mom loved it. I figured he made it an apology to mom for whatever they were arguing about that same day in the morning.

But I figure that I might also use what we already have than prep another thing of beef. Even though the dish might not taste as great since the meat is not freshly prepped.

Meagan slightly nods her head, pressing her lips tightly together in a straight line. "I can always just catch the bus back."

I scoff. *Yeah right. Or I could just invite you to stay for dinner.*

"What?"

My heart nearly pounces out of my chest when I hear Meagan's voice, and I fumble with the wooden spoon.

Shit. I said that out loud?!

I clear my throat, tapping the spoon against the rim of the skillet. I set it aside in the empty kitchen sink and wipe my hands with the small towel over my shoulder. I rub my hands together as I face Meagan. I try to think of something quick and believable to say as I lean back on the edge of the countertop, wishing I could go back in time to a couple seconds ago and tape my mouth shut.

"Nothing." I shrug. "Just thinking about something is all."

When she chews on her lip, I feel my throat close up, and it becomes impossible for me to speak. She looks down at her shoes and rubs her arm. For some reason, she feels as though she's in the way. But she's not.

"Welp," she pops her head back up and tries to force enthusiasm in her words. "I'll let you get back to it."

Dammit.

"Hey, kid."

Meagan sharply stops moving where she stands and looks at me with her lips parted and eyes wide. My heart thumps loudly in my ears like drums. I open my mouth, but nothing comes out.

"Donny?" She takes a small step towards me. "You good?"

Speak, you idiot.

I chuckle, standing up straight. "Yeah. Just wondering if you wanted to stay tonight. For dinner." I check the time on the microwave. It's half past five. "I know you have to be home by a certain time, but I gotta finish this up, and I don't know how long that's gonna take. Plus, one meal at the Gonzalez residence can't hurt, right?"

The look on Meagan's face says it all—her eyes wide in shock, her mouth slightly agape, but nothing comes out.

Way to go, Gonzalez! You really nailed it this time!

I wouldn't blame her if she kneed me in the balls, grabbed her stuff, and stormed out to catch the bus home. I probably sounded as though I wanted to keep her hostage. Like I wasn't giving her a choice. I'd kick myself in the balls if I could. I don't even know why I said anything or where all that even came from. The words just came out of nowhere. It was like a vomit of words.

More like a vomit of bullshit, I think to myself.

"Kid?" I try to keep my voice straight as the nickname I gave her slips out softly.

Meagan blinks and runs her hands down her sides as she stands up straight. "Yeah." Soft chuckle. "Yeah, that sounds like a plan to me. I'll let my mom know." She bites down on her bottom lip in an attempt to hide the smile creeping on her face before she walks back into the living room and sits on the couch.

A wave of relief runs through me, and I let out a sharp breath, leaning back on the countertop. My heart beats so rapidly that I picture it just bursting in my chest at any second. I turn around to grip the edge of the countertop, feeling the sharp edge sink into my palms a bit. I let out a slow breath, and I felt my heart start to settle down. A chuckle escapes my lips, and I slap my hand over my mouth, praying to God that Meagan didn't hear me. When I quickly peek over my shoulder, she has her head down as she forcefully pulls off the cap to one of her highlighters to go over her notes.

Sigh of relief.

El burro.

I turn my focus back to cooking, and I suddenly hear Meagan call out to me that her mother is cool with her staying over for dinner. I feel my heartbeat too quickly for my own comfort. Even though it's for a millisecond.

I just nod and tell her, "Good to know."

. . . .

"Oh my God, c'mon!" Meagan stomps her foot, glaring at me. "I got it! You cooked! Let me help." She turns her body away from me, trying to block me from snatching the dishrag and plate from her hands.

Still, I manage to tower over her and grab the rag from her soapy hands. She huffs and tries to get it back, but I hold it up out of her reach and lean back to keep her from grabbing it from me. I've never seen her this hellbent before on helping out. It's almost impossible for me to not laugh. And the more I laugh and prevent her from helping me wash the dishes, the more irritated she looks. Despite her dark skin, I can tell she's getting flustered, and somehow, it's irresistible.

My back lower back bumps into the stove, and Meagan pushes her hand against the edge of the countertop, attempting to reach higher to get the rag from me. I stand up on my toes and switch hands to keep her from getting the rag.

She grits her teeth and leans her body in closer, still reaching.

I try to stop laughing, but it's beyond impossible at this point.

"You're going have to try better than that, chica," I snicker. Meagan grunts and stomps her foot.

"Doooonny!" she whines as she leans in further.

Suddenly, my back roughly presses up against the stove as Meagan's body falls onto mine. My arms think before I do as one comes around her waist while the other securely comes around her upper back. Her hands tightly grip onto my shoulders, and she drops the plate onto the stovetop, but it doesn't shatter.

When she lifts up her head, I realize just how close her face is to mine. I can see how faint her dark spots really are underneath her makeup, and I can also see just how rich and brown her eyes actually are due to the bright kitchen light. The tightness in my chest fades and is replaced with an unfamiliar sensation that makes me question whether or not I'm actually breathing.

It isn't until she taps on my shoulder and pokes my cheek that I realize that I still have my arms locked around her.

And that I'm sandwiched between her and the stove.

I feel her right hand slide down my arm, setting my skin on fire before she reaches behind me and grabs the rag from my hand. She looks away from me and clears her throat.

I loosen my arms from around her. She reaches behind me with her other hand to grab the plate from off the stovetop. When she takes a step back from me, the space between us suddenly seems so far, even though it's not.

I shake my head and rub the back of my neck.

Snap out of it, moron. Don't be a weirdo.

I let out a soft chuckle. "I'll dry, and you wash?"

Meagan stands up straight, dragging the rag over the rim of the plate. I watch the corners of her mouth curl upward, and she slowly lifts her eyes up to meet mine.

She nods. "Deal."

As she swerves on her heels and makes her way back to the sink, I run my hand over my face and softly exhale. I can't believe what just happened. I honestly could've made her fall. If it wasn't for my body reacting on its own, she would have.

Although, it was worth seeing her like that—so damn determined. It was unlike anything I'd ever seen before. I can't describe it.

Instead of dwelling on it, I uphold my deal to Meagan, dry the dishes, and put them away while she washes them.

Week 2, Sunday.

I call out to Yago from the bottom of the stairs as I tightly tie the laces to Gabriel's boots. Gabriel sits on the bottom steps and is already wearing his dark blue jacket, making him look marshmallow. Half of his face is buried into the coat, bringing out the roundness of his cheeks, making him look like a chipmunk. He wiggles his thin, tiny fingers in his dark blue gloves that fit like giant oven mitts over his hands.

He points over to the table by the door. I figure it's because he wants to put on his hat since it's on top of the table, but I shake my head, telling Gabriel to wait since we're not leaving yet.

I decided to take the boys out to the playground since the snow has melted during the week, and the sun is shining bright today. The forecast called for rain this morning, but the sky proved otherwise. Plus, if I hadn't thought of taking them out, they—mainly Yago—would've begged me to take them to the playground, whining that they were bored from being stuck at home.

So, after I fixed the boys' lunch and cleaned their dishes, I told them to throw on something warm so we could go to the playground. As expected, Yago was excited— waving his hands in the air as he ran up the steps to get dressed. Meanwhile, Gabriel waddled over to me and tightly wrapped his little arms around my leg, giving me an opened-mouth smile.

I sent Yoselin a text beforehand about us going to the playground, and she finally responded once Gabriel came downstairs, wearing his heavy boots and a long-sleeved shirt with a train on the front. I was surprised that he beat Yago in getting dressed. Not only is Yago older, but whenever he's excited about something, he's quick in preparation since he's a great ball of energy.

Anyway, Yoselin responded that she was okay with me taking the boys to the playground, but she reminded me to be careful. I replied that I would guard the boys with my life, and she knew I would keep my word. That's why she always trusts me to babysit. Yoselin is not the parent to let anyone just babysit her kids, unlike the boys' father. Yoselin is very particular in who she trusts to look after them—especially since their father is not the brightest bulb, nor is he reliable.

Whenever he comes to pick the boys up for specific days, I can tell that all the color just drains from her out of worry for the boys' well-being. But their father wasn't always so reckless. It wasn't until after Gabriel was born that he started drinking and staying out late hours doing God knows what.

But once Gabriel hit three, that's when the boys' father started turning himself around. Slowly. But it was only because Yoselin was able to bribe him in a way. She made him promise that if he began attending therapy and got clean, he could spend more time with the boys, and he did just that. I'll give him props for sticking to it too. It's not like he bailed after trying a certain amount of times. He continues to uphold his end of the bargain between him and aunt Yoselin. Yet, he's still despised whenever he attends family gatherings. He'd not participate in them if he had things his way, but he only goes because of the boys.

I know Yoselin could care less if he attended or not. Even if she still had some love for him deep down, she replaced it with resentment for him and worry for her sons.

It's a miracle that she even trusts me with the boys so easily. Probably because they like being around me so damn much, and she had no problem using that to her advantage. And it should probably bother me if she feels that way, but it doesn't. The boys hardly give me any trouble, and I don't mind doing things for the family. That's how I was brought up—you do for family.

So that probably settled her nerves, too, and made it easier for her to trust me with them.

I pick up Gabriel from the steps, and he latches his arms around my neck and nuzzles his head against the crook of my neck, whimpering. I sigh.

"I know you want to go, but not yet, alright?" I tell him.

I sit him down on the couch and click on the TV with the remote. The channel is already on some kids' cartoon show with a talking dog dressed as a detective. Gabriel sits up and giggles.

I ruffle his hair and tell him that I'll be right back. I doubt he even cared since his eyes were still glued to the cartoon of the talking detective dog on the screen.

One down. One to go.

I shift my focus to Yago and call him downstairs, but he doesn't respond. I tap my fingertips against the railing and look back at Gabriel as he continues to watch the TV. Unlike Gabriel, I doubt Yago has trouble getting dressed since he's older and knows how to dress. And it's not like Yago wouldn't want to go to the playground since he's always excited whenever we go.

I think.

I heard him moving around to help Gabriel get dressed.

So, what's the problem?

"Yago?" My voice is a bit softer as I walk up a couple steps and stop. "Yago?!" I try not to sound too demanding of him, but I start to think worst-case scenario once I see his door is closed.

And it's quiet. Too quiet. Upstairs, at least.

A giant ball forms in my throat, and I practically sprint the rest of the way up the steps and to his bedroom door. I put my ear to the door and heard nothing. My lips become dry as my mind suddenly goes back to when I found Morris-Lina. This is precisely what happened. It was tranquil in her room. Even though she kept her windows open, I couldn't even hear anything from the outdoors.

I knock on Yago's door, the same way I did with Morris-Lina's. And just like her door, his pushed open with no problem. The only thing that is missing is the sound of a creak the more I push it open. I take a small step into Yago's room. His walls are perfectly smooth and painted midnight blue. Instead of posters, there are shelves on his walls with trains and action figures settled on them. My eyes then trail to his bed, which is terribly covered by a white-and-blue checkered comforter.

I notice a small bump under the covers as if someone is hiding underneath. I suddenly feel that my heart is about to come up my throat, followed by my other organs. I forget how to breathe as I dare myself to approach the bed. Every step is like walking on pins and needles, and the closer I get, the more strain I put on my legs. I have to tighten my jaw to keep my teeth from chattering.

I don't even want to move my hand to pull the comforter. My mind goes back to when I did that once before. Morris-Lina had the leftover pills in her hand. Her eyes were closed. She had me fooled that she was sleeping…but she wasn't. No matter how much I rocked her and shook her, nothing happened.

My palms start to sweat as I reach for the comforter. I'm unable to pull it back because it lifts on its own, and I practically fall backward, but I manage to catch myself. All I see is the flash of colors dance in my vision before the rest of the room becomes clear to me. My heart thumps loudly in my chest and rapidly. My lungs try to retrieve as much air as possible as I grip my right hand onto the dresser beside the bed.

When I lift my gaze, I see Yago standing up on his bed, bouncing. I can hear him singing and laughing all at once, but his voice is somehow faint as I try to hold grasp to reality.

"I got you! I got you!" he sings clearly.

He jumps off his bed, and I can see him making his way to me from the corner of my eye. My blood rushes through me, and my skin feels like it's on fire.

What the hell is wrong with this damn kid?!

I grit my teeth and grab him by his shoulders. All I see is a flash of colors from the comforter—like it's mocking me. The tightness in my chest is unbearable, and it's all thanks to this little hellion and his silly amusement!

"What the hell is wrong with you?!"

The sound of my voice makes my throat tighten from the venom within the words. I no longer see colors dancing in my vision. Just Yago. The softness of his eyes that are practically glossy, like he's holding back tears. The slight quivering of his lip, followed by the look he gives me—it's nothing I've seen before. Then, I realize how tightly I am gripping his shoulders.

My breath hitches.

I clear my throat as I look at Yago in his delicate, big brown eyes. I run my hand through his hair and loosen my other hand off his shoulder.

"I'm sorry," I say, trying to keep my voice straight, but it's almost impossible. The words quiver due to the ball forming in my throat.

I clear my throat and wrap my arm around him to pull him in close to me. Surprisingly, he doesn't try to fight me or push away after the way I just blew up at him. Maybe he's in shock because I've never done that to him before. I've never thought I would do that to him. Or Gabriel.

I crouch down and somewhat sit him on my lap. Yago's not tiny like Gabriel, so he's standing, even though I keep my arm around him like he's sitting on my lap to keep him steady. He looks down and fiddles with his fingers, not saying a word.

I sigh. "Look at me, Yago." I make sure my voice is soft, and he gives me his attention. "I thought you were hurt. Don't do that again, okay?"

"Why would I be hurt? Didn't you see me hiding?" The sound of his voice reminds me that he's still a kid and doesn't get what I mean. Even though he and Gabriel were there for Morris-Lina's funeral service, they didn't see the burial. They don't understand the concept of—

I shake myself out of my thoughts.

"I know," I say, trying to force a smile on my face. "But you could've hit your head or something." I manage to wiggle my fingers against the side of his neck, making him squirm into a fit of soft giggles. I chuckle, "I wouldn't want anything to happen to my favorite bobblehead."

I move my hand away from his neck and press a light kiss to the side of his forehead. I pat his back, telling him to put his coat and stuff on so we can head out. I watch as he sprints out of the bedroom and goes down the steps to do what I asked.

I fall back, sitting on the floor and leaning back against the dresser. I rest my head back against the dresser drawer behind me and run my hand down my face. Honest to God, I don't know what came over me. The look Yago had on his face replays in my head like a broken record. The knots in my stomach intensify, and I feel something stirring inside. I can feel a burning swelling up in my throat, and my lungs feel like they're going to burst.

I rush into the bathroom and slam the door shut behind me. I lift up the lid to the toilet, and I'm not even able to get on my knees when the burning in my throat travels up to my mouth. It feels like someone took a jar of nuclear acid and pumped it through me as my stomach bubbles, giving the vomit the initiative to jump out of my mouth. I keep my head over the toilet as another rush of acid comes flying up my throat. The second round is just as unbearable as the first one, and I grip onto the toilet seat. It feels like another one is up, but nothing happens.

I spit out what remains in my mouth and flush it down the toilet.

I turn on the sink water and wash my hands. The warm water sends tingles throughout my body, and I look at myself in the mirror.

I don't look sick, so I shouldn't feel sick.

I notice a few light circles under my eyes, but that's how I've looked for these past couple of days. Rarely, I'll actually get good sleep, and it's not because mom and dad are constantly arguing late at night. I've managed to block them out when they do, but it's not every night.

I rinse the taste of acid out of my mouth and splash some water on my face. I turn off the water before patting my face dry with a paper towel. I let out a sigh when I take one last glance at myself. I fix the color to my plaid button-down shirt that I keep open while wearing my solid white tee-shirt underneath. I'm surprised I didn't get any stains on it after what just happened.

I fix the front of my hair, pushing back and off my face, but a few strands still tickle against my forehead. I leave it and tuck my tee-shirt into my black jeans. I take a step back to get a better look at myself.

I sigh. *You're fine. Just pull yourself together. At least for the kids.*

I cut off the bathroom light and head downstairs. When I get to the bottom of the steps, the boys sit in the living room, watching television. It's the same one with the detective dog. Gabriel looks like he hasn't moved an inch since I went upstairs, and Yago is all suited up for the outdoors, with his coat all zipped up, his face practically buried into his fluffy scarf, while wearing his hat and gloves.

I grab my coat from out of the closet and throw it on.

I bring my two fingers to my mouth and let out a loud whistle that catches both of their attention as they whip their heads around to look at me as I stand by the front door.

I clap my hands together. "You boys ready?"

Yago clicks off the TV with the remote and grabs Gabriel's hand. They both run up to me with so much enthusiasm—like it's their first time going outside since God knows how long.

"Can we play on the swings?" Yago asks as I kneel down to meet Gabriel's level, putting his hat on his head.

Gabriel moves his arms, but it looks like he's trying to flap like a bird since his coat makes him look like a giant marshmallow. I can't help but laugh a bit as I stand up to my feet. I hold Gabriel's hand and open the door.

"If you don't run ahead on our way there, then you can play on the swings if there's any open," I reply to Yago, earning a bright smile from him.

He gave me his word that he wouldn't run ahead on our way to the playground, but I could tell it was hard for him not to run ahead—even the slightest bit—since he couldn't contain his excitement. So, the whole way to the park, he just kept telling me how much farther we had to walk until we actually got there. He even counted how many blocks of cement we stepped on as we walked and then how many blocks of ice still remained in the street. Meanwhile, Gabriel waddled in silence, and even though he was holding my hand the entire time, I could tell walking bothered him due to the heaviness of his coat and boots.

So, I carried him on my back. Gabriel's little fingers rested on my collarbone while the soft texture from the sleeves of his puffy coat pressed against my throat and the sides of my neck.

We get to the playground, and Yago gasps when he sees that no one uses the swing set. It's not like there's no one else there. A few other kids run around while their parents or guardians are off to the side, hardly watching them. One woman looks up from her phone and tells her kid to stop running up the slide. The woman looks young. She can't be that much older than me. She looks like she's probably in her late teens or early twenties, maybe.

I crouch down to let Gabriel climb off my back, and Yago asks me if he can play the swings.

I sigh. "Ask me in Spanish." I arch an eyebrow and twist my lips into a smile.

He groans. "Whyyyy?" he whines.

I chuckle. "C'mon, bobblehead. Just do it."

"But I speak Spanish for mamá all the time."

"As you should, and you should be proud." I take a quick glance at Gabriel as he leans on my thigh. I scoop him up and sit him on my lap. I look back at Yago. "I wish my parents made me speak Spanish all the time when I was little. I wouldn't have struggled as much."

Yago rocks on his heels. "Really?" he asks, genuinely curious.

I nod. "Mhm."

It makes me kind of jealous that Yoselin is on top of the boys with their Spanish, making sure that they know the value of the language and of our culture. When Morris-Lina and I were growing up, our parents were different. Our dad would try to stay on top of us by speaking Spanish frequently, but our mom hardly wanted to teach us anything. I think that's pretty ironic since abuela was always on top of her and mi tía Yoselin when they were younger. All abuela would speak was Spanish, even though she knew English. Whenever we would go over to her house, abuela would only want us to speak Spanish, and if there were certain words we didn't know, she'd teach us.

She wasn't ruthless about it, though. Abuela would never pop us in the mouth if we spoke English. She'd sigh and pat our heads and then correct us in Spanish.

I press my lips tightly together in a flat line and pat the top of Yago's head, like abuela used to do with me.

Yago then sighs and asks me, "Por favor?"

I tilt my head, arching my eyebrow. "Por favor qué?"

He twists his lips. "Um..."

I chuckle. "Puedo por favor jugar en los columpios?"

Yago nods. "Puedo por favor...jugar en...los columpios?"

"Excelente!" Even though he is wearing a hat, I ruffle the top of Yago's head, making him giggle. I nod my head in the direction of the swing set. "Sí, adelante. Be careful."

Yago sprints off to the swing set, and I realize the ground could still be icy. "Don't run!"

I watch him jump onto one of the swings, and he starts rocking to swing. I shake my head, snorting.

I look over at Gabriel as he keeps his head rested against my shoulder. I bounce my leg to get him laughing. He likes it whenever I do that for some reason.

"Want to go on the slide?" I ask him.

He nods, rubbing his eyes.

I move Gabriel up and off of my lap and walk with him to the jungle gym. There aren't many kids playing in the jungle gym, surprisingly. Most of them are just running around in the open, either playing tag or hand games. I help Gabriel up the steps to get to the long, spiral slide that's like a tunnel. Gabriel looks up at me with pleading eyes. I know he wants me to go down with him, but I shake my head.

I crouch down to his level so I can look him in the eye. I fix the collar to his coat and push his hat down back on his head, covering his eyebrows.

"Are you a big boy?" I ask him.

He shakes his head in denial.

I chuckle. *This kid.*

"Yes, you are." I rub his cheek with my thumb, and he sniffs. "Do you want me to meet you at the bottom?"

He shakes his head in refusal. He tugs on my arm, wanting me to go down with him. He makes a crying sound but doesn't cry. I rub the back of my neck and roll my eyes.

"Alright," I groan. "I'll go with you. But just this once, okay?" He nods.

I hug Gabriel tight as I sit behind him and prop him up on my thighs. It is dark when we go down the slide, and I practically have to scoot to get down the slide since I'm not a little kid. Still, Gabriel's laugh echoes as we reach the very bottom of the slide, making it out the spiral tunnel. I let Gabriel go, and he flaps his arms.

"Can you go on your own now?" I ask him as I stand up from off the slide, dusting off the back of my pants.

Gabriel nods and makes his way back up the steps of the jungle gym to go down the slide on his own. I stuff my hands into the pockets of my jacket once the cool breeze hits me out of nowhere, making my teeth chatter.

As I walk around the jungle gym to watch Gabriel go down the slide, I notice the woman sitting on the bench, yelling at two guys standing close to her. One guy is laughing while the other keeps trying to touch her, but she backs away from him. It's the woman who told her kid to stop running up the slide earlier.

I can't hear what they are talking about, but the guy that keeps trying to touch her grips onto her wrist and has a stern look on his face. She starts cussing, demanding for the guy to let go of her.

My blood boils, and I take a breath. I've seen this happen before. Once with Morris-Lina. It happened with her first boyfriend. The guy was a total prick. She would try to walk away from him whenever they were about to argue, and he would always grab her and yank for her to turn around and face him. It pissed me off.

Assholes.

I quickly glance at Gabriel as he plays with the blocks that are attached to the wall. I then look back at the woman as she curses for the guy to leave her alone. She even says his name, implying that she knows him.

I walk over to them and clear my throat. I think fast.

"Hey! I didn't expect to see you here! What's up?" I try to sound convincing. All three of them are looking at me, and my stomach does backflips.

I keep my focus on the woman. She furrows her eyebrows at first, not realizing what I'm trying to do. She probably thinks I am a loon or has her confused for someone else. I can tell even the guys are lost. So, I continue.

"I tried to call earlier, but it went to voicemail. I thought you'd call me back." I raise my eyebrows to give her a hint.

The woman finally catches on. She chuckles and nods her head. "Oh my God! I'm so sorry!" She manages to get up from the bench, collecting her purse. "I didn't expect you to be here!"

I laugh. "Small world."

I turn my attention to the two guys. They're both tall but not gigantic. The one who was grabbing at her has broad shoulders, but he's probably around my height. He has a tattoo of an X by his right eyebrow and a thin, dark caterpillar on the top of his lip. The other guy looks taller than him and is much leaner.

"Who's this?" I ask the woman, moving off to the side to stand in front of her a bit.

The woman grabs my wrist. "Just a friend." I look over my shoulder so I can see her face. Her eyes are glossy, but she pushes herself to smile and play along. "C'mon, let's go. I'm about to take Ricky home. We can chat and walk."

I smile. "Alright."

I stay behind her as we walk away from the guys to ensure they don't try anything. I slightly turn my head back to see if they are following us, but instead, they back away and walk off, heading towards the back gate.

"Thank you," I hear the woman whisper as we approach the jungle gym.

I walk up beside her and get a better look at her face. Her freckles are dark but compliment her smooth caramel skin. Her dark raven hair is pulled back into a ponytail, but a couple strands in the front drape over her right eye. Her round face makes her look like a doll, as do her big eyes. She's like one of those cute dolls that Morris-Lina used to make me play with her when we were kids.

I clear my throat. "It's no problem." I look behind us to see if those two pricks are gone, and they are. I look back at her. "Do you need me to call someone for you or...?"

"Oh no, it's all good." She looks over to the jungle gym and watches her kid. She lets out a deep sigh. "He's just some jerk."

"Asshole seems more accurate," I mumble.

She chuckles. "You don't even know him."

I shrug. "I can spot a dickless prick from a mile away."

The woman laughs. I notice her tuck a strand of her hair behind her ear as she looks away from me. The wind sends the loose strands at the front of her hair flying in different directions that I'm sure it's getting on her nerves. I look back to the jungle gym, watching Yago as she swings high enough to almost reach the clouds, and then Gabriel as he hangs from the mini monkey bars that are meant for more minor children his size.

I blow warm air into my palms and rub my hands together, sighing as I watch them.

"I'm Aitana." I swiftly shift my attention to the woman as she extends her hand out for me to shake. Her full lips pull upward into a faint smile, and she squints her eyes a bit to block out the brightness of the sun.

I press my lips together in a tight half-smile as I shake her hand.

"Donald."

She arches her eyebrow and snorts. "Really? *Donald?*"

I chuckle, shaking my head. "Yeah. My parents didn't really wanna give me and my sister traditional names. Thought it would be best to stun college interviewers, I guess." That last part was a joke, although it could've been a possibility.

The woman—Aitana—just nods her head and crosses her arms over her chest. She then asks, "And what's your sister's name?" She sways side-to-side but keeps her feet planted to the ground and doesn't touch me.

I clear my throat. "Morris-Lina." I sniff from the cold breeze. "But we called her 'Moe' for short."

Aitana stops swaying, and she looks as though she's suddenly having a great realization of something. With her lips slightly parted open and her gaze off to the side, it's like she's trying to put something together in her head. She even goes, "Huh," as if what I had said was interesting. I mean, it probably was since not many girls are named Morris-Lina or are called "*Moe.*"

I honestly don't know what our parents thought when they named us. Seriously, abuelo and abuela's names are not hard to spell or sound out.

I would've had abuelo's name—Armando Luca.

My sister would've had abuela's name—Juanita Marie.

Yet, our parents decided to nix the idea and went with *"Donald"* and *"Morris-Lina."*

I scratch my eyebrow and huff. Aitana asks me if we could have a seat on the bench while the kids play, and I nod. We sat on the bench and started doing small-talk, which I usually am not a fan of, but I didn't just push her aside. So, I participated, and eventually, we started having ice-breaker conversations. She figures that I'm probably in high school since I look young, and I nod, telling her that I'm in my senior year. She asks about my college plans, and I tell her that I've applied to several places.

"Have you considered which one you'd want to attend if you hear back from 'em?" she asks, crossing her right leg over her left while shifting around on the bench to get comfortable.

I rub the back of my neck and lean forward, resting my elbow on top of my thigh as I shrug. "Yeah, but I don't know if I'll get in."

"Oh yeah? Where?"

I don't like to brag, but I'm honest. "Welmur's University and Charleston Clinton, but they're overseas."

Immediately, her jaw practically drops to the ground. I should feel proud that I took a bold step and applied to two schools overseas that offered the best medical programs. But my parents didn't take me seriously when I announced where I was planning to attend college. Morris-Lina was the one who wanted me to go through with applying to Welmur's and Charleston.

When I announced the idea of going to college abroad to my parents during dinner a couple of months ago, mom choked on her drink, and dad almost dropped his fork of food.

Mom asked me, *"Are you serious?"*

I told her, *"Yes."*

Then dad was like, *"You really think that's a good idea?"*

I told him, *"Yes."*

They still didn't think I was serious, and it really pissed me off. I tried going to bed right after dinner, but I couldn't sleep to save my life that night. Then, I heard a knock at the door, and it was Morris-Lina. I let her into my room, and she sat down with me on the floor and talked to me. She told me that she thought I had a chance of getting into wherever I decided to apply for college, especially the schools abroad. She wanted me to go for them because she thought I had dreams that were bigger than my head, and I had a shot at making things work out.

I took her words to heart and decided to apply to Welmur's and Charleston— and a few other schools, but they were within the states. I should hear back from them later this month or next month, but just the thought of actually going to Europe sends chills down my spine and makes my stomach churn.

Aitana suddenly stands up from the bench and calls out for her kid—Ricky. I watch as she zips her coat entirely up to her chin and pulls at the collar since it looks tight on her.

"Well," she sighs, "it's been real. Hasn't it, Donald?" She crooks her neck side-to-side, keeping her gaze on me as her lashes flutter.

My throat suddenly feels dry, and I clear it up.

"Yeah." I jump up to my feet. "Yeah, it has been." I look over at the kids playing in the jungle gym as she calls for her kid again. I look back at her. "Do you need me to walk you somewhere? Just to make sure you're good?"

Aitana chuckles. "So chivalrous you are. It's like you're trying to swoon me, and we just met."

A laugh quivers from my mouth, and I rub the back of my neck. "You can never be too careful these days, huh?"

She slightly nods. "Well, thank you, but I'll be fine. We're parked right across the street, so." She then points over to where her car is parked, and I assume it's the shiny blue car that looks too luxurious to be parked in this neighborhood.

I'll be damned.

I notice a small child run up to us and the kid immediately hugs Aitana's leg. She rubs his head that is hardly covered by the hat on his head.

"Ricardo." Aitana sucks her teeth and fixes the kid's hat, so it's entirely on top of his head, which is a mop of dark curls. "No te lo vuelvas a quitar."

"Pero mami—" her kid starts to whine.

"Cállate!"

Aitana then grabs his hand takes one last look at me before telling me goodbye with a smile on her face. I watch as she exits the playground and looks both ways before she and her kid hurry across the street to her shiny blue car. Once she and her kid are in the car, I sit back down the bench and throw my head back, now looking up at the sky.

I don't know what just happened. Everything happened so quickly. I just wanted to take the boys out for a *lovely* day at the playground, not have to deal with people. Although, I couldn't just sit back and do nothing when I saw Aitana being harassed by those goons. Even though she is incredibly short, she's not tiny. She looks like she works out and probably could've kicked their asses if she wanted to. She probably didn't because there were other people around, and she probably didn't want someone to call the cops on her for using physical violence, even though it would've been self-defense.

But our society sucks. Someone probably would have recorded what happened but only get footage of Aitana beating the guys up instead of everything that occurred beforehand.

I groan.

A familiar tiny hand latches onto my hand, and I sit my head up, meeting Gabriel's eyes as he stands between my legs. I pick him up and sit him on my lap, bouncing my leg.

"Everything okay?" I ask him, pushing the front of his hair out of his eyes, and I fix his hat.

Gabriel points over to the swing-set, which is now occupied by two more kids and Yago, but a seat remains open. I sigh.

"You want me to push you?" I ask Gabriel, and he gives me a toothy smile, showing off his chipmunk cheeks. I poke his nose, making him laugh. "Okay, I'll push you."

He scoots himself off my lap and wastes no time running over to the slide, but his run looks more like a bounce, and his arms are extended out and flap due to the puffiness of his coat. I stay right behind Gabriel and help him up into the only available swing seat.

As I pull him back a little bit, I hear Yago call out my name. When I look up at him, he waves to me and tells me to watch how high he can swing.

"I'm a bird, Cousin Don-O!" he tells me, kicking out his legs as he makes it up higher.

I laugh after hearing him call me the nickname Yoselin rarely calls me, but Yago decided to use it forever. I remind Yago to be careful as I turn my attention back to Gabriel and lightly push him on the swing.

Week 2, Tuesday

I couldn't sleep the past couple of days. I felt terrible for what I did to Yago. Even though he forgot about it—me yelling at him and all—I still felt awful. I couldn't tell my tia about it because she'd probably never let me see the boys ever again. I didn't want that. But I don't even know what happened—it wasn't me.

Meanwhile, mom and dad have been nagging me about making sure I sent all my stuff to the colleges I want to go to. I still don't think they're taking me seriously when I tell them that I want to go somewhere abroad. I know I can get in, but I also...don't want to? I mean, Morris-Lina would've wanted me to get the hell up outta here, but I don't know if I'd really like to go that far yet. It would be nice, though. Not having to deal with the shittiness of the city. It's all shit. It wasn't always shit, but now it's becoming shit. After that kid's death a while ago, and then what I heard during homeroom, I wouldn't mind getting away. But I wouldn't want my folks to think I'm just abandoning them, even though they'd probably care less. Maybe.

I don't know why I'm writing all this out. Counselor Malik will probably use all this against me, anyway.-- D.G.

Counselor Malik lets out a low chuckle as he sits my journal face down on his right leg crossed over his left. It gives him a real thrill, reading my writings aloud. But just hearing the nonsense that I jot down makes me cringe a little. I can't believe I wrote all of that, and for what?

So we can have something to talk about?

It's like I set myself up for this.

I sink into my seat, crossing my right ankle over my left. My lips feel chapped, and I bite at the skin, but I remind myself not to peel it off since I don't like the taste of my own blood. Plus, I know I'll regret it later—peeling the skin of my lip.

I tighten my jaw as I look down at my hands, picking at my nails while praying to God that Counselor Malik doesn't ask me anything too ridiculous as to why I wrote all that junk. But then again, it won't surprise me if he does ask me anyway. It's sort of his job to ask me ridiculous things and whatnot.

Besides, I know I set myself up for it.

I didn't have to mention Yago and the way I scared him. I know damn well that I scared him. The way his eyes looked at me as if he was going to burst into tears. I was waiting for him to cry. It's not that I wanted him to, but I knew there was a chance it was going to happen. I don't even know what came over me. The thought of him being in that bed, possibly lying face down, not breathing—

A sudden familiar rush of acid starts bubbling up my throat, but I can hold it down. I put my fist to my mouth as I tighten my jaw, hoping I don't let anything out. It doesn't even feel major, probably just acid reflux or something.

It makes me hiccup, and then I sit up in my seat.

Counselor Malik takes another look at the journal, reading the same page he just finished reading while mouthing the words to himself. He clears his throat.

"So, I'm curious." *Here we go.* "What happened with Yago?"

Should've guessed he'd ask about that one. Good luck.

I shrug my shoulders, shaking my head. "I just kinda..." I pause.

Counselor Malik arches his eyebrow, expecting me to say more, but I don't know what else to say. I don't even know how to describe what happened. All I know is that the kid was scared of me, and that's never happened before. It's not like I hit him. I just kind of freaked out a bit. Maybe?

I take a deep breath. "I just kinda freaked a bit. I guess."

"You guess?" Counselor Malik was unconvinced. "Why?"

I can't help but suck my teeth and roll my eyes. Obviously, I don't want to talk about it, so why keep bugging me about it? Still, the man's relentless. He's not going to let it go. He'll just keep on picking at my brain about it until he's satisfied with my answer. And there's no point in making up something because he knows me all too well at this point. So, I give in.

"Look," I start off, trying to maintain eye contact with him, "the kid did a bad prank. I was trying to find him to take him and Gabe out for the day, and I couldn't find him. Then, when I did find him, he just startled me a bit."

Counselor Malik squints his eyes a bit like he's trying real hard to figure me out for a second. I started to question whether or not my answer was enough for him, but it should be because that's what happened. What more could he want from me?

"Where was Yago hiding?" he asks, still looking at me all funny.

"In his bed," I sigh. I look off to the side since I'm getting tired of how he's looking at me. "He was under his bedsheets. I should've known he was there. I just thought that it was empty. I don't know why it scared me so much. I just freaked for a second."

Counselor Malik is nodding from the corner of my eye, and he sits up with his hands folded. The way he looks at me this time, he's more relaxed, but I can tell he's still trying to figure me out a bit. When I give him my full attention, I notice his thumb grazing over his knuckle. Then I look him in the eyes. They are soft, but his jaw is tight, and his nostrils flare when he breathes.

My throat tightens.

"Donald." Counselor Malik leans forward a bit, still looking me in the eyes. "How would you describe yourself at that moment? Like what did you feel?"

I furrow my eyebrows. "I just told you I was startled."

"I know, but..." He pauses. He then takes a quick breath. "How did you feel at that moment? Were you scared?"

I snort and shake my head. "No. I wasn't scared. I was annoyed. Like I am now."

"Why are you annoyed?"

"Because!" I try not to raise my voice as I look away from him. "I don't know. One minute I knew he was there, but I wasn't sure. Then the next, I don't know what happened. I was just mad and confused and...I don't know. Then, when I saw that I was grabbing him too hard and how scared he looked, it made me sick, and I ended up throwing up and—"

"Wait for a second," Counselor Malik cuts me off, holding up his hand for me to stop. "You grabbed him, and then you threw up?"

Dammit. I said too much.

I nod. "Yeah." I can't keep my voice straight, and my eyes wander off to the side, looking down at the floor. "But I didn't like, hit him. I would never do that. At least, I don't think I did." I shake my head. "I don't know, it's all a big...something."

"A big blur?" Counselor Malik chimes in.

His gaze feels heavy on me, and it becomes almost unbearable. My stomach starts twisting in knots, and my throat becomes dry. Even when I clear my throat,

Counselor Malik's gaze doesn't change. He just keeps his eyes on me with his lips parted while drumming his fingers against the hardcover of my journal that still sits in his lap.

"What?" The question blurts out of me with slight hostility.

Counselor Malik just takes a deep breath, exhaling through his nose, making his nostrils flare due to the tone of my question. I can tell he's two seconds away from smacking me with either my journal or the clipboard sitting atop the small table beside him.

"Donald, based on what you've been through and what you've experienced, Post Traumatic Stress Disorder is common in these circumstances."

My heart drops to the pit of my stomach. "Post...what?"

"PTSD." Counselor Malik clarifies. "You finding your sister, going through all you went through..."

His words start to drift off, even though he's clearly talking. My chest feels tight, and my heart thumps loudly in my chest. I open my mouth to speak, but no words come out as I watch his lips move. All I can grasp are a few words, like "panic," "insomnia," "flashbacks," and "nausea."

Everything else slips my mind. He says this like I'm stupid. I know what PTSD is, but there's no way I could have PTSD.

PTSD from what? It's not like I fought in the war or was in an accident.

I cut him off from whatever else he's saying and shake my head. I try to remain calm as I speak, but I practically fumble with my words as I try to gather my thoughts and make a case for myself.

"I'm not loony here," I tell Counselor Malik, looking him straight in the eyes. "Not to say that people who do have PTSD are loony. But I'm not...there's no way I have that. I wasn't in some accident or in the army. I'm not freaking out every two minutes from looking at something or when I hear something pop off."

"There are many other triggers and forms of PTSD, Donald," Counselor Malik clarifies in a *"matter-of-fact"* tone. "You and your sister were close. You were twins and spent almost every second together." *Shut up.* "Then you go into her room, and you find her in her bed, completely drugged out."

"She wasn't *'drugged out,'*" I hiss through my teeth.

"She died of a drug overdose, Donald."

"I know that!" My voice practically bounces off the walls of the room, but my blood continues to boil inside me, and a rush of colors conquers my vision. All I can do is hear myself. "I know what I saw, and I don't need to be reminded of that! And I certainly don't need to be diagnosed by some damn high school counselor that thinks he's too good but actually has to buy his clothes from the clearance rack like everyone else because he tried all his luck for nothing and works minimum wage!"

When I rest back in the chair, I feel my hands start to shake as I take in the sudden silence. I notice the look on Counselor Malik's face without breaking eye contact. His lips are in a straight line, but his eyes stare me down like he's trying to concentrate on capturing some part of my face. It suddenly hits me what I just said, and I bring my fist to my mouth. I close my eyes and take a breath.

"I'm sorry." I drop my hand, letting it drape over the armrest as my leg bounces. "I didn't mean that."

Counselor Malik shakes his head, sitting up in his chair. "Don't worry. It's nothing I haven't heard before."

I arch my eyebrow. "Really?"

He hands me my journal. "No." He sits back, crossing his legs. "But you're a good kid, Donald. I'm not stupid, I know what other people say about you, and I know it gets to you. I went through the same thing growing up."

No way. Him?!

I guess the look on my face is a dead giveaway to my disbelief because Counselor Malik snorts a chuckle. He sighs, his smirk slowly fading. "I'm an Israeli man living in the US. All I do is walk into a store, and people label me as a terrorist. Even in my own neighborhood. Doesn't matter that I've lived here for most of my life. Ignorance is contagious and inevitable." He briefly licks his lips and lowers his eyes to the ground. "But it's important to not let those assumptions consume you. Otherwise, you'll become what they say about you."

When Counselor Malik slowly lifts his gaze to meet mine, all the oxygen in my body suddenly gets lost, and my heart tries to climb up my throat.

The bell suddenly sounds off, signaling the end of the fourth period and of our counseling session. Counselor Malik clears his throat and tells me that we will meet next week. He makes a note of it, writing on the sheet attached to his clipboard.

I nod.

I gather my things and bolt out of his office before he has anything else to say. I rest my head back against the door when I close it shut behind me. I can suddenly breathe again, and I take in the commotion of students moving up and down the hallway, slamming and opening the doors to get up and down the steps to wherever they have to go.

I walk through the crowds of people and make it to the bathroom on the other side of the hallway. The second I step foot inside, and the door closes behind me, the ground seems to move under my feet, and the walls start closing in.

What the hell is wrong with you? Relax!

I get to the sink and fumble with the knob to turn on the cold water. I can hear my heart thumping in my ears no matter how much I try to block it out. I don't know what's going on with me. My session went fine. At least, I thought it did—despite Counselor Malik trying to play doctor all of a sudden. He had absolutely no right to try to pull that shit on me.

What the hell?!

I get that it's his job to help, but he didn't have to do that. Then for him to accuse Morris-Lina of *"drugging out"* when that wasn't the case at all.

Asshole.

She was *my* sister. He even said it himself—we were *twins*.

She didn't mean it, I'll bet.

It just happened.

It wasn't her fault.

I could've hidden the pills, maybe.

But why would I have to do that?

A familiar feeling in my stomach starts to arise, and I manage to get the water turned on as my breathing becomes rapid. I dunk my head under the faucet, letting the water splash all on my face as I keep my eyes closed. The cooling sensation makes the hairs on the back of my neck stick up, and I lift my head out of the running water. I cup my hands and splash some water on my face.

I start to relax as I grip the sides of the sink. I flutter my lashes open, looking straight at my reflection, slowly panting.

You're fine. You're perfectly fine.

I turn off the water and snatch a paper towel from the dispenser above the trash can to wipe off my wet face. I toss the paper towel in the trash and slip my bookbag back on my back. I stop myself from rushing out into the hallway and take another quick breath, reminding myself to relax.

I'm fine.

I just keep telling myself that, and I step back out into the hallway and hurry my way to my fifth class period.

Week 2, Wednesday.

My mother called me downstairs, pulling my attention away from my textbook for Economics as I was reviewing the different terms required for me to know for my next class. I rub my eyebrows, groaning to myself before having the will to get up from my seat at my desk, facing the bedroom window, allowing me to see the soothing outdoors. The sun is set but still burns from afar, causing red-orange streaks to mix with the sky's dark blue and soft purple colors. I can tell that the breeze isn't too harsh compared to yesterday from how the leaves sway. It's relaxing.

"Donald!" my mom calls again, her voice getting louder this time. I bet she's at the very bottom of the steps. "Come here now!"

I sigh. "Sí, mamá."

I push the chair back in after getting up, and I make my way halfway down the steps. I look over the banister, and I realize that she's actually in the kitchen. Her back faces me as she stands over the stove, stirring up something in the pot with her favorite wooden spoon that she would use to whack Morris-Lina and me when we were little and disobedient. It was big and heavy.

Abuela used to cook with that spoon. I can't remember when she gave it to our mom, though. Unless mom took it after abuela died.

I walk down a few more steps, and then I realize that she is talking to herself in Spanish, which is weird. Her voice is quiet, like she's trying to be secretive, but fails because she doesn't know what it means to keep her voice entirely down.

"Eso es ridículo, Yoselin." She taps the spoon to the side of the pot and sits it on the countertop. She has a paper towel underneath the wooden spoon, so it doesn't mess up the countertop.

I furrow my eyebrows as I quietly reach the bottom of the steps. Mom's on the phone, talking to tía Yoselin about God knows what. It's not usual for the two of them to speak to each other in Spanish. I mean, they do, but not often. I guess tía Yoselin's belief in valuing the Spanish language is rubbing off on mom a bit.

I stand behind the wall to the kitchen entrance, leaning on my toes to get a small glimpse at my mom as her back remains facing me. Even though I can't tell precisely what Yoselin is saying, I can hear her voice since she's just naturally loud like my mom. But it doesn't bother mom, though. She still keeps the phone pressed to her ear, trying to interject and interrupt whatever it is Yoselin is rambling about.

When mom finally gets a word in, she raises her voice, speaking expressively with her free hand to emphasize what she says. Mom urges Yoselin to stop being emotional, and that she's being outright ridiculous. I can hear Yoselin chiming in, and soon enough, they are speaking over each other on the phone.

My head starts to ache, and I completely hide behind the wall. I bite down on my lip to ensure that I'm quiet and don't make it evident that I'm here. The last thing I need is for my mom to be all up in my face, scowling me down for eavesdropping, which isn't something I usually do. But her trying to be so secretive isn't something she usually does either.

Mom suddenly mentions the boys and criticizes Yoselin for depriving them of the *"real world"*—whatever that means. All I know is that I have to cover my mouth with both hands to prevent myself from making a sound. I can only imagine how Yoselin feels now.

Just like my friends and I made vows to never say a word about each other's mothers, mi mamá y mi tía made vows to never question each other's parenting. That's next-level line crossing.

All I know is that mi tía Yoselin could get the final say before hanging up on my mother, and I can't say I blame her. But that's not like my mom. She'd never stoop that low to criticize Yoselin like that. Mom knows damn well that it's tough for Yoselin to raise the boys alone, but she's doing a damn good at it. It's not like Yoselin's living paycheck to paycheck, either. She has money, but it's a lot of stress and emotionally draining, especially after abuela passed away.

From the look in her eyes, I can tell that Yoselin stays up late at night and hardly gets any sleep. I also know that the boys try to be as good as possible because they're not stupid. Although, I doubt she told the boys outright that abuela passed away. She probably came up with something clever, filling their heads with beliefs of abuela traveling to the sky above to chill for a bit, not specifying when or if she will ever come back.

I take a deep breath, exhaling through my nose while making sure that I'm quiet. I get myself together, step out from behind the wall, and take small steps forward, approaching mamá. Mom still has her back to me, and she picks up the wooden spoon and halfheartedly starts to stir in the pot.

I clear my throat to get her attention. She practically jumps out of her skin and grips onto her chest as she turns around. I press my lips together, trying to prevent myself from smirking at the fact that I nearly scared the wits out of my own mother. I don't know why, but seeing my mom like that has always made me crack up. Morris-Lina and dad would always work together to prank mom, using every trick in the book. From fake spiders to leaving fake vomit on the bed, mom would fall for all of it. It was always so funny, seeing her eyes bulge out of her head, almost like in the cartoons.

Luckily for them, mom eventually learned to laugh with them rather than cuss them out like she used to when Morris-Lina and I were kids.

Mom lets out a sigh of relief when she finally realizes that it's just me, and a warm smile washes over her face once she catches her breath. When I ask her if she's alright, she shakes her head, giggling that she's okay. She leaves the spoon in the pot, and it tilts forward but doesn't fall into the stew she's stirring up.

She takes a small step back, resting her hands on my shoulders. I squint my eyes when she comes over and grabs my chin, pressing a gentle kiss to the side of my face. I keep my lips pressed tightly together as she examines my face as if she hasn't seen me in God knows how long.

It does feel as though I haven't seen my mom in a while, though—her and dad. Whenever I come home, they're nowhere to be found. I'm used to dad working long and late hours, but mom? It used to be a rarity. Then, all of a sudden, I stopped seeing her as much. I'll be lucky if I see mom or dad in the morning before school. But it's a rarity for dad to still be home when I'm getting ready for school. He's usually out the door before the crack of dawn to get to work. I'll hear him moving around a bit, but he tries to stay quiet for the most part since he knows we're all sleeping.

A few times, Morris-Lina used to text me around the time dad would be getting ready for work, and she would ask me random questions since she could not go back to sleep. I would try to ignore her messages, forcing myself to get as much sleep as possible, but I couldn't ignore the bright light from my phone. Sometimes, I would answer her back, telling her to either figure out how to get back to sleep or just respond with *"IDK"* and call it a day. Other times, I'd read her messages but not answer them because I was annoyed.

"You called me downstairs?" I suddenly ask mom, scratching my eyebrow. I have to stay focused on reality.

Mom snaps her fingers and walks out of the kitchen, heading to the closet by the door. "Yes. I need you to go to the store for me and buy a thing of milk and sourdough bread." I watch as she digs through her big black purse hanging on one of the hooks attached to the back of the door.

I arch my eyebrow. "Doesn't dad hate sourdough bread?" I lean against the wall to the dining room.

Mom finally retrieves her wallet and uses her foot to kick the closet door shut as she digs through to find some cash. I try to offer to just use the money I have saved up in my room, but she whips her head up to me, glaring at me intensely. I feel my stomach do backflips, and my heart starts to come up my throat. I try to tell myself that it's nothing personal and that she's just trying to be motherly since she doesn't like it when I have to use my own money to help pay for things. But at the same time, I can't tell if she's really trying to be motherly...or if she just doesn't like me whenever I offer to help out financially.

She would always give Morris-Lina that look too. Whenever Morris-Lina said or did something that wasn't "lady-like"—or mom just didn't like—mom would give her that same look to shut down whatever Morris-Lina had said or did. For some reason, it always felt like there was venom in mom's eyes. Like she just didn't like her. I often wanted to say something, but mom would just shoot me the same look, and I would shut up.

Like I was way out of line, even though I wouldn't do anything.

But to mom, Morris-Lina always did something.

She'd always give her that look.

I rub the back of my neck, trying to soothe myself a bit as goosebumps form on my arms. Mom pulls out a twenty-dollar bill and holds it out for me to take.

I look at her and look back at the bill. I take it and fold it up before slipping it into my pants pocket.

"Your father will just have to suck it up for tonight," she mutters, heading back to the closet to put her wallet back into her purse. "He doesn't like it, then he can drink it down with some milk for all I care." She doesn't even bat an eyelash when she speaks and stops in her tracks to give me a quick kiss on the cheek before making her way back into the kitchen, tending to the pot of stew.

My lips are terribly dry all of a sudden, and I refrain myself from biting the skin off. I figure that mom and dad probably had another fight about God knows what. I bet it's over something idiotic that would even make a small child-like Yago question their logic. But what do I know? Whenever I try to step in and voice my thoughts, the two of them waste no time reminding me that I'm their son and don't know any better.

You sound pathetic. Get over it.

I shake myself out of my own delusions and hurry upstairs to my room. I sit on the edge of my bed, put on my sneakers, and throw on my heavy black jacket since I refuse to put on a different shirt. I step out of my room, closing the door behind me. I look over, eyeing the closed mahogany bedroom door that is across from mine. I feel my throat tighten at the thought of what my sister's room could possibly look like now.

Did anyone bother to fix her bed? Are her windows still open?

I bet she has some clothes still in her laundry hamper that need to be cleaned. I can't remember the last time mom even bothered going into her room. I don't even think dad gives the door a second glance when he walks by.

Am I the only one who wants to go in? It's not a big deal.

It isn't—it isn't a big deal.

Yet, my bones freeze when I think about opening the door.

Get a grip. Just go to the damn store before mom yells at you.

Right.

I hurry down the steps and snatch my keys off the small table by the door. Before I shut the door behind me, mom calls out to me, reminding me to keep my phone on in case of an emergency—she means the sound.

I assure her, "Voy a mamá, no te preocupes!"

I close the door behind me.

. . . . . .

I park my car down the street from the market and cut off the engine. The second I get out, I'm hit with a breeze that makes my teeth chatter. I zip my jacket up to my neck and chills still rush down my spine.

I push in the wing mirror and lock up my car.

HOOONK!!!

I flinch and bump back into my car as a red sports car zips right past me. The loud music causes a terrible vibration to swim through my head. It slowly goes away as the car starts to vanish down the street. I feel my heart begin to ease its pace, and I clear my throat.

I stuff my hands into my jacket pockets as I walk down the block to get to the market. As I walk, I look over to the other side as a couple of guys hang around the corner, speaking to each other and laughing loudly. Some of them are drinking while the rest of them are smoking. Usually, Morris-Lina would always say something sappy at sights like that. She'd probably say, *"It's better to see 'em laughing than shooting."*

The sudden sound of two large pit bulls barking pulls my attention away from the group of guys across the street. I don't flinch when the pit bulls charge to the metal wire fence, barking at me as I pass by. I just let out a soft breath and kept moving. That sometimes happens, too, even on my block.

The young couple who lives across the street from us owns two dogs—one pit bull and one rottweiler. They trained their dogs well, but sometimes they would get too playful and bark excessively at people.

I check both sides of the street before quickly crossing over to get to the market. I tightly grip onto the metal handle since the door is heavy when I pull it open. A bell—almost like music—jingles as I step inside. There are a couple people inside, roaming through the few aisles of the small market. Usually, no one is in here around this time of the evening, and it's not even late.

I check the time on my phone—*7:43 PM.*

I shrug—*still a bit early.* It's just dark.

"Hola, Donald!"

I look over as Mr. Pérez comes up to me with a big smile on his round face as he pats his large hand on my shoulder.

I grin at him. "Cómo está, señor Pérez?"

He has a bit of a waddle in his step as he steps back and stands tall with his stomach poking out a bit while remaining tucked under his shirt. "Todo bien, todo bien!" He then leans forward, placing his hand on my shoulder. He whispers, "Cómo está tu familia y todo?"

The smile on his face softens, and I can tell there is genuine concern in his eyes for wanting to know my family's well-being. The man has good intentions, and I know that he cares. He's one of the few people who doesn't think it's better to have one Gonzalez kid. But at the same time, he should understand that this isn't something I can answer quickly. I don't even know how my family feels most of the time.

I'm not a mind reader, and I can't speak for everyone.

So I nod my head and tell him that everyone is good, which is probably a bald-faced lie. I mean, I'm good. Mom and dad are just...mom and dad.

Either way, Mr. Pérez beams and pats me on the chest, telling me that if I ever need anything, he's here for me.

I force myself to smile as I thank him.

"Excuuuse me!" a woman with short blonde hair calls out to him, waving her hand to get Mr. Pérez's attention. "I'm ready to check out!"

I snort. She could've just hit the bell on the counter.

Mr. Pérez gives me a quick look, pressing his lips tightly together while raising his eyebrows. He's thinking the same thing I am—*arrogance.*

He just pats my shoulder with a wide closed-mouth smile before going over to tend to the lady, standing impatiently at the counter with her groceries.

I'm not in the store long. I get what I need to get—sourdough bread and milk. I assume that mom wants me to get our usual oat milk since she didn't specify anything in particular. So, that's what I get. Oat milk and sourdough bread.

I suddenly feel my phone vibrate, and the familiar text tone goes off as I grab the milk. I tuck the milk carton under my arm and pull my phone out of my pocket. I tap on the notification to silence the text tone and read the message from my mom.

Mama: You can get something too, mi niño pequeño!

I stuff the phone back into my pants pocket and sigh. I honestly just want to go home. I take out my phone again to check the time.

8:03 PM.

My eyes widen. How is it past eight o'clock already?!

I walk up the produce aisle and get in line for check out at the front of the store. There are only two people in front of me, and despite his age and size, Mr. Pérez is quick on his feet.

The door suddenly opens, and the bell jingles sweetly. And like his usual jolly-self, Mr. Pérez greets the person in Spanish, waving at them with a kind smile. I look over to the entrance as the two guys who walked in nod their heads to greet Mr. Pérez, but they don't smile. For some reason, they look familiar. I try not to stare as I take small glances at them while seeming to look forward.

They're both tall, but one is more fit and has a ridiculous mustache on his lip, while the other guy is lanky but has a decent-looking face. They both wear their jackets open, and they both look like they fighting to stay awake. I notice that the one with the mustache has a tattoo of an X near his right eyebrow when he turns his head—

Ay, joder. Puta mierda.

"Donald! Ya estás arriba!"

I snap my attention to Mr. Pérez as he gestures for me to step forward to the counter. I didn't even realize that it was my turn. My stomach knots up as I approach the counter, feigning a grin when meeting Mr. Pérez's gaze. I slowly cut my eyes over to the guys as they stood by the front entrance, looking on.

The one with the X tattoo shifts around where he stands, stuffing his hands in the pockets of his jeans that are barely secure around his waist. His gaze remains on me while the other guy looks at the different chip bags on display at the front of the store.

My throat dries. I know he probably recognizes me.

"Diez dólares y cincuenta y ocho centavos."

I reach in my pocket for the twenty-dollar bill mom gave me as Mr. Pérez places the plastic bag containing the groceries on the countertop. I hand him the money. As Mr. Pérez goes into his cash register to get my change, I notice that the guy with the X tattooed on his face is standing on the other side of the display of chips, but he isn't looking at me. His attention is elsewhere as the leaner guy waltzes into one of the aisles.

Mr. Pérez clears his throat to get my attention, handing me the change. I smile, taking the change from him, and I stuff it deep into my pants pocket while grabbing the bag of groceries.

I give him a small nod. "Gracias, señor Pérez. Buenas noches."

I don't keep my head down or try to hide my face at all as I bolt straight for the door. I figure that if I keep my eyes straight forward and just get out of there, I'll be good.

I hear Mr. Pérez tell me to have a good night, but the door shuts behind me before he even has a chance to wrap up his sentence. I feel bad, but it's late. There's no chance that my mom will blow up my phone, asking where I am since she doesn't find it necessary. If something happens, I'll be the one to call her.

She trusts me.

I stop walking when I reach the street corner as a long line of cars start to move once the light turns green. I take out my phone to check the time and text my mom to let her know that I'm on my way home. I don't have to, but I do it anyway.

Me: On my way back.

I hit SEND and put the phone back into my pocket.

Everything becomes quiet, and when I look up, there are no cars in the street coming from either direction. The light turns red, and I'm given the go-ahead to cross to the other side, even though I can take my time.

Suddenly, I am being choked by my collar and yanked from the back of my jacket. A flash of darkness conquers my vision, and my mouth is covered all at once by a...hand?

My heels scrape against the ground as I am dragged, and my arms are forcefully held behind my back. My wrists are in a twist as I try to pull myself free, but it's pointless. The next thing I feel is my backside being pushed up against a solid wall, and my arms are held above my head. I can suddenly see again, and before I can even blink, the wind is knocked out of me by the swift fist that plunges into my stomach.

Then another.

And another.

As I lean forward, I am thrown back up against the wall, hands being forcefully held above my head, tightly. When I look up, I realize that it's the guy with the X tattoo and his lanky weasel. But for a lanky weasel, he's got a tight grip as he manages to keep my hands above my head. I can't even kick them in the balls since they're both pressing themselves up against me to hold me up against the wall with all their might, practically crushing me.

I wince at the tight grip the guy with the tattoo has on my hair, lifting up my head so I can face him. A sharp sting shoots through my face after his fist swiftly collides into the side of my face. He does it again...and again...and again.

The lanky guy hypes up the one with the X tattoo as the punches keep coming. Finally, the guy with the tattoo stops for a quick second to get a look at me. I can taste the blood in my mouth coming from my lip. I wiggle my wrists around, trying to break free from the lanky one's grip, and he cackles.

He lifts my hands off the wall, only to slam them back into the wall. "You ain't going nowhere, muchacho."

The guy with the tattoo uses his finger to lift up my chin, so I look at him. I tighten my jaw, still trying to wiggle myself free. He snickers, taking a step forward to get up in my face while standing over me.

He holds my chin in place. "Got a lot of nerve coming between me and my girl, *cara culo.*"

I tighten my fist, and my nostrils flare. I close my mouth, mixing the blood with my spit. The guy stumbles back when my blood and saliva contact his face, giving me the advantage I need to break free. I kick the lanky guy off of me, and he loses his grip on my hands. I plunge my fist to his jaw, and he stumbles to the ground, groaning.

I look up as the one with the tattoo of the X charges at me, his arms locking around my waist as he lifts me off the ground and throws me into the wall. A sharp pain shoots all along my spine as if it had shattered, and I wince. I grip onto his shoulders as he backs away, intending to slam me back into the wall again. I don't give him a chance, using my elbow and sharply jabbing him on the temple multiple times until he finally drops me. Oxygen enters through my lungs, and I can get myself together once he releases me.

I go to knock him out, but I am roughly shoved into the wall on the other side of me, and I hiss from the sudden pain that shoots through my arm. I quickly look up and realize that it's the lanky guy this time. He manages to swipe his fist into my face and plunges his other one into my gut, nearly taking the wind out of me. He grips me up by the collar of my jacket and draws back his fist. My knee roughly connects to his crotch, and he lets go of me, wailing as he leans back on the wall.

The guy with the tattoo swiftly turns me around, crashes his fist into the side of my face, and plows his foot into my stomach. I hit the wall and feel every bone in my body practically shatter. I can hardly stand up as I remain on one knee, holding my stomach. I cough, and blood drips from my mouth. The colors of the ground and everything else around me seems to blend together and are a blur. I blink, trying to snap out of it.

Get up. Get back up!

I notice the hunger in the guy's eyes as he approaches me with tight fists, making the veins to his hands practically bulge out. I put my hand to the wall to keep myself steady as I use all of my strength. With one arm draped over my stomach and my other hand making a tight fist, I'm ready to take this guy on—

THUMP!

The guy with the tattoo comes down to his knees, arching his back, grunting. He hisses through his teeth, and a mix of emotions plasters on his face. He's fuming, but at the same time, he doesn't know what hit him from behind. As he goes to turn around, a flash of silver flashes by, colliding into his shoulder. This time, I hear a *CRACK*, and the guy hollers, holding his shoulder while lying on his side, rocking like a wounded child.

My vision becomes more apparent as I look up at the boy, who looks around my age, standing over the guy while holding a metal pipe in his hand. The dude wears a jean jacket like it's 70-degrees outside, keeping the sleeves cuffed up to his elbows, which reveals intricate tattoos on his arms. His jeans fit him perfectly, coming close to his legs and down to his ankles, showing his white socks and black-and-white converse sneakers.

The guy with X tattoo huffs, glaring up at the boy. *"Alejandro?!"* His eyes widen, and he shrieks at the realization of who has dominated him. "What the f—?!"

Instead of finishing his words, the guy lets out a brutal cry as Mr. Jean-Jacket slams the pipe down onto the guy's right now. I notice the twisted smirk that forms on Mr. Jean-Jacket's face as he watches the guy hold his knee while rocking in unbearable pain.

Mr. Jean-Jacket holds the pipe like a bat, having it settle against his shoulder while keeping a tight grip. He rocks on his heels, keeping his eyes on the guy. "You make me laugh, Diego." He crouches down to meet the guy's eye level. "You wanna make a fool of my sister like that and thought I wouldn't find out?" Mr. Jean-Jacket suddenly draws his eyes to me, and the one side of his mouth curls upward. He then looks back at the guy with the X tattoo. "Two against one? You know I ain't about that, right?"

Mr. Jean-Jacket finally stands tall and holds the pipe to his side. He looks over at the lanky guy, still groveling from when I kneed him the ballsack. Mr. Jean-Jacket snorts.

"If you wanna fight, at least fight like honest men."

He whips his attention back to the guy with the tattoo, noticing him starting to rise up from the ground. Mr. Jean-Jacket uses the end of the pipe to lift up the guy's chin, making his head go back a little bit. He's so cocky and mocking. It's almost irresistible.

The guy with the tattoo quivers. "Don't do this, Reyes."

I arch my eyebrow at the last name. *Reyes?*

His first name—*Alejandro?*

Alejandro...Reyes? Alejandro...?

I shake my head, quieting my thoughts. When I try to stand straight, the sharp pain along my ribcage fights against me, making me have to rely on the wall again. I bite down on my bottom lip, not wanting a peep to come out of me as I wince from the unbearable sensation. Mr. Jean-Jacket—I mean, *Alejandro Reyes*—lets the guys go, telling them to get up while keeping the end of the metal pipe pointed at them as they slowly move.

The lanky guy still finds the audacity to try to have the final word as he rises from the ground, hand over his crotch. "You wouldn't be so lucky if it wasn't for that brother of yours."

Alejandro chuckles, drumming his fingers against the metal pipe before holding it like a bat with one hand. "You're actually lucky I showed up and not him. I could give him a call if that's the case."

Both of the guys widen their eyes before hurrying off, not even looking back as they coward away. I sigh of relief, my head resting against the wall. I close my eyes, fighting the pain inside me as I push up off the wall to stand on my own. I can't even take my first step without feeling needles shoot through my spine. I hiss.

When I open my eyes again, Alejandro speed walks over to me, resting his hand on my shoulder to keep me steady.

"Take it easy," he suggests, eyes locked on me.

I try to take in his features now that he's up close. His undercut hair is nicely kept, styled pompadour with streaks of silver visible along the top. He has thick eyebrows, naturally long lashes surrounding his incredibly hazel eyes, and his jawline and cheekbones are sharp and defined. I notice the tattoo on the right side of his neck, under his ear. An eight-pointed star inside a circle, but the star is bigger than the circle. For some reason, his tattoos look perfect on his tan skin. But his face...I can't stop looking at him.

Those eyes. That cocky grin. That name.

That damn name. It gives me heart palpitations.

Still, I manage to get out, "Thank you."

He nods, lips still curled in a grin. "Don't mention it." He takes one foot back and leans to get a look at me, his eyes going up and down. "You don't carry anything on you, do you?"

I arch my eyebrow.

Shaking his head, he adds, "In case you get in these situations. Something to give you an upper hand? No knife?"

I snort. "We fight like honest men, don't we?"

A smirk. "Touché."

Alejandro looks behind him and walks towards the opening of the alleyway. He reaches down and picks up the bag of groceries that I dropped while being dragged by those gilipollas. My breath hitches as I walk up to him so he doesn't have to come back to me.

Alejandro hands me my bag of groceries, smirking. "Luckily, it wasn't anything glass, huh?"

I nod, forcing a smirk on my face as I take the bag. "Yeah."

He licks his lips, looking at me while squinting. My throat tightens. The look on his face throws me off, and I want to call him out for it, but at the same time, he did have my back a couple minutes ago. I don't want to be *that* kind of guy—dismissive and snobby.

Still, it's something about him that makes my stomach do flips. His eyes seem familiar, or it could be that he looks around my age but stands taller than me by a couple inches while holding a metal pipe like he's going to do something. But he doesn't do anything. Instead, he asks me if I need a lift to wherever I got to go, but I shake my head, telling him that I parked right up the street.

He offers to walk with me, and my eyes fall to the pipe he keeps clutched in his hand. I could refuse, but every step I take is like walking on a plank of nails. I clear my throat, looking him in the eyes, and I nod.

As we step out of the alleyway and into the open street, Alejandro extends his hand for me to shake while introducing himself—even though I heard his name being announced earlier.

"Alejandro Reyes." His smile is nearly blinding.

I shake his hand, forcing a similar smile to cross my face. "Donald Gonzalez. Thanks again for what you did back there."

We cross the street, no cars coming. Alejandro snickers, waving his hand dismissively. "Eh, you don't gotta mention it. I had a score to settle with them, jokers anyway. You being there made things easier for me."

"Really?"

"You took them on pretty well by the looks of things. Had one on the ground already by the time I showed up."

I shrug, a slight chuckle slipping through my lips. "It's nothing."

"You still got your ass handed to you, though."

I roll my eyes. "Gee, thanks."

Alejandro lightly nudges me, chuckling. "You always sucked at taking on a fight up on your own."

I wrinkle my eyebrows, and I stop in my tracks. I open my mouth, wondering what the hell that was supposed to mean, but no words come out. Alejandro looks back at me, his one hand stuffed in his pants pocket while the other clutches tightly to the pipe. He finds some sort of sick amusement from the expression on my face and starts snickering, rocking on his heels.

He tilts his head. "Donald, has it really been that long? It's like you don't remember me." He takes a giant step forward, so there is no space between us. He puts his hand on my shoulder and stares me down as if he's trying to read my mind.

I look into his eyes. His name starts ringing in my head. He flashes a devilish smile with a sinister look in his eyes.

I choke.

That smile. That damn smile. And then that name…

…*Alejandro. Reyes.*

My throat feels tight when his name echoes in my head, and the realization hits me. The same Alejandro Reyes grew up not too far from me and went to the same school as me. Memories start to clump together, and my heart pounds heavily in my chest.

My lips part open as Alejandro backs a couple steps away from me, smirking. His eyes don't leave mine as he steps up beside me and leans in close to my ear. His warm breath sends shivers down my spine as his words stick with me.

"Start carrying that knife, shot glass."

Shot Glass. Only one person has ever called me that.

I look back as Alejandro walks in the opposite direction, heading to the street corner while twirling the metal pipe in his hand. My stomach twists in knots, and the familiar acid sensation starts to bubble in my throat, but nothing comes out.

I take a sharp breath and rush to my car, looking to get home as soon as possible.

Week 2, Friday

"You're so slow! C'mon!"

I pant. "I'm not slow!" Pant. "Just a little behind."

I managed to reach the top of the gate, meeting Alejandro at the very top. He arched his eyebrow, nudging his head downward in the direction of the ground. Once I managed to swing my legs over, I gripped onto the bar as I looked down. The ground seemed farther than I anticipated, and I gulped.

I heard Alejandro snort under his breath. "You're not scared, are ya?"

I brushed him off. "No way." I waved dismissively.

I narrowed my eyes back down to the ground below us. But, of course, it didn't help that the summer sun was intensely beaming down on our necks, adding to the humid air that was practically suffocating me. I chewed on my bottom lip, feeling my bones quiver at the thought of jumping off from the top of the gate.

"Ehhh!" Alejandro nudged me lightly to get my attention. "Don't get scared now, shot glass." He leaned over, so he was close to my face. He smiled, shaping his apple cheekbones. Now I understood why most girls in our grade liked him so much. "If you want, I'll hold your hand."

With a 'pft,' I rolled my eyes and looked straight forward at the skyline. The sky was mixed with wild red oranges and cool purple blues. It was finally reaching sunset, but that didn't make it less humid.

I heard Alejandro sigh, and the next thing I knew, his hand was on my shoulder. When I looked at him, he pressed his lips together in a straight line, but his eyes looked soft as could be.

I huffed, feeling defeated. I hated that face.

"Okay!" I blurted. "I'm a little bit...nervous." I looked back down. "But I'm not scared." The fact that my voice softens and is a bit quieter this time contradicts what I said.

Alejandro snorts, shaking his head. "I'll go first and show you it's all good. Then, I can catch you."

I furrowed my eyebrows, whipping my attention to him. I opened my mouth to speak, but he kicked his legs forward, pushing himself off from the top of the gate. I watched him fall down in a swift move, and then he hit the ground, landing on his feet. It happened so fast. It didn't seem that far down.

As I watched Alejandro dust himself off, I tightened my grip on the gate and gulped. My heart was pounding so hard in my chest, I thought it was going to burst. Alejandro could probably hear my heartbeat if he was still right beside me. This was embarrassing. I should follow him without hesitation, yet, here I am, still up at the top of the gate like a big baby. At least I wasn't crying, though.

Alejandro looked up at me, a wide smile taking over his face.

"Let's go, shot glass! You're up!"

He's too confident in me. It's almost scary.

Still, I took a deep breath did the exact same thing he did, except I closed my eyes. I kicked out my legs while pushing myself off the gate. Instead of me hitting the ground, the ground hit me. But at the same time, I felt myself being held up by two strong arms locked around me. When I opened my eyes, Alejandro was looking down at me with a grin on his face. I realized that his arms were wrapped around me to hold me up after I jumped, and my feet were planted on the ground almost perfectly.

I stood up straight, and Alejandro let me.

He dusted off my shoulder. "Told you, you could do it, shot glass."

I rolled my eyes. "Stop calling me that." I tried not to sound like a baby. He was older than me and taller, so I didn't want to give him any more reason to think I was a baby.

"Why?" Alejandro shrugged, throwing his arm around my neck, pulling me closer to him. "It suits you. Don't take it as an insult."

"It makes me feel small."

"But a shot glass is cool!" He noticed me arching my eyebrow, and he sucked his teeth. "When I think of a shot glass, I think of something for dignified people. My dad had one, and he only used that one shot glass for every drink he had. You're like my shot glass in a way. You may be short, but you're definitely my favorite person to be around."

My throat was dry when I looked him in the eye. "Really?"

"Fuck yeah," he boasted.

I gasped at the word he said so confidently. He just laughed.

"You know you wanna say it too," Alejandro urged. "C'mon. No parents are around, and I bet they say it all the time. Just shout it out!" He cupped his hands by his mouth and echoed, "FUCK YEAH!"

I laughed, shaking my head. He had his arms around my shoulders, telling me to give it a shot. I felt my heart race in my chest as I slowly cupped my hands by mouth and looked up to the sky.

"FUCK YEEEEAAAH!!"

Alejandro's laughter filled the air with my echoed words, and he patted me on the back.

• • • • • • • •

I can't believe it was him.

It was actually him.

Ay, Dios mío! What the fu—!

"Can you pass me the glue, please?"

I look up, being pulled away from my thoughts when I hear Meagan's voice all of a sudden. Her eyes are on me, and I notice her pointing to the glue stick right beside my arm as I sit, leaning forward with my arm sprawled out on the wide wooden table.

"Oh..." I pass her the glue and sit up in my seat. "Mn."

Meagan gives a slight head nod, smiling. "Thanks."

I wink, smirking. "Don't mention it."

I watch as Meagan rubs the glue all on the back of the sheet of paper as if she's coloring. Her hand is steady, and she presses her lips tightly together, concentrating like her fate depends on it. I can't help but chuckle.

She only lifts her eyes up to get a quick look at me before shifting her attention back to the paper as she seals the cap onto the glue stick. "Thanks for coming, by the way," she says, pasting the paper down onto the large, thick brown paper lying flat on the table. "Preston would've had my head if I didn't get this poster done ASAP. He wants it up by the end of the day, but thanks to you, it'll be up after lunch."

I shrug, leaning back into my seat while stretching my legs out under the table. "It's no sweat, kid. But I hardly did a thing. You're the one doing all the gluing and whatnot."

Meagan shrugs, already spreading glue over the next sheet of paper. "Yeah, but you're the one who cut out the pictures."

"I do got some steady hands." I lift up my hands and wiggle my fingers, earning a laugh from her when she lifts up her gaze.

I then fold my arms and look around. After our first class period, Meagan had sent me a text asking me if I could help her make a poster for theater promoting their show, *Odella*. Apparently, Meagan is excited about doing the show since it's her favorite musical. Meanwhile, I know nothing about it, but I could only imagine how great she would be up on stage, doing her thing. I've seen her perform before—last year. I forget the show's name, but I thought she was good, even though I didn't know Meagan at the time. After that, I only knew of her.

Anyway, when she texted me and asked for my help, I told Meagan I would help her out. She responded happily, telling me that I was her life savior since Preston became impossible to deal with because of his demands. I don't know how she puts up with that guy. He seems like a handful.

So now, Meagan and I are sitting in the library during our lunch period. She has been on top of her game since we got here, and all I did was cut out the pictures she needed for the poster. She's the one who printed them out and is now gluing them in place on the brown poster paper. She's so focused, I can't help but smile. I try to hide it, but the way she tilts her head as she presses the paper smoothly down onto the poster—it's almost impossible to not admire her.

I use my chin in my hand, propping my elbow up on the table as I watch Meagan spread the glue on the back of another picture for the poster. She suddenly asks me, "Is everything okay? A couple minutes ago, you were kinda like..." She waves her hand all around her head in different motions since she can't find the right word to complete her sentence. Then the word comes to her. "Dazed."

I realize that she's probably talking about how I was a few minutes ago when I thought about Alejandro. The fact that I saw him the other day still blows my mind. It's not that I've completely forgotten about him, even though it's been years since we've seen each other. The last time I thought about him was probably five years ago. I don't know why. I just did. Then, the thoughts just stopped. But I didn't entirely lock him out of my mind. I guess that's why I was able to recognize him. It might not have been right away since it's been years since I've seen him, but I was able to put the pieces together.

We first met in third grade, and we stopped being friends when we reached fifth. We didn't grow apart—sort of—but I wasn't allowed to see him anymore.

I forget why, but my parents just didn't seem to like him. Alejandro and I were supposed to do something together one night, but I couldn't meet up with him. Dad wouldn't allow me. Alejandro wasn't a horrible guy. He was the first person I knew who was decent and didn't make me feel less of a person.

I was his equal, and he was mine. So he was the first person I actually considered a brother.

I don't know what happened between us. But whatever it was, it must've been for a reason. The Alejandro I saw yesterday would've never thought to beat someone up with a pipe. Alejandro didn't like to fight, but he would if someone swung at him first. He wouldn't have told me to start carrying around a weapon myself, either.

I have to stop thinking about this.

I shake my head, smirking. "You worry too much sometimes. Not that I mind, but you're too good for your own good."

Meagan wrinkles her nose, looking up at me. "Not true."

I chuckle. "Don't worry. It's cute."

Her lips part, but no words come out. Instead, she looks at me with a mix of emotions, all thanks to my dumb mouth. In a way, I kind of look at her the same way once it really sinks in what I just said.

Why did I have to say that out loud? You friggin' dunce!

I think fast, clearing my throat. "So, what's your part? In the show, I mean?" I have to change the subject.

Meagan blinks. "Oh." She sits up and snaps on the cap to the glue stick. "I, uh, don't know yet." She sets the glue stick aside and pastes the last picture onto the poster paper. "We don't have auditions until next month. So." She shrugs, pursing her lips.

I slightly nod my head, pressing my lips together in a straight line. "Well, I'm sure you'll get the lead role. You certainly got the skills for it."

Meagan sits up, crossing her arms over her stomach. "I doubt it. In the original musical back in '68, the leads were black and brown, which was huge, but not many people thought it was realistic even though the writer wanted it that way. But over time, the leads were predominately portrayed as white or somewhat tan. Dexter usually tries to stick with what's popular for everyone's comfort, so." Meagan can hardly look me in the eye, and she twists her lips while eyeing the poster she just finished.

I feel bad. I know she'd do a great job playing a lead role. Hell, she deserves it. I don't know what the requirements are for lead roles, if there are any, but Meagan would probably kill it. It makes me sick to my stomach just thinking about Meagan being overlooked for a role she probably deserves. All because some people get a kick out of whitewashing the arts.

Plus, it's 2013, and our school is predominately black and brown anyway. So Meagan should have a shot.

Meagan tries to smooth out the cut-outs she glued to the poster so they don't look too lumpy, and I clear my throat. "I'm sure you got it in the bag for a lead." I chuckle. "I bet you know it all like the back of your hand too, huh?"

Meagan shrugs, still trying to smooth out and flatten some of the cut-outs. "I've only seen it once, but I kind of fell in love with it. I did some research about the show, and that's how I found out about the changes to the casting and whatnot." She sucks her teeth, sitting back in her chair with her arms crossed over her stomach. "I'm okay with whatever outcome. I'm just glad we're doing it." She tries to be optimistic, but I can still tell that she's a bit doubtful of her chances. I can see it in those brown eyes of hers.

I sigh. I don't know why Meagan beats herself up the way she does. It'll be their loss if they don't give her a lead role. To be honest, she and Preston seem like the only ones really giving their all with this theater program anyway. I always see the two of them doing something together. A few times, I mistook them for dating or having been interested in each other, but then I remembered that Preston was gay, and Meagan very much knew that. It's not like it bothered me whenever they were together. I just didn't expect Preston to be close with anyone. He seemed like the type of guy to have a strong disliking for people and would want to keep the hoods of his hoodies pulled tight as a way of blocking people out.

But if he's friends with Meagan, then I'm probably wrong. Still, he always walks around with a deadpan look on his face like a stoic, speaking in his mono-toned voice. It's hard to know what the hell that guy is thinking. Then, add that he's dating Erik Petrov from the lacrosse team on top of it—I read that guy *totally* wrong. I never would've seen him dating Erik. We might not be close, but Erik is a pretty decent dude. Many people like Erik, and when rumors spread about him sophomore year that he was bi, he basically owned it and gave anyone who disregarded him the middle finger. I can honestly say that I respect the hell out of him.

Meagan pushes her chair back when she stands and holds up the poster in admiration. A small grin curls on her lips, and her eyes wander as she takes in the masterpiece she's made. Chances are that she'll never admit that she did most of the work and insist that I helped her immensely, so I don't say anything. I stand up out of my seat and walk up behind her to look at the poster. The letters **O-D-E-L-L-A** are spaced out evenly at the top of the page and written in black marker. Inside each letter are multiple small red dots of glitter glue to make the title stand out a bit. At the center of the poster are two sign-up sheets—both containing information about the audition process. The rest of the sign consists of different cut-outs of drama masks, theater curtains, and other shapes of stars, and they're all spread out.

"Looks great to me," I tell Meagan, getting her to look at me with a shy smile that makes me wonder if she's flattered.

She might be. I don't ask. I throw my arm around her, letting it sit over her shoulder and come around the back of her neck.

"Thanks again, Donny." She tucks the poster under her arm to hold it while looking at me. "I couldn't have—"

"No, no." I hold up my finger, pointing it at her while squinting. "Don't even." I tap the tip of her nose. "Don't start going soft on me now, kid. It's non-negotiable, got it?"

Meagan rolls her eyes. "Yeah, okay." She's not taking me seriously, which is great because nine times out of ten, Meagan takes everything seriously.

The bell finally sounds off, signaling for the next period. I help Meagan pack up the art supplies she used—scissors, construction paper, glue sticks, and multiple glitter glue tubes—before snatching up my book bag so we can head out.

I hold the glass door open for her, letting her out first. "I'd offer to take you home after school, but I got a feeling that you've got your hands full, being artsy."

Meagan shakes her head, smirking. "It's set-building for the show. Not painting a mural, FYI."

I gasp. "Such sass. Why I'm appalled." I pretend to be taken aback, keeping my hand over my chest as I huff and lean back with wide eyes.

Meagan bites down on her bottom lip, trying to restrain herself from laughing while looking down at her shoes. I notice the smile creeping across her mouth as she continues to bite down on her bottom lip. A strange feeling erupts in my chest that sends my heart into a minor fit for speed.

She then snaps her head up, her mouth forming an 'O' as she comes to a sudden realization. All she's missing is a light-bulb flashing right above her head. She hands me the poster, asking me to hold it for her real quick, and I do. I watch as she slips one arm free from the strap to her book bag, and she hastily unzips the front pouch. I arch my eyebrow as she mutters to herself, digging inside, looking for something. She lets out a sigh of relief, and a smile plasters across her face when she finally pulls out a small box that is wrapped nicely in shiny red wrapping paper with a blue ribbon attached to the top.

Meagan takes the poster from me while slipping her book bag back on her back. I feel my heart wanting to jolt right out of my chest when she hands me the box. It's a jewelry box, for like earrings or rings or tiny necklaces.

"In case I don't see you tomorrow, I wanted to give you that, so. Happy birthday." She twists her lips to the side, trying to cover her smile.

A soft chuckle slips through my lips as I rub my thumb across the sharp corners of the wrapping paper that are taped securely. I draw my eyes to Meagan. "You spoil me, kid."

She rolls her eyes, snickering to herself. "You're one to talk."

She then sticks out her wrist, showing off the bracelet I gave her for her birthday. She likes it since I hardly see her without it.

I smirk.

Meagan sharply inhales and checks the time on her phone. "Well, I better get going." She shakes her head. "Well, *we* should get going."

I nod. "Yeah. I'll catch you later."

She nods. "Yeah." She then looks at the box. "But really, happy birthday. And thank you."

Meagan takes a small inhale as she leans forward on her tiptoes, somewhat closing the space between us. A strange sensation pulls within my throat, and my cheeks start to burn when her lips gently touch my cheek, almost hesitantly—but contact was clearly made. My skin suddenly feels as though it's on fire, but it's not excruciating. It's like a thrilling, tingling sensation meant to last forever but unexpectedly comes to an end.

When Meagan draws her face away from mine, my lips part, but the gap between us is still thin. I can tell that she's trying to process what she just did from how she looks at me. Her eyes are big and glossy, lips parted like mine, and her breathing hitches.

Still, manages to get herself together and tells me, "See you."

I watch as she walks in the opposite direction down the hall, practically speed-walking away from me. She sways to the side, almost bumping into the wall, but then she's walking straight again. Even though her back is facing me as she darts to the double doors to get to the stairs, I figure she's probably mumbling all sorts of things to herself. Criticizing herself because that's what Meagan does.

Like I said—she takes everything seriously.

I shouldn't find it amusing, but strangely, I do. It makes the corners of my pull upward, and I can't help but laugh a little.

Yet, when I shift my attention to the wrapped gift in my hand, my laughter dies down, and I feel my smile fade. The sensation I felt from before starts to creep back to me. I have to remind myself that it was only a harmless kiss on the cheek. It hardly meant anything. It didn't mean anything, I'll bet.

But then why did she look at me like that? After the fact?

Nah, you're in your head too much. Knock it off.

I roll my eyes, exhaling deeply through my nostrils. Friends give each other kisses on the cheek, sometimes. I'll admit, it did shock me a bit because I never would've taken Meagan Wright for being the bold-type. I'll also admit that it felt nice a bit for some reason. Probably because her lips felt soft. It wasn't a direct kiss, but I've kissed girls before, but they've never thought to kiss me on the cheek. But I can imagine Meagan's lips being softer than theirs—

Basta!

You sound like a certified manwhore and a perv right now!

I groan.

I start making my way to my class period, which is literally up the hall. I take my time getting there as I unwrap my gift from Meagan. I toss the wrapping paper in the trash can in the hallway and eye the black, satin box. I flip it open and lick my lips since they are suddenly dry. The ring is silver with emerald accents along the rim, and the engraved designs intertwine like twigs and vines all over. The sapphire gem in the center of the ring is small and is outlined by thin gold accents.

She didn't...NO WAY!

It's an exact replica of Jaxton Chyde's moonlight ring from *Allegiance Society*. I can't even imagine how much this must've cost Meagan. I don't even know where she could've brought it from since a delicate ring like this isn't made and sold in any kind of store. This is a specialty item.

I notice the small white card hidden underneath the cushion where the ring sits upon, and I read it. I can tell right away that it's Meagan's handwriting, and it amazes me how she could write clearly on such a small card. If it were me, it'd be impossible to read.

Through blood and fire, the midnight sun favors you. – Meagan.

I chuckle.

Only Meagan would remember the Ancient Blessing of the Circles.

She's such a sap.

I slip the ring onto my right ring finger and put the card back into the box, closing the lid. As I shove the box into my jacket pocket, I waltz right into my fifth-period class as the bell finally sounds off, and Mr. Throne writes on the chalkboard the different things we will need for today's experiment for A.P. Chemistry.

Week 2, Saturday

Today's the day—feliz cumpleaños. Surprisingly, mom and dad didn't come busting into my room like they'd do every year, singing and dancing like weirdos. Then again, this is the first birthday I'm celebrating without Morris-Lina. I can't even call it a celebration. Sure, I got phone calls and texts from relatives that I haven't seen in God knows how long, wishing me a happy birthday. But that doesn't mean that I wanted to get up out of bed, feeling great about being eighteen. It's not like I can go out drinking with the boys if I want to. None of us are 21 anyway. Then again, I wouldn't want to drink. Dios mío. If I could have it my way, I'd be in bed all day. It's not like my parents can ground me for wanting to spend my birthday the way I want to, right? But I know me. No matter how much my headaches from the thought of getting older, I can't stay in bed all day. This blows.--D.G.

The familiar ringtone that chimes repeatedly from my phone draws my face from my pillow. The slightly pounding in my head becomes excruciating as I press my hand against the side of my temple, turning on my side. The warmth from the sunlight hits my bareback through my window, and I feel my muscles relax.

The phone doesn't stop ringing, and I groan.

I sit upon my elbows, causing my bed sheets to drape over my waist in a scrambled mess. Rubbing my eyes to clear my vision, I grab my phone from off the top of the dresser and read the name.

Chris.

I sigh.

Right above his name is the time. *12:13 PM.*

I can't believe I slept that long.

I answer the phone, tiredness still seeping over me. "What?"

"Oi! You haven't been drinking, have you?" Christopher remarks. I can tell he's probably outside doing something since I can hear cars passing by him loudly.

I huff. "I don't drink." I massage my two fingers against the one spot on my head, trying to relieve the pounding in my head. "Chris, I'm tired. Can we talk later?"

"No, we cannot!" I pull the phone from my ear, wincing. I've never heard him get that loud before over the phone. Carmen is definitely rubbing off on him. Jesus.

Still, Christopher adds, "And you're not tired. You just got your head up ya bum, and we're going to get you out of it. You only turn eighteen once."

I catch his words. *"We?"*

"Just get out of bed, mate. I'll see you in a sec."

He hangs up, not even giving me a chance to speak.

I groan, placing my phone back onto my dresser. I fall back onto my bed, my head hitting the soft pillow. I figure my parents probably aren't home since it's too quiet. There's no commotion coming from downstairs, and I don't hear anyone upstairs. I could quickly get up out of my bed to check and see if either of their cars were still in the driveway, but the pounding in my head resurfaced when I tried to sit up.

I lie back down and sigh. With my hand over my eyes, I block out the sunlight. The darkness becomes comforting, along with the silence. I feel my body start to relax, and I let my eyes close, still keeping my hand over them. I can hear myself softly breathing.

. . . .

"I saw it first!" I barked at Morris-Lina, pointing at the TV screen after the cartoon girl asked us to find the missing shape to the puzzle.

"No! I did it!" Morris-Lina crossed her arms over her chest, pouting.

"No! I did it!"

"I did it!"

"Alright! Hey! Hey!" Dad's voice boomed as he clapped his hands to get our attention. "No fighting on your birthday, you hear?" Dad then crouched down to meet our eye levels and sighed. This time, he spoke to us softly. "Now, a big shark just told the entire ocean that two little sharks just turned five today, so all the fishes want to see them very much. Saaay, at the aquarium?"

Morris-Lina and I whipped our heads to each other, big grins on our faces. We rarely get to go to the aquarium since it's so far away. At least that's what mom would always say. She would be too tired to take us when we wanted to go.

Dad ruffles our heads. "That sounds like a plan?"

Morris-Lina and I jump up, waving our hands in the air. "Yeah!"

"Alright!" Dad stands up, looking like a giant again. "Go! Get your jackets on! Let's go before the fish miss us too much!"

· · · · · · · ·

CLAP! CLAP!

I flinch at the sharp sound ringing through my ears, and my lashes flutter open. My eyes slowly adjust to the brightness of my bedroom, and the sunlight still hits my bare chest. I realize that I am lying on my back with my arm behind my head like a pillow. When I move my arm from behind me, there is a strange but quick tingling sensation in my arm, making my bones tighten. I turn my head and gasp at the sight of Christopher standing over me with a cheeky grin on his face.

How did he even get in here?!

Dude!

I sit up, feeling the bedsheets slipping down further from my waist, and I pull my legs close to my chest. I'm in my boxers, and it's not the first time Christopher's seen me in nothing but my boxers either. We've been friends for a long time, after all. But I wasn't expecting him to be standing at my bed, smiling like a weirdo. A tall weirdo who looks like he's hit the jackpot.

"What the hell, man!" My voice shakes, and I gulp.

Christopher welcomes himself on my bed, sitting down on edge, still looking at me with a smirk. I notice he's holding a small glass of water in one hand, and in the other, a white pill in a thin napkin. He has both of them up to my face, telling me to take it.

"You sounded like shit over the phone, lad. You're gonna need this." He tilts his head, softening his smirk and looking at me with gentle eyes.

I sigh. It's a pain reliever.

I sometimes forget how clever Christopher actually is and how he amazingly picks up on things. Even if I tried to sound like a bubbly moron over the phone, Christopher is not gullible. He's many things, but naive isn't one of them, which pisses me off sometimes when I want to get him off my back about certain things. I already have Counselor Malik to deal with for that. I don't need Christopher as an addition. He's the last person I'd want to be on me about some things.

I take the pill and swallow it down with some water. I take a couple gulps before placing the glass down on my dresser beside my phone. I lean back, letting my back touch the headboard of my bed, which is unbearable cold for some reason. Still, I manage to relax, letting my head rest back while looking up at the ceiling.

"Did my mom let you in?" I ask him, crossing my arms over my stomach as I close my eyes.

I feel Christopher sit back a bit further on the bed. "Actually, I let myself in. With the spare key. Your folks aren't here."

I pop my head up, opening my eyes to look at him with furrowed eyebrows. I forgot all about the spare key we keep buried in the flower pot outside. But I also can't believe that my parents aren't home. It's not like them to just up and leave so early in the morning without telling me—let alone on my birthday. Then again, like I said, it's my first birthday alone. They probably didn't want to face that, and I can't say I blame them.

Mom was probably called into work too. Same for dad.

I shrug it off, leaning my head back against the headboard of my bed while looking up at the ceiling to my room. "Oh."

Christopher sucks his teeth and leans in towards me. He grips my shoulders, making me wince from the sudden tightness, and he yanks me up from off the headboard. I always knew Christopher was strong, but not *that* strong. *Mierda!*

"Ah! Jesus, man!" I hiss, rubbing my shoulders once he lets me go. "People usually give birthday punches, not dislocated shoulders."

Christopher shakes his head. *"Lag."*

I flip him off.

He pushes my hand down onto the bed, snickering. He pulls one leg up onto the bed so he can turn his body to face me more but keeps his foot off the bed since he has his sneakers on. The way he pursed his lips and adverts his eyes makes me wonder what could possibly be going on in that head of his. It's so easy for Christopher to figure me out. I forget how easily jealous I get that I can't do the same with him unless he makes it obvious how he feels whenever he looks at me a certain way. Sometimes, I know what he's thinking by the way he curves or twists his lips and arches his eyebrows. Other times, I'm completely lost. It's agitating, but I'm not bothered because of him. Kind of. It's the fact that he knows me so well that gets to me.

Christopher crosses his arms over his stomach, leaning back a little bit, but he's able to hold himself up. His eyes are locked on me, but I purposefully avoid his eyes at all cost, looking down at the bedsheets sprawled over my legs. "I get today may not be the best of days, but for bloody sake, man. Can you at least let the lads and I make things up to you? Hm?"

I let out a low huff. "There's nothing to make up for."

I know what he means, though. Christopher isn't dumb, and he knows that I don't want to celebrate anything about today. Yet, he's still pushing me to get dressed and act like everything is okay. Deep down, I know Christopher thinks I'm unreasonable, telling him to drop it and just let me be. But on the flip side, I know he has good intentions. As I listen to Christopher talk about how he, Benton, and Peter had this whole day planned out for me as a surprise, I huff. He could've just called, wished me a happy birthday, and that be the end of it.

Instead, he planned a day for me. Him, Benton, and Peter. But I was most surprised to hear that Benton even thought of contributing since he's always so...Benton. He doesn't seem like the outgoing type. Not unless Peter somehow managed to wheel him.

After hearing Christopher ramble for a solid five minutes, I lift up my hand to silence him. I cut my gaze to him, taking in the shock in his green eyes. They're like jewels, thanks to the sunlight. I realize he has the front of his hair swept to the side and up out of his face. I never really noticed how thick Christopher's eyebrows were until now since he's so close, I guess. They're not super thick, as if they're close to looking like fat caterpillars, but they're nicer than mine.

I lower my hand. "I don't like surprises."

Christopher scoffs. "But aren't you full of 'em?" It actually sounds more like a statement than a question, and I roll my eyes. Christopher jumps up to his feet and pats my shoulder. "I'll let you get dressed, lag."

I tighten my jaw as he heads out of my bedroom. "Cabrón!"

Christopher laughs maniacally, heading down the steps.

I pinch the bridge of my nose, shutting my eyes tightly. I know it will be a while until I feel the effects of the pain reliever, but until then, my head is pounding as I drag myself out of bed to get dressed.

I strip off my clothes so I can take a shower. I make sure the water is warm before I jump into the tub to wash. The second my body comes in contact with the water, the pounding in my head starts to ease, and my bones start to relax. I let the soap run down my body as I scrub myself with the smell of french vanilla filling the air.

I always liked fragrant soaps—ever since I was little, mom says. I never cared for the soaps that dad would use since they felt chalky. I also didn't like cologne that smelled too strong, making my eyes water. Dad never seemed bothered that I favored fragrant soaps and wasn't too fond of strong-smelling cologne.

Personally, I think he just felt indifferent about it. Like it didn't really matter since it never really meant anything.

I laugh at the thought.

I eventually got out of the shower and dried myself before heading into my room. I moisturize my skin and slip on a pair of boxers from the top drawer of my dresser.

My phone suddenly vibrates against the small dresser near my bed. I take a quick look at the screen and roll my eyes when I see the message from Christopher, asking me if I'm almost ready to go. As I pull out a pair of black jeans from the bottom drawer of my large dresser, I think about responding to him. Maybe telling him that he insisted that I get dressed and take my time since it was *my* day.

Instead, I put on my jeans and slip on my black leather belt to hold my jeans in place since they are somewhat slipping off my waist. They're not baggy. They fit me just fine, coming in close to my legs a bit as they should. But at the same time, I've noticed most of my jeans fitting a little looser lately, which is fine.

I go through my closet and decide to throw on my plaid black and navy blue flannel shirt, leaving the top two buttons undone, showing off my collarbone a bit. After I throw on my usual black-and-white high-top converse sneakers, I grab my phone and head downstairs.

The second I reach the bottom of the steps, my phone vibrates again. Another text message—this time, it's Peter.

Pete: we out here!!!

Stalkers.

I don't get why they're in such a rush. I get that they made plans for this day to be *"special"* and whatnot, but they don't have to be so pushy. If anything, I'd be okay with us just hanging out at my place, watching a movie or something.

I wasn't totally in favor of surprises. I know I seem like someone who's down for whatever, but not today. Today, I wanted things to be at ease. That's not so much to ask.

I throw on my thin black jacket and grab my keys from the small glass bowl that sits on the table by the front door. I step outside and lock the house up behind me. As soon as I turn around, I see Peter, Benton, and Christopher standing by Christopher's car parked right in front of the walkway.

I sigh.

As I walk to them, keeping my hands stuffed in the pockets of my jacket, Peter goes, "It's about damn time! We thought you fell in the bathroom or something."

Benton chuckles at the thought while Christopher gives Peter a look that makes Peter's pearly-white smile fade. I shake my head, knowing that Peter was only joking around. Christopher had to have known that too.

"And if I did, you'd have to get me out," I say, trying to lighten the mood.

Peter shifts his gaze to me, and I wink at him, earning a smile.

Christopher then steps forward, pulling out a black cloth from his pocket. He holds it up to my face, and I furrow my eyebrows.

"Turn around." His voice is soft but also demanding.

I stare at the blindfold and then back at him. I want to think he's joking, but the look in his eyes says otherwise.

"If this is your idea of a surprise..." I can hardly comprehend the situation. He knows damn well that this is way out of line.

A blindfold?! Really?!

"I told you it'd be too much," Peter hisses to Christopher in the form of a whisper. "You done did it now."

"Shut up," Christopher bites back, making Peter shrink closer to Benton while scrunching his nose from Christopher's attitude.

Geez. Talk about 'tough-love.'

"C'mon, Don. You know me," Christopher says as if I'm an airhead. "I'd never do anything—"

"Are you *kidding* me?!" I try to keep my voice low since I don't need the neighborhood to get in on this. Plus, I'm trying to pass a headache, and this is only making it worse. "Chris. I'm not wearing that. Wherever you guys wanna take me, I gotta be able to see. I'm not doing..." I point to the blindfold, "*that.*"

Christopher lets out a huff, and I notice his face getting a bit red. His nostrils flare, and he drops his arm swiftly to his side. I know I'm acting difficult right now, but I have a reason. It's not that I don't trust them. I just don't like wearing blindfolds. I like knowing what's going on around me. For all I know, if something happens and we get kidnapped, I won't even know we're getting kidnapped. I won't know until *after* the fact.

He should know that!

Peter then steps forward and takes the blindfold from Christopher. Peter looks at me, holding the blindfold tightly. "Don, we promise we won't do anything sketchy. We know this day is hard for you, and we just wanna do something for you. We're going to take you somewhere, but if you see it right away, it won't be as fun."

I scoff. "How?"

"Because it won't be! And we worked real hard on it, so..."

Peter then holds out the blindfold, but I doubt he expects me to take it. When I look up at him, his eyes are soft, and he bites the inside of his lip, which I hate. His aunt always yells at him for doing that, and I hate the thought of Peter getting scorned for something he just does out of habit when he's nervous or scared.

That's kind of like whenever Meagan bites her nails. I bet her mom gets on her case about it all the time. Plus, the very thought of Meagan being nervous or scared about anything just makes me feel funny. Like my stomach always twists in knots, and I feel sick.

I close my eyes, needing to look away from Peter.

Dammit.

"Fine." I turn around so that way he can put the blindfold on.

I open my eyes as the thickness from the cloth presses over my eyes, and darkness conquers my vision. A very tiny amount of sunlight comes through, and I can somewhat see tiny dots of color from the outside, but hardly. My head jerks a bit as Peter—I'm assuming—ties on the blindfold, and I suddenly hear someone walking their dog. I know it's a dog because it barks, and loud footsteps follow.

"Afternoon!" Peter pipes up as they pass.

Shut up, please.

I can only imagine how weird this all looks. Four dudes standing in the middle of the sidewalk. One is getting blindfolded, and God knows what could happen. This whole thing feels like one of those fanfictions Morris-Lina used to read in her spare time. If she knew about this, Lord knows how much she'd clown me for it.

I suddenly feel someone grab my hand, guiding me to the car.

"Watch your step." It's Christopher.

I manage to step down from the curb and onto the street. I let Christopher be my eyes as he guides me to wherever he wants me to sit. I hear him open the door, and he goes, "Birthday boy gets shotgun."

I snort. "Of course."

Meanwhile, I know this whole thing probably looks so wrong right now. Knowing my neighbors, they're probably on the edge of their seats, wondering what's happening. This could've been kidnapping, and none of them would give a damn to intervene.

Someone was literally walking their dog and kept it moving as I was being blindfolded! No questions asked. Nothing.

I guess if this were a kidnapping, I'm just going to die then.

This shit.

Once everyone is strapped in, and I hear all the car doors shut, Christopher starts up the engine. I know Christopher is driving because he's like me. No one is allowed to drive his car. Not even Carmen, as much as he loves her. Then again, Carmen wouldn't want to drive his car anyway since she knows deep down that she'll probably wreck it if she tried to take it for a spin. Plus, she has her own car. It's nicer than his too.

I rest my head back against the headrest, and Christopher turns on the radio to fill the car with some kind of sound.

Stupidly, I ask, "How long is this going to be?"

I already know that none of them will tell me, so I don't know why I asked. Christopher is probably glaring at Peter and Benton, so they keep their mouths shut for all I know. Better yet, the three of them are probably smiling at each other, not saying anything, knowing that this will kill me.

The car starts moving, and I roll my eyes.

Surprise my ass.

…….

I heard someone open my door for me after I unbuckled myself from the seat. At this point, I can't tell if I'm keeping my eyes opened or closed. It feels like they're closed, but I can still see tiny glimpses of light. Although, it's mostly darkness that conquers my vision.

I reach out, and someone takes my hand, guiding me up and out of the car. The fresh breeze hits my face gently, and I can hear birds chirping and a few buzzing sounds. There is a crunch beneath me when I step out of the car—like little rocks rubbing together with every step I take.

"We got ya, Don." It's Christopher.

The entire car ride was quiet in terms of interaction. The music helped fill the awkward silence that soon became unbearable and made me want to slam my head against the dashboard. I actually started to believe that the guys were holding something against me since they refused to answer any of my questions.

"Are we almost there?"

"Are you guys good?"

"Could you at least tell me where it is?"

I get that they wanted to keep things a surprise, but they could've answered me just once. Knowing Peter, he probably wanted to, but Christopher would've clocked him so he wouldn't get the chance. Hell, I doubt Benton could hold his tongue either.

With a couple more steps, I hear Peter's voice suddenly as he holds my other hand, telling me to watch my step. I step up and feel concrete. I step forward. More rocks. The buzzing sound around me starts to become faint, but I doubt we're far.

We then come to a stop. Christopher's hand settles on my lower back, and he tells me, "Close your eyes."

I huff.

What's the point of the blindfold if you still want me to close my eyes?

I don't argue, though. I just close my eyes. I feel Christopher start to untie the blindfold, and I know it's him because Peter is still holding my other hand. I even hear Peter giggling and feel him rocking a bit. He can hardly keep himself together.

He's like a little kid that's too hyper for his own good.

It's kind of adorable.

The blindfold slides right off, and Christopher tells me to open my eyes. Once my eyes adjust to the brightness, I can take everything in. All I can do is gasp, staring out at the pier up ahead. The water sparkles in the sunlight like something out of a movie and stretches out far and seems endless—it hardly seems believable. I look over to my right and see many large logs stacked up like a fireplace, and boulders surround the logs in the form of a square. Meanwhile, we're out in a wide-open space surrounded by trees and glistening water.

Everything about this place seems all too familiar. The memories of me, Christopher, and Peter coming here during the summer of our sophomore year and into junior year start rushing back to me. We'd come here on weekends to get away from our problems. It'd be a nice drive too—a solid fifty-minute drive all the way to New Jersey, listening to music, talking about whatever. We'd try to come up here at least once or twice a month to disappear from our folks, but then we just stopped.

Maybe because of time and distance.

All I know is that this was one of my favorite places. This place and the lake where dad used to take Morris-Lina and me.

"I'll start the fire." Peter pats my shoulder, grinning as crinkles form by his eyes.

The corners of my lips instantly curve upwards, and I watch as Peter makes his way over to the stack of logs. Benton is right behind him, and Peter looks back at him, smirking as Benton starts to pull his back, using the hair tie on his wrist.

I feel Christopher settle his arm on my shoulder while placing his other hand on his hip. He sighs with a smirk playing on his lips.

I shake my head, scoffing.

He furrows his eyebrows, looking at me. "What?"

"Nothing." I look forward, watching Peter and Benton gather a few rocks together to try to start the fire. I mutter to myself, "You stunner." Although, I know Christopher probably heard me.

"What's that?" He's not very convincing in sounding oblivious.

"You heard me."

"Actually, I didn't." He leans in closer to me as if he's trying to hear better. "Could you repeat what you said? I didn't catch it."

I suck my teeth, hating how smug he is right now.

"I like it."

"What's that again? I'm sorry, I just—"

"I like it! This is quite the surprise!" I can hear my voice echo, but Christopher doesn't shrink back from my booming voice. He just smiles like a gloating idiot, dusting off his shoulder. I snarl under my breath. "Jesus Christ."

Christopher inches closer to me as if he's trying to whisper, but he doesn't. He's not loud either, but only I can hear. "To be fair. This was Pete and Ben's idea."

I swiftly turn my attention to Christopher and arch an eyebrow. I would expect Peter to come up with something like this since we used to come here. But Benton? He doesn't know a thing about this place. I doubt Christopher or Peter even dared to take him up here without me knowing.

Christopher notices the look on my face and laughs.

"Peter was the mastermind, and Benton was sort of his accomplice. Peter sort of figured you'd like it since it's a bit of déjà vu. But this is just half of the gift, mate."

"Half?" I smirk.

"Don't worry about it." Christopher sighs. "I say we spare the two hopeless souls with setting themselves ablaze, yeah?"

I chuckle, watching Benton and Peter struggle to start the fire like two children. Still, they laugh at each other as they mess up while also barking orders to each other. It's very entertaining, watching them go back and forth with each other in different ways. One second they're laughing, and then the next, they're bossing each other around. It's like they can't pick and choose.

Although, I'm not sure when those two got so close all of a sudden. Usually, Benton is kind of quiet around Peter, even though he'll often laugh at Peter's comments or whenever Christopher smacks Peter upside the head or something like that. For Christopher to say that Benton was Peter's "accomplice" on this whole arrangement, the two of them must've been spending some sort of time together.

Christopher and I make our way over to Peter and Benton as they continue to struggle to start the fire. Christopher rolls his eyes at them and reaches into the pocket inside of his jacket, pulling out a box of matches. Peter's jaw goes slack when Christopher strikes a match across the box, igniting the flame before tossing the match into the pit.

The laughter that spills from my mouth is inevitable, even when I try to cover my mouth to hide the smile. The looks on Benton and Peter's faces are to die for. Peter looks as though he's been betrayed, and Benton seems as though he just decided to give up on life. He probably has since he throws the rocks and sits himself down on one of the bolder, muttering to himself while gazing into the fire as it starts to rise in the pit.

Peter settles his hands on his hips, still stunned by Christopher flicking a match into the pit. "You had matches?!"

Christopher slips the box back into his pocket, raising an eyebrow. "Yeah." It's as if Peter was supposed to know.

Peter folds his arms over his chest like a child. "You could've said so earlier! We were struggling here!"

"I know. That's why I used the match, dumbass." Christopher flashes a cocky grin making Peter scowl at him.

For some reason, Peter even looks younger when he's angry. Probably because his nose scrunches a bit like how kids would. Kind of like Yago. Christopher finds it amusing, and he throws his arm around Peter, who just looks away from him with a "Hmph!"

"C'mon, Petey, let's call it a truce. For the sake of our lad's day, yeah?" His accent has never sounded so thick, especially when he calls Peter *Petey.'* The only time Christopher calls Peter that name is unless he's really sorry about something.

Peter lets out a deep sigh, his nostrils flaring. "Fine."

I chuckle, shaking my head at how much of a kid Peter can be at times. Although I know that out of all of us, he can handle himself just fine. Living with his aunt and dealing with his mom has really made him tough. But there are moments where I worry about him. So does Christopher.

Yet, Peter still smiles and laughs like usual. And just like that, he hurries over to Benton and takes out two wooden rods and a bag of marshmallows from the duffel bag that is behind Benton. He hands Benton one of the rods and opens the bag of marshmallows, allowing Benton to take one.

I feel Christopher gently nudge me on my side with his elbow to get my attention. He tilts his head in their direction, insisting for us to sit down and join them, which we do. It's just the four of us, sitting around the fire, roasting marshmallows while talking about God knows what. We're there for a while, just talking and laughing about ridiculous things.

At one point, Christopher brings up Jen Li, asking Peter if he's set up a date for the two of them yet. Despite his dark skin, I can tell Peter's probably flushed at the thought of taking Jen Li out on a date. I doubt the guy's ever been on a date before with anyone, let alone Jen Li. I notice how Peter chews on his bottom lip while twirling the rod in his fingers, looking down at his shoes.

"It's complicated," is all Peter manages to say before sticking his seventh or tenth marshmallow to the tip of the rod to roast. It's incredible how much this kid can eat and still look fit.

I snort at Peter's words, knowing that's total bullshit. We all know it's bullshit. When he talked to Jen Li, we were there. She even admitted that she wanted to ask Peter to prom for a while—meaning she liked him.

"Sí, cómo no!" I blurt, making Peter lift his gaze to me. He looks like such a puppy with those big eyes of his. I sigh and scoot forward a bit. "The girl likes you, Pete. The last thing you wanna do is take a page outta Chrissy's book and wait until it's the end of the world to ask out the girl of your dreams."

Without even batting an eyelash, Christopher throws a hard punch to my shoulder. I laugh it off while rubbing the spot, knowing it'll probably bruise on the way home since Christopher punches like a pro boxer on steroids.

"Just because it's your birthday doesn't mean you can call me that, mate," Christopher scolds.

I roll my arm, trying to relieve some of the pain. I still can't help but laugh through my words. "Alright, alright. I gotchu." From the corner of my eye, I can see Peter starting to smile at how ridiculous Christopher and I are being.

At least he feels better.

Christopher looks at Peter and clears his throat. "Seriously, Pete. Trust your gut. She seems like a great girl, and you're a decent guy. I'm sure you two will work if you tried."

Peter shrugs. "I guess." He pauses. "I'm not just 'decent' either. I'm a gentleman." Peter takes a bite out of his crispy marshmallow that is close to black all over. He mutters, *"Diablo."*

Benton then chimes in, telling Peter, "If it makes you feel any better, I get where you're coming from. It's hard talking to people that way, you know. I'm still trying, but you're good. So."

Peter's eyes are practically wide as he tries to register everything that Benton has just said. That's probably the most Benton has ever said to him. Around any of us. I know he talks a lot around Meagan, but that's because he likes her. As a friend, I mean. They're friends. Close friends.

Anyway, Peter finally comes back down to planet Earth and gives Benton a slight head nod. "T-T, thanks, Benton. I-I, um, I don't know what to say, actually." Peter chuckles nervously. "That's pretty, uh, pretty insightful. Really!"

Benton nods. "And Christopher is right. She is great. I have psychology with her. She's fluent in Korean."

"Oh yeah?" Peter takes another bite out of his marshmallow.

Benton nods, smirking. "Mhm." Pause. "If you want to impress her, I can teach you a thing or two."

"Really?"

"Yeah, especially if she says anything you might need to know. Like..." Benton then says something in Korean. He then looks at us as if we're all supposed to know what he said. I'm the one who asks him what it means, and with a sinister grin, Benton responds, *"Faster."*

Christopher and I explode in laughter while Peter holds his head, looking down while chuckling. None of us would've expected something like that to come out of Benton's mouth. Ever. I doubt he even realizes how smooth and strange that sounded coming from him. If anything, something like that would've come out of my mouth, and no one would've had a reaction since that's something I would say casually.

Benton, on the other hand, is the kind of guy who seems timid. Too timid for his own good. Like an innocent bystander who just witnessed hellfire by being at the wrong place at the wrong time. Yet, here he is, smirking as if he's just accomplished something big. Perhaps, he has because none of us were expecting him to say *that!*

I'll be damned.

Once we get ourselves together, I ask them if they're ready to wrap things up. Christopher looks at Peter, who then looks at Benton, who then looks at Christopher, who then looks up at me.

"What?" I ask.

"Well." Christopher stands up and throws his arm around my shoulder, pulling me closer to him. "We'll call this Part Two of your birthday surprise." He gives Peter and Benton a head nod.

I watch as Peter scrambles through the duffel bag and pulls out a pack of fireworks. I whip my attention to Christopher, noticing the smirk on his face and the way he arches his eyebrow. When we used to come here, we would always set off firecrackers and fireworks. Kind of like what Morris-Lina and I did whenever she and I would go to the lake.

I smile at the thought.

"Let's light 'em up," I tell them.

We go to the farther part of the field since it's more open and away from nature. We start off with three fireworks, and Christopher sets them off, lighting them up with his matches. Christopher hurries over to the rest of us before the first firework has a chance to pop off. And when it does, it's like a strike of lightening the way it shoots up in the air.

Then, it explodes into a bunch of random colors, sprinkling over the sky like sparkles of dust. The second one is the same, only it's golden and bigger. The third is a bright blue. The way the colors somehow manage to blend together is hypnotizing.

From the corner of my eye, I notice Peter with his arm settled on Benton's shoulder as the two of them watch the fireworks in astonishment. As if they have never seen anything like this before. Benton probably has at least once in his life, for all I know. Meanwhile, Christopher just admires the fireworks with a slight smirk on his face.

I softly chuckle to myself.

I can only imagine how Morris-Lina would've thought of today. She might've spent the day with Meagan and Carmen, doing God knows what. I doubt they would've blindfolded her like the guys did with me. Just thinking about it makes my stomach twist in knots, and my throat goes dry.

I hear Christopher mutter to me, "Moe would've loved today." He doesn't pull his eyes away from the sky either.

My lips part open, but nothing comes out. I just watch as Peter digs in the pack for another thing of fireworks, and Christopher hands him the box of matches to set them off.

Week 3, Monday.

"Are you sure you can get them? Because if not, I'll call their father and—"

I chuckle, pressing the phone closer to my ear as I slam my locker shut after switching out my textbooks for what I'll need to study for homework tonight.

During economics, tía Yoselin messaged me, asking if I could pick the boys up from school and watch them for a bit until she came home. Usually, she hires a babysitter to pick the boys up and watch them when she's working later than expected, but the babysitter was out of town. I texted Yoselin back, letting her know that I didn't mind picking up the boys and watching them.

It's better than going home to nothing, anyway.

Mom is probably going to work late again. Same with dad.

I didn't have anything better to do.

Still, I could tell Yoselin felt terrible since it was on such short notice, but like I said, I didn't mind.

"Tía, está bien!" I reassure her, leaning against my locker. "I promise, it's all good. Y'know I like them anyway."

"Sí, sí," she sighs against the phone. "Ay, sobrino. You're a life savior. If you need anything at all once you get them, let me know, okay? I owe you one."

I snort. "You don't owe me anything. I promise."

"Okay, well I have to go. Adiós. Te quiero."

"Te amo también, tía."

The call ends, and I sigh, stuffing my phone into the pocket of my jacket. I go down the steps, blending with the crowd of students as we try to get out of this prison called school. I usually don't think of Gabe-Day as a prison, but after the day I've had, it sure felt like it.

The day felt slow, and there were moments when I considered gauging my eyes out with my pencils during my classes, but I kept myself together. Things were going fine this morning, though. I'm pretty sure I passed the quiz Mr. Enrique gave us for Honors Algebra II, and Meagan actually felt pretty confident in herself after taking it. But, as usual, she was still skeptical of herself, thinking that she probably bombed the quiz since she felt it was "too easy."

She said, *"I dunno. It was easy, but usually, it's not good if that's the case, right? At least for me."*

Meagan started biting her nails, and I held her hand to get her to stop. She looked at me with so much worry in her eyes, I felt my heart sink. No matter how many times I try to tell her how smart she is, it's like it all goes in one ear and out of the other. She's never failed any of Mr. Enrique's tests. I bet she passes every test she takes for all of her subjects.

Still, she worries herself to death over nothing, and that's something I hope she gets over, not for my sake, but for hers. I know what that's like. My parents were always on my neck like crazy growing up. But they were even tougher on Morris-Lina, and I hated that. Especially after her diagnosis.

I bet if it wasn't for that, things really would've turned out different. But I could never tell them that. No matter how much the thought kills me.

As soon as I get outside, I rush to my car and sigh of relief once I get in it. I rest my head back, thinking about how I will manage taking care of the boys while also getting my assignments done. I have a paper due for Mr. Acosta in two weeks that focuses on *Brave New World's* premise, which he assigned our class to read in January. It's not a bad story. It's certainly better than that Jace Gregg book I forced myself to read—*Chasing Aubrey Hunter. Brave New World* is a classic, so I shouldn't have been surprised that Mr. Acosta assigned my A.P. English class to read it since the story stirs up a conversation on how we utilize mass media for our own pleasures and whatnot. Not to mention how our pleasures define us as people in general, which is the premise of the paper he assigned for us to write.

Five to ten pages, 12 point font size in Times New Roman...and single-spaced. Single-spaced! I don't get how Meagan gets such a thrill from taking Mr. Acosta's class. She has him for regular English III as her second class period, and I can only imagine what stuff Mr. Acosta assigns for them. Probably a bunch of vocab work and a few reading assignments.

But I shouldn't be stunned with how many reading assignments and essays I'm required to write for this guy. He gives us enough time to do the work, but actually, doing the work is tricky. I still get the shit done, nonetheless. It's an A.P course—the expectations are at a much higher standard.

I sigh.

I strap myself and start up the car engine before driving off to pick up Gabriel and Yago from school. Their school isn't far from where they live. I've only been there a few times. It's a pretty decent elementary school with a nice set-up. There is a smaller playground for the smaller kids set up in the front of the school that is hardly a playground since it's nothing but concrete and has limited space.

Meanwhile, the playground at the back of the school for the bigger kids is expansive and stretches out far and has all sorts of fun things for the kids to enjoy. A jungle gym that looks like a castle, swing sets, a few playhouses. It's like a wonderland.

It always stays so well-kept because the school keeps it closed off from the public, so no one can just waltz onto the playground and have their fun. It's school property, not public property.

I decided to park my car outside Yoselin's house and walk down to pick up the boys from school since it's a couple of blocks away.

When I arrive at the front side of the school to pick up the boys, I spot them immediately. Gabriel is holding Yago's hand as they stand up against the wall inside the playground, waiting to be called for dismissal. I get out of the car and walk up to the gate. I notice a heavy-set woman standing at the gate door with a clipboard in hand and a whistle around her neck. Her round sunglasses remind me of the ones abuela used to wear whenever she was reading, letting it slip past the bridge of her nose.

The woman looks up at me as I make my way to the gate, and she purses her lips. "Name?"

"Donald Gonzalez. Here to pick up Yago and Gabriel Ortega-Howard," I tell her, stuffing my hands into my jacket pockets.

The woman twists her lips and pushes her glasses up on her nose while keeping her eyes on me. She looks at me as if I'm suspicious, but I let it roll off my back. It doesn't surprise me that someone with as many wrinkles would consider me to seem suspicious.

The woman blows her whistle and calls for Yago and Gabriel. As soon as the boys look up and see me, smiles spread across their faces, and their eyes are wide.

While running up to me, Yago calls out, "Cousin Don-O!"

Gabriel just giggles with his arms stretched out as if he were a plane, zipping past Yago to get to me.

I crouch down and catch Gabriel in my arms as his little arms lock around my neck. Yago then jumps onto me, his arms wrapping around Gabriel and me as he buries his face into my shoulder.

I laugh. "Good to see you too."

Yago then lets me go, and Gabriel lifts up his head.

Yago asks me, "Are we going over to your house?"

I shake my head. "No. I'm taking you home."

He pouts.

"But!" I add, ruffling his hair. "I'm watching you guys until your mom comes home. I'll even make your favorite dinner while we're at it, yeah?"

Yago gasps, bouncing up and down on his toes. "Yeah!"

At that moment, someone calls his name, and Yago whips his head back and waves at a little boy who runs up to him. The kid has a mop of curls on his head, going in all sorts of directions on his head. Some of it even falls over his eyes but barely. The boy has the roundest cheeks and the deepest dimples I've ever seen, with perfect hazel eyes shaped like almonds.

I notice someone walking behind the kid, and I look up.

Suddenly, all the air in my body escapes me as I forget how to breathe. I blink a few times to make sure my eyes aren't playing tricks on me, but they aren't.

You've got to be kidding me.

It's Alejandro Reyes. It's really him. He wears his jean jacket but keeps the sleeves rolled down past his wrists, and underneath is a solid black crewneck tee-shirt with them hem draping over the waistline of his dark blue skinny jeans that are somewhat torn at the knees, revealing the skin there. His hair is styled the same from when I first saw him—undercut pompadour with streaks of silver along the front and top of his hair.

I notice the look in his eyes, and he's just as baffled as I am. Unlike me, the only thing is the one side of his mouth pulls upward, and sudden confidence radiates from him.

"Donald!" I sharply shift my gaze to Yago as he stands next to the boy with curly hair. "This is my friend Ricardo! Can he walk home with us? He lives a few blocks away!"

I furrow my eyebrows, shaking my head. "Wait, wait. I-uh..."

"That's his uncle!" Yago points to Alejandro, who just stands a few feet away from them while smirking. My throat tightens, and I feel my thump heavily in my chest. Yago adds, "He's okay. He picks up Ricardo sometimes."

I blink.

You've got to be shitting me!

Of all people—Alejandro had to be *this* kid's uncle.

I look at Yago, resting my hand on his shoulder.

"Yago," I say, trying to keep my voice straight as I gather my thoughts. "We don't really know them like that. I don't think that'll be a good idea, you know."

Yago huffs. "Yes, we do! You helped Ricardo's mom the other day at the park, remember? Ricardo said you kept the bad guys away from her."

I take a sharp breath as the memory floods through my mind. Those two jerk-offs who jumped me the other day were the same guys who kept harassing the woman from the park. I think her name was Aitana or something like that. I pretended to be a friend of hers to get the guys off her back. She and I ended up talking, but briefly. She seemed nice, and then...

That's right! I have seen Ricardo before. He's her kid. I hardly recognized him because he was wearing a hat the last time I saw him, and half of his face was buried in his coat to keep him warm.

I remember Alejandro having a sister, but I didn't know that *she* was his sister! His sister was taller, I thought. I remember her being cute, but I was a little kid then. She probably seemed taller because I was younger.

Yago clings to my arm and starts to rock back and forth, pulling my arm in the process. He pouts, whining, "Pleeease?"

Between Yago's whining and pouty-face and then seeing Alejandro as he stands a few feet away while looking on, my head is spinning. I honestly want to scoop the boys up and deal with Yago hating me for a day rather than look at Alejandro any further. It's not that he's repulsive to look at—far from it, actually. It's just the sight of him that makes my stomach churn, and I can't think.

I close my eyes and take a deep breath.

"Alright," I sigh out, and Yago stops rocking.

I open my eyes, smirking when I see Yago and Ricardo throw their arms around each other, grinning. Yago then challenges Ricardo to a race to the street corner, and the boys bolt.

"Don't run off!" I call out to them, but they're already halfway gone.

I suddenly feel Gabriel rest his head on my shoulder, and I press a light kiss to his forehead. I figure the kid's probably tired, even though there's not much he could've done since he's in kindergarten. Those are usually the glory days.

Something stands over me, blocking the sun's light, and I gulp. I already know it's Alejandro. I don't even have to look up. I see the ripped jeans and the white high-top converse sneaker that he wears. Then he goes, "Started carrying that knife like I suggested, shot glass?"

A discomforting taste comes up my mouth. My chest starts to feel tight from Alejandro's presence, and I clear my throat to get rid of the roughness that suddenly crawls up my throat. I can tell from the sound of his words he probably has a cocky smirk plastered on his face, which was usual for him based on what I remembered of him. That was just Alejandro.

I pick up Gabriel in a swift move, his face burying into my neck as I stand up. When I look up, I realize the small distance between Alejandro and me, and I also note how much taller he is compared to me. I already knew he was taller, but I only thought it was by a few inches. Maybe it's his sneakers.

Regardless, I tighten my jaw, keeping hold of Gabriel while looking Alejandro in the eye. His smirk starts to fade.

Sternly, I tell him, "Stop calling me that."

I turn on my heels to get away from him, but as expected, he's right on my tail. Laughing. Friggin' laughing. If it weren't for Gabriel being in my arms, I would've decked him. But then I remember that Yago and his friend...Ricardo...Alejandro's nephew is here too.

I roll my eyes, and Alejandro titters.

"So you *do* remember me?" he coos.

I can feel him looking at me as I pick up the pace to get to Yago and Ricardo as they wait for us at the street corner so they can cross the street. I use my free hand to grab hold of Yago's hand before crossing the street. Alejandro holds Ricardo's hand as we cross the road, and as soon as we get to the other side, the boys break themselves free and run off, laughing with each other.

"Giving me the cold shoulder after I saved your butt the other day? And it's been so long since we've talked?" Alejandro scoffs, lingering over my shoulder. "How rude." I notice him getting closer, leaning in, so he's looking directly at Gabriel, who lifts his head up from my neck. "Don't be like your cousin here, chico pequeño. Having no manners will get you nowhere in life. Believe that."

I halt as my blood starts to boil. I breathe through my nostrils and put Gabriel down. Forcing my smile on my face as he looks at me with his big eyes, I calmly ask him, "Can you be a big boy and walk the rest of the way? I'll hold your hand."

Gabriel nods, reaching his little hand out for me to hold, and I do. My smile drops instantly once I stand back up and cut my eyes to Alejandro. He has no right to talk to Gabriel, especially about me. But obviously, he could care less. Even when I tell him to back off, Alejandro laughs, insisting that I have no manners, which is ironic since he was always the reckless one between the both of us.

As we continue to walk, I notice the look in his eyes start to change, and his cocky smirk flattens into a straight line upon his lips. He sighs and looks ahead before asking me, "How have you been? It's been what? Six...seven years, maybe?"

I keep my eyes forward, watching Ricardo and Yago as they continue to walk down the block, side-by-side, talking and laughing. It's as if they're best friends meant to be. I chuckle at the sight of Yago jumping up and down from whatever Ricardo tells him, and Ricardo laughs before throwing his arm around Yago, pulling him in closer as he starts to talk to Yago.

"It's like looking in a mirror, isn't it?" Alejandro speaks up, watching them as well.

He's not entirely wrong. Back then, that used to be us—me and Alejandro. We were always together, whenever we were given a chance to be. And it's not like I spotted Alejandro and decided to follow behind him like a lost puppy. He chose me. Honest to God, he did. But it wasn't meant to happen. I was in a fight with some kid from my class during recess. Alejandro then stepped in and clocked the kid's lights out.

Alejandro helped me up and dusted me off. I remember him looking me square in the eyes, telling me that I had a lot of heart for a little guy, which really pissed me off because I didn't like it when people called me "little." Hence why the fight happened in the first place. But ever since that day, Alejandro had been by my side, teaching me how to fight on my own.

It was a blessing and a curse, but I liked being around him. Even when my parents didn't want me to be around Alejandro. They were very vocal that he came from trouble, considering that his older brother—I think—was always involved in some shady business, and their parents were no better. But I was a kid. I didn't care. Alejandro was the one good friend I had at the time. I even remember Morris-Lina having a stupid crush on him, and Alejandro would get annoyed, but he would never mistreat her.

But then, one day, everything between us just stopped.

Alejandro dropped out of school and vanished off the face of the earth. No matter how many times I tried to call him, he never answered. I would sneak off to his house, and he never responded. No one would ever answer. Even though my parents made me stop seeing him, I still thought about him, but he didn't give a rat's ass about me.

Now, here he is years later, walking beside me, insisting that whatever bond Yago has with Ricardo is similar to the two of us. I get a bad taste in my mouth at the thought and snort.

I think to myself, *Sí, cómo no*, and roll my eyes.

"Maybe in an alternate universe," I mutter under my breath as I step over the uneven part of the sidewalk.

With a smirk and a 'pft' escaping his lips, Alejandro shakes his head, looking down. "I won't take it personally. I mean..." He shrugs his shoulders, stuffing his hands into the pockets of his jean jacket. He lifts his head, and I feel his eyes on me. "You did help my sister out, after all. So, you can't be too cold, then."

"I was never *cold*, to begin with," I blurt, whipping my attention to him. "Plus..." I shrug. "She didn't deserve that." I can barely look him in the eye. "It's the least I could've done."

I clear my throat, hoping to get rid of the ball that suddenly forms in my throat as we get closer to the next street corner. Yago and Ricardo stand back from the street crossing and are near the white picket fence outside somebody's house.

As we reach the boys, Alejandro goes, "I'm sorry about your sister, by the way." I freeze and look at him. His eyes are soft, and his lips are parted as if he regrets mentioning her. I doubt he does, but all I'm wondering is how the hell he knows about Morris-Lina. It's been years since he's talked to her...since he's spoken to me. There's no way he should know about her. But then Alejandro adds, "Word gets out. One day I was at Pérez's shop and heard him talking about it with someone. It was your dad, I think. The man hasn't aged a day since I last saw him."

Of course. That makes total sense. Just by chance, Alejandro happens to be in the same door as my dad and learns about what happened to Morris-Lina. I should be angry, but it's not his fault for hearing about it. If anything, my dad didn't have to share anything with Mr. Pérez. It doesn't matter how long we've known the guy and how close he is with the family. They're talking about our private family matters in the middle of Mr. Pérez's store—a public place. It's bad enough people at school don't cut me a break about it. It's no one's business, especially not Alejandro's!

Then I wonder how long Alejandro's probably known about it, and I figure that if Alejandro was really sorry, he could've reached out then and said something. But instead, he chooses *NOW* to say something? Now, as I'm standing here around children! But then, I also have to consider the fact that I doubt he would've had any way to contact me since it's been so long since we've seen each other.

Regardless of the case, dad shouldn't be talking about *my* twin sister all willy-nilly. Not everyone needs to have the inside scoop on the Gonzalez household. It's bad enough we're already the freak show of our neighborhood.

I feel a tug on the sleeve of my jacket, and I look down at Gabriel. I bend down, asking him what's wrong. As usual, he just points instead of actually speaking. He points to his stomach and then to his mouth. I figure he's probably hungry. So I nod and ruffle his hair.

"We're going home, okay? I'll feed you." I smile at him.

I stand up straight and clear my throat. "Yago!"

Yago whips his head around, looking at me, and I motion for him to come with me. He sighs, giving Ricardo a fist bump before coming over to me.

"Hold on!"

I look back at Alejandro as he digs in his pocket and takes out a small piece of paper with the edges ripped and a pen. I watch as he scribbles on the paper, using his palm as a surface before handing the piece of paper to me.

"That way, you don't forget me this time," he says, a smirk curling on the one side of his mouth.

I take the paper and realize there are different numbers on it with his initials above the numbers. I gulp.

Then I think about his words...

"That way, don't forget me this time."

What is that supposed to mean?

He's the one who left me when I tried to reach out to him!

I shake myself out of my thoughts, and I slip the paper into my pants pocket before grabbing hold of Yago's hand so we can cross the street. I get another glance at Alejandro as he grabs Ricardo's hand before turning back to me.

He winks. "See you around, shot glass."

My jaw tightens as he and Ricardo cross the intersection to get to the opposite side of the street.

I feel another tug on my sleeve, and I look down at Gabriel. He makes a whining sound, and I sigh.

"Okay, we're going, we're going," I reassure him as I tighten my hold on him and Yago as we cross the street.

April.

Week 2, Tuesday

Everything absolutely blows. The past couple of weeks have been absolutely "riveting." My previous counseling sessions with Counselor Malik have been a complete and total bust, which shouldn't have surprised me, considering that all the guy does is look at me up and down, ready my journal, and then come up with some bullshit philosophy on whatever my "issues" are. The issues he says I have, I know damn well that I don't have. My only issues are people who think they know everything when they don't—like him. I don't care that he's just doing his job anymore. He sits there and diagnoses me without even batting an eyelash, and then he'll sit there, wondering why I don't like talking to him. It's because Counselor Malik is insane. Him, my parents, everyone—especially Alejandro. My God! That guy just won't get off my back. Everywhere I turn, he's there. I have seen him since I bumped into him while picking the boys up from school a few weeks ago. It's like he's tracking me down, which I don't understand because I haven't called him. I doubt he knows where I live either because I'll never see him around my neighborhood, which brings me sweet relief! Dios mío!

Maybe I should call him and tell him to back off. But then again, I don't want him to start tracking me once he does have my number. I haven't told anyone about him either. Not my parents, not Counselor Malik, not even my friends. How can I? My parents will probably think I'm crazy, Counselor Malik will probably ask me many questions on how I feel, and my friends....especially Christopher...will likely encourage me to talk to him, which I don't want. They don't know him like I do.

I don't know what Morris-Lina would do if she were in my shoes. Honest to God, I wish she was, and then I'd be in hers. It'd be better that way, maybe.--D.G.

I hold the door open for Meagan, allowing her to enter the parlor, and she looks back at me with a slight smirk on her face as she thanks me. I nod.

I decided to treat her to some fried ice cream right after school since she was feeling a bit anxious about her personal reflection essay that she turned in to Mr. Acosta for her English III class with him. The essay was due a while ago—about a month or two ago, actually. But Mr. Acosta recently decided to hold individual meeting sessions with students in that class to discuss their papers. Turns out, he wasn't impressed by the majority of the essays he's read, but I assured Meagan that her paper was probably the best overall. She said that he gave her a few critiques, but she wished she had done better.

I remember her going, *"It wasn't as in-depth as he wanted it to be. God, I should've known!"*

And I remember thinking to myself that Mr. Acosta needed to remove whatever stick was up in his ass pronto. The others—Chris, Car, Pete, and Benny—even tried convincing her that she probably did okay, but Meagan was in her own world, stressing. So, after the fifth class period, I messaged Meagan, asking her if she'd be down for some fried ice cream from the parlor in Chinatown. She sent me a thumbs-up followed by a smiley face as confirmation.

I would've invited the others, but I know Meagan has a curfew, and if everyone else tagged along, we'd be out late. Plus, I know Christopher had made plans to spend time with Carmen tonight. I think he's taking her out to some Italian restaurant. I remember him telling Peter and me about it, and the two of us were clowning him, asking Christopher if he was going to propose, and he just glared at us for not taking him seriously.

Honestly, it wouldn't surprise me if Christopher did hint at proposing to Carmen *eventually*. For now, he might as well whip out a promise ring as a start-up. Both of them remind me of Jaxton and Renei from *Allegiance Society*—only Carmen and Christopher are more lovey-dovey than Jaxton and Renei. Their journey to each other, however, seems similar. It took almost forever for Jaxton and Renei to realize their feelings for each other, and once they did, it took an eternity for them to finally get together. I remember reading some comments on this fandom website, and people swore up and down that Renei would end up with Agron, but that was a massive *no*! Not only would it have seemed typical for the male lead to end up with the troubled girl who was trying to find her way through life, but their story would also be tedious and insanely toxic.

Meanwhile, Jaxton and Renei are fantastic together. They're real because they're not perfect, and they don't try to be. Plus, they bring out the best in each other.

I remember when Meagan asked me how I felt about Renei and Jaxton being together, and I immediately responded, *"Team Renaxton, all the way,"* much to her dismay. It didn't surprise me that she was Team Agrenei since she's a sucker for Agron Melhart.

Ugh.

But the thing is, it was bound for Renaxton to happen in the anime, anyway. It happened in the manga. The writers for the anime would've been flogged and shot by the fandom for changing *that* part of the storyline since Jaxton and Renei's relationship is extremely crucial to Renei's character development.

Sheesh.

I feel Meagan bump her elbow against my arm as she lightly rocks side-to-side, playfully. I shift my gaze away from the large menu board of different flavors, and my attention falls to Meagan. The one side of my mouth pulls upward as she gazes at me with a childish grin while rocking on her heels before whipping her gaze to the giant menu board as we stand at the counter.

"What're you going to get?" she asks me.

I shrug, looking back at the menu. "The snickerdoodle? Maybe the cheesecake? Either one sounds good. You?"

She sighs, pressing her lips together, still eying the menu. "The cinnamon crunch seems good." Her eyes widen, and she practically springs up on her toes. "Ooo! How 'bout the crunchy birthday cake?!"

I swear, if she were an anime character, there'd be giant stars in her eyes and little stars sparkling around her. I'd be a liar if I didn't admit that her enthusiasm was kind of adorable. In a friendly sense, of course.

Still, I chuckle, shaking my head. "Whatever your heart desires, my fair lady." I feign an English accent and take a step back to bow, earning a tiny giggle from Meagan.

When I stand upright, one of the workers makes his way to the counter and asks us what we would like. I decide to go with the snickerdoodle while Meagan orders the crunchy birthday cake, asking for rainbow sprinkles as a topping.

The worker smiles at her and winks. "Sure thing."

I feel a strong tug in my throat and press my lips together. I figure the guy is just a decent guy, but at the same time, he didn't have to overdo it. When I look to Meagan, she twists her lips into a faint smile, looking off to the side of the different tubs of ice cream behind the glass. Judging by the smirk, she must've been flattered by his charm. Then again, I doubt it. I doubt they even know each other—he's just a guy who works here and uses his charm to earn some tips.

I roll my eyes, telling myself to shrug it off as I pay the guy.

The guy gives me a look, arching his eyebrow, and I tighten my jaw. I watch as he starts up the iron to do whatever he has to do, and Meagan taps my shoulder, gesturing for us to sit at one of the available booths. We sit at a booth near one of the windows as we wait for our fried ice creams.

As we sit across from each other, I notice Meagan unconsciously picking at her nails as she keeps her hands on the table while blankly staring out the window. The neon colors from the OPEN sign flash on her face, and her eyes suddenly look vibrant. I notice how plump her lips are as she keeps her head turned to the side, and her face seems smoother without her makeup, even though she resents her dark spots.

I clear my throat. I knock on the table, and Meagan snaps back into reality, looking at me with her eyes big and concerned. She chews on her bottom lip, still picking at her nails.

I snort, shaking my head. "Cut your nails a break, kid. You're going to end up with nothing but skin."

Meagan realizes that she's picking her nails and swiftly stuffs her hands into the pockets of her black cardigan. She slumps down into the seat, her bottom lip slightly poked out and her cheeks looking rounder like plums.

I sigh, knowing she's still beating herself up about that damn essay she had to write for Mr. Acosta. I lean forward and knock on the table.

"Earth to Meagan! Hello!" I whisper while continuing to knock on the wooden table.

Meagan swats at my hand, making me stop.

"Cut it out," she huffs, sitting up with her elbows propped up on the table and her chin resting on the back of her hands. She takes a quick glance at me as I wiggle my eyebrows, and then she looks away. A chuckle slips from her lips. "I can't with you."

I shrug. "Made you laugh, though." I sit back, stretching my legs out a bit under the table, crossing my right ankle over my left to get comfortable. "But seriously, what's going on in that big brain of yours?"

Meagan furrows her eyebrows. "Are you saying that I have a big head?" She tries to sound offended, but the smirk that plays on her mouth makes her seem amused.

"I also said you have a big brain, so," I smirk.

Meagan rolls her eyes, the one side of her mouth slightly pulling upward.

When the guy calls for us, we turn our heads, letting us know that our ice creams are done. I grab them from the counter underneath the sign PICK-UP, and Meagan gets us our spoons and a couple of napkins.

As soon as I give Meagan her fried ice cream in a cup, she takes a small bite with her spoon once we sit down. A soft, low moan comes from her the second the ice cream enters her mouth. I feel my cheeks burn a bit, but at the same time, I can't help laughing at how ridiculously childish she looks right now.

Meagan opens her eyes, looking right at me.

"What?" she asks, taking another bite out of her fried ice cream.

I shake my head. "Nothing."

I take a bite out of mine. Instantly, I taste the cinnamon and the swirl of vanilla. My taste buds start dancing from the flavors exploding in my mouth as a crunch comes after. I breathe through my nose, taking it in.

Suddenly, I hear Meagan ask me, "How's yours?"

I nod, taking another bite. "Good." I point to hers with my spoon. "Is yours as good as you make it seem?"

"Shut up," Meagan mutters from embarrassment as she puts another spoonful in her mouth.

I raise my eyebrows, tilting my head. "It's good that you like it. If not, I'd find somewhere else for us to go to cheer you up."

"It's fried ice cream, Donny. Of course, I like it."

"Noted."

As I return to my fried ice cream, Meagan reaches over, her spoon taking a small amount of mine from my cup. I look up as she quickly draws her spoon back and puts it in her mouth, letting it linger so she can take in the taste of my fried ice cream. I just look at her, smirking, but she stares out the window again.

I honestly don't mind. Even if she wants to take another bite out of my ice cream, I still wouldn't care. It's just funny how nervous she suddenly looks. Knowing Meagan, she's probably wondering why the hell I'm not saying anything to her about it. Regardless, I just press my lips together, looking down at the spot where she snatched herself a scoop of my ice cream.

I take a bite.

Meagan finally turns her gaze back to me as she proceeds to eat her own fried ice cream, and I narrow up my gaze. When her lips curve sweetly, I feel my heart thump heavily in my chest, but I just take another bite out of my fried ice cream.

Once we're done eating, we throw our trash away before heading out of the parlor.

I check the time on my watch.

It's only 5:15 PM, which isn't bad.

I ask Meagan if there's anything specific she would want to do, and she shrugs, insisting that taking her out for fried ice cream is enough. She then nudges her arm against mine playfully.

"Thanks. I haven't had fried ice cream in a bit," Meagan says as we start walking down the street.

I throw my arm around her, pulling her in closer to me. I told her that it was no problem, and she looked up at me, smiling faintly. Her arms then come around my waist to hug me, and her head rests against my shoulder. I feel my cheeks start to burn as I keep my arm around her, letting my hand fall over her shoulder.

I snicker, trying to settle the rapidness of my heart all of a sudden. "C'mon, you're such a softie, kid," I tease, trying to keep my voice straight as Meagan lifts her head to get a look at me.

Meagan snorts, rolling her eyes. "You're the one who took me to get fried ice cream."

"And? You earned it."

"Oh really?" *So doubtful.*

I look her in the eye. "Really."

She grins. Meagan lets her arms fall from my waist, and she pulls her cardigan closed as a breeze hits us. I pull her closer into me, hoping that'll somewhat help keep her warm as we continue to walk down the street.

As we turn the corner to get to my car, I hear someone say my name, and my chest tightens. I tell myself to keep walking without even looking up, but stupidly, I dare myself to lift my eyes up from the ground. My legs stop moving, and my lips become terribly dry in seconds.

You. Have got. To be. SHITTING ME!

Alejandro looks right at me with a smirk plastered on his face. With every step he takes to approach me, I tighten my jaw and feel my fist tighten by my side.

How the hell did he even find me?

I swear to God, he probably snuck into my room and planted a chip in my head or is tracking my car somehow! Of all days and times for him to pop up out of the blue, it's NOW!

Dammit.

"What's good, shot glass?"

My blood boils, and it takes everything in me to not cuss him out. Maybe if I had in the past, he'd get the hint that I didn't want to be bothered with him. Better yet, a square, solid punch to the face would make the message real clear to him.

I glare at him.

"Alejandro—"

"Who's this?"

I realize that Alejandro's referring to Meagan as his eyes lock with hers and a playful grin curls on his face. I tighten my jaw, repeatedly telling myself to hold it together.

Then, Meagan smiles at Alejandro before telling him her name.

"Meagan," she grins.

Alejandro's smirk turns sinister as he switches his attention to me. "You sly dog, you. Your charm always did get you the pretty ones." He then cuts his eyes to Meagan, winking at her.

She lets out a shaky chuckle, waving her hands defensively. "No, no. We're just friends."

Alejandro shrugs. "I know *you* probably believe in that theory."

That's it!

I take a step forward, evading Alejandro's personal space while looking him right in the eye. I feel my fist tighten by my side as I speak to him through my teeth.

"Why are you here?" I ask him, my blood pressure rising.

Snickering, Alejandro folds his arms over his chest, unfazed. "I'm meeting up with someone." He tilts his head. "Hope that doesn't seem to bother you. After all, you seem to have your hands full." He winks at Meagan.

I notice Meagan chew inside of her bottom lip as she fidgets, playing with her fingers. She is probably just as uncomfortable as I was in Alejandro's presence. Or maybe she feels embarrassed for some reason. I don't know why she would, but I know Meagan more than he ever will.

I clear my throat and tell Meagan to give me one second before I grab Alejandro's arm, pulling him off to the side and away from Meagan. He yanks his arm from my grip, hissing from where I grabbed him. It would've brought me joy if I had done some type of damage to his arm somehow. Maybe then he'll wipe that dumb smirk off his face.

I get up in his face, keeping my voice is low, so only he can hear me since I don't want Meagan to question what's going on. "What the *hell* is your problem?"

Alejandro keeps his eyes on me, not even blinking. "I don't have a problem. You're the one with the problem."

Is he serious?!

"Bullshit!" I hiss through my teeth. "You keep following me everywhere, so what gives?"

"Who says I'm following you? Just because we happen to be in the same places doesn't mean you're the attraction of my day. Get over yourself."

"You get over *yourself*!"

Alejandro rolls his eyes. "Look. We just happened to bump into each other. If I was stalking you, I would've done something at this point, but I haven't, so relax."

I sigh, studying his face. I can tell from the softness of his eyes that he's trying to be sincere. I also pay attention to his eyebrow since it usually twitches when he's lying—from what I remember.

Nothing. He's in the clear.

I turn my attention over to Meagan, and I see her walking in circles while on the phone. I figure her mom probably called her to check on her since...that's just what her mom does. I can't really say it's a "mom-thing" since my mom hardly calls me.

"She seeing anyone?" I hear Alejandro ask, pulling my attention back to him from his stupid words.

I tighten my jaw. "Why?" I ask firmly.

"Well, you two are only friends, right? You could've fooled me. She's cute. *Real* cute," he eggs on.

"No way." The words come out harshly as intended.

Alejandro holds up his hands defensively. "Okay, okay. No need to get so possessive."

My eyes widen, and my breath hitches. "I am not possessive!"

He arches an eyebrow, looking me up and down with that dumb smirk on his face. My blood starts to boil as I tighten my jaw. He has some nerve saying such ridiculous things. The only reason why I'll never let him three feet near Meagan is that he's...*him!*

Not because I'm possessive.

Meagan deserves someone worthy, and Alejandro isn't that someone. I don't even think she's been in a relationship before. Her mom is *way* too protective, and Lord knows what her dad is probably like—even though I remember Meagan telling me that her parents aren't really together anymore. Plus, Meagan is smart. She wouldn't set herself up for that. She'd wait it out, I'll bet.

Then, here comes Alejandro—saying all sorts of bullshit.

I try to walk away because I know that I'll end up punching his lights out, but Alejandro manages to grab my shoulder, making me face him again.

I push his hand off me as he steps forward, shrinking the space between us.

Alejandro sucks his teeth. "You don't have to be so cold."

I snort. "You've got some nerve."

A chuckle comes from him. "I know." He clears his throat. "But in all seriousness, Don. It's been God knows how long. The least we can do is catch up."

Is he joking, or for real?

I shake my head, trying not to laugh. He shows up after all these years and expects us to "catch up" as if we hadn't seen each other in weeks. He's right—it has been a long time. He's the one who didn't answer my calls and didn't reach out to me when I tried reaching out to him! *I* at least tried to make an effort to stay in touch with him. He never did.

I scoff. "No chan—"

"It's been years, Donald. Yet, here we are. Reunited from *you* getting *your* ass kicked, and I had to help you out. Like old times." I feel his warm breath against my ear when he leans in closer to whisper, making my heart lodge up my throat. "If you ask me, it seems like you're the one with the problem."

I give him a side-eye look as he tightens his jaw, taking a step back while his hazel eyes remain on me through his long eyelashes.

The feeling in my stomach starts to bubble, and an unsatisfying taste comes up in my mouth. The more Alejandro looks at me, the sicker I feel. I take a quick look back at Meagan, seeing that she is still on the phone, nodding her head and huffing.

I have to get Meagan home.

I don't even bother checking the time. I just know that I have to get her home, or else she'll face her mother's wrath.

I turn my attention back to Alejandro, letting out a deep sigh.

"Fine," I get out.

Alejandro arches an eyebrow. "Fine?"

I roll my eyes. Judging from the smirk on his face, Alejandro knows what I mean, but he continues to play dumb to piss me off.

Still, I tell him, "I'll do whatever you want. We'll catch up or whatever."

He nods, pursing his lips. "Sounds good. Free tomorrow?"

I nod, looking away from him.

"Cool. I'll see you tomorrow then. Five o'clock at Papa Dicky's."

I furrow my eyebrows. Papa Dicky's is the old pizza joint we used to go to when we were kids, sometimes after school to hang out. It's not far from our old school, but I thought it was closed down at some point. I remember mom telling me that she didn't want me around there anymore since it was closing down for infestation problems, and she didn't want me to get sick. Unless she lied.

Alejandro pats my shoulder, about to walk by me, but then he stops in his tracks. Close to my ear with a smirk on his face, he says, "Seriously, work on getting that knife, shot glass." I notice his eyes falling on Meagan, and he smirks. "You got precious cargo."

As he walks past me, my nostrils flare as I breathe through my nose. My jaw tight, I ball up my fist, keeping it by my side. I turn around, only seeing his back as he walks away.

"Don't call me that!" I blurt out.

Alejandro just waves me off, still keeping his back to me as he reaches the crosswalk. I watch as he crosses the street to get to the other side. I look past him, seeing a guy with a shaved head and wearing a dark grey hoodie standing by at the street corner. Once Alejandro makes it across the street, the two of them greet each other, smacking their hands together in a handshake before bumping their shoulders together.

He really was just meeting someone.

Obviously. Why would he lie?

I shake my head.

I notice Meagan stuffing her phone back into her pants pocket before coming over to me. She looks drained. Her eyes are tired, and her shoulders are a bit hunched forward. If Alejandro hadn't popped up out of nowhere and been so damn weird, I would've had Meagan home by now. If that was her mom on the phone, her mom probably had some words for her.

I dare myself to check the time on my watch—*5:50 PM.*

Mierda!

That probably was her mom on the phone. Dammit.

"Hey, kid," I say to Meagan as she rests her head against my shoulder, groaning. I wrap my arm around her, guiding her over to my car. "I'm sorry about all that."

Meagan looks up at me and shrugs her shoulders. "All good." She lifts her head off my shoulder when we get to my car. I dig through my jacket pocket, pulling out my car keys so I can unlock the car and open the front passenger's door for her. Then I hear her ask me, "Everything good with you?"

My throat tightens, but I nod, smiling weakly. "Yeah."

I open the door for her, and she steps into the car. I close the door shut and hurry over to the driver's side and get into the car, closing the door shut once I'm in the seat.

As I start up the engine, Meagan asks me, "Who was that, by the way?"

I strap myself in. I exhale through my nose, feeling my shoulders tense up as I focus on pulling off.

"Neighbor's kid," I respond, keeping my voice straight.

Week 2, Tuesday

I really don't feel like going to school. After the run-in with Alejandro yesterday, I'd rather just stay put in bed, not having to deal with anyone. But, mom and dad made it clear that I have to go one way or another no matter how I'm feeling. Meagan texted me that she didn't get in trouble with her mom since her mom still wasn't home yet. Lucky her, but I'm glad that she didn't feel her mother's wrath. Me, on the other hand, my parents had plenty to say to me last night. They didn't care that I didn't come home right after school because...why would they? They were just in my ear about college and skipping out on my counseling session with Counselor Malik yesterday. The only reason they found out about it was that Counselor Malik reached out to them, wondering if I was at home, sick. Honestly, after my last session with him, I would've been able to sit still and listen to whatever Counselor Malik had to say to me. That's something my parents will never seem to get through their skulls. It's one thing to sit down and actually feel like you're getting help, but it's another thing when someone makes you feel helpless. One thing I'm not is "broken," and Counselor Malik enjoys pushing that idea out there.

And the whole "college talk" is a bunch of nonsense. My parents already know that I've applied to four colleges—two in Europe and a few here in the U.S. Whatever the outcome is satisfactory for me as long as it keeps them happy and out of my face. Jesus. --D.G.

Everything about today was a total bust. Classes. My session with Counselor Malik since I bailed yesterday. Everything. My morning started off like usual—me waking up to the sound of my parents arguing over God knows what. Then, I dragged my butt to school against my will, and that was a shit show. Surprisingly, Meagan wasn't in school since I didn't see her during our first class period. I sent her a text asking her where she was, and she responded that she had a cardiology appointment this morning. I figured it was probably because of something important since Meagan takes attendance very seriously. I feel bad that she had to miss out on today since Mr. Enrique had the class play this bizarre math game, and the class was divided into two teams. It was pretty fun, but everyone on my team was an asshole since they wouldn't choose me to represent the team on specific questions unless I blurted out an answer against their wishes. They should've been grateful because I got most of the questions right. So.

Then, Mr. Aziz thought it would be a good idea to split our gym class into two teams for a volleyball game, and of course, Nathan had to be on my team. I swear, the universe just kept trying to find ways to screw me over. I wanted to make it evident to Nathan that I was not in the mood to talk to him since I had enough on my mind, but he still tried to make an effort to speak to me, asking me "small talk" questions—*"What's up?", "Anything new lately?"* and my personal favorite, *"How are you feeling?"*

God, I hate that question. *"How are you feeling?"*

That's a dumb question to ask someone. Unless the person is bleeding or in obvious physical pain, no one should ask someone that. Mainly to make small-talk.

Luckily for Nathan, I didn't ignore him the entire time. As much as I wanted to roll my eyes, not respond, I thought about Meagan and how much she wanted me to make an effort to be fair towards him. I thought about how she started calling him "Nate" whenever he was near or referred to him. I thought about how comfortable she's starting to get when around him in a matter of months. It seemed like yesterday when he approached her as part of a dare, and he made a fool of himself while clowning her. Nathan joined the theater eight months later, and Meagan calls him "Nate" as if they're buddy-buddy. Next, they'll probably be holding hands, laughing with each other. Maybe he'll stir up the courage and end up taking her out or something. But then, he'd hurt her, like he hurt Morris-Lina when they dated.

The hell am I saying? No way!

Blah!

Besides, I doubt Nathan even has feelings for Meagan. I know she doesn't have feelings for him. At least, I don't think she does. She couldn't. Not a chance. Meagan is not the type of girl to fall for the first guy she sees. Especially not a backstabbing clown, like Nathan Hendricks.

Sigh.

Aside from Nathan, there was Austin Brown I had to put up with also. Of course, we would be on opposing teams—Mr. Aziz probably thought he was doing me a favor since the last time Austin and I were on the same team for something, it ended with half the class having to pry us off of each other as I gave Austin a good punch in the mouth.

That happened a couple months ago, and I was surprised that neither of us had been suspended or got detention. Instead, Mr. Aziz gave us a warning, as did Principal Vickins. I usually don't get warnings. I'll get scolded, and Principal Vickins will double-down on my counseling sessions with Counselor Malik as my punishment—although she didn't see it as a punishment, and more so as a way of helping me as if I have a HELP WANTED sign on my back.

I didn't need more counseling sessions with Malik. So, I had to keep myself together during the rest of the gym period. No matter how many times Austin called me "wetback" or dared himself to get all in my personal space in the locker room, I did all I could to let it roll off my back. I even stayed in the showers a little longer, hoping that he'd be gone by the time I was done. But he wasn't. It was like he was waiting for me.

Even as I was getting dressed, Austin wouldn't shut the hell up.

He asked me, *"You got something to hide, Gonzalez? We've been over this. We're all men here. Unless you got a dolly situation down there."* He referred to the fact that I had kept my towel wrapped around me as I was trying to change.

I flipped him off, earning a cackle from him.

He looked at his minions. *"Awww. I must've struck a nerve."*

I heard movement all of a sudden, and when I turned around from my locker, Austin towered over me, bumping me back into the cold metal of my locker. I clenched my jaw, wanting to deck Austin right in the face to wipe that damn smirk off his face.

Instead, someone called out to him, telling him to, *"Fuck off!"*

We both looked over, and Erik Petrov started to approach Austin with a stern look, and he kept his fists tight by his sides.

Austin scoffed at Erik's attempt of intimidation. It's not that Erik was a little guy. Austin was just a huge dick.

He glared at Erik, going, *"I don't think anyone scheduled a tea party for you, Petrov. So shut it."*

Another voice went, *"Seriously, Austin."* It was Nathan. *"Beat it."*

Nathan was all up in Austin's face, giving him the most intense glare I've ever seen. I thought daggers were going to start shooting from his eyes.

Austin snorted a chuckle before cutting his eyes to me. If he had said one more thing, I probably would've ended up clocking him. But he just looked at me up and down with disgust written all over his face before finally walking off as if he had just proven something of himself.

Erik then asked me if I was alright, and I gave him a nod. I was a bit taken aback because Erik had the balls to tell Austin off since I sometimes saw them hanging out in the hallway. Them and a couple other guys on the lacrosse team. And yet, Erik patted my shoulder and told me to take it easy. Before he left, Erik gave Nathan a fist bump, telling him that he would see Nathan later.

Nathan then gave me this weird look—like he was sad but was also relieved. He asked me if I was good, and I just nodded my head rather than opening my mouth. Still, Nathan pressed his together in a tight half-smile.

"I'm surprised you didn't knock him out when you had the chance."

Nathan was trying to make small talk again. I could've just shrugged and left it at that, but I kind of did owe him one. He and Erik stepped in, preventing me from being sent to the main office, only for Vickins to add another counseling session to attend this week.

So, I shrugged and responded with, *"Next time, I won't be so merciful."*

Nathan just snorted, a faint smirk forming on his face. Nathan told me that he would see me around, and I watched as he walked by me. I wanted to slam my head into a brick wall until my brain became nothing but goop and mush.

I should've been grateful when school had ended for the day, but as I was getting my things together, I remembered that I had agreed to meet Alejandro after school at Papa Dicky's. I wanted to scream, ask God why He couldn't just spare me this one time. It's bad enough that I had to put up with bullshit all day at school—I didn't want to deal with more bullshit outside of school. I wanted to go home, do my homework, maybe cook something for dinner to get my mind off things, and then go to bed.

Instead, I'm in my car, driving to Papa Dicky's to meet the last person I would want to talk to right now. Or ever.

Make a right turn on Thelmen Street, the GPS notifies me.

I sigh.

I've already passed the elementary school where Alejandro and I attended before the building was condemned. The playground filled with nothing but tall weeds growing in between the cement cracks, vines stretching all on the walls, windows busted, and graffiti terribly sprayed on random parts of the building. I remember when they decided to have the school up for a lease, but I guess no one ever took action since the school is now another rundown lost cause in Philly. I remember how it used to look. I remember the hallways always been clean, the floors would gleam from the bright indoor lights, and the tips of sneakers would speak when rubbed against the floor just right. I remember round tables in the cafeteria and how every room in the school seemed to stretch out, looking more extensive than expected. The gym was better than the playground, having more space and even a pool for students on the swim team.

I remember thinking that I wasn't good enough to go to a school like that—Bishop Cardwell Academy. I remember getting shoved in the hallways by the other kids, and they would never fail to remind me that I was beneath them since most of them came from upper-class lifestyles. To them, there was no such thing as "middle-class." You were either rich or poor. But not all of the students were like that, though.

I remember this one girl—Sabine Chase. She came from a good home, was adopted by a wealthy white couple, and always wore her hair in a puffy ponytail. She never straightened her hair, and I remember her getting mocked for it, which really pissed me off since I thought she looked lovely. Sabine was just a nice person overall. She never bad-mouthed anyone, and she'd always sit with me at lunch. She even invited me to a few of her birthday parties.

Now that I think about it, Sabine was a bit like Meagan, only I was the one who approached Meagan. Sabine had come to me. I also remember having a bit of a crush on her at some point, and Alejandro dared me to kiss her, but I never did.

I didn't have my first kiss until I was ten, and it was with Amanda Rose—a red-head with freckles and dimples. I don't even remember why I kissed Amanda Rose. I remember feeling sick about it because it felt weird at first. We were on a field trip, and Sabine was supposed to be my partner, but instead, she was partnered with Alejandro, and she didn't like Alejandro since she—like everyone else—thought he was a troublemaker. I ended up being partnered with Amanda Rose, and at some point, Amanda and I wandered off to check something out. We were alone, and for a second, I guess I thought she was kind of pretty—but looking back, she was a bit weird-looking. Her eyes were way too big for her head, and her lips were hardly visible. And yet, I kissed her for some reason.

I probably should've waited to kiss the right person, but I was ten. What the hell did I know?

Besides, the look on Alejandro's face when I told him that I kissed Amanda Rose that same day was priceless. His eyes wide, his jaw practically on the floor, and the corners of his mouth curled a bit. He ruffled my hair, saying that he was proud of me. I could tell he meant it too since his smile was huge, and he threw his arm around my neck, pulling me close to him. It was probably the first time I actually felt proud of myself because Alejandro was happy...for me—

About a quarter-mile, the destination is on your left. Papa Dicky's Pizzeria.

The GPS brings me out of my thoughts, and I tighten my grip on the steering wheel. I feel my stomach twist in knots at the very thought of sitting across from Alejandro. I should be used to the idea of being around him since he's been like a ninja, popping up at random everywhere I turn. Running into him yesterday shouldn't have surprised me as much as it did, now that I think about it.

Although, Meagan being there made things ten times worse.

Not cool at all.

As much as I wanted to shove him and make it clear to him that I wanted him to leave me alone, agreeing to meet up with him was probably the best option. I had to think about Meagan being there. Yesterday was about *her.* I wanted to make sure that she was feeling better. So causing a scene because of Alejandro would've been the wrong move for me to make.

Just keep it together, Donald. Keep it together.

I turn my car into the parking lot the second I spot the familiar flashing neon sign outside the pizzeria. I find a spot to park and turn off the GPS on my phone before going in.

. . . .

"Would you like a refill?" the waitress asks me in her perky voice, pulling my attention up to her and away from the window. She holds the pitcher of ice water while keeping her doe-eyes on me.

I clear my throat, nodding slightly. I watch as the waitress pours the water into my glass.

"Still waiting for someone?" she asks.

I shrug, still watching the water rise in the glass as a few ice cubs fall in. "Kind of," I tell her.

I cut my gaze to the clock behind her, mounted on the wall. It's been over twenty minutes. I thought Alejandro would've been here already once I pulled up. It baffled me that he wasn't already here since the Alejandro I remembered didn't believe in tardiness. No matter the circumstance, Alejandro was always on time—especially for something *he* arranged.

Maybe this is a sign. Honestly, I can just up and leave and pray to God that I don't ever run into Alejandro ever again.

I turn my attention back to the waitress as she finally stops pouring the water. I take the glass, bringing it to my lips as I tell her, "Thank you."

She nods. "Of course." She watches me as I take a sip, and I notice the expression on her face suddenly shift. It's as if she feels guilty or sad. She then sighs. "Don't beat yourself, hun. Dating is hard, but getting stood up isn't the worst thing. Trust me."

I catch her words, and I nearly choke on the water I'm drinking as I notice the waitress walk away. I whip my head around, looking back at her, but she's already back in the kitchen before I can say anything.

I groan, rolling my eyes.

I grab a napkin from the holder and wipe my mouth. I take another look at the clock, watching the seconds tick away.

This is stupid.

I rub my eyebrows and take another sip of water. I suddenly feel something brush against my leg, and I flinch. I notice the tattooed hand stretched out on the surface of the table as movement comes from across the table.

"Sorry I'm late," Alejandro grunts as he makes himself comfortable. "I had some business to take care of."

I dare myself to look up at him, and I feel my chest tighten at the sight of his cheeky grin. His hair is styled in a side fringe, pushed off to the left side of his face, showing off the undercut on the right side of his head and most of the streaks of silver in his hair. Still, he wears his jean jacket but keeps the sleeves rolled halfway up his forearm, showing off some of the intricate tattoos on his skin.

"Wanna take a picture?" Alejandro pipes up, propping his elbows upon the table before resting his chin on top of his laced fingers. "I've never seen that look in your eye before. Is it the hair?"

Son of a bitch.

I clench my jaw. "Screw you."

Alejandro jerks his head back, putting his hand over his heart.

I roll my eyes, taking another gulp of water. I waited almost half an hour for this clown, and now he wants to make jokes as if everything's all good. The only reason I agreed to meet him is that I want him to get off my back. After this little "catch-up" session is over, that's it. The next time I see Alejandro, I'll probably knock his lights out.

Alejandro grabs the menu off the table and opens it up, letting it cover the bottom half of his face as he sets it up in his lap.

"Did you order yourself something already or…?" Alejandro trails off, his eyes still skimming down the menu.

I roll my eyes, sitting back in my seat with my arms crossed.

"No," I tell him, looking down at the table.

Alejandro gasps dramatically, his hand covering his mouth. I narrow my eyes to him as he coos, "Aww, you waited for me? That's so sweet." He snickers, the one side of his mouth pulling upward.

My pulse starts to race, and I tighten my fist as I keep my arms crossed over my stomach.

I glare at him. "You're not funny."

Alejandro snorts, eyes on the menu. "I'd always make you laugh, though."

"That was in the past." Frustration rings through my words effortlessly as I hold my gaze on Alejandro, even though he's not paying me any mind.

Alejandro cocks an eyebrow. "Doesn't mean it's a lie." He looks up at me, keeping his lips in a straight line as he puts the menu places the menu down on the table.

Dryness starts to tickle in my throat, and my palms start to sweat from tightening my fist. Alejandro folds his hands on the table, keeping his eyes locked on me as if he's trying to get a read of me. A strange feeling starts to stir in my stomach, and I drink some more water as the waitress suddenly pops up at our table.

As I lower my glass, I notice the twisted smirk on her lips.

"Well, looks like all's well end's well, huh?" She's talking to me.

I shake my head. "On the contrary."

The waitress chuckles before asking us what we would like to order. Alejandro orders himself a basket of rolls with olive oil, an appetizer, but he clarifies that's all he wants. I order myself a chocolate-chip cookie, and both the waitress and Alejandro look at me with confusion written over their faces.

I honestly don't care. I don't intend for this to take long anyway.

The waitress shrugs, taking the menu off of the table and tucking it under her arm. "I'll have your orders out in a jiffy." She looks back and forth at both of us. "Enjoy mingling." There is way too much enthusiasm in her voice, and she walks away, heading into the kitchen.

Alejandro watches as the waitress walks off. Once she's in the kitchen, he leans in, furrowing his eyebrows.

"Does she think we're...?" He points back-and-forth between the both of us, and I catch what he's implying.

I lightly shake the glass cup in my hand, hardly rattling the ice.

"Why do you think I only ordered a cookie," I tell him before taking a small ice cube into my mouth from the cup.

Alejandro huffs, shaking his head as if he's disappointed. "Just ordering a cookie doesn't necessarily scream something *not* being a date."

I roll my eyes, chewing the ice cube in my mouth until it dissolves.

"Whatever," I huff, gulping down the bits of ice. "This isn't a date."

Alejandro tilts his head, scrunching his face a bit. "Eh."

"Piss off," I mutter, looking away from him.

Alejandro quirks an eyebrow, letting out a small 'tsk' before sitting back in his seat. He reaches over and takes a napkin from the holder. I watch as he rips a tiny piece from the edge off of the napkin and leaves the rest of the napkin pushed off to the side. He starts to fiddle with the small piece in his hand, not looking at me once as he starts to speak. He asks me questions about my parents, wondering how they've been. He admits that it's probably a stupid question, considering what happened to Morris-Lina, but he insists that it's the thought that counts.

I find that statement quite amusing coming from him, of all people. *"It's the thought that counts."*

I have to bite down on the inside of my lip to prevent me from bursting into laughter, but a slight noise still manages to slip through my lips. Alejandro narrows his eyes up, giving me a deadpan look on his face as he suddenly stops fiddling with the piece of napkin in between his fingers.

He tilts his head, slightly leaning forward. "You got something you wanna say, Don?" There's a hint of mockery in his words as he squints his eyes a bit.

I shake my head, looking off to the side. "I'm all good. Just going with the flow. It's been like what, years since we've last seen each other, and here we are talking as if it was just yesterday you popped back from oblivion." I force myself to flash him a quick smile before I bring the glass of water to my lips, hoping to catch another ice cube in my mouth.

Alejandro shakes his head. Despite the slight grin playing on his mouth, I can see spite in his eyes as his jaw tightens.

"You've always been bad with your words." He starts to fiddle with the piece of paper in between his fingers. "No one wonder you always got your ass handed to you." A faint chuckle.

My grip on the cup tightens, and my pulse rises. If I could turn back time, I would. Then maybe he'll remember that most of the time I did get into fights, it was because of him. The way people looked at him and talked about him—it never sat well with me, and Alejandro knew that. The more I spent time with him, the more I started to notice how much people resented him. I never saw anything wrong with him. People would just make shit up so that way he'd fit how they wanted to see him.

Alejandro Reyes: The troublemaker. The good-for-nothing.

To me, he was anything but those things, and Alejandro knows that whenever someone thought otherwise, it'd piss me off.

And I remind Alejandro of that too, which shuts him up. He just looks at me with wide eyes as I remind him of all the times I would take up for him whenever someone bad-mouthed him or tried to make a fool of him. I do my best to keep my voice down as I feel my heart starting to race and my pulse rising. The only thing I can really hear is the sound of my heart thumping in my chest.

Alejandro just sits in silence, his nostrils flaring and his jaw clenched. I sit back in my seat, giving myself a chance to breathe. I nearly jump when a hand reaches in front of me, placing down a small basket of freshly baked rolls and then a small cup full of olive oil. I look up, realizing that it's only the waitress giving us our orders.

I clear my throat, forcing a faint smile on my face as she gives me my cookie on a small plate. She then asks me if I would like more water, and I realize that this will probably be my fifth glass of water. Still, I nod, and the waitress smiles.

"You boys enjoy yourselves. I'll be right back." She scurries back into the kitchen to get the pitcher of water.

I sigh, turning my attention to Alejandro. The way he looks at me makes my stomach twist in knots. His lips somewhat pursed, his right eyebrow quirked, and his eyes locked on me through his perfect lashes. The lighting in the restaurant somehow manages to show off his features better as the sun goes down outside. Probably because the restaurant lights are hardly dimmed, showing every detail of his face while making his eyes seem darker compared to when he's in the sunlight.

Alejandro shifts down to the basket of rolls in front of him and gestures towards them.

"Want one?" he asks, slightly pushing the basket forward to the center of the table.

I shake my head, breaking off a piece of my cookie. It breaks easily, and the chocolate chips are a bit gooey, indicating that it's fresh out of the oven. I pop the piece of cookie into my mouth, letting the taste melt into my mouth, sending me into an indescribable sensation.

I watch as Alejandro grabs a roll and breaks it in half. He puts one half back into the basket but dips the other into the plate of olive oil. He takes a bite and exhales.

As I take another bite out of my cookie, Alejandro comments about the food, saying that it's good. I couldn't agree more. I nod. He sits up straight and leans in so that I can hear him as he keeps his voice low for only me to listen to him.

"I didn't forget about all that stuff, you know." Alejandro licks his lips, keeping his eyes on me. My throat tightens, and my palms start to sweat, but I keep my hands in my lap. Alejandro clears his throat before adding on. "I thought about you too, you know. I thought about calling, but I figured after all these years, your number probably changed."

His eyes are soft, and he shifts his gaze down to the table. For the first time in a long time, I've never seen Alejandro like this. It's as if he's actually sorry, but he doesn't say the words. He just bites the corner of his bottom lip, tapping his finger against the wood of the table.

It takes me a second to actually process this.

Suddenly, he lifts his head and sits back into the seat with his arm stretched and his hand still on the table.

A chuckle spills from his mouth, and he smiles.

"Remember the last time we hung out? We were at my place, and we stayed in the basement because my brother and his boys were doing God knows what upstairs.

The two of us started talking about how shitty our lives were and how much we wanted to make a run for it." His smile starts to fade as he looks down off to the side. "I told you about how much my dad hated me, so you devised a plan for us to meet up that same night at the school and make a run for it. Maybe live with your grams for a while."

His jaw tightens, and his nostrils flare. His words start to quiver, but he clears his throat each time. "I tried calling you that night to see if you would come, but you never answered your phone. I tried about three times and still got nothing. Eventually, my dad found me at the school, dragged me back home."

A chuckle. "Next thing I knew, he brings me home, beats the crap out of me, and then…." He pauses, taking a sharp inhale. "…he dipped. My aunt took in me, Aitana, and my brother for a while. Then, my brother ended up skipping town for some time. I can't say he was any less harmless compared to my dad, though. He actually blames me for dad leaving us and has hated my guts ever since." The look in his eyes softens, and his face loses some of its colors. "But Aitana and I stayed with our aunt until we could move out on our own. Aitana was able to get our old house back, and we moved back here to Philly."

Alejandro quirks an eyebrow, looking at me with his lips in a straight line. I feel every function in my body suddenly shut down as I take in every word he says. I remember our last time together before he left.

We were at his place right after school. His older brother—God, I can't remember his name—was in the living room with a couple of guys who looked way older than him. Alejandro and I were in the basement, listening to music through his MP3 Player. I don't remember exactly what he told me about his dad, but I remember feeling sorry for him. I also remember spotting a bruise on his side, right above his hip. I told him about my abuela and how she loved helping people. I swore to him that he'd be able to stay with her until things cooled down with his dad. But then, my dad came and picked me up and took me home. When I came home, my parents took away my phone, telling me that I couldn't see Alejandro anymore since they thought he was a bad influence, even though nothing wrong had been done.

The next day rolled around, and he didn't show up for school. That was the last time I saw him. The last time I heard from him. Every time I tried to call his number, I got nothing. Then, I just stopped trying. I assumed he didn't want to be bothered. So.

An unbearable feeling swims through my chest, and I clench my eyes shut for a second, trying to collect my thoughts. I'd kick myself if I could. I'd punch myself out if I could.

Shit.

I sigh. "Alejandro, I—"

"Don't." He holds up his hand, cutting me off. "Don't. You didn't know. I may have needed you, but you didn't know."

I gulp, feeling a strange lump form in my throat.

He needed me. He needed me, and I wasn't there.

But you didn't know.

Still, he needed me.

Alejandro turns his attention back to the basket of rolls, and he offers me the other half that he didn't eat from the first roll he had. I look at him, and then I look back at the half of the roll.

Just take it, I urge myself, even though I don't want it.

Still, I take it, earning a tiny grin from Alejandro. He grabs a fresh roll for himself and dips the whole thing into the olive oil. The tightness in my chest returns as I dip my half of a roll into the olive oil and take a bite.

The waitress eventually returns with a pitcher of ice water in one hand and our bill in the other. As she pours the water, I try to explain that Alejandro and I were planning on paying separately since we weren't together. The waitress steps back, looking at both of us.

"Oh.." she gasps, realizing the situation. "Oh! *Oh my God!* I am so so sorry!" She practically fumbles with her words, and I notice a sly grin curling on Alejandro's lips as he watches her struggle to explain herself. "I shouldn't have assumed. I'm a modern woman, and we get a few couples in here from time to time, so I—"

Alejandro cuts her off, giving her a flattering chuckle with a smile. "It's all good, Miss. You can't help it. Two good-looking guys with this kind of set-up. It's only reasonable to assume."

My foot jolts, making immediate contact with Alejandro's leg from under the table. He winces and whips his head around to me.

I turn my attention to the waitress. Her face is entirely red, but she tries to laugh everything off. I still assure her that it's all good and that we take no offense to what she thought before. If anything, I had my chances to correct her, but I never did. I just let it slide and allowed her to think what she thought of us.

The waitress reaches for the bill, offering to split it, but Alejandro reaches over and offers to cover everything. I open my mouth to protest, but he cuts me off, suggesting that we play a quick round of Rock-Paper-Scissors to decide for us.

I roll my eyes. "That's stupid."

He snorts. "It's not stupid. It's reasonable."

He balls up his left hand, keeping over his right hand as he holds it out. I sigh, holding my hands out while keeping my left hand balled up over my right hand.

We go once.

Rock. Paper. Scissors. Shoot.

Alejandro smirks, holding out two fingers for scissors while I have my hand out for the paper.

"I win," he chuckles.

I roll my eyes as he pays in small bills and leaves a nice tip for the waitress.

When Alejandro and I leave, the sky is almost dark, and the street lights are already on.

I check the time on my phone—*7:32 PM.*

"Shit!" I blurt.

Alejandro snickers, bumping my arm with his elbow. "Got a curfew or something?"

I sigh. "No." I stuff my phone back into my pants pocket. "I got homework to do, though. I have a test tomorrow, I think."

Alejandro arches an eyebrow, confused. "You think?"

I shrug. "School is a lot, alright? I can't really keep up. We get tests almost every day now." *Not really.*

"Huh." Alejandro rocks on his heels. "Well." He claps his hands together. "I guess we should call it then. Can't have Mister Perfect dozing off in class, can we?"

I snort a chuckle. "Piss off." I lightly shove his shoulder, making him stumble back a bit, laughing.

Our laughter starts to quiet down as we remain looking at each other. I remember us being like this when we were younger. Before he left. I feel my heart dislodge into the pit of my stomach as I recall his words from in the restaurant—about how he needed me back then, but I just assumed that he could care less about me. Then again, I didn't expect to ever see him again.

So, there's that too.

Alejandro wishes me a safe drive home and starts to walk off.

I think fast.

"Wait!"

He turns back to me, stuffing his hands into the pockets of his jean jacket. I clear my throat.

"Let me see your phone." I try to keep my voice straight as I look up at him.

Alejandro just shrugs his shoulders, pulling his phone out from the front pocket of his jean jacket. He hands it to me, and I feel my fingers fumble as I take it. I shake my head, trying to get over whatever nerves are stirring inside of me right now.

I punch my number in and click ADD CONTACT. I put in my name and saved the number.

"Here," I say, handing Alejandro back his phone. He looks at his phone with his lips pursed. "In case you need anything."

The one side of his mouth pulls upward, but it's not out of mockery. I press my lips together in a tight half-smile, and he nods. As I watch him walk away, the familiar discomforting feeling in my stomach starts to bubble, but I manage to ignore it as I head to my car. I throw my head back against the leather headrest the second I get in and pull the door shut.

I close my eyes, exhaling through my nose.

I try to get my body to relax before I start the engine.

God help me, I think as I dreadfully start to head home.

Week 2, Thursday.

I sit between Meagan and Christopher at our usual lunch table, and I rest my head down on the surface of the table, taking in the strange combination of disinfectant spray and bitter pineapples from the fruit cups. I let my eyes close for about a second until I felt a finger poke the top of my head, twirling at my scalp.

I groan, swatting the finger without lifting my head.

I hear Peter remark, "Looks like it's that time of the month."

I flip him off, still keeping my head down on the table.

Carmen scoffs. "Serves you right. That's actually pretty sexist."

"How?" Peter asks with some food stuffed in his mouth since he sounds a bit muffled. "It's not like I said it to you or Miss Thang over there." I know he's referring to Meagan since he'll call her that sometimes, which I assume she's grown fond of since she never complains about it. Either that or she could care less.

As I close my eyes, I hear Meagan speak up, going, "He does have a point, Carmen."

"I don't care!" Carmen retorts. "It's the principle."

"What principle?" Peter's voice gets pitchy at the end, and I groan. "You know I ain't about the patriarchy!"

"Well, what way to stick it 'em," Carmen replies sarcastically.

An ache starts pounding at my head as the two of them go back and forth, and it becomes almost impossible for me to block them out.

"Why are you on my head today?!" Peter raises his voice, possibly drawing attention to our table, despite the commotion of other students talking loudly from other tables. "All I said was—"

"Enough!" I blurt, lifting my head up and slamming my hands down on the table. "Jesus Christ!"

I notice how Peter is looking at me with his eyes wide in shock and his mouth agape. I realize that everyone else at the table has the same expression, taking in my sudden outburst. I didn't mean to react that way, but for the love of God, I wanted them to just be quiet for two seconds.

The pounding in my head starts to ache against the right side of my temple, and I gently rub the spot, hoping that it'll ease down a bit. I sigh.

"Sorry," I mutter to Carmen and Peter.

I slouch forward, letting my folding my arms on the table, but I still sit up a bit.

Meagan puts her hand to my shoulder, and her eyebrows wrinkle with worry. "Are you alright, Donny?" she asks softly.

"Yeah, mate," I hear Christopher chime in. "You look like..." He then says something in Irish, but I shrug it off since I don't know what it means. I'm pretty sure it probably relates to something shitty if that's what he's going for. I wouldn't be mad at him if he said it in English, either.

I woke up this morning, hardly being able to function.

I spent the night tossing and turning, trying to block out the sound of my parents' bickering. And then, I woke up to the sound of them going at it again. It was like they didn't care that we had neighbors or that I was even in the house, trying to sleep since I had to wake up early for school. It's like arguing was their energy booster.

If I really cared about what they were arguing about, I would've tried to listen and figured out a possible solution to the best of my ability. But I can't say anything to my parents. Even if I tried, they wouldn't give a damn. So I did my best to block them out, yet I could barely keep my eyes open during class, and I was dozing off at lunch.

I can't say anything to my friends, though.

Especially not Christopher.

So, I shrug, telling them that I just had a slight headache. I tell them that it's nothing serious, but Meagan insists that I go to the nurse if it makes me drowsy.

Christopher nods. "I agree."

I snort, shaking my head. "You guys worry too much."

"You're not invincible, Don." Christopher practically looks down at me, giving a stern look with his arms folded across his chest. "Seriously, it wouldn't hurt to just get a quick check-up. You don't look so good."

I roll my eyes. *Why can't he just drop it?*

"Listen," I say through my teeth. "I'm fine, okay? Just drop it. All I need is some water. That's all." I get up and out of my seat. "Excuse me."

Christopher tries to stop me from leaving by grabbing hold of my wrist, but I manage to pull away before he gets a chance to touch me.

I head out of the cafeteria, making my way to the men's restroom. I push open the door, letting the back handle hit against the tile part of the wall before it bounces off the wall, and the door gently closes behind me. I go over to the sink and turn the water on. I let it run for a bit before splashing some cold water on my face to wake me up.

I tell my body to wake up, knowing that I still have a couple more hours of hell to go through before I can head home.

I groan.

I look up at my reflection in the mirror while pressing my palms against the edge of the sink. I think about all the times Morris-Lina and I would overhear mom and dad's arguments, but the two of us would try to distract either from them. Morris-Lina was always better at figuring out ways to tune out mom and dad whenever they argued. She knew that it killed me whenever they would go at each other's throats, especially as Morris-Lina and I got older.

········

I pinched the bridge of my nose, closing my eyes. I wanted to turn up the volume to my headphones to block the sound from the two of them arguing, but if I turned the volume up any louder, I'd go deaf.

Morris-Lina was sitting in the chair at my desk by the window. She had her hair pulled up in a messy updo, and her thin black glasses were pushed up on the bridge of her nose. She sat cross-legged in the chair, and her body was turned facing me as she kept one elbow propped up on the desk, resting the side of her face against her fist.

I could tell by the way her eyes lazily skimmed the page of the book she had rested on her lap that she was hardly intrigued by whatever she was reading. Usually, Morris-Lina doesn't mind reading, but I guess the sound of another one of mom and dad's arguments has her in the dumps as much as it has me wanting to rip my ears off my head.

My jaw tightened as I focused on blocking out our parents' voices. It just seemed as though they were getting louder and louder, and I felt myself starting to sink as I pulled my knees into my chest as I sat on my bed. I don't even know what they could be arguing about—every day, it's something new and stupid. It's like they pick something out of a hat for fun and make a big deal out of whatever it could be.

If it's not about Morris-Lina or me, then it's about something with the house or finances, or God knows what else. My stomach churned as I tried to figure out what stupid thing could have our parents at each other's throats for the third time this week.

Suddenly, I felt a hand rest on my shoulder, and I opened my eyes and met Morris-Lina's soft brown ones. She was sitting on the edge of my bed, and her lips curled into a half-smile. She gestured for me to make room for her, and I scooted over, giving her room to lay back on my bed. Morris-Lina purposely kept her legs were stretched out, bumping into mine, and crossed her hands behind her head as a cushion when she leaned her head back against the headboard.

I rolled my eyes, crossing my right leg over my left as I sat up in my bed. I kept my pillow tucked beneath my lower back, serving as a cushion between me and the headboard. I tried to focus on the sound of the music that pounded against my eardrums through my earbuds. The raspy voice of Jay Von Joyce from HAVOX soothes me as he calmly sings in sync with the smooth rhythm of the instruments. Next comes Perry T's guitar solo, and it sounds close to perfection.

How could anyone not like HAVOX?

They've been around since the early 1990s, and they're still underappreciated, which goes to show how sketchy the industry can be. It's not like no one's heard of HAVOX. They've performed all over the world, sold millions of albums, but people still like to pretend that they're not good, which I don't get. If they weren't good, they wouldn't have sold as many records as they did. Plus, everyone forgets that they've won many awards and were even inducted into the Rock & Roll Hall of Fame! They just haven't released anything recently, unfortunately.

And people think bands like Runaway Capsules are the next big thing, completely kicking HAVOX to the curb, which is total bullshit. Runaway Capsules is just another pop band that'll have its reign for about one or two years until they're molded into the general pop culture and are soon forgotten in the next decade.

But not HAVOX. No one could ever forget about HAVOX.

And damn, whoever thinks otherwise.

I flinched when one of my earbuds was taken out of my ear, and I whipped my head around, eyeing Morris-Lina as she put the one earbud into her ear. She wrinkled her nose and furrowed her eyebrows.

"Seriously?" Morris-Lina snorted as she shifted her weight around, turning her body around to face me.

I rolled my eyes. "No one asked you to listen to my music." I snatched the earbud out of her ear and slipped it back into mine. I muttered under my breath, "Bruja."

Her jaw dropped, and she punched me in my arm. It wasn't super hard, but it did hurt a little bit. I just laughed, rubbing my arm. I noticed the look on her face slowly start to change. Her lips curled, and she quirked an eyebrow. It was as if she felt a slight sense of pride in herself.

I arched an eyebrow. "What?"

She shook her head. "Nothing."

I snorted, knowing that something was up. "C'mon, tell me."

She sighed, resting her head back so she was looking up at the ceiling. She kept her fingers laced together with her hands behind her head. The faint smile on her face started to stretch into a full smile.

She shrugged her shoulders, feigning innocence. "I got you to laugh." She then gave me a side-eye look. "Made you forget about things."

I realized what she was talking about—mom and dad. I just snickered and continued to listen to the sound of HAVOX through my earbuds.

· · · · · · · ·

The sound of one of the stall doors swinging open brings me out of my thoughts, and I look up at the mirror. Nathan freezes when he spots me, and I feel my body stiffen when we make eye contact through the mirror.

Just my luck, I think.

Nathan approaches the sink beside me, and I quickly avert my attention away from him. I decide to wash my hands, even though there is no need for me to, but I don't want to just stand at the sink while looking at myself like some pompous weirdo.

I hear Nathan clear his throat as he pumps the dispenser, filling his hand with foam before rubbing his hands together.

"Hey," he says almost quietly.

I clear my throat, rinsing the soap from off my hands. "Hey."

I slowly dot my eyes up to look at him through the mirror. I'm expecting him to say something like he always does and make small talk. Instead, he's quiet, looking down at his hands as he runs them through the warm water spilling through the faucet. I don't know what it is, but something about him not saying anything just doesn't sit with me all too well. Part of me doesn't mind since Nathan is the last person I would want to talk to right now, but another part of me wants him to say something else to put my nerves at ease.

I figure that it's probably because I got so used to him always having something to say whenever we were in a room or space together. I know the only reason he tries to make such an effort to speak to me is out of guilt and wanting to make things right after all the shit he put Morris-Lina and me through. The way he hurt my sister was by falling for Diana. How he tossed our friendship away like it was nothing and then talked so much shit about us because he wanted to please his skank of a girlfriend.

I still want to hate him for that, but then I think about Meagan. I see how he looks at her and how he treats her. It's better than I would've ever imagined. She's okay around him, and I believe her when she says that he's trying. I see him trying through her.

I sigh.

Nathan turns off the water and dries his hands with a paper towel. Before he has the chance to walk out of the bathroom, I call out to him.

Nathan slowly turns around, and I can see the confusion sprawled all over his face. He's probably wondering if I meant to say his name, but I did.

I tell myself to look him in the eye, but all I can do is look down at his shoes. His nice white sneakers look expensive as hell and are in too perfect condition to be worn at a school like ours. A ball forms in my throat, but I manage to stir up the strength to speak to him.

"Do right by her," I muster out, making sure my words are clear. My chest tightens, and I can tell that Nathan is probably confused by what I mean since he's quiet. I take a quick breath before standing up straight, and I dare myself to look in him dead in the eyes. "If you want me to make things up with me, you'll do right by Meagan. Whether as a friend or something else. Do right by her. Got it?"

He just stares at me with his lips parted open in disbelief, probably still taking in what I just said to him. He should know that I'm serious. I trusted him to make my sister happy. I gave him my approval, and he promised me that he would take care of Morris-Lina and show how much he cared about her. But then, he dumped her out of the blue, not even giving a valid reason. Then, Christopher and I spotted Nathan hanging out with Diana Clovis, and I tried to provide Nathan with the benefit of the doubt because I didn't think Nathan could ditch my sister for some bimbo who thought she was better than everyone else. But then, Nathan made it clear that he cared more about Diana than us by ditching us all.

Nathan tarnished that trust, and I know he wants it back. But if he wants it, he'll need to earn my respect first. I can tell from the look on Nathan's face that he realizes how serious I am.

He nods his head, confirming that he understands.

I then watch him head out of the bathroom as the bell sounds off, signaling the end of my lunch period.

. . . .

My phone buzzes in my pants pocket as Ms. Phan informs the class for the third time about what pages she wants us to read in our textbooks for tomorrow's group discussion. A couple students in front of me start packing up their things since the bell is about to sound off, signaling the end of classes for the day. As much as I want to move and start packing up, Ms. Phan begins to scold the students who packed their things, telling them that it wouldn't be the end of the world if we were dismissed after the bell.

I hear the girl behind me gasp in shock from Ms. Phan's comment and from the tone of her voice. Ms. Phan will sometimes have her days when she's super strict with us, but it's a rarity since this class is pointless. At least, I find it pointless. But still, I don't ever question Ms. Phan when she gets stern. I just sit back and keep my mouth shut.

The whole class falls silent and still, letting Ms. Phan continue explaining the agenda for tomorrow's group discussion. She reminds us that participation is essential, and she wants everyone to be as thorough as possible with their comments or responses to her questions.

The bell sounds off, but no one dares to move until Ms. Phan gives us the cue to leave. She rolls her eyes, telling us that we're dismissed. The sound of chairs being pushed back and starting to disperse from the classroom echoes throughout the classroom. I pack up my notebook and pen and slip my arm through the one strap of my bookbag, letting the other strap hang freely.

As I walk out of the classroom and head to my locker to switch out what books I'll need for homework, I pull out my phone from my pants pocket and read my notifications. A text message from an unknown number appears on the screen, and I furrow my eyebrows.

I read the message: **wat's good shot glass...**

Alejandro?

How did he get my——?

Then, I remember giving him my phone number the other day after meeting with him at Papa Dicky's Pizzeria. I remember telling him that he could text me or give me a call if he ever needed anything. So, what could he possibly need from me already?

Maybe he's just checking on you? I think to myself.

Nah. It's not like we're in grade school, being friends again.

I decide it's whatever at this point. The only way to find out for sure is by responding back, which I do.

I just respond with: **What's up?**

SEND.

I then save his number.

"You feeling better?"

I snap my head up, meeting Christopher's curious eyes after his voice catches me by surprise. He quirks an eyebrow as I let out a sigh of relief, slipping my phone back into my pants pocket.

"You need a bell or something. Jesus Christ," I sigh as my heart rate beats at its average pace.

Christopher snickers, shrugging his shoulders. "Don't be bloody dramatic." He walks with me as I head to my locker. "But seriously, are you okay? You looked like hell earlier, mate. We were worried about you."

I sigh. "I know."

"Especially Meagan," he adds.

I nod, sighing at Christopher's words. "I know that too."

Christopher nudges my arm with his elbow. I look at him while rubbing my arm, and he just gives me an unamused look. "Don't be an ass." His accent thickens.

"I'm not," I tell him as I stop walking once we reach my locker. I enter the combination to my locker and swing the door open. "I just think you guys worry over nothing. It's not like I'm dying."

Christopher leans his back against the locker beside mine while crossing his arms over his chest. He tilts his head, looking at me with his eyebrow arched. "Well, we're dying every day we live, mate. So, you might want to reconsider that phrase."

I roll my eyes as I put my textbook for A.P. Chemistry into my locker before shoving my textbook for Honors Algebra II into my bookbag.

"Piss up a rope," I mutter to Christopher, making him laugh.

"Aww," he goes, poking out his bottom lip out of mockery. "Does it hurt knowing that there are people who care for you?" He tries to tickle under my chin, but I swat his hand away. Christopher chuckles. "Don't be such a wanker."

I slam my locker shut before looking at Christopher. He arches his eyebrow, waiting for me to say something, and I snort.

"Puto," is all I say, and he lightly punches my shoulder.

Christopher walks down the steps with me to head out, and as we're going downstairs, he asks me if I want to come over to his place this weekend for movie night since his dad will be out of town.

I smirk. "I don't know, man. I mean, you, me, and a movie? If the mood set and you play your cards right, Carmen will get a little suspicious, don't you think?"

Christopher scoffs as irritation washes over his face.

It's so easy for me to push his buttons.

It's hard for me to not laugh at him.

"Thanks, but Carmen is just fine for me. Trust me," he says, not even looking at me. "It'll be a squad hang. All five of us."

I shrug. "Yeah, I'll be there. I don't think I got anything to do."

Christopher nods. "I'll let you know when to be over."

Just then, my phone vibrates in my pants pocket. I pull it out and read the text message that appears on my phone screen.

Alejandro: busy tomorrow? I gotta see you. Peace.

I wrinkle my eyebrows in confusion. I text him back.

Me: Why? Got school tomorrow.

SEND.

Of course, Alejandro wants to meet me after school. But why does he want to meet with me at all? I just saw him the other day.

"Don?" I hear Christopher's voice, and I look at him. He looks up at me from the bottom step. "Everything good?" The concern in his voice makes my throat go dry, and I gulp.

I nod and tell him, "Yeah." I stuff my phone back into my pants pocket as I head down the last set couple steps to meet Christopher at the bottom. "I just gotta get home. My folks are bugging me again about dinner." *That's very convincing.*

Christopher presses his lips together, and I notice the color in his face start to drain as his gaze falls to the ground.

"What?" I ask him.

He shakes his head. "Nothing." He looks up at me, trying to force a smile on his face. "Just let me know if you need anything, okay?"

I look him right in the eye, and I take in the softness of his voice. I know he cares when it comes to me having to deal with my parents. And I know that he doesn't think they are terrible, even though their arguing keeps me up at night.

Still, I couldn't just tell Christopher about Alejandro. Alejandro is someone that I don't think Christopher would understand like I do. Plus, Alejandro just waltzed in out of the blue after years of not talking to each other. Christopher and I...he's like my brother. I mean, people say we're like brothers, but over time, I started to realize what they meant, and I believed it.

But Christopher doesn't need to know about Alejandro.

At least, not right now.

I shrug it all off, bringing myself out of my thoughts.

I look at Christopher, giving him a faint smile, nodding my head. I tell him, "Yeah, I know."

He smiles, patting me on the shoulder. "See ya."

I wink at him, clicking my tongue. "See ya."

We part ways, and I waste no time getting to my car. It isn't super cold outside, but the wind isn't too kind either. As soon as I get in the car, I turn on the engine and strap myself in. I sent my mom a text that I'll be making dinner tonight, even though she probably didn't care since I usually make dinner on weekdays, anyway.

It never took me long to get home since traffic was light, which rarely happens since my school is within the inner city. But as soon as I pull into the driveway of my house, my phone buzzes in my pocket.

I groan.

I park the car, wondering if it's my mom texting me about what she'd prefer for me to make for dinner.

It's not.

Alejandro: after school. We gotta talk.

A knot forms in my throat, and my chest tightens as a million thoughts start to swim through my mind. I try to suppress my thoughts as I get out of my car and head inside my house.

What could he possibly want to talk about? We just saw each other the other day!

I keep telling myself to relax and to let it go. From what I know about Alejandro, he loves to play mind games. It's amusing to him. He used to play tricks on me all the time, and I'd always feel like a fool for always falling for them.

It was like a sport for him, kinda.

My phone vibrates again, and I read the message that appears.

Mama: Anything with pasta, mi niño pequeño!

I roll my eyes, sucking my teeth.

Of course, she'll say "anything" with pasta.

Mom doesn't like "anything." She's incredibly picky.

I sigh as I head upstairs to my room to change. I tell myself to focus on deciding what to make for dinner to please my picky mother, rather than whatever it could be that Alejandro wants to talk to me about tomorrow.

Week 2, Friday.

"What about number two? Anyone want to give that one a crack at it?" Mr. Enrique asks, holding a dry erase marker in one hand and the open math textbook in the other as he stands up at the front of the classroom. He eyes all of us, waiting for one brave—or petrified—soul to volunteer to solve one of the math problems we are going over from our textbook.

We have been going over rational functions and graphing rational functions this entire week, which isn't all that hard. At least, it doesn't look hard to me. But I'll be damned if I am the one to go up to the board and solve the problem. It's not like I'm going up to the board or giving answers every time Mr. Enrique asks for a volunteer. It's just that people sometimes expect me to solve the problem, even when I don't want to.

So, I sit with my hands clasped together in front of my mouth while looking off to the side, praying to God that Mr. Enrique wouldn't pick me. And thank the Heavens that he doesn't.

Instead, Mr. Enrique calls out Meagan, causing her eyes to go wide with anxiety and her lips part slightly open. Mr. Enrique holds his gaze on her, and she whips her head around to face me. The anxiety plastered on her face is almost unbearable. I feel bad for her, but I know she can solve it. Meagan is intelligent. Every time she studies, she is always on her A-Game, like a hawk on its prey.

I give Meagan a sincere look of reassurance, letting her know that I believe in her. I always tell her that I'd bet my car on her whenever she's nervous about something because I wholeheartedly believe in her. There's no reason for me not to.

Meagan finally turns her attention back to Mr. Enrique and rises out of her seat to approach the board with her textbook open to the page to reference the problem. Her hand quivers as she takes the marker from Mr. Enrique. Meagan takes quick glances at the page of the textbook while solving the equation on the whiteboard. I can't help but watch in admiration as she writes everything carefully, as if she's afraid of breaking the board. But at the same time, she's a tad bit fierce, her determination and concentration showing in her work. She takes up a decent amount of space on the board as she finishes solving the problem. I notice her hand starting to shake again as whispers begin to rise from a couple of watching students.

I tighten my jaw, cutting my eyes to where the whispers are coming from. I notice a few students smirking, pressing their lips together in grins to silence their giggles. I see a few guys eying Meagan up and down as if they're checking her out, and a strange feeling stirs in the pit of my stomach as I tighten my jaw. It's not a sick feeling, but it's not easy to stomach down either. The only way to bring me some kind of relief is picturing myself swinging at one of them—teach them some manners.

I cut my attention back to Meagan as she placed the marker in the holder attached to the side of the white erase board. I can tell by the way she fiddles with her fingers and chews on her bottom lip that she's dreading every second she remains at the front of the classroom, waiting for Mr. Enrique to allow her to sit down. Instead, he just examines her work, pressing his lips tightly together while rocking on his heels.

I sit up a bit to get a better look at the masterpiece written on the board. My eyes wandered, taking in every detail and every step Meagan made to get to her final answer.

Everything is right. One-hundred percent correct.

Judging by the smirk that starts to stretch across Mr. Enrique's lips, he, too, knows that Meagan is right. Yet, Meagan begins chewing at the skin of her bottom lip while clasping her hands behind her back.

Mr. Enrique gives her a look. She grows stiff as a robot when it's set to power down.

Instead of saying anything, Mr. Enrique holds his hand up for a high-five. Shock washes over her face, but Meagan manages to keep herself together and smacks her hand with Mr. Enrique's, making the sound slightly echo throughout the classroom.

Mr. Enrique then gestures for Meagan to have a seat, and she clutches onto her textbook against her chest. The room grows quiet, but it's still evident that some people are still eyeballing her. Meagan looks at me as she approaches her seat, and I wink at her, hoping that'll settle her nerves.

The curves at the corners of her mouth confirm my success as Meagan takes her seat.

The bell soon sounds off, and I snatch up my bookbag from off the floor, zipping it up before throwing it on my back. I sit halfway on top of my desk as I watch Meagan as she gets her stuff together, stuffing her textbook into her bookbag before pulling out her purple notebook with the word **ENGLISH** written on the front of the notebook in black marker along with a shiny black folder containing packs of papers that I'm assuming are essays and worksheets that she had to complete for her class with Mr. Acosta.

Meagan groans under her breath, pushing a strand of her crinkly hair out of her face and tucking it behind her ear.

She struggles to zip her bookbag shut, pulling and tugging at the zipper relentlessly until she's finally able to get the zipper moving. Her eyes bore tiredness, and I can tell that she tried to cover the bags under her eyes with makeup. No such luck.

Meagan groans as she finally stands up, slipping on her bookbag and grabbing her notebook and folder for her next class.

She pushes the chair in. "This is going to be the death of me."

A chuckle mistakenly slips through my lips, and I immediately put my hand to my lips to hide the smile creeping on my face. Meagan practically glares at me, but her tired eyes make her less intimidating. Instead, she looks exhausted and kind of…helpless?

Innocent, maybe, as a better choice of words.

Regardless, it's kind of adorable—seeing her like that.

Meanwhile, Meagan is unamused, rolling her eyes. "What?"

I let my eyes wander around in an attempt to avoid hers, and I shake my head as I stuff my hands into my pants pockets.

"Nothing," I tell her, trying to sound convincing. I hold my arm out, gesturing for her to walk to the door. "After you, milady."

Meagan snorts. I notice the smile curled at her lips and the corners of my mouth pull upward when we make eye contact. I admire how crinkly her hair is as it falls perfectly over her shoulders. When I complimented her hair this morning when I saw her before homeroom, she said she had taken her braids out, and then BOOM—beautifully crinkled hair. I remember telling her that I thought her natural hair looked pretty, and she had a dumbfounded look on her face, but she couldn't look me in the eye.

I don't get why she doesn't realize how pretty she is—seriously!

She's gorgeous, I think to myself.

I press my lips together in a tight smile as Meagan walks ahead of me to the door, but she waits for me at the doorway as a few students enter the classroom for their class with Mr. Enrique.

As I walk out of the classroom with Meagan, I ask her if she wants me to walk with her to her next class, but she shakes her head, insisting that it's out of the way for me.

I roll my eyes. "You're too considerate for your own good."

I then throw my arm around her, and Meagan clenches her notebook and folder tightly into her chest but allows her body to relax against mine as we walk down the hall. My face starts to feel warm all of a sudden, but I shake it off as Meagan looks up at me. Her eyes are fighting sleep.

I can't help but wonder. "Did you get any sleep at all, kid?"

Meagan sighs, looking away from me.

Shit. Way to go, Gonzalez.

I clear my throat. "Not saying that you look bad, I was just—"

"No," Meagan cuts me off, still staying close to me. "I know what you mean." She groans, pinching the bridge of her nose while shutting her eyes. "I was up working on this essay for English." She opens her eyes and lets out an agitated huff. "God help me."

I stop walking, and I grab hold of both of her shoulders. Wild confusion spreads all over Meagan's face as I whip her around to look at me and hold her in place so I have her full attention. She's been beating herself up about this essay she has for Mr. Acosta's class, and I'm honestly getting sick and tired of it. Not of her, but the doubt she has in herself.

For the love of God, the girl radiates incredibility.

She has to get that.

I hold my gaze on her while making sure that I'm not gripping her shoulders too tightly as I talk to her. "Listen, kid. You gotta chill and let yourself breathe for a second. This paper ain't nothing. Don't lose sleep because of it. I know damn well you did it right. Just…trust yourself a bit more. Got it?"

Then, Meagan's eyes looked off to the different students walking past us, but I could care less about them. It's not like we're standing in the middle of the hallway. We're out of everyone's way.

Her eyes then come back to me, and she opens her mouth to speak, but nothing comes out. So, she closes her mouth and just gives me a nod. I can still see the doubt in her eyes as she looks off to the side, letting her gaze fall to the ground.

If I could, I would pull her close and tell her how incredible she really is. Hell, I'd even show her. I would find some way to prove that she's not like anyone I've ever met. Even if she finds it hard to believe, Meagan would eventually realize that I'm not just bullshitting because she's my friend. I'm dead serious.

Yet, I say nothing, and she tells me that she'll see me at lunch—which she does—before heading to her next class.

By the time lunch rolls around, Meagan is already sitting at our table next to Benton. The two of them are practically mushed together, watching something on Benton's phone, and Meagan has a giant smile on her face. When I come over to the table with my lunch, Meagan looks up at me and smiles.

I smile back at her. "Looks like you're feeling better."

Meagan looks back at Benton as he places his phone face down on the table. Meagan nudges him. "Show him."

I wrinkle my eyebrows, and Benton picks up his phone to unlock it. "Show me what?" I ask.

Benton leans forward, putting his elbows on the table. "My cousin had a baby yesterday." He shows me the screen of his phone. The baby is tiny and wrapped up in a white blanket. The baby's eyes are closed, and there is hardly any hair on the baby's head. "Her name is Yoon-ah."

I smirk, hardly able to take my eyes off the picture. "She's so small." A tiny chuckle mixes in with my words.

Meagan chimes in, "That's what I said! She's so cute."

Benton pulls the phone away and puts it back in sleep mode while Meagan starts gushing about the baby. Her smile becomes wide as she talks about how small the baby looks, and she asks Benton how much she weighed. He tells her that the baby was about five pounds and six ounces, and Meagan coos, going, "Aww." I just sit there, watching her becomes swoon by the baby.

And all of a sudden, Meagan has this glow about her that makes me even more intrigued. I didn't expect her to like babies so much. Although, I can't say I blame her. There are many cute babies out there, and Gabriel and Yago are proofs of that. I remember when they were born. Yago was about seven pounds and something ounces. He was crying at the top of his lungs, but when I had the chance to hold him, he stopped and just made soft noises. And then came Gabriel. He was much smaller than Yago, but I can't remember his weight precisely. All I know is that when Gabriel was born, the room stood still. Tía Yoselin was worried out of her mind that something was wrong with him since he wasn't screaming and crying like Yago had when he was born. But the doctors did something to Gabriel that made him cry, ensuring that he was alright.

I remember Yago not wanting anyone to hold Gabriel except for him. Every time Morris-Lina and I would come over, or if the family would get together, and someone tried to pick up Gabriel to do whatever, Yago would swoop in and try to swat everyone away.

He'd be like, *"No! My Gabriel! Mine!"*

He'd even throw fits when Yoselin wouldn't allow Yago to feed Gabriel. Honest to God, I thought it was hilarious. Looking back, I still laugh at how protective Yago would get when it came to Gabriel. If Gabriel hurt himself while playing with one of his toys, Yago would hit the toy, telling the toy to not hurt his little brother. I doubt Morris-Lina and I were *that* protective of each other when we were little.

I flinch when I hear my phone suddenly ring in the pocket of my jacket. I take a look at the screen, wondering who the hell could be calling me in the middle of the day because I know it's not my parents. I furrow my eyebrows when I see the name on the screen.

Alejandro.

I clear my throat before standing up to step away from the table. I notice the others looking at me with confusion and concern on their faces.

"I'll be right back," I tell them as I leave.

I head to the back of the cafeteria and stand by the window. I clear my throat before answering the phone.

"What?" I make sure my words aren't too harsh as I keep my voice low.

Alejandro snickers on the other end of the phone. "Good to hear your voice too, shot glass."

I roll my eyes, hearing the twisted mockery in his words. He's the last person I'd expect to call me in the middle of the day, especially while I'm at school. I made it clear to him yesterday when he texted me about wanting to talk that I had school. He even responded that he'd speak with me *after* school.

Not *during*.

Not *before*.

After school! Meaning when school is over for the day.

I exhale through my nose, closing my eyes as I try to choose my words carefully. I can imagine the cocky grin on Alejandro's face as I remain silent, thinking about what to say to him. He can probably sense my irritation, which will only fuel his smug nature.

I let out a sharp breath, but I make sure that I keep my voice low and my words steady to hide the irritation stirring inside me. "I thought you'd talk to me after school. It's what we agreed. I got class in a few minutes." I catch my voice starting to rise, so I speak through my teeth and push the phone up closer to my ear.

I hear Alejandro moving around before sirens start blaring in the background. Like an ambulance. The sound begins to fade out, and Alejandro huffs. "And I told you that I'd speak to you after school." He grunts and the sound of a door slamming shut follows. I furrow my eyebrows. "I'm just chilling 'til then."

The sound of a loud car horn going off in the distance pulls my attention. The same sound echoes outside the school, followed by someone screaming. I can't help but ask Alejandro exactly where he is, and he gives me a mocking chuckle as if we're kids, playing games with each other. He then tells me to take a "wild guess," and my heart leaps up into my throat.

I dare myself to look out the window, and I look down to the street, praying to God that this was some sick joke. There's no way Alejandro would actually show up to my school like some weirdo. He doesn't even know where I go to school.

There's no way—!

Son of a bitch!

I stand corrected. There down below, looking right up at me and waving up to me, is a smiling Alejandro Reyes as he stands leaning up against his car as if he owns the block.

"Hey, shot glass," he coos into the phone before clicking his tongue.

My eyes widen, and I feel my chest tighten as the air in my lungs escapes my body. He's here. Alejandro Reyes. He's here…at my friggin' school!

I feel my grip on the phone tighten as my blood starts to bubble in my body like a boiling pot. He acts as though this is normal and fine, but really, it's not. It's definitely *far* from being fine!

He has some nerve showing up at *my* school, acting as though this is the new norm between us now where he just shows up out of the blue. Even if what happened the other day was a coincidence, it shouldn't have happened—bumping into him when I was hanging out with Meagan after school.

Yes, I did give him my number if he needed something, but that doesn't mean he has to track me down like a bloodhound. I can't even formulate the right words to tell him off for just showing up at my school out of the blue.

Plus, a million thoughts are soaring through my mind, trying to figure out how he could've figured out that I attend Gabe-Day. I never told him about me attending Gabe-Day. Mainly because I wanted to avoid situations like this.

Just then, Alejandro waves at me again and speaks into the phone. "I know you see me. I don't get what the problem is, shot glass." He tries to sound innocent—like he's done nothing wrong at all. But that's total bullshit.

As much as I want to tell him off for just showing up at my school and calling me in the middle of the day like some weirdo, I end the call. The last thing I want to do is give him the satisfaction that he caught me completely off-guard, although he probably already knows he did since I didn't say anything to follow up his comments. I just let him say whatever, and I hung up the phone.

I stuff my phone into my pants pocket as I watch Alejandro from the window. I can see him laughing to himself while putting his phone away inside his jean jacket. He then gets into his car, but he doesn't pull off. Instead, he just sits there as if he's waiting for some show to come around.

I roll my eyes. *Prick.*

. . . .

I dread having to go outside when school ends for the day. Christopher is blowing up my phone, sending me messages, asking where I am since he and the others are waiting for me outside the school. Meanwhile, I'm pacing back and forth in the men's bathroom, trying to think of the best way to get to my car without Alejandro spotting me. I was praying to God during my classes, begging that something would happen to make Alejandro leave.

But when I checked from the window after my last class to see if Alejandro was gone, his car remained parked outside the school. I still don't get how he knows where I go to school. That just doesn't make any damn sense.

I grunt, running my hands down my face as I lean back against the bathroom wall.

My phone then starts to buzz in my pants pocket, and a familiar jingle starts to sound off. I groan, pulling my phone out before pressing my thumb against the screen to answer the call.

"I'll be down, Chris," I say, leaning my head back against the wall, looking up at the ceiling.

Christopher lets out a deep sigh on the other line. I guess it didn't surprise him that I figured out why he was calling me. He's already sent me about a million text messages asking me where I am. I could've responded to give him some type of reassurance that I was alright, but it just slipped my mind. I was trying to strategize how to dodge Alejandro. I know I told him that I'd listen to whatever he had to say to me after school, but that was before I found out that he knew where I went to school.

What the hell kind of stunt is that?! Just showing up here?!

I push my thoughts aside, though, when Christopher asks me if I need him to come inside and meet up somewhere. My heart sinks at the sound of his voice. Christopher is naturally too caring for his own good, and a wave of guilt swallows me whole.

Crap.

I try to lighten the mood by chuckling. "You're such a dad." I push up off the wall to stand straight before heading over to the mirror attached to the wall above the sink. I fix the collar of my burgundy polo uniform shirt and pop the collar to my leather jacket. I make sure that I keep the phone pressed up against my ear as I talk to Christopher. "I had to ask Miss Phan something about our next assignment, and then I took a piss."

I swallow thickly, hoping he buys it.

"Ugh," Christopher grunts in disgust on the other line. I can imagine him rolling his eyes as well. "I didn't need to know that last part."

I snicker as a wave of relief puts me at ease. I have to keep it up. "You wouldn't quit bugging."

Christopher sucks his teeth. "Whatever."

I smirk. "I'm heading down now. See you in two."

"I'm counting down." The laugh that ties in with Christopher's words assures me that he brought everything I was saying.

Then, the call ends.

As I stuff my phone back into the pocket of my jacket and head out of the bathroom, I contemplate the different ways I can avoid being seen by Alejandro. But each idea that comes to mind is impossible once I remind myself that I have to get to my car parked in the parking lot across the street.

Just suck it up and deal with it, I tell myself as I head down the steps. That's all I can really do at this point.

I spot Christopher the second I make it outside the school through the front entrance. He stands at the bottom of the steps to the front, his arms locked around Carmen's waist as she rests her hands on his chest to keep a small amount of distance between them. She laughs at whatever he whispers to her, and the smile on his face expands.

I roll my eyes at the sight. Usually, I pick at the two of them, interrupting whatever moment they have with each other. But it's not because I can't stand to see the two of them like this—all lovey-dovey. Besides, Christopher deserves this.

Still, a ball forms in my throat whenever I see them kiss. Even if it's a quick peck to the lips or the cheek. They make it look so easy, being intimate with each other. It makes me green with envy sometimes, but not often.

Christopher then draws his eyes in my direction, and my body stiffens. He waves for me to come down to them, and I sigh. As I head down the steps to meet Christopher and Carmen at the bottom, Carmen gives Christopher one final, semi-lingering kiss on the lips before telling him that she will call him later.

He smiles, watching her get to her car that is parked in the lot across the street.

Christopher licks his lips when she makes it across the street, and a sly grin stretches on his face. "Get home safe, love!" he calls out to her, keeping his hands behind his back as he slightly sways his hips.

Carmen just waves him off as she enters the lot and gets to her car.

I tilt my head, narrowing my eyes to Christopher.

He notices my gaze and arches his eyebrow. "What?"

I snort, shaking my head. "Talk about being whipped."

Christopher shoots me a look as if he's ready to kill me, but I laugh it off. He knows that I'd never badmouthed his relationship with Carmen. Besides, I was his hype-man for them getting together—that's a fact.

I throw my arm around him, letting my hand brush against his shoulder. "Lighten up, will you?" I pull him close towards me, even though he's a couple inches taller than me, so it makes it hard for me to not really pull him down to meet my height. "Just do me a favor and let me be your best man for the wedding, alright?"

Christopher snorts. "Ta!" I expect him to push me away as we start to walk across the street, but he doesn't. Instead, he lets me lean on him for support, but he keeps looking forward. "You're full of yourself. What credentials do you have to be my best man?"

"I certainly know how to handle that stick up your ass."

Christopher purses his lips. "Up mine or yours? Because I think yours is *waaay* up farther than you realize. Even your eyes look bigger from it."

I punch his arm, and Christopher lets out a low chuckle through his teeth while keeping his eyebrow arched. A sinister smile slightly spreads across his lips.

"Is that all you got?" His voice is low, making his accent much thicker. It's like he's mocking me.

I look away from him, feeling my cheeks flush. "Verga," I mutter as we make it across the street.

Christopher moves in closer to me, bumping his arm with mine in an attempt to lighten the mood, but I just roll my eyes. I hear someone call my name just then, and it takes me a second to recognize the voice. I freeze, looking up as Alejandro is making his way over to me—well, *us* since Christopher is here too.

Alejandro—with his hair styled in an undercut pompadour, showing off his silver streaks along the front and top of his hair, and his white tee-shirt tucked into his ripped blue jeans while wearing a jean jacket vest on top—looks shockingly intimidating up-close. I don't know if it's because I still can't get over how he knows where I go to school or if it's just the vibe he gives off. But whatever the reason, I don't go cowering behind Christopher or anything.

I look Alejandro in the eye as he inches closer towards me. He looks down at me but keeps a fair amount of distance between us. The corner of his mouth on one side pulls upward as he arches an eyebrow.

"You weren't planning on ditching me, were you?"

A shiver runs down my spine, and I feel the hairs on the back of my neck stick up.

Maybe.

"No." The word comes out straight and firm.

Alejandro shakes his head, chuckling in disbelief. His eyes then cut over to Christopher, and I notice the look on Alejandro's face suddenly drop when he realizes Christopher's presence. Christopher just stands there, keeping one hand gripped on the strap of his bookbag while the other is down by his side. There is an unfamiliar and strange look in Christopher's eyes as he looks at Alejandro as if he's trying to read him.

Alejandro slightly lifts his head up, gesturing to Christopher. "Who's this? Your bodyguard?" Even though he's joking, I can still sense some hostility in Alejandro's words. He tries to play it off by chuckling at the end.

Christopher just twists his lips into a half-smile, staring right at Alejandro. "You couldn't pay me a million dollars to protect this guy." Christopher glances at me. "He's pretty much got himself under control."

Alejandro shrugs. "Perhaps. But he does have his moments, doesn't he?"

I groan. "I'm right here, you know."

I can't stand being talked about as if I'm not even present. That's the worst feeling ever. My parents will sometimes have full-blown conversations about me while I'm still in the room, which pisses me off.

Alejandro then takes the initiative to introduce himself to Christopher, sticking his hand out for Christopher to shake. Christopher shakes his hand, and I feel my chest tighten when he tells Alejandro his name.

Alejandro raises an eyebrow. "What're you? British?"

Christopher chuckles at Alejandro's ignorance. "Irish, actually."

"Ah." Alejandro stuffs his hands in the pockets of his jean vest. "Interesting." He looks at me, giving me a sly smirk. "Out with the old and in with the new, huh?"

I roll my eyes. "Alejandro—"

"Nah, I get it." He holds up his hand, cutting me off. "It's all good. I can take a hint." Alejandro takes a small step back and switches gears to Christopher. "Good to meet you. I'm sure I'll see more of you, huh?"

Christopher presses his lips together in a tight grin, but not out of pleasantry. It's as if he's forcing himself to seem delighted by the idea of seeing Alejandro again, even though the chances of that happening are probably slim.

Still, Christopher nods. "If the universe allows it."

The look on Alejandro's face softens, and he licks his lips. My chest tightens at the sight of the two of them, suddenly glaring at each other as if it is the ultimate staring contest. Luckily, Alejandro cuts things short, telling me that he'll talk to me later.

Part of me is relieved when Alejandro finally turns on his heels to walk away to his car. But then, as I look at Christopher and then Alejandro as he gets in his car, part of me feels uneasy. I know Alejandro, and I know he probably thinks I stabbed him in the back, even though I didn't meet Christopher until my freshman year of high school.

We might not be the best of friends anymore—or friends in general. But I do have some type of care for him, and I wanted him to know that. It's just…times have changed. Even Alejandro has to admit that deep down.

Christopher lets out a deep sigh, crossing his arms over his chest. I look at him, quirking an eyebrow. When I ask him what's wrong with him, he just gives me a look that makes me question my existence all of a sudden.

What's his deal?

Christopher then comes out with it. "How do you know him?"

I sigh. *Should've seen that coming.*

There's no point in making up stories, and I realize that as much as I hate the thought, there could be a chance of them bumping into each other again. So, I tell Christopher the truth. But at the same time, I don't want to overwhelm him. So, I keep it short and sweet.

"We used to be friends back in grade school." I try to keep my voice straight as I look Christopher in the eyes. My palms start to sweat, but I tell myself to keep it together. "We bumped into each other recently. In a fight. He sort of helped me out."

Christopher rolls his eyes. The way he presses his lips together, pouting, I can tell he either doesn't believe me or isn't satisfied with what I gave him. Regardless, it's the truth, and that's all.

"What fight?" Christopher asks, slightly raising his voice.

I shrug. "Just a couple of guys. They jumped me. Not a big deal."

Concern washes over his face. "Why didn't you tell me? When was this?" Christopher looks about an inch taller for a second as he turns his body around to face me, towering over me a bit.

I shake my head.

There's no reason for Christopher to be so uptight about this. The fight happened weeks ago. Besides, what would he be able to do? There's no point in him worrying about it now. It's over and done with, and that's what I tell him.

"Chris," I say, trying to suppress the annoyance in my voice. "It doesn't matter. Besides, I'm not five. I came out alive, didn't I?" I try to keep my voice calm, but my frustration somewhat gets the best of me.

Christopher just looks at me, trying to make sure that he chooses his words wisely. I know he doesn't mean to be all up in my business, but I get why he is. We've been friends for a long time, and he's like my brother. Anytime something goes down, I tell him. Honestly, I trust him more than I trust in my folks. It's like I can breathe when I'm around him. He'll tease and scold me about some things, but not to the point where I feel as though I'm drowning in shame. The only reason why I didn't tell him about this is that I didn't want him to act like this. He gets worked up so quickly now, and it's annoying. But I'll never hate him for it.

Like I said, he's like my brother. My tall, white Irish brother.

Christopher lets out a sigh, closing his eyes while pinching the bridge of his nose. He mumbles something under his breath in Irish, knowing that I won't be able to understand whatever he's saying.

I snort, shaking my head.

"You worry too much, you know that," I tell him.

Christopher looks at me, licking his lips. "And you're the reason for that, mate. You don't care enough at all."

"Hey. At least I'm aging a lot better than you are because of it."

Christopher punches my shoulder, and I wince.

"Prick," he hisses, glaring at me.

It becomes impossible for me to not laugh, and Christopher just walks away, and I'm right behind him as we enter the parking lot to get to our cars.

Week 3, Sunday.

The cold air hits my skin, sending a shiver down my spine as my teeth chatter. I tightened my grip on the comforter, pulling it over my bare chest, so it's up against my neck. The thickness is comforting, and I nuzzle my face into the pillow, letting the warmth consume me.

Another strong breeze hits me—this time against my back.

I can't take it anymore.

I sat up on my elbows, letting the comforter drape over my waist. I whipped my head to my bedroom window. My eyebrows knitted together in confusion once I realized that the window was cracked open. Not even cracked. It was halfway up, letting the wind enter my room.

I swore that I closed it shut before going to bed.

It's like fifty degrees outside.

I swung my legs over the edge of the bed and got up to close the window. The breeze becomes more chilling as I try to close the window shut. My bones tighten, and I use all my force as I push down on the edge of the window, finally getting some kind of movement from the window.

It closes with a hard slam, and I let out a sigh of relief.

Still, I swore I had that window closed, though.

I shook my head and rubbed my eyes as exhaustion crept up on me. I turned on my heels, ready to get back into the warm comfort of my bed when I heard a noise come from the other side of my bed. It sounded like a combination of footsteps and heavy objects being moved around.

I quirked an eyebrow. "Papá? Mamá?"

I made a fist, but I kept my hand down to my side as I took small steps towards my bedroom door. I could feel my palms starting to sweat as my heart thumped heavily in my chest.

What am I doing? I thought.

I should just get back in the bed and force myself to get some sleep. But God forbid something is actually going on. And I'll be damned if I didn't try to do anything about it. Knowing dad, he'd scold me if I let anything happen to mom or Morris-Lina. Hell, it could be him. He's probably just moving boxes around in our sad excuse of a guest room.

Still, I have the urge to see what's going on.

It's now or never.

I firmly grasped the doorknob to my bedroom door and swung the door open. I swallowed thickly when I saw that nothing was there. Everything became quiet, and I felt my heart starting to beat back to its regular pace.

A sigh of relief.

I was about to turn around and go back into my room when I noticed Morris-Lina had her door cracked open. I wrinkled my eyebrows. Usually, she keeps her door closed when she's going to bed. In her words, it helps her block out all the distractions that prevent her from sleeping.

I can't say I blame her, though.

I, too, like peace and quiet. So, I'll usually sleep with my door closed. Even though mom hates that we do that, she worries that we won't hear her if there's an emergency. But mom doesn't realize how loud she is, which is funny to us.

I take a peek through the crack between the doorframe and Morris-Lina's bedroom door to look into her room. She lays sound asleep with the side of her face nuzzled against her thick pillow and comforter barely covering her shoulders.

I shake my head, knowing that she'll probably catch a cold since she's wearing a tank top. I can't be mad at her. I mean, I'm not even wearing a shirt. Although, I'm wearing sweatpants to make up for it.

I dare myself to push open her bedroom door, giving me enough space to slip inside her room without making a sound. I have to walk on my tiptoes to make sure that I don't make a sound, disturbing her sleep. Otherwise, she'll have my head on a silver platter.

Luckily, I manage to make it beside Morris-Lina's bed without waking her up. She's so quiet, so peaceful. It's unlike anything I've ever seen. Morris-Lina sometimes snores, even though she'll swear up and down that she doesn't, and it's hilarious whenever I tease her about it.

Still, I can't help but feel envious of how peaceful she looks asleep. It's as if nothing can disturb her. Like she's in some kind of trance.

I pushed the hair out of her face when I noticed something closed up in her fist, which was near her face at the edge of the pillow. My eyebrows furrowed. I know I should probably just forget about it since I don't want to wake her, but something compels me to check and see what she holds. For all I know, it could be a piece of paper that she probably meant to throw away but fell asleep and forgot about it.

I opened up her hand.

My eyes widened at the number of pills that were in her hand. It had to be more than what the doctor prescribed for her to take. Of course, it was—who takes that many pills?

Why would she be sleeping with them in her hand?

"Morris?" I whisper as I gently shove her a bit.

Nothing.

I sigh. Either Morris-Lina's in that much of deep sleep, or she is purposely ignoring me.

I poked her cheek this time since I know she hates that, but she doesn't even make a sound.

A ball starts to form in my throat.

"Moe?" I call her by her nickname, but it hardly comes out clear.

I grip onto her shoulder, shaking her this time. My heart plummets to the pit of my stomach, and I can hear myself breathing rapidly. I tried taking deep breaths, hoping that'll calm me down, but Morris-Lina still being unresponsive makes that almost impossible.

My voice grows louder and louder as I say her name, and each time, her eyes never open, and her face never changes.

······

My vision is blurry as my heart beats faster than a rabbit. I sit up, gasping for air as the humidity starts to close in on me. I can feel the sweat trickling down my forehead as I blink, hoping to make sense of where I am. I should know where I am, though.

I grip onto the surface under me, trying to familiarize my surroundings. Darkness consumes most of what I see, but small glimpses of light come from the window on the other side of the room.

That's right. I'm in my bedroom.

I can't stop panting, though. It becomes impossible to pace my breathing as my heart climbs its way up my throat, thumping louder and heavier.

The air is closing in way too much, and I have to get out of here. I waste no time getting myself out of bed, but my legs wobble as I stand. I lean against the wall as I make my way to the door and swing it open. I reach my hand out, searching for some kind of light switch.

Dammit!

A tight feeling pulls in my chest, and my stomach churns. I can feel a terrible rush starting to swell up inside me. I manage to make it to the bathroom, and I close the door behind me once I hit the lights on. My vision becomes vibrant once I manage to spot the toilet.

I swiftly lift up the seat as I succumb to the terrible feeling that stirs inside me. I fall to my knees, keeping my face over the toilet. A rush of acid spills out of my mouth. My throat burns, and I can feel my lungs wanting to burst as my chest heaves.

I clutch onto the rim of the toilet as another wave hits through me. My vision becomes a blur as tears form in my eyes as the burning spreads through my chest. I don't know what came over me, but I want it to stop whatever it is.

And finally, it does.

The sickening feeling in my mouth, the burning—it just stops. I gather whatever residue is left in my mouth, and I spit it out into the toilet water before I flush. I lift my head up, trying to slow down my breathing.

I pinch my eyes shut, wiping away the tears that still remain before opening my eyes again, blinking. My cheeks feel terribly warm, but I doubt I even have a fever. I just puked my guts out.

That could be the reason.

I'm just surprised that neither mom nor dad came barging in, asking me what's going on. I tried to be as quiet as possible, but it's hard to be quiet when something like that happens.

The feeling is so nauseating, it's painful to bear.

The bitter taste still remains in my mouth, so I spit into the toilet one last time and flush before gaining the courage to stand up. My legs shake, and I have to grip onto the sink for support. Once I'm up, I feel weightless, and the side of my head starts to ache. I have to grasp onto both sides of the sink as I look at myself in the mirror. The bags under my eyes are horrendous, and I know that if abuela was still alive, she would have a fit and blame my parents for my lack of sleep, even though it has nothing to do with them. This time.

I run my fingers through the front of my hair, pushing it out of my face. The redness in my eyes started to lighten up from when I was getting teary-eyed. I wasn't crying. Honestly, what is there for me to cry about?

It was just a dream.

It doesn't matter. I mean, it does matter because it was Morris-Lina, but I can't let that get to my head. I already mourned about it. I was locked in my room for a few days, reminiscing all the good times I had with her, and that was it. I don't remember crying at her funeral. I don't think mom or dad did either, which surprised me because they were always on her case. Maybe that's why they didn't cry.

God, that's awful.

The only reason why I didn't cry was that…well, I don't know. I just couldn't, but I still miss Morris-Lina. A lot.

Just forget about it, I tell myself.

I splash some cold water on my face before heading back to my room, taking slow and deep breaths. As I close my bedroom door, my phone repeatedly vibrates against the top of my dresser. I sit down on the edge of my bed before checking to see who the hell is calling at me at four-thirty in the friggin' morning.

I groan when I see Alejandro's name on my screen. I know that I told him he could call me whenever he needed me, but not this early in the morning. Someone better be dead, so help me, God.

Still, I answer the phone.

"What?" I don't try to hide my annoyance with him.

"Don't you sound shitty?" He tries to be funny, but I'm clearly not in the mood.

"Thanks." I roll my eyes.

"So, I want to talk to you. I kind of need a favor."

I groan. "It's four in the morning, Alejandro." I pinch the bridge of my nose as the need for sleep increases inside me. "Can't this wait 'til later?"

Alejandro huffs and mutters under his breath. "I was hoping to talk to you the other day, but you looked pretty busy with your boyfriend."

I choke, realizing that he's referring to Christopher. "First off, he isn't my boyfriend. Second, you still could've told me whatever you wanted to tell me that day, so don't blame me." I try to keep my voice down as much as possible so I don't wake up my parents.

Alejandro snorts in annoyance. Probably because he knows that I'm right. After all, he didn't have to leave after meeting Christopher. I don't even get why he did.

Alejandro could've just pulled me to the side and told me whatever he wanted to say. Instead, he just left.

Alejandro then asks me, "What's your address?"

I wrinkle my eyebrows in confusion. "What?"

"Give me your address, and I'll come to see you."

He can't be serious. I shake my head. "Alejandro—"

"Five seconds until I'm pulling off."

"You're crazy. It's too early for this."

"Three seconds."

I hear a car engine turn on.

He's not playing around? He's serious!

"Dude, just call me la—"

"Two seconds. I'll just be driving around all over until I find you." Now that, I believe.

I groan. *"Alright!"* I slap my hand over my mouth, realizing how loud I must've been. I have to be quiet. "Alright, fine." Frustration mixes within my words as I try to whisper into the phone. I give Alejandro my home address, and he tells me that he'll be there ASAP.

And he was.

One second I was lying in my bed trying to force myself to get some kind of sleep, and the next thing I heard was my phone vibrating against my pillow, bringing me back into consciousness. Rather than call me, Alejandro sends me a text, telling me that he's sitting outside of my house in his car.

I look outside my window and see his car.

I sigh.

I throw on a long-sleeve shirt, a pair of sweatpants and slip my feet into the first pair of sneakers that I can find. I manage to quietly leave my bedroom, close the door behind me, and head downstairs. I go through the backdoor since it's a sliding door, and I shut it behind me.

I walk around to the front of the house, heading straight to Alejandro's car. He probably sees me coming his way since he reaches over and opens the door for me to get in. I snort.

"Such a gentleman," I tell him as I get into the front passenger's seat. I shut the door once I was inside. I feel Alejandro's eyes on me, and I look at him. "You wanna take a picture or…?"

"Ta! Please," Alejandro laughs. "You're not even my type. So."

I dramatically roll my eyes. "Well. Ex-cuuuse me."

Alejandro shakes his head, grinning. "You're definitely bushed. I can see it in your eyes."

I gasp and slowly clap my hands to give him applause for stating the obvious. "Great job. And the sooner you tell me whatever you want, the sooner I can get back to sleep."

Alejandro quirks an eyebrow. "Got church or something?"

With a 'pfft,' I shake my head. I can't remember the last we've been to church. It's not that we're non-believers. I know that God is real. It's just that our church doesn't really have the best people to spread the word. They like to twist things around for their own benefit and then act like they're superior. We went to mom's church until abuela died, and then we went to a different church, but that didn't last very long.

It just wasn't the right fit. I also think the priest just didn't like us. He never mistreated us, but he always had this look that had a hint of disdain in his eyes.

Tiredness sweeps over me, and I let out a quiet yawn, covering my mouth with the back of my hand. Alejandro sighs.

"This won't take long, and then you can go back to sleeping and having good dreams."

I feel a tug in my throat from his words. I know he feels terrible, but I wouldn't call my dreams good. But I wouldn't call them bad either. It was like a twisted memory of what actually happened.

But I don't want to think about that right now.

Instead, I listen to Alejandro and what he has to say. He starts by asking me if I remember the two guys who jumped me in the alley weeks ago, and I nod. Alejandro tells me that for the past couple of weeks, one of them has been harassing his sister, Aitana. Turns out, the guy with the X tattoo on his face is named Diego, and he and Aitana had some history. Alejandro already gave him a warning, but Diego didn't take him seriously. Alejandro tells me that he got a phone call from his nephew, Ricardo, late last night that he heard screams outside of her bedroom door and sounded like she was crying. Alejandro was running errands and was out last night, but he rushed home. When we got there, he told Ricardo to go to bed and rushed to Aitana's bedroom. He opened the door, and she was on the floor, crouched in a fetal position, sobbing. The bedroom window was wide open, and he noticed her pants on the other side of the room and her underwear pulled down to her ankles. When he tried to help Aitana up, she kept grunting in pain, and that's when Alejandro realized what happened.

"It was Diego. He broke in through her bedroom window, and he..." His words drift, and he bites down on his bottom lip, trying to hold in the rage stirring up in him. I can see the veins in his neck as he grits his teeth. "It's bad enough that he is the father of my nephew, but after the way he treated her, he has himself to blame for her leaving him. And for him to do this! Fuck!"

My eyes widen. "That guy is Ricardo's father?!" The question comes out more so as a surprised statement than a question. I would have never put two and two together.

Alejandro sighs and clenches his jaw. "I don't know how the two of them ended up hitting it off, but it was while we were still with my aunt. When Aitana found out she was pregnant, Diego basically turned a whole one-eighty and treated her like shit. So, she broke it off with him. He wasn't even there for Ricardo's birth. I was. Me and..." His breath hitches.

I quirk an eyebrow and lightly nudge my elbow into him. Alejandro lifts his gaze, and I can see a surprising look of concern in his eyes. It's like he's too afraid to finish his words. Otherwise, he'd be summoning the Boogie Man or something. Still, he sighs and sits up so he can speak.

"Remember my brother? Álvaro?" he asks.

I remember his face, now that I think about it. He had a muscular build that made him petrifying, but he didn't look inhuman. He had tattoos all down his arms and even some on his chest. I remember admiring them when I was little, and Alejandro swore that he'd get tattoos like his brother once he was old enough. And his hair was surprisingly long, not long like Benton's, but longer than Alejandro's. His eyes were also a piercing hazel brown.

So that's his name.

Álvaro.

Alejandro proceeds to tell me that Álvaro was also present for Ricardo's birth before he left and went off to God knows where. He says that Álvaro found better opportunities for himself out of Philly, but Álvaro never specified what exactly those opportunities were. But as he was preparing to leave, Álvaro told Alejandro that it was his responsibility to look after Aitana and Ricardo and make sure that things in their area were *"under control."*

"So is he like a gang leader or in the mafia?" I ask, keeping my eyes on Alejandro. I try to bury the unsettling feeling bubbling up inside of me.

Alejandro just huffs and rests his head back against the headrest. "It's not like that. It's just..." He sighs. "Look, he never told me what he does. Even if I knew and could tell you, you wouldn't understand."

I quirk my eyebrow, shrinking back a little. "What is that supposed to mean?"

Alejandro snorts, rolling his eyes as if I'm a silly child asking silly things. "C'mon, Don. I know about your dreams and wanting to go to college and all that sappy shit. There's no way you'd ever get the life I have to live. Period."

My face feels warm. His words pierce through me like daggers with how condescending he sounds. "Try me," I mutter under my breath, but he still hears me.

Alejandro shakes his head. "I can't promise you that, Don." He turns his head, looking me in the eye. "But what I can tell you is that Álvaro put Aitana and Ricardo's safety in my hands, and I let her..." He grits his teeth, his eyes getting darker. "...that son of a bitch, he..." A frustrated exhale. He punches his fist into the steering wheel, growling under his breath. His nostrils flare as he looks forward, tightening his jaw.

There is a fire in Alejandro's eyes that I've never seen before. A giant ball forms in my throat, and I stiffen up. I understand that anger, that hunger he has. If it were Morris-Lina, I'd be ready to kill someone too. And I'd blame myself too for what happened to her. Hell, sometimes, I still think it's my fault that I hardly helped her out after her first boyfriend forced her into having sex, and then she ended up getting pregnant. Even though I took her to the clinic and made sure our parents never found out, I feel like I could've done more. And I could've. I know it.

I sigh. "Alejandro—"

"He needs to pay," Alejandro says, still glaring forward. "He needs to pay, and I can't let this get out to Álvaro. Not by any chance."

I wrinkle my brows. "Why?"

He turns his gaze to me. "Because he'll kill me. That's not me being dramatic either. He said that if I slip up once, he'll kill me, and Álvaro is a man of his word, Don. He says what he means and sticks with it."

Before I know it, Alejandro is speaking too fast, and I can hardly process anything he's saying. The idea of his brother finding out what happened to Aitana and letting Álvaro down frightens him. From what I remember, Álvaro was always an intimidating guy, but he was always quiet. He would never yell when he scolded Alejandro. He always spoke in a calm voice, but the way he looked whenever he'd scold him was the scary thing. It was like he was ready to shoot him with bullets coming out of his eyes.

I sharply inhale, finally mustering the courage to silence Alejandro. "Alright, alright." Sigh. "I-I, I'll help out."

Alejandro shuts up and looks at me with wide eyes. "Seriously?"

I nod. "Yeah."

The look on Alejandro's face makes my stomach churn as the corners of his mouth slightly curve upward, and I finally realize the words that I just let escape from my mouth. *Shit.*

I clear my throat and sit up, turning my body away from him as I look forward. "What're you going to do?"

Alejandro deeply sighs, turning his gaze forward into the empty street. "I don't know yet. I just have to make sure Álvaro doesn't get involved."

My throat feels dry. "When you figure it out, give me a call."

"Count on it."

I didn't give him the chance to add anything else, and I let myself out of his car. I told Alejandro that I would see him later, and he just flashed a sinister grin as if he's the devil with a couple tricks up his sleeve. I step back far enough and watch as he pulls off, tires screeching against the road.

My teeth chatter as I keep my lips pressed together. My mind slowly processes everything that just happened, and I feel like punching myself in the balls right now.

You're a friggin' dumbass, Donald, I hiss to myself.

I know!

Why would you agree to this? Puto!

I kick at the ground, letting out a defeated groan as I realize how much I'll probably regret this later.

Week 3, Tuesday

I was up late last night, puking my guts out. I didn't expect it to happen again, but it did. I guess the idea of helping Alejandro carry out his plan to "take care" of the guy who assaulted Aitana is really starting to sink in. But I can't back down now. What does that show? Besides, I owe this to him, don't I?

I think I do. Probably not, but I don't know. Now is not the best time to be second-guessing myself. Usually, I'd call abuelo or abuela, ask them for guidance, but I can't summon the dead. If I could, well, I still don't know what I'd do. Maybe things in this house would eventually get better.—D.G.

"Mister Gonzalez?"

My head snaps up from my journal, and I lock eyes with Mr. Hua. His thin lips are slightly curled into a faint grin, and he holds his gaze on me through his square glasses that sit perfectly on the bridge of his nose.

I clear my throat, sitting up in my seat. "Mister Hua?"

"Shouldn't you be getting to your first class period? The bell just went off." Mr. Hua folds his arms over his chest, giving me a look.

I look around, realizing that everyone in my homeroom is gone, and the classroom is now being filled with students who have Mr. Hua for the first period. I slam my journal closed and quickly gather my things, apologizing to Mr. Hua for delaying his class. Quite frankly, I don't know what happened.

I was writing in my journal one second, trying to make up for the number of days I haven't jotted down my thoughts as recommended by Counselor Malik. And now—now I'm about to be late for class. That never happens!

Get it together, Gonzalez.

I mentally slap myself.

Suddenly, I feel Mr. Hua's hand grab onto my arm as I'm about to walk past him to leave. He holds his gaze on me, but the look on his face unexpectedly changes. It's like he's worried for me, but I don't know why. I just lost track of time, I guess.

Then, Mr. Hua asks me, "Are you okay, Donald?" He speaks to me softly, and I also realize that it's the first time Mr. Hua's called me by my first name.

I nod, telling Mr. Hua that I'm fine. I look him in the eye as I tell him, hoping that he believes me. But through his forced smile, I can tell that there is a bit of doubt. I just walk past Mr. Hua and hurry off to my class with Mr. Enrique.

I couldn't get the look on Mr. Hua's face out of my mind throughout the day. Nor could I forget the sound of his voice. I know Mr. Hua cares about his students, but he can be stern as hell. He doesn't play games, and he sure as hell does not like it when people dilly-dally. I'm surprised that he didn't push me out of the classroom while scolding me down.

I must've really been out of it for him to go easy on me.

Although, it is kind of weird that he was that way towards me.

I just let it go.

I manage to get through my first three class periods before it reaches my lunch period. Although, I have to skip lunch because I have a session scheduled with Counselor Malik. I think about ripping out the journal entry I wrote this morning or maybe "forgetting" to bring my journal.

But Counselor Malik is impossible to fool.

It's like he wears glasses that detect bullshit spot-on.

I let out a sigh, puffing my cheeks as I enter Counselor Malik's office. I knock on the doorway to his office, getting his attention. Counselor Malik looks up from whatever he's working on at his desk and pushes his thick, square glasses on his face.

"Come on in." He smiles, gesturing for me to enter.

I close the door behind me as I step inside.

I walk over to the usual chair that Counselor Malik makes me sit in during our sessions, and I slip my arms out of the straps of my bookbag before I sit down. I hear Counselor Malik clear his throat, and I look at him over my shoulder. He looks up at me while shuffling the papers together on his desk to make a neat pile.

"You can sit, Donald." A small chuckle at the end of his words. "Make yourself comfortable."

I snort at his words, rolling my eyes as his attention goes back to the papers on his desk.

Make myself comfortable.

I practically plop myself into the seat, sitting back into the cushion of the chair. I pull out my journal from my bookbag, tossing it onto the small table beside me. I then notice a small foam ball on top of the table, and I pick it up. I lean back into the chair, tossing the ball around in my hand to distract myself as I wait for Counselor Malik.

. . . .

I swap out my textbook for Honors Algebra II for my Economics textbook as Peter rambles on and on about how he has what he calls "the perfect date" arranged for him and Jen Li tonight. I try to listen, but I'm hardly interested in his plans with Jen Li.

I am happy for him, nonetheless. Peter deserves this. Besides, I've never seen him so nervous about something before. It is rather adorable of him. Benton even teases Peter a bit, saying that Peter's smitten, but Peter denies it. But I wouldn't be surprised if Peter does end up calling me next week, saying that he's practically in love with the girl. He falls hard too fast from time to time, and he does get hurt because of it, and that's because his heart is probably the biggest organ in his body. He's easily manipulated, and I guess that's why Christopher is usually so hard on him and protective, which isn't always right.

But I'm barely listening to Peter now, but luckily, the others seem pretty invested in what he has to say. Especially Benton since he finds some humor in all of this.

My mind drifts off to my therapy session with Counselor Malik, still trying to process how well it went. I mean, it's not like Counselor Malik is terrible at his job, but he always has to nitpick on the things that don't matter. Like, there was a moment during today's session where Counselor Malik wouldn't let go of the fact that I threw up the other day and then again last night. He kept pushing the idea that it was because I have PTSD from Morris-Lina's death since this had happened before when Yago was hiding under his bedsheets as a joke, and it scared the shit out of me.

I just shook my head, knowing damn well that couldn't have been the case. I don't have PTSD. I just don't like thinking about Morris-Lina that way—so I try not to, even though it does occasionally happen. That's all. It doesn't mean I have PTSD, and I wish Counselor Malik would get that through his thick head!

Dios mío.

But other than that, everything else was fine. I was surprised that he didn't ask any questions about my parents since he bugged me about my thoughts on Morris-Lina, but I guess he figured: *what's the point?*

Thank God.

I close my locker shut, slipping out of my thoughts. Rarely, I'll actually look forward to going home, but today is that type of day. Although, I did tell Meagan that I'd take her home since it's been a while since I've taken her home. She refused at first, insisting that she'd take the train and bus home with Benton, but Benton corrected her, saying that his older sister, Roselle, was picking him up after school since he and his folks were going to visit a relative or something.

That meant Meagan would be heading home alone. But she made it clear that she was a big girl and could fend for herself. But then I asked her, *"Don't you have to get home before the street lights come on?"*

She nodded, *"Yeah?"*

"And what if transportation is delayed and you're coming home by yourself? You know how your mom gets, right?"

Once that sank in, Meagan gave up, and I was victorious. I could tell she felt terrible, even though I kept telling her that I liked taking her home. Well, actually, I said to her that it was no big deal and that it was my pleasure. Meagan would just shrug, saying she didn't want to seem like a burden since I "looked tired," and she wanted me to get home ASAP.

I just laughed, trying to rub off what she said. I know she doesn't mean any harm by it—I know she's just looking out for me. But she worries about nothing. So, I assured her that I wasn't tired.

And I'm not.

Maybe a bit, but not to the point where I'll fall asleep behind the wheel. I'm still able to operate a moving vehicle.

As we're all heading downstairs to leave through the school's main entrance, I hear Peter ask me for my opinions about his plans tonight for his date with Jen Li. As if hearing the views of everyone else wasn't enough.

Don't be an ass, Don. This is Peter. He just wants your help.

I sigh.

"You didn't get candles, did you?" I ask.

Peter's eyebrows wrinkle in confusion, and his eyes scream unnecessary concern and worry. "I didn't even think of that!" He smacks his forehead, calling himself an idiot.

I suddenly feel something pinch me under my arm, and I hiss, jolting my arm up. I whip my head around, meeting Carmen's dagger-like eyes as she glares at me with a stern look on her face. She probably thinks I'm causing Peter to worry about nothing, but she didn't even give me the chance to finish what I was going to tell him. I just roll my eyes at her.

I settle my hand on Peter's shoulder, trying to get him to relax.

"Bro, chill, alright?" I sigh. "I was gonna say, leave candles out of this one. It's your first date, right?"

Peter nods, looking at me. "Mhm."

"Yeah, so just keep it simple. Like, offer a sneak peek on what she can expect from you." I wrap my arm around his neck, letting my hand drape over his chest.

Benton then chimes in, "So she doesn't think you're predictable?"

I shrug. "That, and also, so you don't scare her off."

The look on Peter's face slowly changes as his lips fall into a straight line, and he takes a sudden interest in his white sneakers. The way he bites down on the corner of his bottom lip is a clear indicator of how much he is overthinking everything right now. It's not like he'll one day have to marry this girl.

I don't get why he's putting so much pressure on himself.

Carmen pushes me aside and slings her arm around Peter as a way of comforting him. She sucks her teeth. "Well, I think whatever you have planned, Jen Li will love it." Carmen then whips her around to scowl at me.

I just look at her, bothered that she somehow thinks I'm in the wrong for helping a guy out. After all, Peter asked for my input. It wasn't like I was telling him to not be considerate of her. I just don't want Peter to be taken advantage of because he falls for people quickly. Christopher and I are the only ones who have seen this happen before. We're the ones Peter will call if something goes down, or his aunt will contact us, asking about his whereabouts if Peter isn't home by a particular time. And then, Christopher and I are the ones who will look for Peter and find him sitting alone somewhere with so much hurt in his eyes, even though he'll try to hide it with a feigned smile.

Carmen's never dealt with that before! She's never seen Peter so hurt. So she has no right to judge me for whatever I say to Peter!

I sigh, moving to stand on the other side of Peter, away from Carmen. Peter looks up at me when I rest my hand on his shoulder.

"She'll like you." The words come out of my mouth effortlessly, but I know that my eyebrow is probably twitching. I have to seem believable. "Why else would she say yes to being your prom date? The girl likes you. You got a big heart, and my *God*, that's one of your best qualities. It's nothing to be worried about. So, chillax."

Peter opens his mouth as if he's about to say something, but he decides to close it and keep his thoughts to himself. He just nods, pressing his lips together in a faint but genuine smile.

As we finally exit the building, Christopher puts his hand on my shoulder, and I nearly jump, turning my attention to him. Meagan waits for me at the bottom of the steps to the front entrance while talking to Benton as he waits for his sister to come to pick him up.

Christopher looks over his shoulder, taking a quick glance at Carmen as she talks with Peter off to the side. She's probably giving him more words of encouragement for his date tonight with Jen Li. He just nods his head, listening to whatever she has to say. But it's not like dismissive nodding—he's actually interested in what Carmen has to say to him. He holds eye contact with her, pressing his lips firmly together, and his eyebrows knit together in a way. All Peter's missing is a notebook and a pen to take thorough notes, even though he's not going to need them.

I roll my eyes, a soft sigh coming from my throat.

"She means well," I hear Christopher say. He looks at me with furrowed eyebrows, and his green orbs practically gleam from the sunlight, making them look lighter than usual. Close to gems.

I shrug, folding my arms over my chest. "I know that." I look Christopher in the eye. I know I have to be careful with whatever I want to say next since Carmen is still his girl. I pause and take a breath. "She just hasn't seen Pete hurt like we have, you know?"

Christopher's nostrils flare when he sighs, but he doesn't look irritated by what I said. He just removes his hand from my shoulder, stuffing his hands into the front pocket of his hoodie. Judging from the way he's looking down at the ground, Christopher probably sees where I'm coming from. Even though Carmen has a right to her opinions, she didn't have to scold me for being upfront with Peter. She may not have said anything outright, but the way she kept looking at me every time I tried to get a word in—I'd be lying if I didn't say that it was starting to piss me off.

Christopher rocks on his heels before shifting his attention back to me, looking me in the eye as his lips pursed. "She's been having it rough at home lately." The way his words come out, it's as if a weight has suddenly lifted from off his shoulders. "She's been staying at my place since the weekend. My dad's not too keen on the idea and wants her to go home, but I made it clear to him that if she goes, I go too." Christopher doesn't even bat an eyelash as he talks, and his words come out clear as he tries—and fails—to suppress his Irish accent.

My throat becomes dry as I take in what he just said. *Crap.*

"I had no idea," I tell him, my words dying off at the end.

You're a real jerk, Gonzalez, you know that?

Christopher shakes his head, and a faint smile starts to pull at his lips. "No one did. She made me not say anything." Christopher then takes another look over his shoulder as Carmen laughs at whatever Peter just said to her as he uses his hands to add more emphasis to his words.

I notice the look in Christopher's eyes as he watches the two of them. Or, maybe it's just Carmen he's watching. Regardless, there's so much admiration in his eyes. I'm waiting for the sparkles to form in his eyes like they do in anime as his smile starts to widen. I notice the redness in his apple cheekbones and just how infatuated he looks from the sight. It's as if he's forgotten his whereabouts and only has eyes for what's in front of him.

The boy is in love, that's why.

I snicker, shaking my head.

"You really hit the jackpot, haven't you?"

A soft noise escapes from Christopher. Christopher slowly turns his head around, so he's looking at me. His eyes dart to the ground as if he's in deep thought on what to say, but then, the words finally come to him from the Heavens.

"She gets it, Don." Christopher's green eyes meet my brown ones as he licks his dry lips. "She knows what it's like to have hopes for someone and then to get played. Long before the two of us got together, and I was always the one who was there for her." A chuckle and a pause. "To be honest, I didn't think she'd trust me, even though I was always there for her. But she did, and here we are. That's all she wants for Peter. For him to find his person."

My chest suddenly tightens when Christopher takes a small step forward, still looking me in the eye. I try gulping to help get rid of the dryness in my throat, but that only makes it worst as Christopher's eyes never leave mine. I already know he probably thinks I'm an asshole for criticizing his girlfriend, but she was nothing more than a friend before Carmen was his girlfriend. She's my friend too, at that.

Christopher then leans forward, smirking.

"You'll get it one day too." A wink.

I snort, shoving him away. Christopher just laughs, trying to catch himself to prevent himself from falling on his ass.

I can hardly look at him as Carmen finally comes up behind him. Her arms reach up to wrap around his tall torso, and she manages to poke her head under his arm, resting against his side. Christopher lets his arm wrap around her, pulling Carmen close to him before he plants a kiss on the top of her head.

I huff. "Get a room."

Carmen scrunches her nose at me, making Christopher laugh a bit. I roll my eyes. The guy is so whipped.

Christopher tells me that he'll see me tomorrow, and we bump each other's fists before he leaves with Carmen in his arms. All I can do is just watch them. It's like they're addicted to each other, but at the same time, it's not a bad thing as some would think. They're not toxic, just happy—and there's nothing wrong with that. But I still get a strange feeling in the pit of my stomach every time I see them holding hands or kissing. Even if it's just a peck on the cheek, I wonder if I'll get hives from just watching them. As if it's something I should repent, but I know that's not it at all.

I then think about Christopher's words: *"You'll get it one day too."*

What is that supposed to mean? I wonder.

I shrug it off.

It probably doesn't mean anything.

I look at the bottom of the steps as a car pulls up to the curb, honking. Benton yells out something Korean, stomping his foot as the car stops right beside him and Meagan. I figure that's probably his sister picking him up. Before he gets in the car, Benton says something to Meagan, making her laugh.

My heart pounds heavily in my chest, and a strange feeling starts to bubble in my stomach. I don't feel nauseous, but my face starts to feel warm.

It's all in your head.

Regardless, I fight through whatever it is, telling myself to get a grip as Benton gets in the car, leaving with his sister. Meagan then looks around like a lost puppy before finally spotting me at the top of the stairs. The corners of my lips pull upward as my legs finally connect with my brain, allowing me to walk down the steps so I can take her home before her curfew.

Week 3, Thursday

I got a text from Alejandro, asking me to come over to his place after school so we could "talk." My plans were to head straight home after school since I have a couple exams to prepare for before tomorrow. I have one for Honors Algebra II, one for A.P. Chemistry, and then A.P. English. To be honest, I'm not really anxious about any of my tests since I have a firm grasp of what to expect. Still, I don't want to be up 'til midnight, trying to cram as much information as possible while losing sleep.

Yet, I still respond to Alejandro's text message, asking him his home address. In the back of my mind, I'm wondering if I'll regret this. I already gave Alejandro my word that I'd help him go on a witch hunt and make the guy who assaulted Aitana pay. We already knew who it was. We just didn't have a plan on what to do. Maybe we'll rough him up, beat the shit out of him, and then wreck the guy's car—if he has one. That'd be a solid plan.

Alejandro gets back to me in a matter of seconds, responding to my text with his home address. I sigh, remembering going over to his house when we were kids. I can only imagine the condition it's in now.

I waste no time getting to my locker once I'm dismissed from my last class period. I figure the sooner I get to Alejandro's, the sooner I can go home. The last time I came home late, mom and dad were on my head, nagging me about where I was, which isn't like them. I told them that I decided to drop Meagan off at home, but Meagan and I ended up talking in my car for a long time. We were talking about school, and then she went on a whole rant about Preston slowly turning into a tyrant with production work for their upcoming production for theater.

I remember my parents exchanging glances at each other when I told them I was with Meagan, and my mom even smiled a bit. I rolled my eyes, telling them nothing was going on between Meagan and me, but knowing them, they didn't give a damn. They always come up with ridiculous assumptions, especially when it comes to things between Meagan and me.

Yes, she is beautiful, and yes, I am guilty of sometimes thinking of "what ifs"—but they're just thoughts. Useless thoughts that'll never come to reality. Why am I the only one who seems to get that?

I groan under my breath. *It's whatever.*

As I close my locker, my chest roughly comes in contact with the door for a brief second after someone shoves into my backside. I manage to prevent my face from bashing into the locker door by pressing my hands against the metal to catch myself a bit. I look over my shoulder as the giant figure walks past me.

The familiar mocking chuckle that comes from the person stirs a burning sensation in my core.

Austin Brown keeps one arm around Diana Clovis, but he looks over his shoulder, barely meeting my gaze, to look back. "Low see-ento, muchacho," he titters. It's becoming insulting now the way he says the words. It's as if he's trying to make it clear that he hates the language by speaking like an ignorant child. And then, that stupid smirk on his face on top of it.

I snort, standing up straight. "Come mierda de perro."

I turn the dial to lock my locker, and as I turn around, a pair of hands grip onto my shoulders, whipping me around, and my back is shoved against my locker. I grit my teeth, fighting the urge to wince as my head practically bounces after making rough contact with my locker door. Austin towers over me, sinking his nails and meaty fingers into my skin through my jacket.

He glares down at me as if I would ever find him intimidating. "What was that you said, beaner?" He keeps his voice low so that only I can hear him.

I feel my blood pressure start to rise as my fists tighten by my sides. The word spills from Austin's mouth effortlessly, and my mind suddenly flashes to the time a guy said that to Morris-Lina. We were hanging out with Meagan, Peter, Carmen, Christopher, and Benton after school at Kenny's Dine-n-Dash, and this pompous Yank bumped into Meagan and didn't apologize. Morris-Lina confronted the guy, even though I tried to calm her down. The guy then looked her square in the eye and called her—well, us—*"beaners."* Morris-Lina snapped and practically beat the shit out of the guy.

Looking back, he deserved it, but at the same time, I couldn't have her getting locked up because that guy was an asshole. Yes, I was pissed at her, and I probably shouldn't have been, but I was. She was only proving his point—that we have no control. I just wanted her to get that.

Now, here I am, looking up at Austin Brown as he tightens his grip on my shoulders. I can feel my bones starting to mash together, sending a terrible sensation all through my chest and backside. I clench my fist even tighter, letting my nails sink into the skin of my palms as a way to bring me some kind of relief. In my mind, I see myself shoving Austin off me and clocking him square in the jaw, shattering any chances he thought he had in being a pretty boy. He'd be spitting out his teeth, but that wouldn't be enough for me. I'd keep pounding down on him until his face was utterly ruined. The hell with medical expenses.

I feel my heart clawing its way up my throat, but I swallow it back down, exhaling through my nostrils. Austin's grip on me starts to loosen once Diana steps in. She has her hand on his chest and a strange look on her face, as if she's actually concerned for him. I almost want to laugh at the thought, but I can hardly find the energy to think of this as a sick joke.

Diana speaks softly to Austin. "Babe, c'mon. We have to get going. You can rile him on another day."

Austin snickers. The relief he grants my body is almost too good to be true. I keep my eyes on him as he straights my jacket, dusting off my shoulders to play nice.

"Don't worry, we're all good here." He smirks. "Besides, I'm feeling courteous today." A wink to me. His arm wraps around Diana, and I watch him walk away with a smug look on his face.

As much as I want to deck him, as much as I want to shove him back, and as much as I want to cuss him out—I tell myself *no*.

I have to get out of here. That's all I can do is get out of here.

. . . .

It doesn't take me as long as I thought to get to Alejandro's house. I hardly had to rely on GPS since I slowly became familiar with the route as I followed the directions. Whenever I would go over to Alejandro's place as a kid, I would take the bus. I remember passing a shopping center near Wadsworth Avenue and then a cemetery. A bit further up, Alejandro and I would get off the bus and get some ice cream from Basil's Swirl, which was right next to the bakery, Dynamic Dough. Then, we'd walk the rest of the way to his place. It was about a fifteen to twenty-minute walk to Alejandro's place from the ice cream parlor.

It takes me almost five to ten minutes to find his place. When I turn the corner, a few kids are playing basketball in the middle of the street. They look no older than ten or twelve. It's like eight of them. Two of them grab the basketball hoop from the middle of the street, moving it out of my way as I slowly drive down the road, looking for Alejandro's address. The boys all looked at me with cautious eyes, watching my every move, but none of them dared themselves to do anything. Besides, they're kids—what could they possibly do?

I eventually manage to find a parking spot that's just a few doors down from where Alejandro lives. I get out of the car, locking the door behind me. I look over my shoulder and then around, taking everything in. Nothing's really changed. The houses are still shabby looking, some cars parked up halfway on the sidewalk, and there is some trash on the ground, but that's always been a thing around here. The kids are playing in the street, just like Alejandro and I used to when we weren't running off to the other side of town without anyone knowing. A couple of people call out to each other from different sides of the street, having short conversations, laughing, and carrying on. Music is blasting throughout the neighborhood as if it were a block party.

I laugh to myself, shaking my head. Nothing has really changed.

I walk up the narrow one-way street, looking out for the address Alejandro gave me. It doesn't take me long to find his place. I recognize it almost instantly. The cracked steps lead up to the porch in fine shape, which sticks out compared to the rest of the house's exterior. I smirk when I spot the rusty black mailbox mounted on the wall next to the front door. Alejandro and I would sometimes sit outside on the porch, tossing small balls of paper into the mailbox if we were bored. Whoever managed to get the most balls of paper into the mailbox was the winner, and the loser had to do whatever ridiculous thing the winner dared them to do. So many times, Alejandro had the upper hand, and he'd have me do the stupidest things.

I ring the doorbell and take a step back from the door.

I can hear the sound of a woman yelling on the other side like she's calling out to someone. Then a loud thud practically makes me jump out of my skin, but I stand still at the door.

The front door swings open, and I'm expecting to see Aitana or Alejandro. Instead, in front of me is a woman with long bleached blonde hair that does not compliment her dark tan skin well while wearing eyelashes that could pass for feather dusters. Her tube top manages to shape her waist, but her chest looks as though it's ready to pop out judging from her cleavage, and her jeans hug into her legs, forcing an emphasis on her curvaceous hips and thighs. I clear my throat as the woman looks at me up and down, tapping her long bright colored nails against the doorframe while popping her hip out.

"Can I help you?" There is a hint of annoyance in that nasal voice of hers.

I nod. "Here to see, Alejandro. Is he here?"

The woman purses her lips and shoots me a glare before looking me up and down again. She smacks her lips and gestures for me to follow her. The woman sways her hips as she turns around, flicking her hair over her shoulder as if she has something to prove. I just roll my eyes and follow her inside, closing the door behind me.

The lighting inside the house is darker than I expected, but hints of sunlight manage to creep in through the openings from the blinds. The wooden floors creak with every step I take, and I can see the particles of dust that flutter around in the air. For some reason, I welcome the smell of the home—storage and mothballs. It's comforting. Ever since I was a kid, I always liked the smell of mothballs. Mostly because my abuela's garage smelled of mothballs.

The woman takes me through the kitchen to get to the backyard. From the back door, I see the top of Alejandro's head as he works on the front of his car, keeping the hood of his car up and in place. The backyard is hardly a backyard at all. It's just another narrow street and driveways to the back of people's homes, and each driveway is secured by a wired gate. Some houses have garages connected to the bottom of their homes for the sake of space.

The woman claps her hands to get Alejandro's attention.

"Hey!" she calls to him.

I hear Alejandro groan. "I'm busy."

The woman rolls her eyes, pursing her lips. "You got a visitor." She looks back at me. "What's your name again?"

I clear my throat. "Donald."

The woman turns back in Alejandro's direction. "Yeah, Donald." She folds her arms over her chest and pops her hip out. "Says he's here for you or something."

I hear Alejandro grunt as he sets the wrench down on the small cart beside the car's front. He then steps out from behind the car's hood, wiping his hands with the small cloth over his tatted shoulder. Intricate symbols are tatted all up and down his arms, even his wrists. But they all blend together really well and look neat—some symbols are smaller than others. Even some tattoos stretch across his bare chest— at least from what I can see through his low-cut tank—and along his collarbone. I can't stop my eyes from wandering up and down his arms, admiring how perfect the ink looks on his toned arms and rounded shoulders. To be quite honest, I'd be lying if I didn't admit that I'm a smidge jealous.

The drawstring to his gray sweat pants are pulled tightly, securing the pants right above his hips, and the hem of his sweatpants are tucked into his black combat boots.

Alejandro cards through the front of his hair with one hand, pushing it back and out of his face to show off his undercut along the sides. The one side of his mouth pulls upward as he looks at me.

"I can take it from here." Alejandro leans against the side of his car, crossing one ankle over the other. "Thanks, Mami."

The woman makes a face, but it's not in flattery. Her hip brushes against me as she walks past me to get back inside the house, and she gives me a side-eye glance. I swiftly turn my gaze from her before I feel myself gag. It's not that she's ugly, and she's not. She's just not my type.

I ask Alejandro once she's gone, "Who's that? Your girl?"

Alejandro grimaces. "The fu—? No." Disgust is one way to describe the tone of his voice as Alejandro furrows his eyebrows. "I plan to remain disease-free, thank you very much."

I try biting down on my lip to contain the laughter that tries to escape through my mouth, but a small chuckle manages to come out instead. It shouldn't surprise me that Alejandro would say something so shallow, but at the same time, I don't remember Alejandro having a "type" in terms of an interest in a lover. Judging from his looks and taking what I know of him, he has the experience, that's for sure. More than me, I'll bet.

Alejandro tells me that the woman is a friend of Aitana's, and she's just stopping by since she has to pick up Ricardo from school for Aitana, who is working late at the Dominican hair salon two blocks away from their house, Alejandro said. He then digs into his pants pocket and pulls out his phone, checking the time.

"How much you wanna bet that she forgot about getting Ricardo from aftercare?" Alejandro asks me with annoyance swimming through his words.

I shrug. "I know nothing about this chick, so."

Alejandro raises his eyebrows. "That's fair." He calls out to the woman. "Constance!" Silence. "Constance!"

Finally, "What?!" The woman—Constance—comes to the back, practically swinging the door open to the point where it bangs into the railing.

"It's half-past four now. When are you getting Ricardo?" Alejandro folds his arms over his chest in authority.

Constance rolls her eyes, scoffing. "I'm getting him now." She sucks her teeth. "I ain't forget."

The door slams shut behind her when she goes back inside the house. Alejandro chuckles under his breath before turning his attention back to his car. He grabs the wrench off the cart and throws his cloth over his shoulder.

"You know a thing about cars?" he asks me while propping the hood of the car up higher.

I sigh. I start to take off my jacket. "If a man can't take care of his car, he shouldn't have one, right?" I put my leather jacket on the bottom row of the car. I do the same thing with my uniform shirt, taking it off and tossing it onto the cart, leaving me in my sleeveless undershirt, which is tucked into my pants.

As I turn around, Alejandro whistles, smirking. "No wonder you get the cute ones." He winks with pursed lips.

I roll my eyes, snorting a chuckle.

I stay beside Alejandro as he works his wrench at the engine, unscrewing the bolts from the transmission. There is so much focus in his eyes, I can't help but admire him. Alejandro does have a nice car, and I can't say I blame him for wanting to treat it so delicately. It looks new, but it's nothing super high-tech or fancy. It just looks like a really nice car.

Alejandro steps aside, wanting me to take over in unscrewing the engine. "Let's see what expertise you've got in cars, shot glass."

I give him a look since he just had to use the name I've genuinely grown to despise, but I still take the wrench from him and work on the car. As I work on unscrewing the bolts, Alejandro tells me that he's come up with an idea of getting back at the dude who assaulted Aitana.

A dry, itchy feeling arises in my throat, and I gulp as I listen to what Alejandro has to say.

"I'm all for giving the guy a taste of justice, but if we're going to catch him, we have to be smart about it. I say we grab when he's least expecting it, take him out somewhere, and then we'll deal with him for there. But we gotta keep quiet about it, you know, and make sure that no one is around when we do it." I look at him once he's done talking, and his eyes are already on me. I realize that he's serious.

Alejandro's really thought this through. He doesn't give it a second thought, and he doesn't even smirk in between his words to indicate some type of punchline. He means it.

I swallow thickly. "You're serious?" I try to keep my voice calm as I look at Alejandro dead in his eyes. I'm all for kicking his guy's teeth down his throat. But Alejandro is basically suggesting that we kidnap him to do it, and I'm the only one who sees the fault in that. "We can't just kidnap the guy and make him disappear. Did you really think this through?"

Irritation is obvious on Alejandro's face as his nostrils flare, and he stands up straight, practically scowling at me. "You told me to call you once I figured something out. Well, I did. And it wouldn't be 'kidnapping,' technically."

"Technically?" I lose all control of how I want my words to sound. "Dude, cut the bullshit."

The look in Alejandro's eyes changes real quick. "*You* cut the bullshit. If this was your sister, wouldn't you have done whatever it took to get back at the guy, huh? That's the Donald Gonzalez I remember."

A surge of warmth—more like burning—erupts in my chest, and I tighten my grip on the wrench in my hand. I can feel my bones lock up in my arms. He has some nerve to say something so boldly. Part of me wants to clock his lights out, while another part of me just wants to put him in check because he has no damn right to question what I'd do for Morris-Lina. Of course, I'd do anything for her, but that's none of his damn business. Alejandro has no right to question me! Not one bit!

"Keep her out of your mouth," I hiss through my teeth.

Alejandro takes a step forward, standing just inches from me. The smirk that creeps on the side of his mouth causes my breath to hitch as he stares down at me. He's only a few inches taller, but that doesn't intimidate me if that's what he's trying to go for. I've dealt with bigger douchebags than him—height and size-wise. Austin Brown is a perfect example. Still, Alejandro doesn't bat an eyelash as he disregards my personal bubble. He crosses his arms over his chest, widening his smirk as if he has something to be proud of.

I bite the inside of my cheek, restraining myself from feeding into whatever he's trying to get out of me. For all I know, Alejandro could be wanting me to snap at him. He gets a kick out of pissing me off like that—always has, and I hate it.

Then, he goes, "You always had that look in your eyes. That anger. No wonder you always like to fight." He walks past me, taking the wrench from my hand as he goes to the front of his car.

I furrow my eyebrows, taking in what he just said.

What look? The look of someone who is pissed off?

I snort, shaking my head at his assumption about me. Just because I'm pissed doesn't mean I *always* like to fight. In fact, I do all I can to not fight. Who the hell wants to fight all the damn time? It's not like I'm involved in martial arts. Shit.

I turn to Alejandro as he starts working on his car.

"I don't like to fight." My voice is stern, but a ball still manages to form in my throat.

Alejandro snickers, unscrewing another bolt. "It's nothing to be ashamed of, you know. People like us are meant to live that kind of life. Always running and fighting." He grunts, managing to unscrew another tight bolt. "But the thing is, wanting to get a little blood on your knuckles doesn't make you a bad guy. That's how you take it as, but that's not it, Donald. And the more you deny that part of yourself, the easier it'll be for people to make the worst assumptions about you. Liking to fight and wanting to cause fights are two different things." This time, he's looking at me. "That's why I need you for this one. I need that hunger to get out all that shit you battling and use it to set things right. Alright?"

The color of his eyes seems to lighten as his voice nearly croaks at the end of his words. My heart stops for a second before resuming its average pace. The look in his eyes reminds me of the puppies I'll usually watch on one of the ads for animals in shelters with some sad song playing in the background to make me feel even more horrible about myself for not donating. I feel a knot form in the pit of my stomach the longer I look at Alejandro in the eye. He's always been so convincing—but this has to be his best attempt yet.

I suck my teeth, stuffing my hands into the pockets of my slacks.

"You always had to be such an evil genius of convincing, didn't you?" I let my eyes wander, trying to find as many ways to avoid looking at him as much as possible.

Alejandro lets out a faint chuckle, sniffing from the cold air that hits us all of a sudden. "I've been told that I'd make a killing in sales. Preferably in real estate."

I shrug. "Eh. I can see you go further than that. Toying with emotions and all. Sure played me."

Alejandro lightly shoves me with a 'pffftt,' and I rock back a bit, chuckling. He puts down the wrench before wiping his hands with the cloth resting over his shoulders. He then gives me a cheeky grin. "You're probably better than I am with being convincing. You know, considering you get all the cute girls and all." A twisted grin.

I snort. "What're you talking about?" I ask him, wrinkling my eyebrows.

Alejandro leans back against his car, tossing the cloth back over his shoulder before crossing his arms over his chest. "Oh c'mon, Donald. Stop being so modest. I bet you managed to hold a few fine ones over the years."

I huff. "Think again," I mutter under my breath.

"Oh yeah?" Alejandro seems almost unconvinced as a smirk comes across his plump lips. "How 'bout that girl of yours? The one I saw you with the other day?"

I nearly choke on my own breath when I realize he's referring to Meagan. My mind goes back to Meagan and I bumping into Alejandro when I decided to take Meagan out for fried ice cream the other day. I wanted to get her mind off of school, you know? Help her lighten up a bit. And she loved fried ice cream, so why not? But then, Alejandro popped up, and he made the bold move to introduce himself to her, being all *delightful* in his own obnoxious and invasive way.

I huff. "She's not my girl."

I hear Alejandro go, "Really?" He sounds as if he doesn't believe me, but a childish smirk is twisted on his face when I look at him. "She's quite fine. She's got a cute face and a nice figure. I'm surprised you ain't try to hit that."

Alejandro wiggles his eyebrows—probably as a joke—and my cheeks feel warm. I clear my throat, trying to block out the feeling of my heart pounding heavily in my chest. "Dude, shut it," I manage to get out as I avert my eyes from him.

Alejandro just giggles like a foolish child as he inches closer to me, invading my personal space again. The corners of his mouth are pulled upwards as he arches an eyebrow in a cocky manner. I can tell he's enjoying every bit of this the more he eggs on. "Oh c'mon, Don, don't even deny it. Them wide hips, thighs thick enough to hold, perfectly busty, and not to mention… she's got quite the ass. Golden in all the right places. And I bet she's hella innocent too. She's probably never been kissed, and you're just the guy to break that for her, I'll bet ya."

My fist knocks right into Alejandro's chest, backing him right up off me as his words start to swim in my head. My face feels like it's on fire, along with the rest of me. All of the blood in my body boils, and my pulse races, but I can't tell if it's because I'm agitated from his foolishness or if it's because of something else.

Yes, Meagan is obviously beautiful and has a nice body, even though she thinks otherwise because she's like a size 12 or some dumb shit like that. She's gorgeous. Her curves suit her in their own way. Hell, some girls would probably kill to have curves like hers. I mean, I'd be lying to myself if I didn't admit that there have been a few times where I'd look at her and think, *wow!* But never in a way where I'd want to…I mean, maybe once or twice, but that's irrelevant now.

Dammit!

My legs start to feel like jelly, and I lean against Alejandro's car, but I make sure to not put all of my weight on it. I shoot a quick glare at Alejandro after he asks me if I'm good.

"Don't talk about her like that," I spit out, my words coming out harsher than expected.

Alejandro sucks his teeth, rolling his eyes. "C'mon, man. Lighten up, will you? All I'm saying is that you'd be missing out if you didn't take a shot at what's right in front of you. I'm sure you'd be perfect considering all the practice you've had, am I right?" He flashes a toothy grin and winks.

My cheeks flush at his assumption. The farthest I've gone with anyone is making out. Maybe occasional caressing, but nothing beyond that. My parents just swore that I'd be the one bringing someone home for them to meet, but Morris-Lina beat me to that punch. But I'm confident in what I know I'm capable of, though. It's not like I haven't considered other things and haven't done my research.

Still, Alejandro's assumption that I can just swoon anyone—specifically Meagan—with what I know is just agitating. I look away from him, not wanting to give him the satisfaction that he's already getting under my skin. But that just riles Alejandro more as he gasps in sudden realization and laughs.

"Jesus Christ, dude," he titters, bumping my arm with his elbow. "No wonder you're so uptight! You're still in your cocoon, aren't you? Haven't found the right one to show what you're made of, huh?"

I punch him in the shoulder this time, but that only adds to Alejandro's amusement as he continues to cackle. If I could, I'd hit him where it would really hurt, but I know I'd gain nothing from it if I did. I just keep telling him to shut up, and Alejandro finally manages to catch his breath, reminding me that he's only messing around. Still, I flip him off.

His arm comes around me, and he ruffles my hair. "Aww, you're so cute when you're all flustered, shot glass." He tries to pinch my cheek, but I smack his hand away and manage to shove him off me.

"Piss off," I mutter under my breath. "Don't you got a car to work on?"

Alejandro snorts. "Don't you got a stick up your ass?"

I jeer. "I'm not uptight." I can feel my face starting to get warm as the one side of Alejandro's mouth quirks into his trademark grin. My nose wrinkles, and my brows furrow as I muster a snort in retaliation. I mutter, "Diablo."

A chuckle. "Hm." Alejandro walks on his toes as he goes back to the front of his car, pushing the hood up a bit further before holding it in place. He takes a step back to get a look at me while crossing his arms over his chest, cocking his hip out. "So, can I count on you? About the plan?"

Oh right. That.

I clear my throat, taking in a quivering inhale as I force myself to nod. Alejandro probably knows that I'm still skeptical of what he has in mind. He sucks his teeth, rolling his eyes. "Fine, we won't kidnap him. We'll still lure him out, though."

"How?" It comes out like a laugh. "With your boyish charm?"

Alejandro purses his lips, shrugging. "*That.* But I do have other ways, shot glass." Wink and a twisted smirk. "Now, I could use a hand here if you don't mind."

I open my mouth, wanting to ask Alejandro what else he has in mind regarding the plan, but the question fades from my mind as Alejandro gestures for me to come over to him and help him with his car.

Week 4, Sunday

Gabriel tugs on the collar of my jacket as I tie the last knot to his shoelaces. No matter how many times I tell the kid to stay still, he just keeps tugging and tugging, wanting me to cave into whatever it is he wants. If he weren't so small and if it weren't for those big eyes of his, I'd pay him no mind. Instead, I groan, grabbing him up by the arms before propping him on my leg.

"Why are you so needy?" I smirk, letting my fingers lightly brush against the skin of Gabriel's neck, making him smile and wiggle around.

Mi tía called me this morning, asking if I could watch the boys since she was called into work last minute to handle some presentation for a client. Even though I agreed—obviously—I still thought it was strange for her to be working on a Sunday. Usually, she works on Saturdays and has Sundays off. Then again, she said it was last minute.

So, I came over to her house, and I decided to take Yago and Gabriel to the playground. Since it's Sunday, I figured that people were probably attending church being Holy or hanging out with family or something. Surprisingly, the park is quiet, but some other kids run around as their guardians or parents watch over them.

Yago is on the jungle gym, swinging on the monkey bars, calling for me to look at him. His legs are like string beans as they dangle while he rocks back and forth to launch for the next bar ahead of him.

"*Oye!*" I call out to him. "Yago, watch it! Don't hurt yourself!"

Yago clearly ignores me as he lunges forward, grabbing hold of the next bar ahead of him. I can only thank God that the kid didn't fall flat on his ass or break his face. Both he and Gabriel are like porcelain dolls sometimes. One second, they're sturdy— can't nothing hurt them. But then, the next, they're crying with busted knees and scarred faces.

Thankfully, Gabriel takes it easy as he remains seated on my lap, burying his head into my chest. I ask him if he wants to play on the slide, but he shakes his head, making a noise. It's like a grunt, but it's also a growl—like he's defiant. I furrow my eyebrows, pulling his hat up a bit so I can get a better look at his face. His face is all scrunched up, and his lips are turned downward into a scowling frown.

I tell myself not to laugh, but the way Gabriel nuzzles his face further into my chest while grunting makes it almost impossible for me to keep a straight face. Instead, I clear my mouth, trying to swallow down the feeling as I tighten my arms around Gabriel.

"What's wrong with you, huh? Do you hate the slides now?" I ask him, trying to bury my urge to laugh.

Gabriel nods his head, and I hear a soft whimper escape him this time. His eyebrows furrow, matching the sudden emotion within his big, glossy eyes. I quirk an eyebrow, taken aback by the look of fear in Gabriel's eyes when I bring up the slide. Typically, Gabriel is pulling me over, practically begging me to go down the slides with him. He'll get excited, jumping up and down, wanting to go again and again—at least three or five times until I tell him it's enough and to play on something else.

Now, all of a sudden, he doesn't like the slides?

What gives?

I use my finger to lift up Gabriel's chin, so he's looking at me. He tries to bury his head back into my chest, but I turn him around, so he's facing towards the jungle gym, and I wrap my arms around him to hold him in place. He makes a noise, squirming in my hold.

"Hey, hey," I say sternly. I tap my hand against Gabriel's thigh, making him whip his attention up at me. Gabriel just stares at me with the same big eyes. I sigh. "Why don't you like the slides anymore? Are they scary?"

He shakes his head.

I try to think. "Are the slides for babies, and you're a big kid now?"

Gabriel shakes his head in denial.

Jesus Christ.

There's no point in trying to figure this out, I realize. Gabriel's not going to talk. Gabriel never talks. He'll just look at me with those big eyes of his, or he'll let out some kind of whine or grunt. But nothing will help make me understand whatever he's trying to say. But I don't hold it against him. How could I?

I just look at him, letting out a small breath. I press a light kiss to the top of his head, and Gabriel stretches out his arms, wanting to wrap his arms around my neck.

"Nah-ah-ah." I pull my head back a bit. "I know that trick. You're not going to stay over here all this time." I look out, seeing how much fun Gabriel could possibly have around the jungle gym. Even if he doesn't like the slides anymore for some weird reason, he can still enjoy other things. "Let's try the swings, yeah?" I smile down at Gabriel. "That'll be fun. And look! It's all open!"

Gabriel folds his arms across his chest in petty defiance.

I take in a sharp breath. If only Yoselin could see what I have to put up with when she's not here. But the thing is, Gabriel's not usually this defiant. He's typically the easy one. At least with me, he's easier to deal with than Yago.

I hold my ground, though. "C'mon." I pat Gabriel's bottom for him to get up off me. "We're going on the swings. Let's go."

A deadpan expression spreads across Gabriel's face, but I flash a smirk at him. Usually, he'll smile back, but instead, I watch as my four-year-old cousin *rolls* his eyes at me before jumping off my lap, and he goes over to the swing set. The fact that Gabriel, of all people, rolled his eyes at me—it's not something I should take lightly. Usually, it's Yago giving the attitude. That's probably who Gabriel's been taking lessons from, obviously.

Honestly, it was only a matter of time before Gabriel picked up on a few things from his big brother. Yago is older, and even though Yago messes with him a lot, Gabriel admires the heck out of that kid—as he probably should.

I just sit back on the bench, letting out a sigh as I watch Gabriel climb up into the swing and a little boy runs up behind him, offering to give Gabriel a push. He smiles, nodding his head. The boy looks around his age and has thick, coyly hair. I can't fight the smirk that pulls at the corners of my mouth as Gabriel's smile widens more and more the higher the boy manages to push him.

I look over in Yago's direction, and I see him running around, playfully chasing after a boy who looks familiar. The two of them are laughing as the boy tries to dodge

Yago every chance he can. Suddenly, a woman's voice calls out to them, making them stop, but they keep laughing. I look over, trying to find the voice's source.

My breathing hitches when I spot Aitana standing tall with her arms crossed over her chest, looking out at the two boys, but she only speaks to her kid—Ricardo.

She goes, "Ricardo, ten cuidado! No corras tan rápido!"

Still laughing, Ricardo calls back to Aitana, "Sí, mamá!" He takes off running again, this time chasing after Yago, who screams in laughter.

Aitana shakes her head and looks off to the side. Her eyes suddenly meet mine, and for a moment, my body shuts down, and I'm frozen. I was not expecting to see her here, but I still acknowledged her presence and gave her a small wave with a slight smile. Aitana takes it upon herself to approach me. As she makes her way over to me, her head is somewhat facing downward, but not like she's ashamed.

I can't say it's easy for me to look at her as she approaches me. I feel my heart sank to the pit of my stomach as I think about the way Alejandro said he found her the other night. I can't even imagine what could possibly be going through her mind. I know Ricardo is probably worried to death about her, even though I doubt she and Alejandro sat down with him and told the little guy what happened.

And it's crazy too because when I look at Ricardo and then think about that prick with the X tattoo, I wouldn't have thought he'd be the spawn of someone like that. Hell, I'd be surprised if Ricardo knew that piece of shit was his father. The kid doesn't need someone like that in his life, and I'm sure if Ricardo was a bit older and had a bit more strength on him, he'd beat the hell out of that guy—Diego, I think is his name?

I sigh.

I figure Alejandro's witch-hunting plans are kept on the down-low and are out Aitana's knowledge, so I make sure to not mention anything when she comes over.

"Mind if I join you?" she asks, knitting her brows together from the bright sun that beams down upon us.

I scoot over a bit, making room for her to sit next to me. I watch as she tucks the loose front strand of her hair behind her ear, sitting down on the bench. Aitana crosses her right leg over her left, relaxing back against the bench.

A small sigh comes from her, and she whips her head over to look at me. Her lips remain in a flat line. "How're you doing, Donald? It's been quite some time." She looks me up and down as if she's trying to figure out what part of my body is best for her to look at.

I shrug, tilting my head back a bit. "I've been better." I take in the swift but gentle breeze that swoops in out of the blue. "The weather is nice." *Ugh, small talking? Seriously?*

"I suppose so," Aitana agrees. "Spring is the best season, in my opinion. Summer will be here before you know it." I catch Aitana staring at me with a faint grin pulling at the corners of her mouth. "Did you hear back from those colleges yet, English boy?"

My lips part open, and I sit my head up. *She remembered?*

I clear my throat and feel a tingle along the back of my neck, making me itch. I scratch the spot for a second and avert my eyes from Aitana.

I tell her, "No. Not yet."

She goes, "Hm?"

I shift my eyes back to her, studying the look on her face. "What?" I can't help but ask as she looks forward with her eyebrows knitting together.

Aitana shakes her head. "Nothing. It's just…." She twists her lips and starts to ponder. "…don't you usually hear from schools by like March?"

Yes.

"I guess so."

That has crossed my mind multiple times. It's not like my application got lost or anything. I submitted everything online, so I should have received something from the schools I applied to by now. The fact that even Aitana is wondering about the delay makes me wonder if I ever had a shot going to either of the schools I planned on attending. For all I know, I'd probably be better off going to community college, even though Morris-Lina would've had my head if she had heard me even consider that as an option.

It's kind of funny too. When I was applying for different colleges, Morris-Lina was hovering over my shoulder the whole time to make sure that I didn't apply for community college. I tried to get her to back off, but she was like, *"I'm just making sure you don't sell yourself short. I know you too damn well, so don't even."*

And then, when I tried to encourage her to apply for schools, she just laughed, saying that college wouldn't have been best for her. I didn't get why she felt that way. Just because Morris-Lina struggled with some of her subjects, that didn't mean that she was incapable of making it through college. She was just as brilliant as she claimed I was.

If only, is all I can think of when looking back. *If only.*

"Donald?"

Aitana's soothing voice pulls me from my thoughts. I blink as I feel my eyes getting dry from staring out for too long. Aitana asks me if I'm alright, and I tell her that I'm fine. I even smile to give her more reassurance.

Aitana then calls out to her son, telling him to stop climbing up one of the poles to the swing set. When I look over, I realize that Yago is doing the exact same thing as Ricardo, and I groan. All I have to do is call out Yago's name for him to realize that he's making the wrong move. So, he hops down and off the pole across from Ricardo, and the two of them run around, chasing each other.

Aitana leans back, shaking her head in annoyance. "Sometimes, I wonder if adoption would've been the best choice, you know?" There is a hint of doubt in her words as her voice remains low. I turn my attention to her, noticing the faint smirk on her lips as a small chuckle comes out. "I love him, I do. But sometimes, I just wonder if maybe, he'd be better off with someone else." The smirk falls into a flat line, and she blinks a few times. "But then I remember that he's all I really have. So, in a way, he's a blessing, and I love him."

I swallow down the lump in my throat. I think about how she's probably been protecting Ricardo from his birth father all these years. I know I'm just going off what Alejandro told me, but as I sit with her, I can tell something is eating at Aitana. Her eyes are glossy as if she's holding back tears, and her bottom lip trembles a bit.

I sharply breathe. "Well," I get out as I scoot closer to her, "if you want my honest opinion, I say you're doing great. I mean, from the looks of it, the kid comes from a good home. He's got you, and that's what matters."

Aitana snorts. "You're so naïve."

"How so?"

She gives me a look, and I arch my eyebrow, anticipating whatever response she has for me. Aitana just rolls her eyes and sits back, crossing one leg over the other while looking out to the boys as they play. "Yes, he's got me. But sometimes I think I'm not always strong enough for him, you know?" She tilts her head, looking at me. "What if…what if something happens to me that I can't recover from, and I want to be strong for Ricardo, but I just…can't?" Her words break at the end, and my chest tightens.

I may not know her like that, but I swear, at that moment, I wanted to hug or something. Seeing Aitana like that—all I saw was my sister. Morris-Lina would get choked about things like this, and I would try to figure out what to do to help her, but I was hardly helpful. I didn't want to be like that for Aitana. I couldn't be.

I put my hand on her shoulder and looked her right in the eye. I lean in and keep my voice low when I speak. "You're doing everything right. You wake up in the morning, and making sure he gets to school on time or making sure that he's safe should be enough for you to know that you're doing alright."

"But—"

"Just trust me, okay?" I swallow hard, feeling my chest tighten. "I may not be around you all the time, but when I do see the way you treat your kid, you keep him smiling. So, you are strong for him. Trust me."

Aitana looks at me with parted lips. I can tell she wants to say something in response, but all the power she has to speak leaves the atmosphere. I guess my words really sunk in.

I sit back. "Besides," I smirk, "the kid will always have Alejandro, so."

Aitana snorts, shaking her head with a twisted grin on her face. She whips her attention back to the boys, still smirking to herself, and I can't help but wonder if I struck a nerve by mentioning Alejandro. I doubt there is any bad blood between them, considering how close they are, but what do I know? Or maybe she *does* know about Alejandro going rouge and wanting to hunt down the guy who assaulted her.

But why would that make her twitch?

Shouldn't she be happy that she has a brother who is bold like that?

So, I ask her, "Are things okay between you two?"

Aitana licks her lips. "Of course, they are. Alejandro has always been there for me. But the thing is…" she pauses and narrows her eyes downward. "…I know he considers me and Ricardo as his responsibility. Before our older brother left, he was strict about Alejandro protecting me and Ricardo. And ever since then, Alejandro has been wrapped up in things that he shouldn't be in."

I tightly press my lips together, wrinkling my eyebrows in confusion. *"What sort of things?"* is what I want to ask, but I keep my mouth shut. For all I know, it could be similar to whatever things Álvaro is involved in. And regardless of what Alejandro says, I genuinely think Álvaro may be in some sort of gang or the mafia. He just gives off that vibe. Plus, he literally dipped on them and left Alejandro responsible for protecting Aitana and Ricardo while also keeping things in their area *"under control."* You can't tell me that doesn't scream some shady shit.

With a faint grin, Aitana shakes her head and adds, "I wish Álvaro never put that on him. Alejandro isn't meant for this life. Sometimes, I even pray to God that I'll walk into his bedroom one day, and everything is just cleaned out. All his clothes are gone, his car is gone, and he's gone. He doesn't even have to explain anything to me because I'll know he's out of this place and on the road somewhere far. Maybe he'll call me when he's halfway to wherever he's going, but at least he's gone. I don't know if that makes me a terrible sister or what, but I'd rather him not be here than suffer staying here." A soft laugh escapes her lips, but it's not in amusement. It's one of those laughs where there's some pain in the mix, but the person tries to fend it off with a smile, but you can still see some of the pain in their eyes.

I sit up, pressing my back against the bench. I chew the inside of my lip as I think about how Morris-Lina used to say the same exact things about me. She thought I wasn't meant to stay here and that my life was meant to be somewhere and to leave everything behind me. But how could I do that to her? How could I do that to anyone I cared about?

College is one thing, but for life…

…That's another story.

"Maybe," I breathe, trying to suppress the ball forming in my throat as I gather my thoughts. "Maybe he just wants to make sure that you're okay, you know? You are his sister, after all. He's just looking out for you."

Aitana lets out a low sigh, leaning back a bit. "I know that." She watches Yago and Ricardo as the two of them sit on the ground, playing some kind of hand game, laughing at each other. The straight face Aitana holds slowly softens as a smile creeps onto her face as she watches them with such admiration. "Want my advice?"

My eyebrow arches in sudden curiosity.

"Go to Europe," she practically demands. "It doesn't matter which school you choose, but don't stay here. You'd be doing yourself and everyone a favor. Trust me." She gives me a quick glance, tilting her head while her lips remain parted.

My stomach starts to do backflips, and an unsatisfying taste forms in my mouth. It feels like I am in the hot-seat, and what Aitana is asking of me is non-negotiable. And once again, all I see is Morris-Lina in the form of Aitana, and I feel sick to my stomach. I try to let it roll off my back as Aitana stands up from the bench, calling out to Ricardo to get him to stop trying to put worms in Yago's hair.

I watch her march over to Ricardo as she scolds him, and Ricardo starts huffing and puffing.

I jump when I suddenly feel something wrap around my leg, and I look down. Gabriel sits on the ground, keeping his arms wrapped tightly around my leg as he looks up at me, flashing a toothy smile.

I sigh.

I reach down, picking Gabriel up off the ground, and I prop him up on my thigh, dusting off his monkey patterned pajama pants that he refused to change out of before we left the house earlier. I ask Gabriel if he's okay, and he responds by patting his stomach.

I know what that means.

"Hungry?" I ask him, just to be sure.

He nods.

I figure that it's probably way past lunchtime since we've been at the playground for quite some time. I call out to Yago, telling him that it's time to go. He gives me a scowl, but I glare at him before he even has the chance to protest.

I put Gabriel down and grab hold of his hand as Yago clomps over to us. He groans. "Do we have to go?" More so whining than groaning.

I don't even bother looking at him. This is expected from Yago, but I just grab his hand and give him my word that I'll make him and Gabriel one of their favorite food for lunch. Instantly, Yago's mood changes, and he whispers a triumphant, *"Yesss!"* before jumping up and down while holding my hand.

I look back as we're leaving, and I see Aitana pushing Ricardo on the swing. Broad smiles are plastered across both of their faces, and Ricardo urges her to make him higher and higher. It's like something out of a movie, where the mother and child are in their own little happily ever after. I've seen it a dozen times in cliché chick-flicks that Morris-Lina used to watch as her guilty pleasures.

I sigh, and then I remember that I have two children tugging at my sleeves, begging me to get them home so I can feed them.

May.

Week 2, Friday

I'm angry. That's how I'll start off. I've been trying to think of a way to start this whole thing off, but I can't really find the right words to put down, other than stating the obvious. But I have every reason to be. This morning, I found out why I haven't heard back from any schools I applied to. MY MOM HAD MY ACCEPTANCE LETTERS! And I know that they're acceptance letters because they were more like bulky packages than actual letters! And she had them in her dresser drawer the whole friggin' time! Only God probably knows how long she's had them for! The only reason I found out about them was that she was asking me to help her find her keys this morning, so I checked in her dresser since she has a habit of placing things in weird places. But instead of finding her keys, I found my acceptance letters from all the colleges I've applied to!

WHAT THE ACTUAL HELL?!

I don't know why I put everything back, though. I guess I was too shocked to say anything about it? So now, I'm writing it all out because...I can't believe she would do something like that! What psychopath does that?! Actually, psychopaths—plural! For all I know, dad was probably in on it. This is such bullshit!—D.G.

I squeeze the foam stress ball in my hand as I exhale through my nose, keeping my eyes closed. Counselor Malik clears his throat as he turns to the next page of my journal. I hear him shift around in his chair as the sound of leather rubs against the fabric of his shirt and pants.

I'm honestly grateful that he's not reading anything aloud. I can only imagine what thoughts run through his mind as he takes in my recent journal entries. At our last session, he wanted me to focus on the positive outcomes of certain situations and do some personal reflection on how it can lead to the improvement of my character. Right away, I knew that was not going to be a success one bit.

My journal entry from this morning is a perfect example.

I barely slept a wink last night, but not because of my parents' relentless arguing. They hardly argued at all. I just couldn't sleep. It was one of those nights. Then, I had to wake up and get ready for school, which bugged me. If I had things my way, I would've slept in and just called my friends, telling them I was sick.

And then, as I was getting dressed, my mom was panicking since she thought she'd be late for work since she couldn't find her car keys. So, I thought I'd be a model son and help her out. As I said in my journal entry, I checked in her dresser drawer because, like I said, my mom has a habit of putting things in weird places.

I looked through the top drawer, and the more I looked through, that's when I found the envelopes from all five colleges I applied to. They were unopened and thick as hell. For a second, I was ecstatic because it was apparent that I had been accepted into all of them. But then, once I was able to process that my mom had them in her dresser drawer for God knows how long, I was fuming. Still, I stuffed them back into the dresser drawer because my mom called up the steps she had found her keys, and then, she was out the door.

I can feel my blood pressure rising from just thinking about it, and I can hear my heart thump against my chest like a drum. I open my eyes while still tightening my grip on the foam ball in my hand. Counselor Malik keeps his eyes glued to the page of my journal. I assume he's reading my recent entry since his eyebrows knit together as he concentrates on what he's reading, taking everything in.

Knowing him, he'll probably want me to put myself in my mother's shoes as a way of tapping into what she might've felt when I got the acceptance letters. Hell, knowing Counselor Malik, he probably has more empathy for my mother and her actions than realizing that she could've possibly jeopardized *my* damn future!

I'm the one taking a chance to go to college to get out of this friggin' place! Even though I'm not sure if my dad knew about the envelopes, I know how he feels about me wanting to go to school so far away. It probably scares the hell out of them, but that doesn't give either of them the right to keep me from shooting my shot at something. For eighteen years, they've always been in control—especially my mother.

How does someone even justify this?!

A sharp feeling pulls on the side of my temple, causing me to wince. The surface soon starts to throb and slowly numbs a bit as I rub the spot. I probably gave myself a damn migraine, thanks to all this shit.

I groan.

"Are you alright, Donald?" Counselor Malik asks, closing up my journal with a booming slam that echoes throughout the room.

I slowly draw my eyes to him as I continue to rub the spot on the side of my head to bring some relief. I just nod my head as a way of telling him that I'm good. I stop rubbing the spot once I feel the throbbing pain start to lighten up, and I sit back in the chair positioned across from Counselor Malik as usual.

Counselor Malik sets the journal aside before crossing his right leg over his left, resting his clipboard up against his thigh while keeping the papers attached facing him. He stares at me for what feels like an eternity, but it's not like he's judging me, which is surprising. In fact, it's like he's studying me while contemplating what to say in response to my journal entries.

I brace myself for whatever critical observation Counselor Malik wants to share upon reading my journal. Part of me just wants to come up with some lame reason to be excused, like using the bathroom and leaving. But I remember that Counselor Malik isn't an idiot. He knows me all too well at this point.

Just forget it. I huff, finally succumbing to my thoughts.

I sink down into my seat, waiting for Counselor Malik to finally get his thoughts together so he can just break the unbearable silence. Even though the windows are open, there aren't any cars going by, which is strange. It shouldn't be this quiet in Center City. It's Center City! There are usually sirens blaring or cars honking from road rage.

I dart my attention to the clock mounted to the wall.

We have ten minutes left in this session. *Thank God!*

I clench my jaw, squeezing the ball once again.

That's when I finally hear Counselor Malik clear his throat, and he shuffles around his seat. "Donald." Despite him sounding calm, I can tell there is some sternness as a way of him showing his authority over me.

I sigh. "Hm?"

"Can I ask you something?"

Oh great.

I chew the inside of my cheek, averting my eyes from Counselor Malik. I take a sudden interest in the cactus plant settled in the corner of his office by the window.

"Might as well," I manage to say, still avoiding his eyes.

With a deep and irritated sigh, Counselor Malik sits up straight in his chair. "What do you want out of all of this?"

I blink. A sharp feeling erupts in my chest as I grasp his words. The way Counselor Malik looks at me as he carefully removes his glasses from his face and clips them onto the opening of his shirt makes my breath quiver. His eyes practically pierce into my soul, and whatever will I had to move leaves my body as I feel my bones stiffen as I remain frozen in my seat.

What do I want out of all of what?

I ponder on what that could possibly mean. Is he talking about this session? Honestly, if I had things my way, I'd be sitting at lunch with my friends to bring me some kind of pleasure.

I shake my head with much confusion. "What?" I realize that I'm leaning forward a bit as I question Counselor Malik's words, and I ease myself into sitting back into the chair.

Counselor Malik just looks at me blankly before placing the clipboard down on the small table beside him where he's placed my journal. He laces his fingers together, restating his question but in a better way.

"What do you want to gain out of these sessions? I know that you probably didn't want to come here initially, but you still do anyway. So, there must be something you want to gain from all of these conversations we have."

I snort. "Are you serious?" A small chuckle escapes from my mouth as I arch an eyebrow. I can't believe he's seriously asking me this *now*, after all this time. "What choice do I have? If I try to ditch, you'll either alert the principal or my folks, or you'll just add in more time for me to come in."

Counselor Malik purses his lips as his nostrils flare from when he lets out a deep exhale through his nose. "Even so, you still can opt-out. I'm surprised you just don't throw in the towel. It's obvious you don't want to consider what I suggest to you."

I feel my body jerk back a bit as I take in his words. "Excuse me?" I sharply bite back, tightening my fist. My nails sink into the foam ball, probably peeling off the surface.

Counselor Malik snickers, shrugging his shoulder as if he doesn't have a care in the world. "Am I wrong?" he questions, a smile playing at his lips. He reaches for my journal and starts flipping through the pages like it gives him some kind of sick thrill. "I mean, each week, I tell you to consider things that'll help you. I suggest for you to write about things that matter to you, tap into your feelings and dig deep, but all you do is just rant."

He can't be serious.

There is no friggin' way he's serious right now!

My skin starts to feel hot as I clench my jaw, glaring at him. If I could, I'd just walk out, but I know that's probably what he wants me to do. This is all probably some sick joke or tactic he's trying to do, but it won't work.

I scoff. "But isn't ranting all a therapy session is?" I sit up straight, never taking my eyes off of Counselor Malik. The look on his face changes as his smirk starts to soften into a flat line. I add on, "You want me to be in touch with my feelings, well, this is it. It's all there in your hand." I point to the journal in his hand, and Counselor Malik just shakes his head.

"Oh yeah?" He tilts his head, slightly squinting his eyes. He leans forward a bit, trying to seem intimidating, I guess, but I remain still and unfazed. Then, in a soft but clear enough voice, he goes, "Donald, I've been doing this job for a long time. I've dealt with students who've walked away, believing their own lies, and that's only led them deeper into the pit of their own tragedy. I honestly don't want that for you. You have so much potential. But right now, all I see is a broken kid who carries the burden of the world on his shoulders and hates the idea of being able to heal."

He doesn't even blink when he speaks, and I feel every breath in my body just leave. My chest tightens as an unbearable feeling twists in the pit of my stomach— like a knot that can't be undone. I lose all feeling in my fingers as I suddenly get lost from Counselor Malik's alarming gaze. His words are meant to be bitter, but they don't sound that way for some reason. It's like he's trying to set the record straight as if he knows everything there is to know about me. It's completely deprecating, and I'll be damned if I give him the idea that he has me all figured out.

I'm broken but don't wanna heal?

The very thought of that makes me want to hurl this very second. I can't even picture how he probably sleeps at night. Probably alone in a cold bed all to himself.

I bite down on my bottom lip, trying to restrain myself from saying something that I know damn well that I'll regret. So badly, I want to tell him just how wrong he is about all that he said. For once, I would just love to see the look of shock and ruin on Counselor Malik's face. The man has a right to a job. I wouldn't want to take that from him. But my God, he's a high school guidance counselor. Not a licensed doctor or therapist who goes around diagnosing students!

"Say it," Counselor Malik suddenly pipes up. I watch as he sits back in his seat to get comfortable, keeping his fingers laced together. "You clearly have something on your mind." He gestures for me to speak. "You now have the floor, Mister Gonzalez."

Mister Gonzalez.

He rarely ever calls me that.

I'm used to teachers like Mr. Hua calling me by my last name, but Counselor Malik? A sharp sting tugs my chest when I hear him call me that, but I don't let my emotions show. I hold myself together as I stare right back at him. The way Counselor Malik looks at me this time, though, is different. It's like he's genuinely interested in whatever I have to say as he raises his eyebrows, waiting for me to speak up.

The knot feeling in the pit of my stomach becomes impossible to ignore, and my heart feels like it's ready to launch itself out of my throat. I blink, trying to get my eyes to adjust as I feel a sudden dryness attempt to take over. I swallow down whatever nerves try to creep up on me as I gather my thoughts.

My mind replays every word from Counselor Malik's outburst.

That's all it is—an outburst.

It's not an observation or an epiphany.

Just a jumble of words that hold no meaning. And yet, somehow, they manage to stick with me. No matter how much I try to push the feeling down, a rush of nerves starts to build up inside of me. Especially as the words *"broken"* and *"burden"* constantly echo in my head like a broken record.

My breath trembles when I softly exhale. I have to close my eyes for just a second to suppress the burning forming in my eyes right now. A lump starts to develop in my throat, but I let out a soft chuckle as a way of getting rid of it.

My lashes flutter open, and I'm staring at Counselor Malik as he awaits whatever I have to say. It's like he's enjoying this.

I look him right in the eye, and I tell him, "I know that I'm a piece of shit." I feel the one side of my mouth slowly but slightly pull upward as I hold my gaze on him. The expression on Counselor Malik's face starts to die down, but I pay him no mind as I continue. "That may seem pessimistic, but when you think about it, we're all a little fucked, aren't we? And not everyone always follows the books on how to hash things out." I gulp as I feel my throat become dry, making my words come out like a croak towards the end.

Counselor Malik just looks at me with his hands now open and on his lap. Judging by the look on his face, he's struggling to find the right words to respond with. So, he just sits there, quiet and in deep thought. I doubt he even has an ounce of regret for what he said earlier. One thing I'll give to Counselor Malik is that he never backs down from his words. He stands by what he says and runs with it.

Perhaps, that is the only thing I admire about him at this point.

I mean, I know he cares. He just has a funny way of showing it, as most teachers and counselors do. It's not like anyone would want to spend a day walking in the shoes of Donald Gonzalez either. So, he just tries to do whatever he can to work with me. Sometimes, even against me.

And today, it feels like he was entirely against me.

Counselor Malik opens his mouth to speak up, but the sound of the bell going off prevents even the sound of a breath from escaping his mouth.

My body immediately jumps up and out of the seat, and I snatch up my book bag from off the floor near the chair. I slip my arms through the straps, and I hear

Counselor Malik stand up from his chair. I turn around and look down as he holds out the journal for me to take. I look up at him, and he holds a deadpan expression on his face.

I sigh and take the journal from him.

I make my way to the door, but before I go, I look back at Counselor Malik as he walks over to his desk and pulls out the swivel chair for him to sit in. He puts his glasses back on his face, pushing back a couple of loose strands at the front of his hair as he looks down at the mess of papers laid out on his desk.

I can't help but wonder if it's all an act—him seeming unbothered by what I said. But I also realize that knowing how he really feels will only make me feel more shitty than I know I'll feel after leaving his office for the day. So, I clear my throat, drawing his attention up to me for a brief moment.

I take a quick inhale. "I'll see you next week."

Counselor Malik just nods his head, not saying a word, and goes back to tending to his paperwork.

I just leave it at that. I close the door behind me, and I let out a breath as a feeling of relief swims through me. But the feeling doesn't last long, and then the knots in my stomach return, and a burning sensation swims through my chest.

I start to hear those two words again that Counselor Malik had said as his voice echoes in my head. *Broken. Burden.*

I take a deep breath, keeping my eyes closed. The burning in my chest is starting to die down as I let out a smooth exhale. Still, I take another deep breath, but this time, I count to three before releasing another exhale.

When I open my eyes, I realize that I still have the small foam stress ball in my hand. A piece of foam is in my nail from where I peeled off the foam from the ball. I swallow thickly, thinking about whether or not I should go back into Counselor Malik's office to return the ball. But at the same time, I figure that going back in would be a mistake.

So I just stuff the foam ball into my jacket pocket, keeping a firm grasp on it as I walk up the steps and head to my next class period.

Week 2, Saturday

My phone vibrates against my pillow as a continuous alarm goes off on my phone, but I immediately turn it off for the eighth and final time as I keep my head rested on my pillow. The time pops up on the screen, and I roll my eyes, flipping my phone over so I can block out the brightness as I stay buried under the covers.

I can't believe it's only a quarter to eleven.

Usually, I'm up and out of bed by eight or nine on the weekends. But after I came home from school yesterday, I told myself that I'd sleep in. I didn't even bother eating dinner or knocking out the homework I was assigned over the weekend. Between my parents and my counseling session with Counselor Malik yesterday, I just wanted to get home, climb into bed, and forget about everything.

I hear a knock on my bedroom door, and I bury my face further into the pillow, groaning.

Though muffled, I manage to say, "Go away."

But the door still opens. I figure that it's probably my mother since she's the only one who is ever home now on the weekends. The only day dad would have off now is Sundays, and that's if someone didn't call out of work for some bullshit reason.

I close my eyes, tightening my grip on the pillow as I keep my face nuzzled. Then, I hear my mom clear her throat. I can tell she's hesitant to speak up, but I don't know why. It's not like I made it obvious that I found the acceptance letters. I left everything the way I saw it. If I was going to bring it up, I would do it civilly. But for that to happen, I had to not be as enraged as I still am. I have a right to be mad, but I don't want it all to be one big screaming match. We do have enough of those, especially my parents.

I hear my mom step into my room, but I don't think she's anywhere near me. If she was, she'd probably pull the covers off me and try to get me out of bed. But she doesn't. Instead, she just says my name in a soft voice, speaking to me as if I was still a five-year-old kid who she's trying to get out of bed with sweet words and a gentle touch to the head.

"Mijo, I'm going to the supermarket, and then I have to visit your tía Yoselin." There is a moment of silence that feels like an eternity, and my mom takes a shaky inhale. "Are you feeling okay?"

I hear her start to approach me, and I lift my head up from the pillow to speak clearly.

"I'm fine," I pipe up, still under the covers. I hear my mom stop in her tracks, and I feel my heart pick up speed for just a second. I breathe. "I'm just…exhausted." A faint but unsteady chuckle comes out of my mouth.

"Oh," mom says. "Well, then." There is a pause, and I hear movement again, but then I hear the door starting to close. The creak stops. "If you need anything, give me a call, okay?"

I exhale, relaxing my head down against the pillow again. "Okay," I tell her, making sure my back is turned, even though I'm under the covers and she can't really see me.

"Te quiero, mi príncipe."

A ball forms in my throat. Now, I know she's just trying to suck up to me and stay on my good side. Her calling me her prince is basically a sign of her feeling bad about something. She rarely calls me that, just like when she would call Morris-Lina su angelita.

I don't let it faze me, though.

"Okay," is all I say in response.

Then, the door closes, and I can hear my mom walking down the steps. A sigh of relief.

I shouldn't feel this happy about my mother leaving the house, but she honestly couldn't have gotten out of my room fast enough. I already know that I'll hate myself later for having this feeling, but right now, I just let the feeling wash over me as I close my eyes. I pull my legs in close to my chest, curling up like a cat as I nuzzle the side of my face deeper into my pillow.

The light that shines through my window barely hits me due to the thickness of my comforter and bedsheets. When I take a sharp inhale, a whiff of lilac swims through my nostrils from my pillowcase, and I become at ease. I forgot that I washed my pillowcases and bed set two days ago, so the aroma is still kind of fresh.

It's actually nice.

I start to drift into a blank state of mind as my body starts to feel weightless when my phone pings from a notification. I ignore it at first, but then it pings again. And again. And again. No matter how much I try to block out the brightness of my phone screen while ignoring the sound, the vibration is what gets to me.

I groan, eventually succumbing to my irritation as I lift my head up from my pillow and sit upon my elbows. I flip my phone over, looking at the screen, and I see a long text message from Christopher. I furrow my eyebrows, trying to figure out what he could possibly want as I read the first few words displayed from his text on the lock screen.

At first, he's just asking me how I'm doing since I seemed pretty "off" yesterday. He says that about me a lot—more times than I can count on my fingers. But this time, I can't say he's not wrong. After my counseling session with Counselor Malik, I wasn't really in the best mood. After school, the six of us went to Chinatown and hung for a bit. Peter was cracking jokes on Benton since Benton's hair was starting to get long again, and Benton felt self-conscious about it since he was debating whether or not he should keep his hair short. Peter joked that regardless, Benton was always going to be the prettiest best boy out of all of us.

Carmen noticed that Benton was blushing, and she called him out on it, and Peter started to mess with Benton again, only making Benton more and more flustered. Everyone thought it was funny, seeing Benton all flustered, and it was, but I could hardly laugh. My mind was somewhere. But I had to put on a face for the sake of the mood. I just smiled the whole time, and Meagan even asked me if I was alright at one point.

I told her that I was, but she wasn't sure I was honest.

But then I told her, *"Kid, if you're this worked up about me, then maybe we should make this arrangement between us official. We can go to City Hall, file some paperwork, and I'll even get a ring."*

I was joking, of course, and Meagan knew that. She laughed, crinkles forming by her eyes and a smile on her face as she nudged me away. I even looked her in those brown eyes of hers and told her again that I was okay. The smile she gave me, followed by the way she softly said, *"Okay,"* was good enough for me to know that I was in the clear.

I just didn't want her to worry, that's all.

Better yet, none of them needed to worry. We were out to have a good time. I just wasn't in the mood at the time, and it's all thanks to Counselor Malik and his dumb ideas about me.

Yawning, I unlock my phone to read the rest of Christopher's text message. I blink a few times, trying to keep myself awake as I start to feel tiredness overwhelm me since I've been in bed all this time, and I'm finally getting comfortable. I roll over, laying on my stomach, but I prop up my elbows while staring at my phone. The rest of his message consisted of him telling me that I could always talk to him if anything was on my mind, and I sighed.

I texted him back, letting him know that I was okay and that I was just tired. It didn't even take him a minute to respond back after I hit SEND. Christopher asked if my parents were arguing again, and I informed him that my folks hadn't argued for the past couple of weeks. I purposely left out the part about me finding my college acceptance letter hidden away in my mom's dresser drawer since I didn't want to give Christopher any more reason to stay on my back.

Honestly, I just wanted sleep. I didn't care that it was close to the afternoon, and I sure as hell didn't care that I had homework and other stuff to do. I can take care of all that other shit later.

I feel my phone vibrate, and the screen brightens, but I don't bother checking Christopher's response as I flip my phone over, keeping the screen facing downward into the pillow. I bury my head into my pillow, turning my body to the side and keeping my back to the brighter side of the room. I curl up, taking in the comfort of the bedsheets and the warmth that starts to consume me. My lashes flutter shut, and I take a deep inhale, soaking up the fragrant scent still trapped in my pillowcase.

•••••••••

"What're you thinking, Luciana?" Dad's rage was visible as he briskly approached mom from what I could hear on the other side of the bedroom door. "You can't seriously think that this is alright!"

"You heard what the doctor said, Nicolás!" Mom's words had much more force than dad's, but I knew that dad wouldn't back down, even if he tried. Mom tried bringing her voice down, but I could still hear her through the walls since her aggravation always got the best of her. "What are we supposed to do, huh? She refuses to take her pills, so this is the best choice we got."

"By sending her away?!" dad shot back. "Luciana, she's our daughter."

"I know that." The way mom said it—it's like she's annoyed.

"If you know, then you'd consider other options."

I felt my throat tighten as I looked up from the worksheet I was working on for my Honors Algebra II. I felt my fingers lock up as I held the pencil over the dotted line just as I was about to fill out my answer. Morris-Lina kept her legs pulled in close to her chest with her arms wrapped around her legs. The side of her face rested against her knee. There was an emptiness in her eyes as I looked at her.

We have been down this road before with Morris-Lina. It's starting to become like a game of cat-and-mouse with her in a way. Since her middle school diagnosis and being prescribed the proper medications to help her out, Morris-Lina just all will to give a shit. At least, that's what I'm seeing. It doesn't matter how many times mom and dad have to bicker within an ear-shot. She always ends up sitting on the couch, staring out like she's in her own fantasy world.

At first, I told myself to not read into it too much since I'll never know what it feels like to be in her shoes. I mean, our abuela—our mother's mom—was bipolar. And if I'm not mistaken, our bisabuela had schizophrenia, but mamá did not know much about her since she was so young when bisabuela had died. But the thing is, even when Morris-Lina and I were younger and wanted to learn more about our bisabuela, mom would get upset—as in angry. She would also get upset with abuela whenever she would try to tell me and Morris-Lina stories of how mom was when she was young. They were never bad stories. In fact, mom was viewed as an angel through abuela's eyes. But mom would get so irritated and so annoyed by abuela. It was as if mom just didn't like abuela at all.

And I sometimes see mom do the same thing with Morris-Lina. Not when we were kids, but now that we're older. Mom will always be on top of Morris-Lina, but not for the sake of being a "good parent." It was as if she, through Morris-Lina, was incompetent, and she always had to Morris-Lina in check whenever Morris-Lina would try to voice her opinions on how unfair mom would be towards her sometimes.

I could never put my finger on it as to why. The littlest thing, whether it had to do with Morris-Lina not acting lady-like or having something to say, mom would just get frustrated with her. But now…I get it.

And I hate it.

As I looked at Morris-Lina from across the room as she stared out blankly as if all hope was lost, I hated the idea of my mom purposely wanting to shun my twin sister. That's not me being bold in assumptions, either. Mom and dad were still at each other's throats, going back and forth because mom thought it'd be a good idea to send Morris-Lina away to some rehabilitation center in friggin' Texas. Mom even had the nerve to ask me what I thought about all this, and at first, I wanted to get up and walk out—maybe spend the night over Christopher's to clear my head. But I couldn't leave Morris-Lina alone with mom and dad bickering.

It's aggravating.

But I had to think about some things too.

Yes, Morris-Lina hasn't been taking her medications.

No, she hasn't been herself lately. She lashes out more, and then she'll get really sad and lock herself up in her room all day. She'll even stare at the blank television screen as if she's watching something that killed her mood, but in reality, the television is off.

So, after some thinking, I found myself telling my mom that it wouldn't be a terrible idea. And then I realized that Morris-Lina was still in the room, but she was hiding. The expression on her face could've killed me, but at the same time, it was as though Morris-Lina kind of already knew that there was nothing she could do.

Dad was at first fine with the idea of Morris-Lina going to a rehabilitation center, but not one that's almost two thousand miles away from Philly. That's the only reason why he and mom are going back and forth—the distance, not so much the idea.

Our parents' voices soon became nothing but background noise as Morris-Lina stood up from the couch and dragged herself to my bedroom door. I didn't understand why she decided to sit in my bedroom since the walls are thinner than hers. I wanted to barge into our parents' room and plead for them to shut up because they were not only bothering Morris-Lina, making her sulk more and more, but they were making me want to blast the music playing through my earbuds so loud to the point where my ears would've bled.

I watched Morris-Lina's every move as she smoothed out the surface on the top of my bed from where she had been sitting for the past ten or fifteen minutes. She turned around and faced me, delivering a cold gaze as if she was hoping that I'd melt like a statue into a puddle of goop. I didn't blame her, though. I would've been pissed, too, if she sided with mom on sending me away somewhere I didn't want to be.

But Morris-Lina needed to go, and I wanted her to understand that I wasn't trying to spite her. I could see it in her eyes that she thought I was plotting for her downfall. But the truth is, I'm not. I'm the only one who's really had her back ever since her diagnosis was brought to the light. I was the one who kept her pregnancy a secret when we were fifteen, and I was the one who took her to the clinic to take care of her business. I made sure no one came at her, and here she is, giving me the stink eye all because I'm trying to make sure she's getting the proper treatment she needs for her disorder.

Still, as Morris-Lina tried to walk past me to get to the bedroom door, I heard her go, "Hijo de puta," under her breath.

I chewed on my bottom lip, trying to hold my tongue. But then I looked at her again, and Morris-Lina just shook her head, scoffing—as if I was some kind of sell-out. I pulled my earbuds from my ears and slammed my worksheet and pencil off to the side. I sprung up to my feet and out of the small chair at my desk.

Morris-Lina stopped in her tracks just as she was about to open the door, and she looked unfazed as I took a step forward and blocked her from her leaving my room.

"What is your problem?" I asked her, knowing damn well that was probably a stupid question. But I didn't care. I was tired of her giving me the stink-eye.

Morris-Lina shook her head, saying that it was nothing, but I knew she was just saying that so I could let her leave. I folded my arms over my chest and looked her in the eye.

She snorted, the one side of her mouth pulled upward. "You have some nerve." The bitterness in her tone was sharp as she looked me in the eye. "About an hour ago, you were on board with me going away to another state. So, why do you care what I'm thinking all of a sudden?"

I swallowed thickly and exhaled through my nostrils in hopes that my frustrations with her wouldn't be obvious. "Don't be like that, Moe," I called her by her nickname, thinking that would diffuse the situation. But then, I realized that there was no point in trying. She obviously didn't care enough to do better by taking her medications. I shook my head, huffing. "Forget it," I said, throwing my hands up in defeat.

As I walked past her, Morris-Lina grabbed my arm and turned me around to face her. With her eyebrows furrowed and eyes burning into my soul, she asked, "What's your deal, Don?"

I pulled my arm free from her grip. "What's with you?!" It became impossible for me to hold in whatever irritation I had swum through me. From mom and dad arguing to Morris-Lina acting as though *we didn't give a shit about her, I couldn't take it anymore, and it showed as I spoke up. "You act like everyone is against you when all we want is to help you, for Christ's sake!"*

She raised her eyebrows. "Help me?!" Her lips curled, but her eyes were getting glossy as she raised her tone. "You want to send me away! You say you care, but you have a funny way of showing it!"

I rolled my eyes. "That's rich coming from you."

Morris-Lina opened her mouth, ready to fire back, but nothing came out of her. It was like she was struggling to find the right words to say as her eyes just peered into mine. It was like she couldn't believe that I would even think to say something like that to her. As if she's some saint.

My blood pressure was rising within every second. She had some nerve playing the victim. No one here is a victim of anything. Morris-Lina is responsible for her actions. If she had just taken her medications as prescribed, we wouldn't be in this mess. It's like she doesn't even care, and I told her that. I couldn't hold my tongue any longer. I didn't care how harsh I sounded or how intimidated she felt. I just wanted her to get through her thick skull the severity of the situation.

"I didn't side with mom to spite you, alright?" My words were low, but Morris-Lina could still hear me as she looked at me with furrowed eyebrows. "You're all I got, Moe. And if you keep this up, then you don't give a shit about me."

At that moment, I felt my heart plunge into the pit of my stomach like a giant ball formed in my throat. I had to blink as I felt my eyes starting to water as I attempted to push back whatever tears were trying to escape. I could hardly look at Morris-Lina anymore. The longer we held eye contact, the more I felt myself wanting to ball up and slam my head into the floor. It was agony. She was my agony. Since day one, I always looked to Morris-Lina and no one else. For her to not take that into consideration, I felt like an idiot. I felt played.

The expression on Morris-Lina's face started to ease up as her eyes glistened and her bottom lip trembled. She opened her mouth, ready to say something, but I lifted up my hand to stop her. I took a step back, avoiding her eyes. She was the one who said I didn't care when all I've ever done was care.

What more do I have to do?

I couldn't take it anymore. I swung open my bedroom door and practically bolted out of my room, wanting to get away from my sister as much as possible.

....

"Donny?" A soft voice coos against my ear, causing me to squirm out.

My lashes flutter open, and my eyes squint from the sunlight peering into my room, hitting my face. I roll over to avoid the brightness as my vision starts to clear. I look up, and all I see are familiar brown eyes gazing at me and a faint smile. I blink.

It's just Meagan, I tell myself as my limbs stretch out.

Wait.

My eyes widen as my brain finally comprehends everything. Meagan is sitting on the edge of my bed, smirking at me right now. I jolt up, sitting up and scooting back against the headboard of my bed. My heart claws its way up my throat as it beats like a rabbit.

"Jesus, kid!" My voice practically shakes as I try to get myself together. "W-W, when did you get here?"

Meagan presses her lips together and averts her eyes from me. "A little bit ago. Chris told me you weren't feeling well, so I thought I'd come to see you."

"He did?" I ask.

She nods, still avoiding my eyes as she takes an interest in the floor. I swallow thickly.

He's a dead man.

A brush of cool air hits my chest, sending a shiver down my spine. I look down, gripping onto my comforter as I pull it over my waist.

Shit!

I realize that I'm not wearing a shirt!

I look back at Meagan as she starts to look around my room, trying to keep her eyes off me as much as possible. In a way, it's kind of flattering that she can hardly look me in the eye because I'm not wearing a shirt. But at the same time, I can't imagine how uncomfortable she probably feels right now. I mean, it's not like I'd try anything on her or vice versa. I'm at least comfortable with not having a shirt on around her, but I have to consider her feelings too. For all I know, Meagan's probably never been around a guy like this before.

Suddenly, my mind flashes back to Alejandro's words the other day about Meagan being innocent and all that nonsense...

"And I bet she's hella innocent too. She's probably never been kissed, and you're just the guy to break that for her, I'll bet ya."

…His words swimming through my head is a pure mockery. I don't know why I didn't sock him when I had the chance to say such ridiculous things.

The idea of Meagan and me—it's just…I can't. Not that there's anything wrong with it. I wouldn't mind it.

God, I really wouldn't mind.

But how would I even be able to contain myself if I was even bold enough to try something with her? Plus, I absolutely doubt she'd want anything to do with me in that way.

Get it together, Donald.

I slowly dot my eyes back to Meagan as she stands up from off the bed and smooths the surface from where she was sitting. I can't help but stare. She wears a dark red sundress with the hem falling against her thighs in waves but barely reaches her knees. The heart-shaped neckline has some support on her chest but still manages to show some cleavage. Her curves are hard to ignore since the dress shapes her perfectly—especially when she stands up straight.

Then there's her hair, which she has styled in a single braid down her back with a few loose strands out along the front. I can also tell that she's wearing light makeup.

Meagan finally decides to look at me, and I feel my face get warm. I don't know if it's because she's in a dress or if it has to do with the fact that she's here—maybe both. My chest tightens, and my heart feels like it's about to explode.

Meagan asks me if I'm feeling alright, and I try to suppress the rush of anxiety I'm starting to develop in her presence. I don't even think it's anxiety. I just feel incredibly uneasy, and like I want to just grab her and—

Shut up! Snap out of it!

I let out a chuckle. "Yeah, I'm good." I sit up, folding my arms over my chest. "You good?"

Meagan's body stiffens for a moment, but she just gives an assuring smile. "Of course. You're the one who's still in bed at…." She checks the time on her phone. "Two o'clock in the afternoon. Did you even have breakfast?"

I snort, smirking. "You really worry over nothing, kid." I can't believe it's already two in the afternoon. Was I really out for that long? It didn't feel like it. I clear my throat. "How did you get in here, anyway?"

Meagan fiddles with her fingers, but she still looks at me questionably. "Christopher told me about the spare key under the mat. I'm surprised you were so typical in hiding a spare key."

I just nod my head. I am relieved that Christopher isn't here right now because I would've probably killed him if I knew he would send Meagan here to "check" on me. For all I know, he probably made me sound as though I was bedridden, and knowing Meagan, she rushed over here without a second thought. Although, I didn't expect to see her looking so good. But she always looks good.

What am I saying? Get your head out of the gutter, Donald.

Meagan clears her throat and rocks on her heels with her hands behind her back. "Anyway. If you didn't eat, I'd make you something." She arches an eyebrow, and the corners of her mouth curve upward. "I make a killer omelet."

I quirk an eyebrow. "Ah, is that so?"

She nods. "Just ask my mom."

I snort. "Moms don't count."

"Yes, they do." Meagan sounds almost offended as she wrinkles her eyebrows and takes a step back with her arms folded like a child. "Does the idea of someone cooking for you make your heart melt?"

I roll my eyes, snickering. *This girl.*

I pull my covers off my body and get up out of bed. I feel my throat start to close up once I notice how much Meagan and I are in each other's space. We're practically chest to chest, and I have to sort of look down at her, even though I'm not that much taller than her. I notice the look on her face, and her eyes kind of wander around. It is as if she's scared to look into my eyes.

My heart starts pounding like a drum as I study her face. Meagan's dark spots are hardly noticeable with makeup, but I always thought she had a lovely look. A pretty face. And I never realized just how light her eyes are 'til now. They're like honey, but just a tad bit dark. The golden highlights on her cheeks for her makeup make her dark brown face shimmer like satin, and it's smooth. I have to keep my hands in a fist to prevent myself from even daring to touch her cheek. Or any part of her, for that matter.

Dammit, Alejandro!

With a shaking breath, Meagan looks off to the side and hesitantly grins. I say hesitantly because it's as if she doesn't know what to do with herself. "I should, um, go make that omelet I was just bragging about."

Do I really make her feel that uneasy? I think.

I smirk, looking down at the floor. I can't help but notice that we're only inches apart, and if I wanted to, I could easily take another step forward to make contact with her. But I don't. I can't.

I just can't.

I lift my head. "Show me what you're made of then, kid."

I use my finger to push back the small loose strand of hair that falls in front of Meagan's right eye, and I tuck it behind her ear. Her lips slightly part open, and I can hear her softly gasp, which awakens the goosebumps on my arms. Still, I just wink and flash a quick smirk.

Meagan just takes that as her cue to head downstairs. She presses her lips together in a smile and turns on her heels to leave my room. Before closing the door, Meagan asks me if I want anything specific in my omelet. I just tell her to surprise me, and she snorts, saying that I'm impossible.

I shrug. "If it still makes you smile, then it's worth it."

Her eyes roll, and then she closes the door, and I hear her head down the steps.

I bite down on my bottom lip and tightly shut my eyes as I feel every emotion within me start to boil. It's not like I'm angry—well, I am, but mostly at myself—but everything hits me like a freight train. I grip onto my hair as I lean back and plop down onto the edge of my bed. I prop my knees up on my thighs and run my hands down my face.

Everything feels like pure agony.

I look over at my phone as it remains face down on my pillow. I let out a frustrated huff and snatched up my phone. I unlock the screen and waste no time texting Christopher.

Me: I'm killing you for this.

I hit SEND and tossed my phone back onto the bed. Even though it sounds like a joke, there is some truth behind it.

Cabrón.

. . . .

After I get out of the shower and moisturize my skin, I throw on a black sleeveless shirt and a pair of gray sweatpants before heading downstairs. The smell of cooked eggs swims through my nostrils with each step I go down.

I can hear Meagan in the kitchen as she taps the spatula against the skillet, muttering to herself. I walk on my toes, trying to stay as quiet as possible while pressing my lips tightly together as I creep into the kitchen. A smile tugs on the corners of my mouth as I come around the corner. I stay on my toes as I lean to the side to get a better look at Meagan. She keeps her back to me as she lays down a slice of cheese into the eggs she has scrambled in the skillet. Her focus is intense on the food she makes, not turning her gaze from the skillet for even a split second.

I smirk.

Honestly, I never would've guessed that she'd treat cooking the way she treats her studies. I don't even have to see her face for me to know that she's probably scrunching her eyebrows as she sprinkles a small amount of salt into the eggs and uses the tip of the spatula to scramble everything together.

Even her posture is intense. She keeps her shoulders back, and they look tense as she looks down at the food in front of her. But at the same time, I can't help but let my eyes trail downward as I admire her concentration as she cooks.

I feel my throat go dry as the hem of her dress sways against her legs at the slightest movements she makes. Even though she was up-close to me not even an hour ago, I can't help but admire her in the dress. I don't know if it's the way it shapes her or the way she looks in the dress, but strange feeling tugs in my throat.

My heart pounds heavily in my chest, and I swallow thickly to suppress the dry feeling in my throat.

Snap out of it, I tell myself as I shake my head.

I take a sharp inhale through my nostrils before I dare myself to take small steps forward into the kitchen. Meagan cranks down the heat as she slightly tilts the skillet to fold the eggs over in a wrap against the rim of the pan.

I hold my breath for a second, trying not to give myself away as I tower over her from behind.

I feel my heart climbing up my throat as I let my arms snake around Meagan's waist as I stand up on my toes.

Meagan practically jumps out of her skin, nearly dropping the spatula out of her hand, but she manages to catch it. She whips her head, and her bulging, startled eyes meet mine as she looks over her shoulder.

I burst into laughter as I settled my chin onto her shoulder with a smile.

Meagan rolls her eyes, letting out a sigh. I feel her body ease against mine as I keep my arms around her.

"What the hell, Donny?!" she hisses, turning her attention back to the eggs in the pan.

I chuckle. "C'mon, even you gotta admit that was a good one," I smirk. I lock my hand over my wrist to secure her in my hold.

Meagan groans. "Let me go so I can get this done." I can hear the displeasure in her words as she tries to pry herself free by tugging on my hands with her free hand.

I roll my eyes. "You know," I say, still holding her in place while keeping my chin against her shoulder, "in a way, you did ask for it."

Meagan turns her head so she can get a better look at me while arching an eyebrow. "Oh really?"

I nod, grinning at her. "Yeah."

Meagan looks at me with a slight smile tugging on the one side of her mouth. Her eyes have a glint of light in them as she stares at me. She keeps her lips slightly parted open, and my face grows warm when I realize how close our faces are to each other. A wave of regret rushes through me as I realize what I just set myself up for.

In my head, I consider being bold. The more I keep my face close to hers, and the more I hold her in my arms the way I am—arms locked around her waist as her back remains against me…

My chest tightens, and a mixture of knots and butterflies twists and flutter in the pit of my stomach.

I clear my throat. I slip my arms from her waist, freeing Meagan from my grasp. I take a small step back from Meagan, and she turns her attention back to the pan. She turns off the heat and settles the pan down on the stovetop.

"Your, um, your omelet," she fumbles to say as she reaches for the plate on the countertop. "I didn't do anything fancy with it, though."

I walk around to stand beside her, and I press my palms against the edge of the countertop. I watch as Meagan carefully pushes the omelet out of the pan with the spatula and onto the plate.

I snort. "You sure you didn't come over just to show off to me?"

Meagan narrows her eyes up to me, quirking an eyebrow. I know that look all too well. She's either thinking, *Bitch, please,* or *Are you serious?*

Either way, I snort a chuckle and gradually take the plate from her once she sets the omelet on top.

I go over to the dining room table and set my plate down before pulling out the seat across from me for Meagan to sit in as we both eat our omelets.

Week 3, Monday

Mr. Aziz blares his whistle as I manage to hit the bottom of the volleyball with my two hands cupped together, sending it to the other side of the net. Erik Petrov is on the other side with a few other guys—including Austin Brown—and he manages to catch the ball in his arms, hugging it to his chest.

"Alright, boys! Hit the showers!" Mr. Aziz demands, keeping his hands on his hips.

I try to catch my breath, settling my hands on my hips as I remain in the same spot. I feel someone pat me on the back, and I look over my shoulder as Nathan grins at me with slight hesitation in his eyes. I can barely find the energy to fully acknowledge him, so I just nod my head as he walks by me.

Since our interaction in the bathroom stall about a month ago, Nathan has been acting as if he's walking on eggshells around me. Honestly, it's bittersweet. I wonder if I really got through to him this time, and that's why he's acting all nervous around me. Like he's worried that one little mishap will set me off, and I'll beat the shit out of him. All I told him was that if he wanted to make things go between us, he had to do right by Meagan. As a friend or whatever they are. Although, Meagan swears up and down that she and Nathan are only friends.

I could care less about what they are. I just don't want to see her get stabbed in the back like Nathan had done with Morris-Lina. Meagan doesn't deserve that. She deserves all the good that's out there, and all Nathan has to do is keep his word, and we're solid.

I head over to the bench and sit down next to my bookbag. I rest my arms atop of my thighs, taking tiny breaths to calm my heart down. Mr. Aziz tosses the volleyball into the ball cart on the other side of the gym, and he turns around, looking at me.

"That means you too, Gonzalez," he orders, practically waddling in my direction.

I sigh. "On my way, Mister Aziz."

I take another deep breath before springing up to my feet. Every time I try to wait for everyone to be out of the showers, Mr. Aziz has to be on my case and still orders me to go in the back with the rest of the guys. I just roll with it at this point.

I suck it up and drag myself into the locker room, but I avoid eye contact with anyone. I get to my locker, and I pull my shirt over my head. I feel my muscles ache along my side from when Austin had served the ball and practically slammed it into my side. I don't know how he did it, but he did. Mr. Aziz asked me if I wanted to sit out, which surprised me since Mr. Aziz doesn't stand for people sitting out after taking a hit with a ball unless they're bleeding. I wasn't bleeding. I was in pain, but that was expected.

I told Mr. Aziz that I was good and did all I could to play it off. I tried serving the ball as much as I could to get back at Austin, but I never got my chance to get him. He'd either hit it, or someone else would get to the ball before him.

I twist my hips a little, slightly turning to the side to better look at the area to make sure it isn't swollen.

"You okay, Donald?"

I whip my head around, seeing Erik looking down at me, but not because he's trying to seem intimidating. He's just taller than me, that's all.

I clear my throat. "Yeah. I'm good."

Erik presses his lips together in a straight line. "It doesn't look bad," he finally says, pointing to the spot where the volleyball had made contact. "But if it does bruise, you know what to do, right?"

I chuckle, shaking my head. This is probably the first time Erik and I have actually interacted with each other. I don't mind Erik. Even though he sometimes hangs around Austin, he's a pretty decent guy. He often acknowledges people, especially the ones that Austin and his hounds like to mess with. Erik tries to show that even lacrosse players have hearts—at least he does. But from what I've noticed, Erik has kind of withdrawn himself from Austin.

I don't even see the two of them hanging around with each other after school. Either Erik has come to his senses that Austin is literal dog shit, or it has something to do with Erik dating Preston Highmore. I still find it shocking that Erik would even date Preston. Not because Preston is a guy, but because Preston is uptight and demanding. At least, from what Meagan tells me about him.

Erik seems like a chill dude 24/7, but Preston is always on alert as if the next big thing is around the corner. It could be good or bad. It doesn't matter. And yet, Erik seems happy around Preston. He probably is happy. Happier, in fact.

Now that prom is around the corner, I'll often see the two of them together in the hallway, talking. Preston will be rambling about something, and Erik will just be looking at him in awe or laughing at how ridiculous Preston probably sounds. Not absurd, but adorable.

I can see why Meagan thinks they're perfect for each other. I remember when she told me about the time she found Preston all beat up in the back of the gym. She said he had blood all over him, and it looked as though he had been put through hell and could've been beaten to death. She was devastated. Hell, I was devastated, and I didn't even know Preston like that.

Preston refused to fess up who was responsible for practically beating him to a pulp, and he urged Meagan to let it go. But that was hard for Meagan to do, obviously. She didn't go off, trying to hunt the guys down, but it never sat well with her that Preston didn't even try to call the guys out who had hurt him.

The reason: *The school doesn't do shit.*

And that's true.

She suspected they were guys from the lacrosse team who probably beat Preston up. And if that's true, there's no way any of them are getting what they deserve. The only thing of value in this school are buff, athletic prodigies who can win a few championships.

I doubt Erik even knows what happened to Preston. But that's none of my concern. I'm with Meagan when I say that Preston deserves Erik, though. He's alright.

The sound of someone whistling pulls our attention over to the side, and my eyes lock on Austin as he holds a twisted smirk on his face. "I didn't know you and Preston were in an open relationship, Petrov. Pretty funny how you instantly thought of Gonzalez."

Austin starts cackling, and Erik rolls his eyes in deep disgust.

"Lay off, Brown." There's a sternness in Erik's words that matches the expression on his face as he glares right at Austin.

Austin just looks at Erik, folding his arms across his chest as he leans against his locker. "What? Nothing wrong with a little teasing, is there? We're all big boys, aren't we?"

I almost laugh.

I turn my attention back to my locker. As I enter the combination, I see Austin eying me with a twisted, smug smirk playing on his lips. I notice the way he gives one of his buddies a side-eye glance as if he's proud about something. I try not to feed into whatever he has going on, and I slowly drag my attention back to my locker.

I swing the door open once the lock pops open. I take a step back when I see something come flying out of my locker and falling onto the ground. I look down at my feet and quirk a brow when I realize a rag doll with raggedy stitching. I bend down and pick it up, and then I turn it over to see the front.

I hear Erik gasp, but I don't take my eyes off the rag doll.

The doll has buttons for eyes, and a terrible curvy mustache is drawn onto the face in black marker right under the black buttons. Across the torso in thick, red thread, the words ALIEN are sewn.

"What the hell?!" Erik's voice rings with rage.

My chest tightens as I tighten my grip on the doll. I can feel my blood start to boil as I squeeze the ragdoll tighter and tighter. I clench my jaw as I breathe through my nostrils. I can hear Austin and Erik going back and forth with each other, but everything starts to come to a blur.

All I can see is red and a few colors as I feel my legs move. I manage to lock my sights on Austin as he rambles about whatever is coming out of that big mouth of his. I want that mouth to be shut permanently. Under no circumstances should he be able to open that mouth of his again. People like him never change.

They need to be taught when to shut up.

So, I shut his mouth for him.

My fist plunges into his mouth, and I land a right hook to the side of his face. I don't let him get away from me as I grab hold of the back of his neck to keep him within my reach. I let my fist practically sink into his gut, which feels more like a wall of bricks thanks to whatever conditioning he does for his beast of a body.

Red dots dance in my vision as I land my fist across his face, sending Austin to his knees. I feel someone grip onto my arms in an attempt to drag me away, but I fight against them. I wiggle my way out of their grasp and turn my attention back to Austin. Before I get a chance to take a step forward, Austin wraps his beastly arms around my ways and lifts me off my feet.

I feel a good amount of oxygen vanish out of my body in a swift blow when my back makes rough contact against the wall of lockers. I have to blink in an attempt to clear up my vision as I feel Austin release his hold on me. I reach out, gripping onto his shoulders for support as I try to stand up from off the lockers.

The side of my face burns as inevitable pain shoots through my cheekbone, and the taste of blood from my cheek is hard to miss. I manage to grab hold of the wall as I feel my legs practically give out on me. My body then jolts when I feel Austin's fingers grip onto the back of my shirt before my back slams into the wall of lockers.

My knees give up on me, and a gust of wind jumps out of me as I stumble forward. I blink as I feel another sharp pain shoot through me—this time through the pit of my stomach. I can see Austin pull his fist back to deliver another blow, but he's been pulled away from me before he even has the chance.

No. You can't go down like this, Don.

I grit my teeth and tighten my fist as I dare myself to charge at Austin against the crowd trying to keep us apart. My fist makes contact with the side of his face, making Austin stumble back into the arms of a few people behind. They struggle to hold him up since they're much leaner than him and barely look like they have any strength. Austin is like a tank—a tank with broad shoulders and a prick of an attitude.

Austin looks up at me with red eyes full of scorn and gritted teeth. I feel my pulse rise, and my heart thumps loudly in my chest. I clench my fist tightly, practically bouncing on my toes as I charge towards him. Austin tries to come at me, but about three or four dudes manage to hold him back. I feel arms lock around my waist and under my arms, pulling me away from Austin.

The voices are loud and all mash together, informing me to back down.

"Donald, chill!" and even "Let it go, Gonzalez!"

Then there's, "Stop! It's not worth it!"

That's like a slap to the face whoever said that one!

Not worth it?!

Assholes like Austin Brown get away with this shit more times than I can count on my fingers! I have every right to blow off some steam—specifically on him!

My bare backside is pressed up against a locker, and my arms are over my head. I look back and forth between Nathan and Erik as they keep me pushed back against the lockers with much force. I demand them to let me go, but they refuse, and their hold on me tightens.

I can hear Nathan practically begging me to relax, insisting that it isn't worth it, but a burning sensation stirs in the pit of my stomach, and my face becomes hot. I pull my eyes away from Austin, and I look to Erik. His eyebrows are practically knitted together as a stern look remains on his face. Even though he doesn't say anything, his eyes are basically speaking for him.

It's like he gets it—my anger.

Occasionally, Austin will call Erik "kraut" or "Commie," even though Erik isn't German and is against Communism in all its forms. Erik would probably be a liar if he didn't admit that he would probably want to sock the daylights out of Austin. But he doesn't. Not because it isn't worth it.

Erik is just…Erik, I guess.

Just then, Erik and Nathan release me as we hear heavy footsteps stomp into the locker room. Everyone grows quiet and slightly breaks away from each other as we're met with Mr. Aziz's stern gaze.

"The hell is going on in here?" His voice booms as his hands settle on his hips.

He stares each and every one of us down, but no one dares to say anything. I keep my fist down by my side, avoiding any chance of making eye contact with Mr. Aziz as he continues to stare us all down from where he stands.

I narrow my eyes up to Austin as he wipes the corner of his mouth with the back of his hand. He clears his throat and folds his arms over his chest, eying Mr. Aziz.

"We're all good here, coach," he assures, standing tall.

Mr. Aziz quirks an eyebrow, unconvinced. "You sure about that, Brown?" Mr. Aziz takes a few steps forward, keeping little distance between him and Austin. "I could hear you boys from my office. Seems like you were doing more than just showering if you ask me."

For a second, a vein pops up in the crook of Austin's neck as he stars Mr. Aziz in the eye. Mr. Aziz, being Mr. Aziz, didn't give a damn. He keeps his eyes on Austin, matching Austin's attempted level of intimidation, but Mr. Aziz still manages to overpower him with a single glare.

Austin blinks, and the one side of his mouth curves upward. A faint chuckle slips past his lips, and he takes a small step back.

"What can we say?" Austin looks around the room at the guys beside him to avoid staring at Mr. Aziz any longer. "We got into a little roughhousing. It's hard to avoid. After all, boys will be boys like you always say, right?" This time he meets Mr. Aziz's stern eyes.

Mr. Aziz lets out a sigh and gives a slight nod, but his gaze still remains on Austin. "I suppose so." Mr. Aziz backs away from Austin while taking a look around at the rest of us. In his usual demanding voice, he goes, "Stop fondling and get to class."

Then, he's out of the locker room.

Relief sweeps over everyone as sighs are let out, and pats on the back are exchanged between some. Nathan and Erik look at me as I exhale through my nose but still keep my fist tight by my side.

Nathan tries to put his hand on my shoulder, but I flinch away before he even gets the chance to touch me. Through my teeth, I tell him that I am fine while looking at him. Nathan's lips fall into a flat line, and his eyes lower to the direction of the floor. I get that he's only trying to help—him and Erik—but the last thing I need is their pity.

It's not the first time a teacher has seen a scene like this and didn't try to properly take care of the situation. Instead, like all teachers here, Mr. Aziz takes the word of his favorite athlete and calls it a day.

Like Preston said to Meagan: *The school doesn't do shit.*

At least when it comes to people like Preston or me. They could care less about what we have to say, but it's all hands on deck when it comes to students like Nathan Hendricks or Austin Brown!

Putos gilipollas!

I give Erik and Nathan the chance to walk away before grabbing my gym shirt from off the bench and heading to my locker. I swing the door open, and the metal rattles against the locker next to me. I close my eyes, trying to tell myself to calm down.

It's over now. Everyone has dispersed.

I slam my fist into the door of my locker without having all eyes on me. I start to feel the flame stirring inside me burn out as I look down at my knuckle, admiring the scrapes and fresh blood that pierced through the skin.

....

My phone buzzes in my pocket as Ms. Phan wraps up her class for the day after the bell finally goes off. I stand up from my seat and dig into my back pants pocket to retrieve my phone as the sound of moving chairs rings through my ears as the other students waste no time getting up and out of the classroom.

I unlock my phone screen and see a text message from Christopher.

Code P. Boys room ASAP.

Oh great. I groan.

Code P, which—in summation—means something's up with Peter. It could be anything, and it's a Code P. For all I know, Peter probably had a falling out with his aunt about something and is just pissed off at the moment. But I can't be upset with Peter for being upset about something. It's rare for Code P's to happen, anyway.

So, I shoot Christopher a text, letting him know that I'll meet up with him and Peter in the restroom shortly—that's where they are. I stuff my phone into my pants pocket, get my stuff together, slip on my bookbag, and then I'm out the door.

As soon as I step out into the hallway, I look to my left, and I see Meagan talking to Nathan by the doors to the stairway. She smiles as he speaks to her, looking down since he's much taller than her. But Meagan obviously doesn't mind the height difference. But if she tried to kiss him, she'd have to stand on her toes.

Wait—why would she even need or want to kiss him?

Meagan doesn't like Nathan like that, I remind myself.

Regardless, seeing Meagan smile a bit when around Nathan isn't so bad. I think back to when I told Nathan that if he wanted to make things right between him and me, he had to do right by Meagan. From what I'm seeing right now, he's actually trying to uphold his vow.

That's all that matters to me. Seeing Meagan smile, no matter how she feels about anyone. Nathan…or even me—

Head shake. *What am I saying?*

I turn on my heels and walk down the hall to get to the boys' restroom. I don't even bother switching out my books at my locker since it's out of the way.

I walk into the bathroom, moving aside so someone can leave. I can hear Christopher mumbling to himself, and I can see him pacing back-and-forth with his arms crossed over his chest. As I walk up to him, I can see the frustration all over his face, but he keeps his eyebrows wrinkled with worry.

"What's going on?" I ask Christopher, keeping my voice low.

Christopher finally stops pacing as he lets out a deep sigh and leans back against the wall. He looks down at the ground, tapping his foot. "Apparently, Jen Li isn't all that nice as we thought." This time, Christopher lifts up his head and digs into his pocket for his phone. I watch as he unlocks the screen before handing me his phone. I look. "Carmen meant to send the picture only to me, but she accidentally added Pete to the chat, and well. Here we are."

A knot forms in my throat as I eye the photo taken of Jen Li lip-locking some guy who clearly isn't Peter. Honest to God, I don't understand how Carmen could screw things up and end up sending the photo to both Peter and Christopher. The girl is a prodigy at texting. I've seen her text up a storm in a matter of seconds.

But it doesn't matter now.

Peter's seen it.

And while Carmen probably regrets him seeing it so suddenly, she did Peter a favor. Still, I can't blame Peter for wanting to isolate himself. I get what he's going through. There have been times where I thought I'd found the right one, but then, shit like this happens. The person turns around and pulls a stunt like this, thinking that no one will find out, but everyone knows that nothing stays a secret for long. People have eyes and ears around them wherever they go.

So, I feel for Peter.

I sigh.

I hand Christopher back his phone and ask him which stall Peter's hiding in. Christopher points to the one at the end, closest to the bathroom window.

I bend down a bit to take a peek under the stall. I spot Peter's white high-top sneakers, and I stand up straight. I slip off my bookbag, setting it down against the bathroom wall before I take another glance at Christopher. He has his arms folded while resting his head back against the wall. I can see the concern in Christopher's eyes as I make my way over to the stall where Peter remains to block us out.

I mouth to Christopher, "I got this," and a slight smirk curves on the corners of my lips. Instead of saying anything, Christopher just takes a sharp inhale and shrugs his shoulders. He stands up straight but keeps his back against the wall and continues to watch my every move as if he's anticipating for me to make one little slip-up.

I can't stand that about him. That intense gaze of his.

Christopher is almost like my father when he watches me intensely. It's as though he's putting money down on me effing up, and I can't stand it. But I shrug it off, and I turn my attention back to Peter.

This isn't about you, asshole, I tell myself. *Focus.*

I clear my throat, getting rid of the lump.

I knock on the stall door. Twice.

"Hey, Pete," I say, keeping my words straight. "Everything alright in there?"

Mumbling, Peter unleashes an irritated, "Piss off," and nothing more.

I whip my attention to Christopher. I notice how Christopher parts his lips as his eyebrows lift in surprise. He's probably been trying to get Peter to speak to him, but Peter wouldn't budge. Then, here I come, and Peter finally says two words: *Piss off.*

Typical.

I'd be lying if I didn't admit that I'm flattered.

I lean against the door, crossing my right ankle over my left as I cross my arms over my chest. "That's the best you got? Telling me to 'Piss off'?" I chuckle. "And you call yourself the King of Comebacks."

I notice Christopher furrowing his eyebrows, looking at me as if I'm doing everything wrong, but I wave him off. Unlike him, I'm doing everything right since Peter's starting to talk more. It might not be a full-blown conversation, but Peter is at least responding somewhat. He'll give short responses like, "Whatever," "Piss off," and even, "I don't care."

But it's better than nothing.

Soon enough, I decided to stop beating around the bush, and I'm upfront with Peter about everything. Peter might be the most bubbly and childish one out of all of us for the sake of making us feel good, but he's not a dumb kid. Peter has to know that he rushed into things with Jen Li. I mean, yeah, he liked her, but the kid was literally stressing over planning dates with her. He'd think big rather than take baby steps.

And the sad thing is that he fell for her along the way. Peter fell for her hard, and now he's got bruises all over.

I swallow thickly and stand up straight. "Pete, you gotta get your head on straight," I tell him, gripping onto the top of the stall door. "She might've been the first one, but she sure as hell ain't going to be the last. It's a miracle you didn't try marrying her." I'm obviously trying to make a joke, but Christopher arches an eyebrow and shakes his head with disapproval. I roll my eyes. "Point is," I continue, pulling my attention back to Peter. "Would you rather have found out now than when you got in too deep?"

Silence lingers between the three of us. I turn to Christopher, who just stares back at me with a similar look of confusion across his face. It's not my rodeo giving pep talks to Peter, but it's usually about something regarding his aunt. I can't even count the number of times the three of us would hang out over at Christopher's place after comforting Peter when he and his aunt would go at each other's throats. Usually, they'd fight about his mom.

Peter liked spending time with his mom, but his mom couldn't really spend time with him by law. His aunt had full custody and was his legal guardian, and while she does take care of him, she's controlling as hell. Sometimes, she doesn't even treat him like he's a teenage boy but a pet. And while it's only "sometimes," it gets under Peter's skin. A lot.

Looking back, that's kind of how I saw my mom treating Morris-Lina. Like a pet. She had to care for a pet but really didn't want to because of some bullshit reason. Mom didn't really have to worry about me. In fact, I remember when Morris-Lina and I got into an argument because she thought I was the *"Golden Child,"* but that was a load of bull.

If anything, Morris-Lina was always the center of attention. From her diagnosis to her medications and then with school, mom and dad loved focusing on Morris-Lina. Unless it had anything to do with baseball, mom and dad would hardly ask about my day or wonder how I was feeling. Not until earlier in the year after what happened to Morris-Lina did mom start calling me her "little prince" like she used to when I was younger.

Dad is still dad, though. He'll look at me and then walk off, but not in a way where it seems to be bad blood between us.

Just thinking about all of this causes my stomach to twist in knots, and I feel my throat starting to burn. Yet, I manage to swallow down whatever feeling starts to come up inside of me. I then let out a shaky breath. I notice Christopher looking at me with a questionable look on his face. I look away. The last thing I need is for him to be on my case, asking if I'm alright.

You're okay, I tell myself. *Just be cool.*

Just then, the handle to the stall door starts to jiggle, and I back up off of the door. Cautiously, Peter opens the stall door and steps out. He avoids making eye contact with Christopher and me as he stares down at the tiled, dingy floor.

Peter tightens the straps to his bookbag, and I notice how he chews the corner of his bottom lip while avoiding our eyes. Christopher wastes no time making his way to Peter, throwing his arm around his shoulders. Peter turns his head away, letting out a shaky breath. Christopher probably doesn't catch it, but I sure do. Peter's never been this uneasy before.

Something has to be up.

"What is it, Pete?" I asked, locking my eyes on him.

Peter lifts his gaze up to me. "Nothing." He forces the corners of his mouth to pull a bit upward, but his eyes then narrow downward. "Thanks, guys." His words grow faint a bit towards the end as if he's unsure of himself.

Yeah, something is definitely up.

Even Christopher catches on.

Peter tries to walk away, but Christopher puts his hand to Peter's chest, gently holding him back. He speaks softly to Peter, wanting to know what's going on with him. Christopher cares. No matter how many times he'll pluck him or smack Peter upside the head, Christopher has always cared for Peter in a way that amazes me. I know it's because Peter's a bit younger than us, so Christopher feels the need to protect him after everything Peter has gone through with his family, especially his aunt and mom. And I get it. I think the same when it comes to Peter. That's why it pisses me off when people mock Peter for his lisp, and Peter has always been so insecure about that.

So, seeing Peter act so closed off from us raises questions.

After hearing Christopher egg him on with telling us what's on his mind, Peter finally snaps. He breaks away from Christopher with one step to the side and looks at both of us.

"Jesus!" Peter's voice practically echoes through the bathroom. "Can't you guys take a hint?! I'm fine! I'm just a big dummy, alright?! I learned that now, okay?! I fall for every trick in the book! Everything you guys warn me about, and I'm still a dumbass!" His words come out shaky and broken as his bottom lip trembles. His eyes become glossy as he chokes up but forces the words to come out as clear as they can, which is impossible.

I feel my heart climb up my throat as I listen to every word Peter has to say. My chest tightens as I take in the boy standing in front of me. It's like his whole world is falling apart. And it's all thanks to some girl who didn't give a shit about him or his feelings.

"Peter." I go over to him, placing my hand on his shoulder.

Christopher comes up and stands behind Peter, slipping his arm around Peter's chest. "Mate," Christopher says softly. "You're not any of those things. Where do you get thinking like that?"

Peter sighs, narrowing his eyes down to the floor. "After she told me she loved me, and we slept together," he mumbles.

A ball forms in the pit of my stomach, and my jaw hangs open. I think my ears must've been playing tricks on me, but Christopher's eyes are wide in disbelief. That guarantees that I'm not crazy. Peter shifts his gaze up to both of us. Even though his skin is dark, I can tell he feels embarrassed and is probably flustered, judging by the regret in his eyes.

Christopher blinks. "You…had sex? With her?" It's like he's hesitant to get the words out because it doesn't seem real. Like, it's not something he'd expect to hear from Peter.

We always suspected that Peter would be the last person to have sex out of all of us. His aunt was stern on him, and Peter was raised with the moral belief that sex 'til marriage was the way to go. I don't know how he'd manage to pull that off. But we always thought he would. He'd get so flustered with the idea of being with someone. In fact, he hated talking about it, sometimes. That's how embarrassed he'd get.

So, for him to sleep with Jen Li after only seeing her for a few weeks is crazy! We couldn't believe it! Hell, even Peter was in disbelief with himself once he cleared the air!

Peter takes a step back and starts rambling about how foolish he was to think anyone good would come from sleeping with Jen Li. He calls himself an "idiot" more times than I can count on my fingers and toes. Christopher and I try to get him to calm down, but Peter just shakes us off and talks about how it just happened—him and Jen Li having sex. He confesses that he didn't want to do it, but she was persistent.

"She said that she's never done anything like that with someone like me before, and she wanted to know what it was like," he sulks. "I thought there was a special meaning behind that, you know? Someone like me who knows how to make her laugh and is a gentleman. Not...*someone* like...*me*."

Peter throws his head back against the bathroom wall before sliding down against the wall. Before he has the chance to make it all the way down, I rush over to him and hold him up by his shoulders. I feel his body shiver from my touch, and his teeth chatter. Peter groans, drawing his eyes up to meet mine. He looks hopeless, desperate for me to say something encouraging.

So badly, I want to tell him to forget about Jen Li and her ignorant flat ass. So badly, I wish to straight-up say, "Fuck her." So badly, I want to remind him that there are other fish in the sea. But I say nothing of the sort. I can't. For once, I can't. Not when he's looking at me with those puppy-dog eyes of his. In the back of my mind, I know that if I dared myself to say anything against Jen Li—despite what she did to him—it would break Peter, and that's the last thing I want to happen.

I sigh.

I loosen my hold on Peter's shoulders and fix the straps to his bookbag. I pop the collar to his burgundy button-up uniform shirt. Christopher walks around from behind me and puts his hand on Peter's shoulder.

"My dad won't be back 'til tomorrow. He's on a business trip," he says through his thick accent. "How 'bout we catch a movie at my place, yeah?"

Peter snorts. "Catching a movie at your place isn't really 'catching a movie,' Chrissy." A twisted smirk.

Christopher's eyebrow twitches as he grits his teeth in a feigned smile. I have to bite down on the inside of my cheek to hold down my urge to laugh. Christopher tries not to let his irritation show Peter calling him *"Chrissy,"* but he's a terrible actor. But it gets Peter laughing, and that's better than nothing.

Week 2, Tuesday

"Where the hell have you been?"

I whipped my head around, meeting the cold gazes of my parents. Mom's eyes burned into my soul as her lips turned downward. Dad was no better as he mirrored the same look of disappointment, though the beard he started growing in made it hard for me to really tell if he was frowning or kept his lips in a straight line. Regardless, he was displeased.

"Do you have any idea what time it is?!" mom asked, raising her voice. "It's midnight, Donald. You owe us an explanation."

Yeah, right, I thought to myself.

As much as I wanted to laugh at the idea of owing them anything, I swallowed down whatever urges I had and just kept a straight face. I barely looked either of them in the eye as I walked to the other side of the kitchen to get away from them.

"I was with Chris and Pete," I told them, not even daring myself to look at them as I walked by them to get to the steps.

"What?" dad asked.

I rolled my eyes, finally getting to the steps. "I was with Peter and Christopher. We had a movie night at Chris's place since his dad was out of town. Happy?" I don't care about the tone of my voice, even though I should.

I watch as mom comes over to me with a stern look on her face. "Watch your tone, you hear me?" she barked at me, pointing her finger at me. She inched closer, getting up in my face. "It's a school night, Donald! You know the rules around here!"

"What rules?!" I almost laughed at the idea of them having rules around here. "There haven't been any rules around here since Morris-Lina was here! And even then, the rules were shit because they were only meant for her!"

Mom's face boiled. Dad was standing at her side. They both knew I was right. Looking back, I have never been pushed around as much as Morris-Lina. She was the one who really couldn't have company over. She was the one who had to be back at home by a specific time unless we were out together. It was bullshit!

I started to head up the steps when I felt mom grab hold of my wrist, pulling me back down to the bottom of the steps. I felt her nails sinking into my skin as she tightened her grip.

"You watch your mouth, you understand!" she hissed, finally letting go of my wrist. "You can't be out this late, Don. It's a school night!" She took a step back and shook her head. "You're better than this."

I snorted. "I'm not perfect."

"No one ever said you were," dad pitched in. "But you know better."

I rolled my eyes. "Whatever," I muttered under my breath.

I turned on my heels, ready to head upstairs, when I felt mom's grip on my wrist once again. I tried to wiggle myself free, but she practically dragged me down to the bottom of the steps, and I winced. She roughly let me go and stared at me with steely eyes. Dad tried to step in between us, but mom brushed him off as I got up to my feet.

She took a big step forward, invading whatever personal space I had left. I could feel her breathing on me, but I didn't give her any chance to think that she could intimidate me. Not like how she would try intimidating Morris-Lina. That wasn't going to work on me.

"You're grounded," mom said, glaring at me. "No Christopher, no friends, no whatever you like. You go to school, and you come home. That's it." Her eyes never left mine.

Whatever I like? Hearing those words made my chest tighten. It shouldn't surprise me that something like that would come from her. She doesn't even know what I like.

I shook my head. "Wow." I licked my dry lips, taking my eyes off of her. "You don't even know what I like." I turned back to look at my mother, and the look on her face changed. She went from being stern and having a sense of authority to looking baffled. I didn't care. "Thanks, mom," I sneered at her.

"That's not what I meant," she blurted, not giving me the chance to walk away. She looked down and took my hands in hers. She sighed and looked back up at me. "I just want what's best for you. We both do."

Are you freakin' kidding me?!

How can she even have the audacity to say something like that? That she cares for my future?!

My jaw tightened.

I snatched my hands out of hers. I felt sick to my stomach just looking at them. I knew that they had no clue that I knew what they did.

"You have a funny way of showing it," I blurted.

Mom's eyebrows wrinkled. "Excuse me?" She sounded insulted.

I swiftly turned on my heels and rushed up the steps to get to my parents' bedroom. I could hear mom and dad coming up right behind me, calling my name and demanding for me to stop walking away.

Instead of listening to them, I stormed right into mom and dad's bedroom and rummaged through mom's top dresser drawer.

I was sick of this! I couldn't take it anymore!

I didn't want to mention that mom hid my college acceptance envelopes from me, but I couldn't take it anymore!

"Donald Nicolás-Manuel Gonzalez, what are you—?"

Mom didn't get a chance to finish her sentence once I pulled out the envelopes from her dresser. Mom looked as if she had seen a ghost with her face going pale and her lips parted open in shock.

Dad stood by the bedroom door with confusion plastered all over his face. He turned to mom and asked her, "What is going on, Luciana?"

Mom took a sharp breath, and her eyes glistened from the tears forming in her eyes. She took a step forward. "Donald," she got out, her words shaking. "Please, listen—"

"When did they get here?" I cut her off, rage swimming through my words.

For all I know, my letters could've come in the mail last month, and she's been holding them ever since.

So, she closed her mouth and looked at my dad. Mom was probably hoping that he'd intervene, but he was lost with everything going on.

Dad turned to me. He took a step forward in my direction. Dad turned to me. He took a step forward in my direction.

"Donald, watch your tone," he warned, pointing his finger at me. "Now, whatever is going on here, we can talk about it."

I scoffed. "C'mon, dad, seriously?" He's got to be joking. "When was the last time we've ever talked things over in this house? All we do is give the neighbors a show, raising our voices."

"Donald," mom croaked. She took another step forward, shaking. "Sweetheart, lower your voice. Please, I—"

"Mom, just stop." I could hardly keep my words straight as I felt a ball form in my throat. My stomach twisted in knots at the very sight of her. I thought I was going to hurl at any moment the longer I stayed in her presence. So, I looked at my dad. I held up the envelopes in my hand, and I explained to him, "I got into the colleges I applied for. But I guess that didn't settle well with mom because she hid them all this time." I felt my skin crawl.

Dad swerved his attention to mom. His eyes twinkled in disbelief as he stared her down, speechless. She didn't look at him. Probably because she couldn't.

I felt my stomach churn. I had to get out of there.

Without even a second thought, I brushed past mom and left the bedroom to get to my room, shutting them out. The second I slammed my bedroom door closed, I threw myself into bed, burying my head into the pillow. I tightened my hold on my acceptance letters and took deep breaths to calm myself down.

••••••••••••

I groan, feeling someone shake me awake as I keep my head rested in my arms as a cushion between me and the lunch table. The sound of students holding conversing with one another in the cafeteria starts to fill my ears as I lift my head up into the light of reality. The memory of last night plays in my mind like a broken record, making me feel nauseous. But I can't let it go.

No matter how much I try, I just can't.

My own mother withheld my college acceptance letters from me, and now, it's out in the air in our house. Turns out, Dad knew nothing of it, and mom acted in all on her own. Part of me wanted to run back into their bedroom and show the words Congratulations and my name printed on each letter, but if I looked at my mom any longer, I probably would've thrown up. So, I kept myself locked in my room, reading my acceptance letters one-by-one. And all I kept thinking about was how Morris-Lina would've looked if she saw that I got into each school I applied for.

Man. Knowing her, she'd probably tackle me and shake me, boasting about how right she was about me getting into those schools.

"I told you so! I told you so!" she'd probably chant so loud that the whole neighborhood would hear her. And then, I'd probably tell her to chill. Otherwise, I'd threaten to stuff one of my socks in her mouth to silence her. Then, we'd be going back and forth with each other over that, maybe. I chuckle to myself.

I reach for my carton of chocolate milk and take a sip through the thin straw that I poked through the carton since there was no way in hell I was putting my lips on the carton. There was a dude in front of me in the lunch line who reeked, and I doubt that he's courteous enough to wash his hands. The lunch lady handed him a milk carton, but he said he was lactose intolerant. So, she gave me the one she intended for him. Unfortunately, I had no choice but to take it since there was a short supply of milk for lunch.

Thanks, school funding.

As I'm sipping my chocolate milk, someone pokes me on the back of my neck, and I wince, shuttering.

"Chiiill," I drag out, grumbling.

It doesn't surprise me at all when I realize Christopher is the culprit. His hair is tousled in different directions as if he had just rolled out of bed. But I'm no better. I hardly had the energy to fix my hair like usual this morning. It took so much effort just for me to muster whatever power I had to get out of bed and get dressed to get to this hellhole of a school.

Still, I'm surprised Carmen hasn't made a fuss about Christopher's hair being all disheveled. Usually, he can pull off the messy look, but today, he looks like he just rolled out of bed like me. Then again, Christopher does have a nice face, and his hair complements his eyes. Somehow. So, maybe that's why Carmen is calm with his hair looking the way it does.

Whatever floats their boat.

Christopher leans in close to my face, and I can feel his warm breath against my ear when he whispers. "You got a minute, mate?" A shiver down my spine.

He draws his face away, but his eyes still remain on me.

I sigh.

I give him a slight nod, and Christopher clears his throat before turning his attention to the rest of our friends as they sit at the table, eating and talking about God knows what.

"We'll be right back," he assures them.

Peter snorts. "Look, if you're going to make out, just say so." His eyes cut to Carmen, who sits beside Christopher as usual. "I'm sure Car could learn a thing or two, don't you think?"

Carmen scoffs, insulted. "How cute." She rolls her eyes and turns her attention to Christopher as he stands up from his seat with me. "Everything okay, babe?"

Babe? That's the first I've ever heard her call him that. It kind of makes me want to hurl.

Christopher just shakes his head, telling her that everything is all good. He boldly kisses her, and I feel my windpipe start to close up as the inside of my stomach stirs. I should be used to seeing the two of them kiss by now. But as much as I ship them together, it's still weird seeing them together. At least, when they're actually being all lovey-dovey with each other.

It's only weird because they're my friends, I guess.

But I am happy that Christopher is starting to grow some balls to boldly express his love for Carmen, as he should. He deserves it.

Meanwhile, Peter points his finger inside his mouth while making a gagging noise. Carmen shifts her gaze to him, smirking.

She just brushes him off, going, "Rude," and turns back to her food.

Christopher and I leave the cafeteria through the back entryway into the hallway, near the restrooms. We stand off to the side so we're not blocking the door to the boys' bathroom. I lean back against the wall, clenching onto the sleeves of my leather jacket as I feel a breeze come through the small opening of the window.

Christopher presses his lips together and leans back against the wall behind him, crossing his right ankle over his left. He sighs.

"Tough night?" he asks, a hint of sarcasm in his voice.

He doesn't know about what went down last night, but he figures that my parents must've been arguing since that always explains why I'm tired all the time. That's sixty-percent true.

I shrug. "Tell me about it." I feel my eyes go heavy, so I rub them with my fingers to wake myself.

Christopher snickers. "Well," he goes, looking down at his shoes. "It's not every day you get accepted into two of the finest schools Europe has to offer, yeah?"

I chuckle.

Christopher was the first person I called this morning and told about my college acceptances. I could tell he was tired on the phone since it was so early, but he was still pleased to hear the news. And quite surprised. He stuttered a few times, trying to muster up a "Congratulations" and even a "Way to go, mate!" without waking up his dad since it was early.

The two of us met up before homeroom, and one of the first things Christopher told me was, *"Remember, I have family around Welmur's and Charleston. They're from my mum's side, so wherever you decide to go, you're covered. Got it? I told them all about you, and they like you. So, they're more than willing to help you out with staying while you attend school over there."*

Of course, I thanked him. I didn't expect his extended family to know a thing about me, but they did. Although, I doubt they know all the parts about me. Probably just the good parts they're aware of since it's Christopher. He only talks about the good parts.

"So," Christopher suddenly pipes up, bringing me out of my thoughts. "Where are you thinking of going?"

I sigh. "Surprisingly, Welmur's seems like the golden ticket for me," I tell him, crossing my arms over my chest.

It's true. While Charleston is a nice campus and has some decent courses, Welmur's has more to offer towards what I want to do. Psychiatry. I know I won't be specializing in psychiatry right off the bat, but Welmur's has the best set-up for it with the programs it offers. Then, I'll have to attend medical school for about four to five years before residency training.

It is a lot, but I'm ready for it. I'm Donald Gonzalez, for crying out loud. I'm not gonna wimp out.

Christopher clears his throat and stands up straight while still keeping his back up against the wall. He looks at me with soft eyes and a faint smile playing on his lips. It's like he's daydreaming, but he's focused at the same time. I know that look.

"What is it?" I ask, stuffing my hands into the pockets of my leather jacket.

Christopher shrugs. "What you mean?"

"You got that look on your face."

"What look?"

"That 'Should I say what I wanna say or naw?' look." I stand up straight, keeping my back pressed up against the wall as I cross my right ankle over my left. "Just spill it, Chris."

Christopher looks down for a moment, chuckling to himself. I can tell he's still hesitant about saying whatever is on his mind, but he knows that I can take it. For all I know, he's probably going to say something all sappy in the spirit of the mood. That wouldn't surprise me.

Finally, he lifts his head and stares at me. The corners of his mouth slightly curl upward as he shakes his head. "Nothing, it's just…" Pause. Then, a sigh. "She'd be proud real proud of you. Moe. You know that, right?"

A ball forms right in the middle of my throat, making it hard for me to swallow. No wonder he was hesitant to speak up.

Part of me wants to believe that she'd help me pack up my bags right after graduation to head on to Europe ASAP since she's always wanted me to get out of Philly. But I also wonder how she'd feel with me not being around. I wonder if she'd tear up and beg me to take her with me or something.

I would've. Really, I would've.

But, I also know that deep down, Morris-Lina wouldn't have wanted that for me. She would like me to go out on my own. Probably. I don't know. I can't think for her.

Although, Christopher is right. She would've been happy for me either way. This is all she's wanted for me since we entered our senior year of high school.

I relax my shoulders and drift my eyes down to the ground, smirking. "Yeah," I say softly. "She would've been." My lips are dry as I chew on my bottom lip.

I notice Christopher inch away from the wall as he takes a step forward in my direction. I narrow my eyes up at him as his lips part open, as if he's about to speak. His words never get the chance to surface since my phone buzzes in my pants pocket, pulling my attention away from him. It's probably for the best that he doesn't get the chance to say whatever he wants to say this time, anyway. Whenever he mentions Morris-Lina once, he never thinks to not mention her again. He just tries my patience, sometimes.

I pull out my phone from my pants pocket and unlock the phone screen. I see that it's a text message from Alejandro, and I gulp. The dryness in my throat is rough, scratchy. I clench my jaw when I click on his name to open up his text message.

I carefully read his text message: **Plan in motion this weekend. Meet me @7pm. I'll send you the address. See u shot glass.**

A dreadful pressure starts to hammer against the right side of my temple, and I wince. I think back to his original plan of kidnapping the guy who assaulted his sister, and I managed to convince him how terrible that plan would've played out if he tried it. So, he must've come up with something better. Something that won't have us end up in jail.

"You alright?"

I lift my head up at the sound of concern in Christopher's voice. I stuff my phone back into my pants pocket and stand up straight.

"Yeah." I clear my throat. "All good." I feel my words shake towards the end, but I hold my gaze on Christopher to seem convincing.

He twists his lips and exhales deeply through his nostrils. "Okay," is all he says, arching an eyebrow.

I feel a shiver run down my spine as he pushes himself up off the wall and approaches me. No matter how much I try to stand tall, Christopher always manages to tower over me.

I bet deep down, he probably finds it funny that I'm shorter than him. When we first met, it was an ongoing joke. He'd swipe the keys to my car and would hold them up and out of my reach so I would have to jump up to snatch them back from him. If I needed a book from the library, he'd purposely put it up on a higher shelf, so I would have to use a stool to retrieve the book. Christopher was a bit of a prick back in freshman year.

Lucky for him, I never took it personally. Otherwise, I would've kicked his ass. But I know he'd probably kick mine also. At least a bit. He might've been a bit taller and stronger, but I was always faster, so that would've worked in my favor.

I snicker.

Christopher turns his head in my direction. "What?"

I rest my head back against the wall and turn my head in his direction. I let my eyes examine him up and down.

"Why the hell are you so damn tall?" The question rolls right off the tongue as my eyebrows furrow, and I squint up at him.

Christopher rolls his eyes, sucking his teeth. "I'm not that tall," he clarifies, folding his arms. "Maybe you're just too short." The corners of his mouth twist into a smug smirk, and he quirks an eyebrow. "I can see if the librarian still keeps that step ladder for you to carry around whenever you need it."

I shove him, and Christopher slightly rocks to the side, laughing.

"Puto," I mutter under my breath.

I feel my phone vibrate in my pants pocket, and I groan. I figure it's Alejandro again, so I check. As I unlock the screen to my phone, Christopher pipes up, "That guy the other day. Well, from a few weeks ago. The one I met. Who was he exactly?"

I choke on my breath, and I feel a strange tingly feeling run through my fingers. I forgot that Christopher and Alejandro had met each other a few weeks ago. Not even a few weeks ago. It was some time last month. Alejandro showed up at my school, hoping to talk, and then Christopher came over and introduced himself. Despite their civil manner, I could tell that they didn't enjoy meeting each other. The look on Christopher's face whenever Alejandro opened his mouth and spoke, it was unlike anything I had seen from Christopher before.

He was more than just irritated by Alejandro's presence. It was as if he was...jealous?

Ha! That's a bold assumption.

I take a quick breath, trying to focus on my phone and reading Alejandro's message. "You met him, remember?" I remind Christopher as I tap on Alejandro's name to open his text message.

"Yeah," Christopher replies. "I know that. But who is he to *you* is what I mean?"

I wrinkle my eyebrows and draw my eyes up to Christopher. He presses his lips together in a straight line and keeps his eyes locked on me, awaiting my response. I notice the way his lip twitches and his nostrils flare. He probably realizes how ridiculous his question sounded since it caught me off guard. And it was, in fact, stupid.

I mean, *"who is he to me?"*

I remember explaining to Christopher when he met Alejandro that Alejandro and I knew each other back in grade school. That's all. I mean, yeah, Alejandro also helped me out when I was jumped, which seemed to rub Christopher the wrong way for some reason. It wasn't a big deal.

Alejandro was just a person that I knew. It wasn't a big deal.

Unless—

"Are you…" I pause, feeling the word get caught up in my throat for a second as I look Christopher in the eye. "…jealous?" The phrase sort of hangs by a thread, even after I manage to spit it out. I never thought I'd ask Christopher something like this. Ever.

Christopher's face somewhat spazzes out, showing five different emotions all at once as he fidgets. "Wha—*pfft!* No!" He scrunches his eyebrows in annoyance. "I'm only asking because he just…." Christopher's eyes wander downward as he loses his train of thought.

I turn my body entirely in his direction to give him my full attention. "He's just what?" I question, unaware of how my tone probably sounds in the moment as I wait for whatever Christopher is planning to say.

Christopher sighs, dotting his eyes back to me. "Look," he starts off, taking a small step back. "All I'm saying is something's not right with him. That's all. I get that he helped you out somehow, but the guy is bad news, Don."

I wrinkle my eyebrows. "You don't know even know him," I counter, stating the obvious. And he doesn't. So, he has no right to judge when he doesn't understand a person's circumstances.

Frustration washes over Christopher's face, but he manages to keep his voice calm when he speaks. "I know," he goes, taking a small step forward. "But Don, you gotta trust me on this, alright? He's not like you."

I shrink back a bit. "What is *that* supposed to mean?" I ask, hardly able to contain the bitterness stirring inside me from his bold words.

Christopher blinks, realizing his words. "That's not what I meant."

Before he has a chance to dig himself deeper than he already is, I suggest that Christopher drop it. He opens his mouth, ready to get the last word in, but I glare at him. So, he presses his lips together and doesn't say a word. His cheeks flush, and his eyes narrow downward as he leans back against the wall.

I don't get why he feels the need to constantly push his ideas on me. I get that he cares and wants to look out for me, but I'm eighteen years old and my own person. He's not my parent. He's my friend. My best friend. I'm not his responsibility.

So, why does Christopher treat me like I am?

I sigh.

Clearing my throat, I inch a bit closer to Christopher as he keeps his eyes on the ground. I bump my elbow against his arm to get his attention. He turns his head, and his eyes slowly drag up to meet mine. Christopher looks at me as if I'm the one plucking his nerves, but I don't get why. He was the one acting like a know-it-all, judging people without knowing the whole story.

If he just got to know Alejandro like he got the opportunity to know me, he'd see that Alejandro isn't all that bad. People thought I was terrible and still do. Yet, Christopher still chooses to stick around me for some reason. It's like—out of everyone, he chose me. And I don't get it. But he did. He still does.

I press my lips together to get some moisture. I look forward at the wall across from us, and Christopher does the same, resting his head back.

Finally, I muster up the courage to speak up. "You're entitled to your opinions," I tell him, still keeping my eyes fixated on the tiled wall. "But the least you could do is get to know someone before you lock your opinions in on 'em." I turn my head to face him. "You did that with me, at least."

Christopher twists his lips, and I notice his jaw clench. He avoids my eyes at all cost, forcing himself to keep staring at the wall. When he speaks, his voice is low, but I can still hear him. "I always said that you were lucky. But lucky doesn't even amount to what you are, mate." He then draws his attention to me, keeping his head rested back against the wall, looking down at me. "I don't want to be in the same circle as my dad and other pricks like him. And I'm sorry if I came off that way. So, I'll try."

A slight curve forms on the one side of my mouth. I can see it in his eyes that he's not just saying this to say it. He truly means it.

The last thing Christopher would ever want to be viewed as is a close-minded racist like his dad. It's not like Christopher goes around treating people nicely to gain credit for not being considered "racist." He genuinely cares about people, and he tries to live up to the type of person his mom was—kind and humble. That's probably why he still sticks around me. His mom taught him to be good and how to be good.

If only he could swap his dad for his mom. I know that's something he wishes for every night before he goes to bed.

Christopher reaches into his back pants pocket and pulls out his phone. He eyes the screen and lets out a sigh.

"We should get back in there," he suggests, shoving his phone back into his pants pocket. "Lunch will be over soon."

I snort. "Wouldn't want to worry your girl, huh?"

Christopher nudges my arm, telling me to lay off.

I feel my phone vibrate in my pocket, and I remember that Alejandro had sent me a text message that I didn't actually open. I'm right behind Christopher, walking back into the cafeteria as I open Alejandro's message. It's the address he wants me to meet him at this weekend. I click on the address, and a picture of an abandoned parking lot appears on my screen.

My heart thumps loudly in my chest.

Another message appears on my screen from him: Thanks again.

I let out a shaky breath.

God help me, I beg, slipping my phone into my jacket pocket as I sit down at the lunch table with my friends.

Week 3, Saturday

It's been quiet in my house for the past couple of days since...well, I don't want to bring up what exactly happened. We'll have dinner together, and it's quiet. More than a few times, I wondered if I should be the one to just cut the cord and speak up. I would probably point out how pointless it is for all of us to treat each other strangely. But knowing my parents, they wouldn't want to hear anything from me. They already know that I've submitted my deposit to Welmur's University on Wednesday. All thanks to Christopher and Counselor Rashad. I wouldn't dare myself to go to Counselor Malik for anything. Not after our last counseling session. His words still dance around in my head once in a while, taunting me. I hate it. I want to hate him, but what would I gain from it? The best I can do is just forget about him. Although, Christopher thinks it'd be a good idea for me to resume my sessions with Counselor Malik, which I don't understand. I've been getting sleep at night, so I haven't looked like a tired mess in a while. I haven't been spitting up at night like I used to. I'm fine. I always tell Chris, hoping he'd understand, that I'm fine. He just doesn't get it.

Speaking of which, Christopher thought it'd be a good idea for him to tag along with me when I meet up with Alejandro later on. It was hardly a suggestion and felt more like a state of fact. He was coming whether I liked it or not. And I couldn't fight him on it because I knew he'd use the excuse that it was I who told him to give Alejandro a chance. So, this would be his way of getting to know Alejandro better. Bullshit. He just needs to relax and trust my judgment. For once, at least. —D.G.

My teeth chatter as the warm air hits my face through the vents of Christopher's car. I sit back into the firm leather passenger's seat, resting my head back. I became fascinated with the dark sky that probably holds about five or six stars within my view.

"You alright, mate?" I hear Christopher ask me, pulling my attention towards him.

I press my lips together, feeling the dryness of them. The white light from the street lamp shines into the car, beaming on half of Christopher's face when he looks at me. His lips parted, his eyes staring with a hint of unease, and his right eyebrow arching. We'd been sitting in his car for probably about a half-hour when Alejandro asked me to meet up with him at seven.

It's *way* past seven, and he's not even here.

When the clock had passed fifteen minutes, Christopher thought it'd be best for us to leave, but I insisted that we just wait it out. I bet he thinks I should've listened to him since we've been waiting here for so long. But Alejandro insisted on meeting tonight to settle things. And that's got to happen.

I look forward, resting my head back against the soft headrest.

A sigh. "Traffic is probably a bitch for him, I'll bet."

Christopher rolls his eyes, sucking his teeth. He faces forward and rests his head back against the headrest of his seat while muttering something in Irish.

"You sure you don't want to head out?" Christopher insists, turning his head to me while keeping it against the headrest. "He said seven, and it's now going on seven-thirty-five." He quickly points at the clock on his dashboard.

My eyes fixate on the time as the two dots blink, and 7:35 changes into 7:36.

I sigh.

"Fine," I groan, looking up from the clock. "Let's go—"

I practically jump out of my skin, and my heart lodges up my throat when a sudden knock comes from my side of the window. I whip my head around, and I see a smiling Alejandro looking through the fogged glass.

I let out a sigh of relief, feeling my heart start to come down from its face-paced rhythm.

I roll down the window, keeping my eyes on Alejandro. Once the window is rolled down all the way, Alejandro settles his arms on the car door, poking his head through.

"Evening," he grins.

"What took you so long?" I ask hastily in irritation. "You said to meet you at seven. You weren't even here 'til just now."

Alejandro twists his lips. "No, I was here," he assures, wrinkling his eyebrows. He nudges his head to the side. "I parked around the corner on the other side of the building. I was on the phone all this time, that's all."

Are you serious?

I can't believe this guy. If he was here, why didn't he text me and say so instead of having me and Christopher sit here all this time?! Even if he was on the phone speaking with someone, he still could shoot a damn text!

Alejandro looks over past me and spots Christopher. I notice the look on his face change as his lips fall into a straight line and his nostrils sort of flare.

"Irish boy, right?" he asks with a hint of sarcasm.

Christopher's jaw tightens, and he slightly presses his eyebrows together. "Yeah." He forces a grin, causing crinkles to form beside his eyes. "The *old* friend, right?"

With his mouth closed, Alejandro swipes his tongue under his top lip before grinning. His eyes, however, are like daggers. Cold, icy daggers that make goosebumps form on my arms.

I clear my throat, unstrapping myself from the seat. I suggested to Christopher for us to get out of the car since Alejandro was here now. Well, he's been here, but he's with us now.

After we get out of the car, Alejandro tells us to follow him. Before walking, he gives Christopher another cold gaze. I look to Christopher, and he has his hand balled up in a fist by his side with his jaw clenched.

"I don't like this guy," he whispers against my ear.

Well, that's obvious, I think, rolling my eyes.

"Chris." My shoulders drop, and my head slightly tilts to the side as my voice sinks with displeasure.

The last thing I need is for Christopher to start back-peddling on his word, which is unlike him, to be honest. It's obvious that he has a lot of thoughts on Alejandro, but he promised that he'd at least try to get to know Alejandro better. I remind him of that. He also insisted on tagging along with me when I shared with him that I'd be meeting up with Alejandro tonight after Christopher asked if I had plans for the weekend. Although, Christopher doesn't know precisely why I'm meeting up with Alejandro. All he knows is that we're doing something important. If I told Christopher that Alejandro and I were going to beat the shit out of the guy who assaulted Alejandro's sister, Christopher would scold me and insist that we'd tell the police instead of taking things in our own hands. But what are the chances that the cops will actually do anything? An amateur's mistake.

Christopher crosses his arms over his chest in defiance like a child, avoiding my eyes. I hear him mutter, "Pian san asal," under his breath. *Pain in the ass.* He calls me that a lot too.

But this time, I don't know if he's referring to Alejandro or me.

Regardless, I throw my arm around his neck, letting my hand drape over his shoulder. I pat his chest.

"C'mon, stop sulking," I urge. "You're doing great, believe it or not."

Christopher snorts in disbelief. "Aren't you being too confident?" He quirks an eyebrow, questioning me.

I shrug. "I mean. You're still here, aren't you?"

Christopher chuckles under his breath, shaking his head. Before he has the chance to open his mouth to speak, Alejandro calls out for us, and I realize that he's already halfway across the parking lot to the abandoned warehouse.

I slip my arm off of Christopher and nudge for us to keep moving. Still keeping his arms folded, Christopher walks beside me to catch up with Alejandro. Once we do, the two of them exchange a look but don't say anything. I make sure that I'm between them because God forbid the two of them start slugging at each other. It'd be a pain trying to break them up, I'll bet. They're both taller than me, and I've seen them both in fights. They match each other's strength, so I'll have to put in twice the effort to pry them off of each other if they did end up going at it.

I almost wish Christopher hadn't decided to join me because now that's something I have to consider. *Ay!*

We get to the front of the warehouse, and I feel my bones start to stiffen. It's like something out of those tacky horror films that Morris-Lina and I used to watch with abuelo when we were kids, even though our parents never liked the idea of my sister and me watching horror movies late at night. But abuelo enjoyed the thrill of doing something fun behind their backs. And so did we.

I swallow thickly.

I exchange a glance with Alejandro, and the one side of his mouth twitches. It feels like little butterflies are tap dancing in my stomach, causing an unsettling feeling to stir inside me as I look back to the warehouse. The light from the street lamp only adds to the eeriness since it shows how dark the windows are from the outside looking in. And I'll bet it's even worse inside. No one has probably stepped foot in this place for years. Many years.

"You're not getting cold feet, are you, shot glass?" Alejandro's warm breath brushes against the side of my face as his words slither through my ear.

I shrink back, snorting under my breath. "I'm standing here, aren't I?" I slightly turn my head to get a better look at Alejandro as he somewhat stands behind me, sticking his head out while keeping his face close to mine. I take a few steps away from him, feeling my breath grow uneasy.

Alejandro smirks, digging into the pocket of his jean jacket. "My car is parked is over there." He nudges his head off to the side in the direction of where he parked his car. I look over and spot it in the distance right away. It's parked right in the middle of the lot, underneath the street lamp. Alejandro then adds, "There's a bag in the trunk that we'll need, so. If you could get that, it'd be great." He tosses me his car keys, and I catch them.

I huff, furrowing my eyebrows. "I'm your fetch-it guy now?"

Alejandro shrugs his shoulders, humming. "You're standing here, aren't you?" He winks, curling the one side of his mouth into a mischievous grin. "Besides…" Alejandro's words trail off, and his eyes drift to Christopher, who remains by my side with his arms folded across his chest. "…I'm sure your little friend here wouldn't mind helping me open up shop, right? The more hands, the better."

Christopher's arms come down to his sides, and he tightens his fists. His glare intensifies. Christopher takes a step towards Alejandro, but I put my hand to his chest, preventing him from reaching Alejandro any further.

"Chris." I feel my heart pick up its pace when I say his name this time, and my voice quakes. And the look Christopher gives me doesn't help. His eyes glared down at me as if I was preventing him from doing something right, but in reality, I'm stopping him from making a total ass of himself.

So, I glare right back at him. "Chill," I say, keeping my voice low but stern. "Seriously."

Sighing, Christopher presses his lips together and looks away from me. The look on his face softens as I move my hand to his shoulder to give him some kind of reassurance that he has nothing to worry about. That's all he's doing, anyway—worrying over nothing. He overthinks. He creates problems in his head when there's no need. If only he could just shut his brain off for a few seconds and stop worrying.

Alejandro walks up to Christopher and stares him up and down. He clears his throat, stealing Christopher's attention.

"You good?" Alejandro questions, keeping a straight face. There is a hint of annoyance in his words, but he twists his lips to prevent his face from reflecting his words.

Christopher takes a deep breath before standing up straight, keeping his eyes locked on Alejandro. He slightly nods his head, and I feel my body relax.

As I turn on my heels to walk away from them, Alejandro warns me not to look inside the bag and just bring it over to him. When I ask him about the bag, he just tells me that I'll find out later when the time is right. He then looks at me with soft eyes and presses his lips together in a thin grin. My mind goes back to when we were kids. Whenever he gave me that look, it was like a promise. A promise of something good.

Still, I roll my eyes, telling him, "Whatever."

I toss his car keys around in my hands as I walk to Alejandro's car. The humidity is unbearable as I walk, but it is cold out here at the same time. I know it is cold because of the bitterly cold breeze that hits me every couple of seconds.

For all I know, I'm probably the only one who thinks it's humid. I touch my forehead to check to see if I'm sweating, and I'm not. It's all in my head, then.

Get yourself together, I sternly hiss to myself.

I walk around to the back of Alejandro's car and pop open the trunk. I hold the lid to the trunk open, pressing my palm into the metal. I stare down at the red duffle bag, wondering what Alejandro could possibly have in there that he doesn't want me to see just yet.

I snatch up the bag and slip the straps over my shoulder. It's not super heavy, but it's not light either. I run my hand over the bag, trying to figure out what could possibly be in here.

Alejandro always tells me to carry around a knife, so maybe it's a bunch of knives? Then again, the bag would've been pierced open if there were a bunch of knives in here. So, no.

It can't be a gun. I doubt Alejandro even knows how to use one. Unless Álvaro probably showed him how to use one before leaving Alejandro and Aitana behind for some "opportunity" elsewhere.

Just take a look.

I swallow down the lump starting to form in my throat. I put the bag down on the ground and unzip it open. The bitter cold air bites at my face as I dig through the duffle bag to see what the hell Alejandro has in here. I pull out some rope, a thick roll of tape, and a small metal pipe.

I gulp. I can only imagine what fun plans Alejandro has for us to put these to use. Although, I am relieved that Alejandro actually went through with not kidnapping the guy. The last thing we need is for a missing person's report to be issued, and then everyone is on our tails.

I shake my head, putting everything back in the duffle bag. I close the trunk and lock the car up before heading back to the front of the warehouse. As I'm walking, I hear someone grunting, and I furrow my eyebrows. When I get closer, I see Alejandro on the ground, holding his face, and Christopher stands over him with a clenched fist. My eyes widen, and I pick up the pace, heading over to them before Christopher has the chance to take another hit at Alejandro. I notice Christopher taking a few steps forward as Alejandro manages to stand up, keeping his hand over the one side of his mouth.

With a twisted smirk, while swiping his finger against the side of his mouth, I hear Alejandro taunt Christopher, "That all you got, Irish boy?"

Christopher tries to take another step forward, but I manage to stand in front of him. The bag slips off of me as I grab hold of his arms, using my strength to hold

Christopher back. Through his teeth, I hear him threaten to kick Alejandro's ass, and his eyes are full of hunger to fulfill that threat.

I tighten my grip on Christopher's arms as he tries to push past me to get to Alejandro. My heart thumps loudly in my chest as it picks up its pace. My bones tighten in my hands the more I try to hold Christopher back.

That's it!

Using all my strength, I shove Christopher back, causing him to stumble, but he doesn't fall to the ground. I take a giant step forward, closing the space between us while looking at Christopher in the eyes.

"Stop it!" I bark in his face, feeling a burning sensation run through me. My whole body feels like I'm walking through the pit of hell right now as I hold eye contact with Christopher, not even daring to look away for a second. I grit my teeth. "What the hell is wrong with you, man?!"

Christopher tightens his jaw, exhaling through his nostrils. He doesn't even try to look away, and he's completely unfazed right now. I can tell from the way he's looking at me. He doesn't want to hear whatever it is that I have to say.

Christopher's hand is around my wrist without saying a word, and I feel my bones crush together. His grip tightens as he practically pulls me forward, following him as he walks away. My sneakers scrape against the ground as I try to wrestle my wrist free from Christopher's unbearable grip.

"Chris!" I manage to get out, feeling his grip cut off circulation in my wrist. "Stop! You're being—!"

"Being what?!" Christopher snaps, pulling me forward. He stops in his tracks, whipping his attention to me. The sudden stop of his movements causes me to trip forward and bump into him, but that doesn't help free my wrist from his grasp.

He sees me trying to break myself from him, but Christopher just tugs me forward, bumping into him again. He goes to walk again, but I don't give him the chance to pull me with him. I stand my ground, fighting against him to free my wrist from his grip.

"Get!" I grunt, shoving him. "Off me!"

I stumble backward, finally freeing my wrist from Christopher's barbaric grasp. I hiss, feeling my bones finally loosen up a bit as I rub the area. There is fresh redness on my skin, and I trace my fingertips over my wrist. I wince.

I hear Christopher start to approach me, and I shoot him a stern scowl. My blood boils. "What the hell is your problem?!" I could hear my voice echo, but I could care less.

A baffled look comes across Christopher's face as he looks at me with wide eyes. "You're kidding, right?" His accent is incredibly thick, but I can still make out what he's saying. He shakes his head, approaching me. "What's your deal with this guy, huh? He's not right in the head, Donald. I'm telling yeh!"

I snort, feeling the one side of my mouth curl into a smirk from how ridiculous Christopher sounds right now. He probably doesn't even hear himself. That's how ridiculous he's acting right now. He's the one who clocked Alejandro, not the other way around!

"What do you got against him, huh?" I shoot back. "You don't even know him. And yet, here you are, acting as though you have all the answers like some—!" I stop myself from saying anything further. I feel my bones shaking, and my teeth chatter as my heart pounds heavily in my chest. My face feels warm, and the side of my temple starts to ache, but I know damn well that I don't have a fever.

Suddenly, I feel an arm hook around me, gently pulling me back. I realize that it's Alejandro. He keeps his back turned to Christopher while wrapping his arm around my torso to guide me back to the warehouse. I spot the cut on his lip from where Christopher had punched him, and I clench my jaw.

Christopher then steps in, using his arms to pry between Alejandro and me. He bumps his chest into Alejandro's while glowering at him as if he expects Alejandro to immediately turn to stone.

"You stay out of this," Christopher sternly demands.

Alejandro rolls his eyes and smirks, not giving a shit.

Hell, I don't give a shit. What gives him the right to tell me who I can and can't stick with?! It's not like he's my dad!

I stand between Christopher and Alejandro, putting my hands to Christopher's chest. I shove him back just enough to get him out of my face. When he stumbles back, I hear him let out a chuckle while looking down at the ground. He turns on his heels, shaking his head.

"You know what," Christopher gets out, turning back to face me, keeping a slight grin on his face. "This really shouldn't surprise me because this is all you do. You create this fantasy where everyone is against you when you know damn well that's not the case! No matter how much I try to help or reach out to you, this is thanks I get?! You do this *every* goddamn time to *everyone* who tries to bail you out of some shit!" His voice booms in the air as he shrieks a bunch of bullshit.

"What are you talking about?!" I blurt, somewhat matching his tone of voice. "What the fuck kind of thinking is that?!"

"It's all you do!" He leans forward, extending his arms out. "You do it every time with me, Peter, Counselor Malik, your parents! Anyone who tries to get through to you!" He pauses to catch his breath. "And when Moe needed you the most, you did the same thing to her! You treated her like shit and used her illness to play the victim again and again!" He scoffs with spite.

I clench my jaw. "Watch it. I swear I'll—?"

"Say what you will about my dad, but at least I'm not a coward. Yours probably should've beaten you better."

Red dots conquer my vision as rage flows through me. I am ready to pounce, but strong arms lock around me. Alejandro keeps his arms wrapped around me, holding me in place as I try to fight myself free from his grasp. No such luck. I wiggle and try to fight myself free, but Alejandro uses all of his strength to hold me in place.

All the fire that burns within me bursts like a bubble, and I shout to Christopher, "FUCK YOU!" The words come out ruggedly, and my lungs feel as though they are ready to burst from the excessive panting.

Christopher slowly backs away, still looking at me with hard eyes. He keeps his fists down by his sides, and in a low voice, he utters the words, "Go fuck yourself, Donald." And then I watch him walk away.

My breathing starts to become steady, and my heart rhythm begins to slow down. I close my eyes, breathing through my nose. I feel Alejandro loosen his hold around me as I let my head fall back against his shoulder. My lungs expand and then ease back down. I swallow thickly, feeling my throat open up again.

Inhale.

Exhale.

Inhale.

Exhale.

Inhale—

"You okay, Don?" Alejandro asks softly.

Exhale.

I open my eyes, and I clear my throat. I lean back against Alejandro as I try to stand up straight. He moves with me, ensuring that I don't fall back down, but I manage to do just fine on my own.

"Yeah," I tell him, avoiding his eyes. "I'm fine." I turn on my heels, fixing the collar to my jacket. "Let's get this over with."

. . . .

A black car pulls up to the front of the warehouse, and I squint my eyes to block out the brightness from the headlights. Alejandro stays by my side, keeping his hands in the pockets of his jean jacket. After I calmed down from the fiasco with Christopher, I helped Alejandro open up the warehouse, which required a lot of heavy lifting since there were a few pillars and industrial equipment in the way. The warehouse has been abandoned for some years, from the smell to cobwebs built up and rodent droppings.

As we lifted things out of the way, I thought back to Christopher standing over Alejandro after punching him in the mouth. The rage in Christopher's eyes was unlike anything I had ever seen. One second, things were calm, and then the next, Alejandro was on the ground.

I had asked Alejandro what happened between the two of them while I was getting the duffle bag out of the trunk of his car, and Alejandro just shook his head, insisting that nothing happened. But I didn't buy that for one second. So, I asked him again, and Alejandro sighed.

He said, *"I called him out on his bull. He made assumptions about me, so I did the same about him. And he didn't like it. But unlike his assumptions, mine was at least right."*

I pinch the bridge of my nose, shutting my eyes.

The sound of car doors opening and slamming shut pulls my attention. The first guy I spot is the one with the X tattoo—Diego?—as he gets out of the car. Behind him are two large dudes with too many muscles, both dressed in black suits.

I furrow my eyebrows. "Who the hell are they?" I whisper to Alejandro, referring to the Secret-Service-wannabes. As far as I know, Alejandro said that he told Diego to come to the warehouse alone to "talk," but he didn't specify the details to keep our plans on the down-low.

Alejandro sighs before leaning in close to my ear. "Let's find out." He sets his sights forward on Alejandro and the three large men and steps forward. The expression on Alejandro's face immediately changes, and he flashes his signature, cocky smirk. "Diego! Long time no see, am I right?"

Diego scoffs, stopping in his tracks. "You're lucky I don't punt you for what you did to me, you little shit." His words are purely venomous as he stares Alejandro in the eye.

Alejandro snickers. "You've always been a funny guy, you know that?" I notice the look of confusion on Alejandro's face as he looks at both of the guys standing beside Diego. "What's with the Secret Service? A little excessive, don't you think?"

Diego scowls. "You got some nerve," he snarls. "Playing your games. This one's on you."

"What do you mean?"

Diego sucks his teeth. "You sent them at my door and had them drag me into the car. No questions asked or answered."

Alejandro looks back at me, confused. He expects me to have some kind of explanation for the two dudes accompanying Diego, but I'm just as lost as he is. So, I shrug, sending the message that I genuinely have no clue what the guy is talking about.

Just then, a silver sports car pulls up to the warehouse. The headlights are more blinding than the ones from the car, and I actually have to shield my eyes with my hand. But once the car is parked and the headlights shut off, I lower my hand and shift my gaze to Alejandro. I notice his hands ball up into fists down by his sides. When I take a step forward to stand right beside him, his breath hitches as his lips part as he keeps his eyes ahead on the car.

I furrow my brows. "Alejandro?"

A man then emerges from the silver sports car and closes the door behind him. As he approaches all of us, it becomes easier for me to see his face clearly due to the light from the streetlamp.

His dark hair is shaved close to his head, with the sides done nicely in a partial fade. His eyes look golden brown as they glisten from the light. His cheekbones and jawline are sharp like blades, and I can tell that he's got a good build on him based on how his clothes fit on him. There are tribal tattoos across his throat, and I'm guessing he probably has more tattoos all over him, judging from how they stretch down into his shirt. I even notice the small tattoos on the back of his hands and along his knuckles, despite him wearing a long-sleeved leather jacket.

The guy suddenly stops in his tracks, standing a good distance from Alejandro and me. His gaze is unsettling as he scowls directly at us as if he's expecting us to burst right then and there. The hairs on the back of my neck stick up, and a sharp chill rushes down my spine.

Who is this guy?

I narrow my eyes to Alejandro as he locks eyes with the man. I notice how wide Alejandro's eyes are and how shaky his breathing has become. It's as if he's seen a ghost.

My lips part open as I switch my eyes back to the man and then back to Alejandro. Then, it hits me.

Wait a second. Is that—?

"Álvaro," Diego croaks, looking on with wide eyes.

My throat becomes dry as I tightly press my lips together, looking to the man who I now realize is Alejandro's brother, Álvaro. He looks completely different from what I remember when I was younger. He is more terrifying. And it's not that he's ugly. He just has the most intense eyes and looks as if he's ready to snap everyone in half. And I bet he can.

Álvaro takes another step towards Alejandro, shrinking the distance between them. He wraps his fingers around the nape of Alejandro's neck, causing Alejandro to sharply breathe while tightening his jaw.

Álvaro sighs, clenching his jaw. "Long time no see, little brother. Though, I wish I didn't have to come back cleaning your mess." Despite the calmness of his tone, his words pierced like daggers to the heart.

Alejandro gulps. "W-W, What are you doing here?" He clears his throat. "I-I, I thought you weren't coming back for a couple more days."

"That was the plan until I found out about Aitana." Álvaro slips his hand off Alejandro's neck, slowly turning on his heels to face a shaken Diego.

Alejandro parts his lips open as if he wants to say something, but the only sound that comes out is a sharp breath. He narrows his eyes to me, and they glisten as water sits along the bottom of his eyelids. I've never seen him this shaken up before. Not even his father has brought Alejandro to the brink of tears, and his father would often beat him and treat him like dirt. So, I can't even imagine what the hell Álvaro would put Alejandro through to get Alejandro all teary-eyed.

Álvaro locks his sights on Diego, and a slight smirk tugs on one side of his mouth. "I heard you've been causing trouble, Diego," he says smugly.

Diego vigorously shakes his head, breathing heavily. "No, no," he pants, clasping his hands together below his chin. "I haven't done anything wrong."

Álvaro rolls his eyes. "Really?" he remarks, glaring at Diego, who now falls to his knees with tears spilling from his eyes. "Then why are you looking like this?"

Diego bites down on his bottom lip, trembling. I don't know what it is about Álvaro that has everyone collapsing around him. Alejandro is hardly recognizable as he remains quiet and looks down to the ground with his cheeks flushed. When I reach out to him, Alejandro flinches and takes a small step away from me as if he is afraid. But I doubt he's scared of me. He turns his head, so he doesn't have to face me.

Knots instantly form in my stomach.

Diego shakes his head, insisting that he has no idea what Álvaro could be talking about. But Álvaro cuts him off, snapping his fingers. Before I can even blink, the two large guys standing beside Diego knock him to the ground with swift blows to the gut. Diego's eyes practically bulge out of his head from the wind suddenly being knocked out of him.

Álvaro just watches, keeping a straight face while Alejandro and I become frozen like statues. In the matter of a millisecond, things escalated from zero to one hundred. None of this was supposed to happen. I mean, yes, Alejandro and I were going to beat the crap out of Diego. But the more I watch the two guys stomp, kick, and punch on Diego, I realize that he's going to be dead any minute. The amount of blood that Diego spits up is unreal as he remains on the ground in a fetal position, taking the beating of a lifetime.

Álvaro whistles while approaching Diego and the two large men. Immediately, they stop beating on Diego and step away as Álvaro hovers over Diego. Diego shakes as if all his nerves have been ruptured as he lies on the ground on his side. Every inch of his face is busted open and bruised. I notice the small slits on his hands from where he was stomped and dragged against the ground. When he lifts his head up, one of Diego's eyes is completely closed shut, and blood drips from the corner of his mouth. A giant slit is across the bridge of his nose.

Álvaro crouches down to Diego's level, and Diego's breathing becomes rapid as he holds up his hands.

"P-P-P, please," he stammers, whimpering. "Ten piedad. *Por favor.*"

Álvaro sighs, settling his hand on the back of Diego's neck.

"It's bad enough that my nephew is your spawn," he gets out, furrowing his brows, "but you had to also come after my family. You hurt my sister—"

"Álvaro, please, I-I—"

"I know it was you, Diego. I talked to her myself. She saw your face."

Silence. Not even a rock moves.

Alejandro lowers his head from the corner of my eye, and I see his fists shake the tighter he clenches them by his sides. My heart sinks. He probably figured Álvaro heard about Aitana through the grapevine. He didn't expect Aitana to tell Álvaro herself, knowing what Alejandro would have to face. I mean, I don't know what he'll face, but I can only imagine after hearing and witnessing the brutality of the Great Álvaro Reyes.

Diego's breathing quakes as he pushes himself up on his elbows while looking at Álvaro. "I just wanted to talk to her," he cries, shaking. "I just wanted to talk, I swear. You and Alejandro keep her and Ricky from me, so I had to see her on my own terms."

A ball forms in my throat as I take in Diego's words.

Álvaro scoffs. "You forced yourself on her, Diego," he corrects, glowering down at Diego, who grows quiet. "Don't try to play the saint here, buddy. You've always been bad at it."

Álvaro reaches inside his jacket, and my bones lock up. I jump at the feeling of someone's hand grabbing at my wrist. I look down at my hand and see Alejandro's hand locked around my wrist. I didn't realize how close he was standing beside me now. Just a minute ago, he was keeping his distance from me. My breath hitches.

I hear Diego whimpering, and I turn my attention forward. Álvaro stays crouched down to Diego's level as he slips his hand out from the inside of his jacket. I scrunch my eyebrows as Álvaro slips something onto his right hand. He makes a fist, and Diego tries to back away, pleading for Álvaro to show him some kind of mercy.

Álvaro sighs, slightly tilting his head. "Would you fucking relax?" He reaches out with his left hand, letting it rest on Diego's shoulder.

Diego shakes, letting tears seep through his eyes as he lowers his head. Loud sobs escape his mouth as he utters, "I'm sorry," over and over and over again. In a way, this is what Alejandro and I wanted. For Diego to look and feel hopeless, begging that we'd show him some kind of mercy. But at the same time, it doesn't take nearly killing the guy for him to learn his lesson. Although, I'm not sure if he'd be able to walk ever again if Alejandro had the chance to use that metal pipe he had packed up in the duffle bag.

I swallow thickly.

A strange look crosses on Álvaro's face. His eyes soften, and his lips part open as he lets out a soft breath. It's as if he actually pities this guy. Does he? Now that he has Diego right where he wants him, Álvaro all of a sudden feels sorry for him?

No way. That's not the Álvaro I had pictured in my mind.

Still, Álvaro nods his head, patting Diego's shoulder.

"I know," is all he says while keeping his eyes on Diego. He removes his hand from Diego's shoulder. "Believe me, I know you are."

In a flash, as Diego slowly lifts his head, Álvaro's fist connects to the side of Diego's skull, sending Diego down on the ground face first. I feel the air leave my body as I watch Álvaro strike down on Diego's head a second time, this time with much more force. Then, he does it again. And again. And again. And one more time.

My breath hitches.

Diego lies still on the ground with his face towards me and his eyes closed. Blood drips down his face from where Álvaro had punched him in the head, which left an open wound. Diego hardly looks recognizable, thanks to all the cuts and blood on his face. I try to remember what he looked like before everything went down, and the dryness in my throat thickens. He was a weird-looking guy with his bushy brows and long nose, but he wasn't the ugliest guy I've ever seen. Now, he looks like a completely different person. I can't even spot the X tattoo due to blood, bruises, and cuts on his face.

When Álvaro rises up, I realize that his knuckles are brass and covered in crimson from cracking Diego's skull. One of the large men steps forward and hands Álvaro a small cloth to wipe his hands. Álvaro wraps the brass knuckles he used in the fabric before handing it over to the large guy beside him. He looks over to the other guy, and Álvaro tells him to "take care of Diego." The guy nods and lifts Diego up off the ground, throwing him over his shoulders.

My palms start to sweat, and I let out a sharp breath.

I feel Alejandro's grip on my wrist start to loosen, but he doesn't let go. He just keeps his eyes frozen forward, and his face loses its color as Álvaro stares right back at him.

I clear my throat. "You can let go," I whisper to Alejandro, snapping him out of the trance he's in.

Alejandro looks down at his hand, and he gently releases me. He rubs the back of his neck, clearing his throat.

"Sorry 'bout that," he gets out, hardly looking at me.

I rub my wrist, feeling a slight soreness from how tight Alejandro was holding onto me. I press my lips together, trying to suppress myself from wincing as I rub the area. He was squeezing the crap out of me. I'm surprised it's not bruised now. I gently pull up the sleeve to take a look.

"You okay?" Alejandro asks, leaning in close.

"Yeah," I assure him, examining my wrist. It doesn't help that it's the same wrist Christopher grabbed me also. It doesn't look bruised, but it doesn't feel great either. Sighing, I roll my sleeve down all the way, shaking my head. I look at Alejandro. "I'm good. Really."

He nods, pressing his lips together in a straight line.

I suddenly feel someone hovering over me, and I swiftly turn around on my heels. Goosebumps explode on my arms, and my heart practically leaps up my throat when I bump into Álvaro's chest as he stands behind me. His chest is hard as stone when I bump into him, and I stumble back a little, but Alejandro grabs hold of me to keep me up.

"Who's this shorty?" Álvaro's raspy, deep voice and intense gaze make my chest tighten. I rub my hands on my thighs, but I can still hear my heart pounding heavily in my chest as Álvaro looks down at me.

Up close, Álvaro is actually around the same height as Alejandro. But his demeanor makes him seem bigger. Tougher. It's no wonder why Alejandro would always get so queasy when talking about his brother. I try to imagine myself having to grow up, living with someone like Álvaro.

My stomach does backflips at the thought.

Alejandro takes a small step forward, slightly extending his arm to create a divide between Álvaro and me.

"He's with me," he says, trying to keep his words straight.

Álvaro rolls his eyes.

"Obviously," he snorts. "I mean, who is he? Why is he here?" There is a hint of disdain in his words as Álvaro keeps his eyes fixated on me, and my face feels warm.

Alejandro takes a small step forward, pushing me aside and behind him as if that's going to do anything good for me. "He's a friend. And we had all of this under control," he snaps, hardly raising his voice the slightest nonetheless.

Álvaro puts his hand on Alejandro's shoulder, and I notice how quickly Alejandro's body stiffens. I hear him take a sharp and quaky breath while averting his eyes.

"If you really had things under control, I wouldn't have to be here, would I?" Álvaro says, inching closer to Alejandro while keeping his voice low, but I can still hear every word that comes from his mouth. "I had a nice talk with Aitana. Diego and a few of his pals have been lingering around at the playground, too, right? You know how I feel about that. Kids go there to play, not worry about thugs like him."

Alejandro blinks. "I swear, I had everything under control. I—"

Álvaro puts his finger to his own lips, sending the message for Alejandro to zip it. And he does. Alejandro's words die down faster than I anticipated as he bites down on his bottom lip.

"We'll talk at the house." Álvaro cuts his eyes to me, and my heart thumps heavily in my chest. "Take him home first. And next time…" He slowly draws his eyes back to Alejandro. "…don't let this happen again. And there better not be a *next time.*"

Alejandro slightly opens his mouth as if he's desperate to say something in his defense, but the words never get a chance to come out. He doesn't let them come out. Even when Álvaro gives him the chance to say something, Alejandro lowers his gaze but keeps his head up. He's scared, and the fact that Alejandro is scared makes me petrified.

The devil himself, I think to myself, chewing the inside of my lip.

Álvaro leaves Alejandro and me behind at the warehouse, making his way to his car. I shift my eyes to the two large Secret Service-wannabes as they both get into the black car. One sits in the back, where I'm assuming they put Diego, and the other guy sits in the driver's seat. As soon as Álvaro pulls off, the black car follows him, and I watch them drive away.

I gulp, feeling the roughness within my throat.

I turn my attention back to Alejandro as he stands with his fists tight by his sides and his jaw clenched. I can see the veins in his fists and his neck as he keeps his gaze towards the ground. He's like a ticking time bomb waiting to explode. I wish I could take a guess at all the things going through his mind right now, but that would take forever to do.

I know he's probably pissed about Aitana talking to Álvaro behind his back, but I doubt she did anything out of spite. Álvaro is her brother too, and even though I know nothing of their bond, I'm sure Álvaro treats her well. Hell, he probably treats her better than Alejandro. Way better.

I know that feeling. Being treated differently compared to your sibling. It sucks when the parents act that way, but I bet it sucks, even more, when it's your sibling. I'm actually glad that my parents didn't decide to have another kid. As much as I love Morris-Lina, I don't know how I would've been if we had another sibling. Would I treat them better than her? Or would I favor her more and treat them like shit?

Mierda.

I reach out to Alejandro, hoping to give him some type of reassurance, but deep down, even I know that's total bullshit. I can't assure him of anything. What the hell do I even know?

Alejandro takes a small step forward, not allowing me to even touch him. He loosens his fists and huffs.

"C'mon," he says, barely looking at me as he slightly looks over his shoulder. "Let me take you home." He walks away, not giving me the chance to say anything.

I swallow down the lump in my throat as I follow behind him.

....

I stare up at the dark ceiling, taking in the silence. A tiny glint of light from the street lights enters my room through my bedroom window.

My skin starts to feel warm, even though I am only wearing my sweatpants and am hardly under the comforter. Every time I blink, all I see is Diego's face. His eyes closed shut, the one side of his face smashed against the ground, his body still and face bloody.

With a hard knock to the head like that from Álvaro, I already know there is little to no chance of Diego being alive. His skull was cracked open, and he took a rough beating from those two large guys beforehand. He was already set up to die.

I know he's probably dead.

That's why Álvaro had his large henchmen "take care" of Diego. Besides, anyone with a brain would know that things were going to end horribly once Álvaro slipped on them brass knuckles. Even though I didn't even realize they were brass knuckles until after the fact.

And now, every time I close my eyes, all I see is Diego's beaten body and bloody face. His beaten and probably DEAD body and bloody face. No matter how many times I tell myself to stop thinking about it, I can't. The feeling makes me sick, and I can hardly breathe.

I spring up out of bed, feeling bullets of sweat start to trickle down my forehead. My heart feels like it's pushing its way up my throat while pounding heavily like drums to my ears. I clutch onto my chest as unbearable tightness and nausea start to consume me. An intense ache pressures down onto the one side of my temple.

I fight against the darkness of the hallway as I make my way to the bathroom without knocking into things and waking up my parents.

I don't reach for a light. I don't even think I shut the door all the way. My breathing starts to pick up, growing more and more unsteady as I land on my knees. I reach out, feeling the familiar hard surface of the toilet lid. As I lift the lid and pull myself over to the toilet, the burning acid welcomes itself to run through me as if my body is some kind of playground. I can feel my lungs being squeezed as the rush of acid forces its way out of my mouth.

I grip onto the rim of the toilet as I push myself to get everything out of me. The burning is more unbearable than all the other times this has happened. My throat feels like it's being ground by rocks, and my lungs are being wrung into nothingness. My vision blurs from the tears seeping through my lashes, and an ache swells up in my cheeks.

Another rush flows out of me, and my body shakes.

I wrap my arms around the toilet. I can hardly open my eyes as I try to catch my breath. I feel empty, like all of my guts are out of me. But at the same time, my chest weighs me down as I rest my head against the toilet.

I think about getting up. I even think about flushing down the mess in the toilet. But I can't move. As much as I want to, I can't. I just lie there.

Week 4, Tuesday

I can hardly stomach down the food on my plastic spork as I twirl at the noodles on the plate. Every time I bite and swallow, my stomach fights back, and the food tries to claw its way back up my throat. Even if it's just a tiny amount—it doesn't work out. I feel nauseous like I'm on the brink of spitting it all back up.

And it's not just now as I'm sitting here at the lunch table.

This morning, I couldn't even swallow down a single bite of a banana without feeling a bitter taste erupt in my throat. All I could do was drink water. I couldn't even drink a small cup of milk.

Dad caught me in the kitchen this morning, tossing out a whole banana. But I played it off, telling him that it was rotten, even though mom had me buy them from the market about a week ago. Surprisingly, dad took my word for it and nodded.

It was rare for dad and me to interact in the morning since he always leaves for work early, and I'm usually still in bed. But this morning, though I was awake, I could hardly stay in bed. I had to get up. I didn't start getting dressed, but I sat downstairs for a while, trying to clear my head. Then, dad showed up, all dressed for work, and I could tell that he was taken aback that I was up.

He asked me, *"Why are you up so early, mi hijo?"*

I snagged a water bottle from the refrigerator. *"Just up."* I wasn't being smart. I was honest. I just couldn't get back to sleep.

Dad had a strange look on his face before asking me if I had a bad dream as if I was still a little kid. But I didn't mock him for it. I made it clear to him that I just wasn't sleepy anymore, and I couldn't stay in bed. I didn't tell him about me puking my guts out the other night, though. Ever since I came home on Saturday after being with Alejandro and dealing with Álvaro and Diego, I haven't slept as much. I would probably shut my eyes for about an hour or two before jumping up, feeling as though I was being suffocated.

Still, I assured dad that I was okay and left it at that.

But before dad left out this morning for work, he walked up to me and put his hand on my shoulder while looking me in the eye. His eyes looked glossy, but he wasn't going to cry. He had a faint smile curling at his lips, and the way he looked down at me—it was almost comforting. He then put his hand on my cheek before telling me in a low but clear voice, *"Estoy orgulloso de ti, Donald."*

And then, he left.

The look dad had on his face doesn't leave my mind. I continue to look down at my lunch, still twirling at the noodles with the spork, as I think about the last time dad has ever looked at me that way. I was fifteen, and dad had asked me to come with him to the garage. It was a late hot summer evening. Mom was cooking one of abuela's classic dishes that everyone loved, and Morris-Lina was in her room doing God knows what.

I remember the look dad had on his face when I met him in the garage. He had his hands on hips, and he looked at me as if I had done something wrong. I had asked him what was wrong, and he just gestured for me to come to him.

I sighed, dragging my feet.

Dad threw his arm around me and pointed to the black Cadillac car parked in the middle of the garage. It was abuelo's car, and for a while, it was dad's car. But dad had got himself a new car about two years ago before Morris-Lina, and I turned fifteen since the Cadillac wasn't working out for him. I thought he was being ridiculous since that Cadillac was everything I wanted.

Sure, it was old-fashioned, but it was a hell of a car. It was still in good shape and was durable. Before abuelo died, he told me that the car would be mine when dad thought I was ready for it one day. But I figured that wouldn't be until I was eighteen since dad never really gave me the best judgment unless it came down to my grades and baseball.

But then, that summer evening, dad put the keys to the car in my hand, passing the Cadillac down to me. I remember being confused at first, but then, a bunch of other wild emotions consumed me. Joy. Shock. Thrill. Excitement. I could hardly keep myself together. But like always, dad had to drag things out before giving me full ownership of the car.

"If you're going to care for the car, you have to really care for it," he told me upfront. *"You gotta know this car inside out. When your abuelo gave me this car, he put me to the test to see how*

much I deserved it. And so did his father. And now...you." He gave me a stern look. *"Entiendes?"*

I nodded.

Dad taught me how to fix the car up from the inside out. But he never did anything for me. He would talk me through everything, watching my every move while standing far back, so I had enough room to work. And once I nailed it all down, the car was mine. I remember the last thing he taught me, which was fixing the engine. Dad sat inside the car the entire time, talking me through everything. I followed his instructions, making sure I had everything done precisely.

Once I finished, I jumped into the driver's seat and turned on the engine. The car hummed nicely, and dad smiled. It wasn't a big one, but it was good enough to know that I had done well. He rested his hand on the back of my neck and softly exhaled while looking me in the eye.

That's when he told me that he was proud of me. He said I had done well. It's not like he's never said that he was ever proud of me before, but at that moment, it felt different. It felt deeper like it truly mattered. Like I truly mattered.

I remember suggesting that we go for a test drive and even hit the sandlot for some catch, even though it was getting dark. But the street lights would've been on, and it wouldn't have been the first time that dad and I played some ball as the sun was going down. Yet, it didn't happen. Dad said that he had to take Morris-Lina to speak with a psychologist or something like that.

It was a bittersweet moment, I guess.

As I look back, I remember feeling enthusiastic about finally owning the car I've wanted since I was a little kid, sitting in my abuelo's lap behind the steering wheel. But I also pictured having my first test drive with my dad—just like he did with abuelo.

I don't think Morris-Lina ruined the moment. I just wish it had gone differently. But hearing how dad said that he was proud of me made things okay.

I flinch back when fingers snap in my face, pulling me out of my thoughts. I nearly drop my spork into the plate of food, but I tighten my hold on it. I look up, meeting Carmen's glare as annoyance consumes her face. She lowers herself down onto the bench, sitting right across from me, and huffs.

"Are you alright?" she asks, looking me up and down. "You've hardly touched your food, and lunch is almost over." She holds up her phone, showing off the time on her bright lock screen.

It is cutting close to the end of our lunch period, and I've only taken two bites out of my lunch. It's chicken parmesan. And as much as I can't stand the school's fake version of certain meals, it does smell and looks good. But, like usual, it kind of does taste like plastic. But I'll still eat the food, nonetheless.

Just not today, though.

Meagan lightly bumps her arm against me to catch my attention, but I keep my eyes on my food. "Donny?" Her words are soft, and she leans in close so only I can hear her. "What's wrong?" I don't have to look at her to know that she's probably worrying herself more than she needs to over this.

"Look, nothing is wrong, guys," I faintly chuckle, addressing everyone at the table. I know they're all probably in on this. "Seriously. Just lighten up, okay? We all know this food is dogshit."

Just then, I hear Christopher mutter something out from the corner of his mouth in a low voice. "All you eat is dogshit."

I draw my eyes to him.

Christopher doesn't even look up at me when he speaks. He keeps his eyes on his food, digging at the plastic meat with his spork before taking small bites.

 Carmen nudges him with her elbow, but he doesn't budge. He continues to look down at his food, acting all nonchalant. I narrow my eyes at him, clenching my jaw. Ever since what happened on Saturday, Christopher has been acting more and more of a douche. Any time he'll open his mouth to acknowledge my presence is if he has something witty to say. It's as if everything he had said about me on Saturday was true. He truly believed that he had done no wrong, when in fact, that's bullshit!

He had *no* right to speak about my family or my sister! So, yeah, I told him to fuck off! He's lucky that Alejandro could hold me back. Otherwise, Christopher wouldn't have been able to walk away that night. He would've been limping or crawling, for sure.

And now, he's looking at me as though I'm the bad guy in the room! Like I said to Counselor Malik that one time, I know that I'm a piece of shit, and I know some things I deserve, but what happened on Saturday! I sure as hell didn't deserve that!

Who does he think he is anyway?

My dad?!

He is telling me who I can't and can't be around because his gut has a *"funny feeling"* about someone?!

Screw that!

Carmen tries to talk to me, but I snatch up my book bag and stand up from the table. "I think I'm gonna head out now, so I don't gotta deal with getting past people," I sigh, trying to suppress the frustration trying to cut through my words. "I'll see you guys later." I grab my plate of food and toss it into the trashcan.

I feel my stomach twist in knots when I get another look at Christopher. He just glares up at me, watching my every move.

Fuck you, I think, but I don't say anything.

I focus on getting out of the cafeteria as fast as possible before anyone has the chance to stop me.

. . . .

I lean back against the wall to stay out of people's way as they walk out of the school building. It's an unusual rush once the day ends. Peter suggested that we all hang out after school, even though I was against it. I didn't say it outright that I wasn't all for hanging out, but I couldn't say no to Peter. Not today, at least. The guy's been through enough, and he probably deserves this to get his mind off things. After the shit with Jen Li, he's been swinging in and out of his moods.

One second, he'll be fine, and the next, he'll be quieter than a church mouse and not even crack a smile. That girl really did a number on him, and if she weren't a girl, I'd get her for it.

Peter sits on the top concrete step to the school entrance, pouting. Benton is next to him, leaning back on his elbows while using his bookbag as a cushion for his elbows. Christopher and Carmen stand across from me, and Christopher does all he can to avoid looking at me. He'll either look past me or keep his focus on Carmen. It's honestly whatever. I don't care.

Carmen groans. "Why is Meagan always the first to get to class but the last to leave?"

I chuckle under my breath. Classes ended about ten to fifteen minutes ago, and we've all been waiting outside of the school for Meagan. It's not unusual for us to wait for her since she's always caught up in something. She'll either be talking with Preston or Nathan about theater, or a teacher will be talking her ear off. And quite a few times, she'll stay behind in class and ask a teacher all sorts of questions about some kind of assignment.

It's nothing new. Carmen should be used to this by now.

Benton sighs, sitting up. "She should be coming out about now." He reaches into his pants pocket and pulls out a hair tie. Benton puts the hair tie between his teeth and starts pulling back his hair, leaving a few loose strands along the front. I notice him look over to Peter, who still sits on the step with a gray cloud over his head. "What's wrong?" Benton asks him, still holding the hair tie in his mouth.

Peter sighs, shaking his head. "All good."

I snort. I use my foot to gently kick his shoulder for a nudge. "Stop lying to yourself, Petey," I say. "You've been sulking like your favorite dog died or something. What gives?"

Peter sucks his teeth. "I don't have a dog. I'm allergic," he states the obvious, turning his head to look over his shoulder. "And I'm fine." He faces forward again. "My aunt's just on my case because she thinks she wasted money on me again because I have two prom tickets, and I don't even have a date." He holds his head in his hands, sighing.

"That's not your fault," Christopher chimes in, looking to Peter. "You explained to your aunt what happened, yeah? I'm sure she understands."

Peter shrugs his shoulders, sighing. "I doubt it." His voice cracks as he pinches his eyes shut. "Dios mío. I'm pathetic."

I exhale through my nostrils. I've never seen Peter like this. So torn up over someone who he's only gone out with for a few months. It's not like they have pawned for each other as long as Christopher and Carmen. They only recently started getting to know each other. But Peter's a soft guy, so seeing him this way shouldn't shock me all too much. But the fact that his numbskull of an aunt is making him out to be the foolish one is appalling. Jen Li played *him*. Not the other way around. She probably did like him, but then he slept with her, and then she cut the cord between them.

Fuck it, she used him. She fooled all of us.

I try to think of the right words to say to bring Peter out of his mood, but Benton speaks up before I even get the chance. He nudges Peter and nonchalantly goes, "I'll go with you."

Peter swiftly lifts up his head and faces Benton with his eyebrows wrinkled. My jaw partially hangs open, and for a second, I look over to Christopher. He holds the shocked expression as I do. So does Carmen, but her eyes are just wide as she keeps her mouth closed. I look back to a baffled Peter and a relaxed Benton.

"Wait," Peter blinks. "What?" He slightly tilts his head in confusion. "You want to go to prom with me?"

Benton presses his lips together, and his shoulders become tense. He pulls his knees in close to his chest, wrapping his arms around his legs. A slight nod for confirmation.

"We are friends, aren't we?" Benton's voice softens. "And friends do nice things for each other, right? So, let me do this nice thing for you, so your aunt doesn't feel like she wasted her money." A short pause as his cheeks flush. "If you want."

The corners of Peter's mouth slowly start to pull upwards. His arm comes around Benton, pulling him in closer. "Benton Son," he chuckles, still stunned. "You really are the best boy, aren't you?"

Benton shrugs, smirking. "I try."

Peter grins. "Seems I'm rubbing off on you, then, huh?"

"Perhaps." Benton reverts back to his usual, shy self as he averts his eyes.

I chuckle to myself. I try to think of when Benton and Peter started to get close since I doubt they hang out outside of school. Then again, whenever all six of us are hanging out, Peter always hangs with Benton, and I guess Benton's grown used to having Peter at his side all the time. Peter will always try to say something to make Benton laugh since Benton is always so quiet, but Benton would never mind. And sometimes, he'd laugh too. Peter is that way with Meagan, too, from time to time.

Deep down, I know that Peter would act like that towards Meagan and Benton because he knows that once Christopher, Carmen, and I graduate, it'll just be him, Benton, and Meagan. But that will only be for a year since he'll be a senior next year, and Benton and Meagan will be juniors.

It's crazy just thinking about it.

Damn.

My breathing hitches when hands come over my eyes, and darkness conquers my vision. I put my hands up to my eyes, trying to get a feel for the hands that cover them.

Then a familiar voice softly peeps, "Hello," against my ear.

I remove the hands from my eyes as I turn my head around. My lips curve into a smile when I meet Meagan's eyes as she grins. I throw my arm around her, pulling her up against me. My heart thumps heavily when she rests her head against my shoulder. I let my arm slip down as my hand settled against her lower back as I held her a bit tighter.

"You're in a good mood since lunch," I say.

Meagan sighs. "Hardly." Her lips slightly turn downward. "Dexter had a quick meeting with us about the show, and now the school won't allow us to do Odella because of its *'mature themes.'* So, now we're not doing a show for the Spring, but we're still going to push forward with funding for production next Fall." She folds her arms like a child, scraping the bottom of her shoe against the concrete beneath her.

I snicker, still looking at her.

Carmen lets out a scoff, easing into Christopher's arms as he wraps one arm around her. I roll my eyes at the sight. I turn my attention to the side, trying to find something else to focus on. Still, I hear Carmen speak, clearly annoyed over Meagan taking forever to meet up with us, even though it wasn't her fault.

"Well, now that you're here, we can get rolling," Carmen huffs. "You good, Donald?"

I give her my attention. Only her.

"Yeah, I'm good." I tighten the straps to my bookbag. "Ready to head out?"

Peter jumps up, groaning. "Yessss," he drawls. "I'm starving! That crap for lunch really didn't do it for me. I think my stomach is starting to eat itself."

I roll my eyes, snorting.

"Lucky for you, I know this great pizza place I used to go to. It's not that far from my house, but it is a drive."

Peter sighs. "Is it really good, though?"

"It is," I assure. "I used to go there with a friend of mine when we were kids. It's hardly changed. You'll like it."

Christopher snorts under his breath, and I notice him rolling his eyes. I feel my blood start to boil, and I bite the inside of my cheek. Carmen nudges him, asking him what's his problem, but Christopher shrugs his shoulders, insisting that nothing is wrong.

He's such a bullshitter. He always has been.

Now that I think about it, Alejandro had every right to call Christopher out for his crap. Christopher loves going around, trying to fix people, but he can't even improve himself.

My lips part open, and my eyes remain on him. "You got something you wanna say, Chris?" I make sure that my words are clear and come out with ease. I keep my fist tight, squeezing tighter and tighter to resist the urge of knocking some sense into him.

Christopher shakes his head, pursing his lips. "Nothing." His green eyes somehow look darker, as if the Devil is inside of him. Perhaps he is, judging by the cocky smirk that plasters on his pale face. "I just think why to bother going all out for someplace that's old. There are so many other places to go close by, and they have served us well. Why take a chance visiting someplace old, and we get let down?" Even his words sound cocky.

He's got some nerve. I click my tongue.

"Well," I sigh. "If you feel that way, then maybe you should stay behind. I understand that keeping an open mind is tricky for someone like you."

I notice the twitch at the one side of Christopher's mouth as his arm slips off of Carmen. He has his hand in a fist by his side as if that's supposed to intimidate me, and he takes a small step forward. "*Someone like me?*" His eyebrows furrow. "Care to elaborate on that one, Donald?"

I shrug, smirking at his pathetic attempt to scare me. Even if scaring me isn't his intention, he sure does look pathetic.

"It's a real pity that you don't even know yourself well enough to get what I'm saying," I say, taking a small step forward. "Maybe someone should call you out on your shit more often."

His glare intensifies. "Is that so?"

"Damn ri—AH!"

My ear falls victim to the tight pressure of Carmen's fingers as she pinches my earlobe. I grab her wrist, trying to free my ear, but she starts twisting at my earlobe. I wince, feeling the bones in my earlobe crunch together like rocks. I look up, seeing Christopher suffer the same fate. Carmen manages to pull him down, twisting his ear for kicks. His face reflects his pain, which is similar to mine.

I can only imagine how comical and ridiculous we both look right now. Still, Carmen couldn't give two shits. She's grown ruthless.

"Listen here, the both of you!" she barks at us as if we're her children. "I don't know what the hell is up with you two, but you're gonna sort this out right now!"

Without warning, Carmen tugs on our ears, forcing Christopher and me to follow her. She pinches our ears tighter and tighter with every step we take. I'm just waiting for her to finally yank my ear off from the side of my head. I'd rather suffer the fate of having the remaining fat under my arm pinched than go through this.

We make it across the street and into the parking lot. I realize that she's taking us to her car. Lord knows why. But once we do make it to her car, Carmen lets us go, and my ear feels like it's on fire. I would've expected it to be numb, but I feel every ounce of pain resurface. When I go to touch my ear, it stings.

I hiss.

Carmen unlocks her car and opens the door to the backseat.

"Get in there," she demands, looking between Christopher and me.

Christopher tries to speak, "Carm—"

"Nah, uh!" Carmen holds up her hand, cutting him off. "I don't want to hear any excuses. The two of you have been acting like jackasses lately, and you're bringing everyone down." Her tone reminds me of how mom would scold Morris-Lina and me if we ever did something wrong.

God, I hate that feeling.

I open my mouth to speak, but Carmen holds up her hand to silence me. She gives me a stern glare, and I feel my bones stiffen. It's something about her acting this way that makes her seem scarier than I could ever imagine. I'd rather be in the presence of the Devil himself than face off against a pissed-off Carmen Richardson.

"Look," she sighs, lowering her hand. "Sometimes, brothers who really love each other will fight each other every now and then. But they don't friggin' quit on each other." She takes a step aside while holding open the car door. "Now, get in. Or I'll punt the both of you." Her tone indicates that it's not a threat but a promise.

I immediately slide into the back seat, sitting behind the driver's seat. Christopher steps in after me and sits down behind the passenger's seat. Before she closes the car door, Carmen makes it blatantly clear that we cannot come out until we sort our shit out.

"Again, if you try me," she leans her head in and hisses, "I'll punt you. And that'll be a shame on your chances of having children."

I gulp.

Once she closes the door, locking Christopher and me inside the car with her remote control key, I feel myself starting to relax. I let out a long, dragging sigh, resting my head back.

Since when was Carmen so petrifying?

Then, I hear Christopher speak up. "I can't think of a time she's been that…." His words drift off as he ponders on how to carefully finish his sentence.

I end up filling in the blank for him. "Scary?"

Christopher lets out a sharp breath. "Yes. That."

I can't imagine what it's like being in a relationship with her. I bet she probably wears the pants, and Christopher doesn't mind. Especially if she gets *that* fed up over things.

Geez, if Christopher even thought of fighting back in an argument, Carmen would probably destroy him without hesitation. He'll probably think twice before trying to argue with her ever again. That is if he already hasn't.

Anyway, Christopher and I sit next to each other in silence. I look out the window, not wanting to make eye contact with him. He just looks forward, staring out. Carmen's words start to swim through my mind as I trace random shapes with my fingers along the side of the door…

"Sometimes, brothers who really love each other will fight each other every now and then. But they don't friggin' quit on each other."

Here's the thing—I have a right to quit on him. After what he said to me that night about me, my parents, and my sister, I can't stand the sight of him. It's taking everything in me to not deck him because God forbid blood gets in Carmen's car. She'll have my head. But ever since that night, I learned how he *really* felt about me. No matter how much I scolded him, no matter how many times I thought he was being an asshole, I've never talked about his mom. I wouldn't dare myself to bring up how things were between him and his mom. So, what gives him the right to talk about how I treated Morris-Lina?! He doesn't even know the whole story of how things were between her and me! She was my friggin' twin sister! I did all I could for her! I loved her as much as a person could love anyone!

I know I did!

I grit my teeth, clenching my fist. *I fucking hate—!*

"I should've left her out of it," Christopher pipes up.

I turn my head, locking my eyes on him. Christopher narrows his eyes down to the mat under his feet while keeping his head up. His arms are folded as he clutches his bookbag against his stomach. He licks his lips, clearing his throat. "I know what it feels like when someone mentions someone you've lost, and they use that person against you. My dad does it all the time when he and I go at it. He says that I could've done better in taking care of my mom and that I should've been downstairs when she…." His words are shaky, and I notice how his Adam's apple bobs.

The memory of Christopher finding his mother is probably resurfacing in his mind as he closes his eyes, trying to get himself together. He coughs into his elbow in an attempt to suppress whatever feeling is trying to come out of him. It's not like I haven't seen Christopher cry before. I remember having to hold him up as he watched his mom's casket being lowered into the ground. It was just the two of us, and Christopher could hardly get himself together even after her casket was lowered. I stayed with him for a long time. So long that our parents had to get on our case, telling us to wrap things up, which was pretty heartless.

To be honest, I never wanted to see Christopher like that ever again. So whenever February 10th rolls around, I make sure that I'm there for him.

Christopher sits up, finally getting his thoughts together before continuing to say whatever he has to say. He still narrows his eyes downward, keeping his head up. But I put the effort in to actually look at him as he talks.

"You didn't deserve that." He turns his head, looking me in the eye. "I'm sorry." His eyes are glossy from the water forming along his eyelids, but he holds himself together and keeps his words straight.

My mouth starts to feel dry as his words begin to sink in. I could tell him that it was alright, but everything was not okay. I know he means what he says, but part of me—a small part—still wants to hate him. But the thing is, he gets it, just like I get him.

That's what made us stick around each other for as long as we have, anyway. Even though it's not okay, I still end up choosing him, just like he always ends up choosing me. I don't get why we're like that, but we are.

"Yeah," I manage to get out. "I'm sorry too." My voice softens towards the end as I feel a ball swell up in my throat.

I ease back into the comfortable leather of the backseat, resting my head. Christopher averts his downward, staring at the car mat under his feet. I go back to tracing random patterns on the armrest of the car door. Silence fills the car, and I don't even bother checking my phone to see what time it is. All I know is that now that we apologized to each other, Carmen should let us out. I mean, it's been over ten minutes, I'll bet.

Then, out of the blue, I hear Christopher chuckling to himself, and I slowly draw my eyes over to him. He keeps his arms folded across his chest, looking down with a faint grin plastered on his face.

I quirk an eyebrow.

He doesn't have his phone out, so it's not like he's watching a video or listening to something funny. It's just him and me sitting in silence. And yet, he's laughing to himself?

Christopher notices me staring at him, and he sits further back into the backseat.

"Sorry," Christopher snickers, shaking his head. "It's just…I've never seen such a look of shock on your face when Carmen grabbed at you." Small fits of laughter come from as crinkles form by his eyes the more he laughs. "Oi, she really got you good, didn't she?"

I roll my eyes. Of course, he'd laugh at that. I can only imagine how ridiculous the scene looked when Carmen pinched my ear as though I was her child. But in my defense, she did it without warning! And it hurt like hell! So, of course, I was shocked and in pain! I thought the bruja was going to yank my ear off my head!

Just thinking about it makes my ear tingle and ache again.

But Christopher has no right to laugh at me. He looked just as ridiculous as I did since Carmen got to him too! How else was she able to bring him over and put us together?

I suck my teeth, turning my body so I can face him better. Christopher's laughter starts to die down, and I lock my eyes on him. "You got amnesia or something? Because FYI, your wifey got you too, and you looked more ridiculous since she had to pull you down because you're such a beanstalk."

"*Pfft.*" Christopher rolls his eyes. "Please. Your face was more iconic than mine was, mate. You're meme-material with that look you had. Trust me."

I flip him off.

His grin widens, and he lightly pushes me back. I press my lips tightly together, trying to prevent a grin from creeping onto my face. Looking back, I can't think of a time I've seen Carmen so pissed to the point where she looked like the Devil was going to come out of her. Her face is so much like a doll. It's hard to imagine her being so…cruel.

But there was one time that I did see her get angry.

I lightly tap Christopher's leg to get his attention, and I tell him, "I don't know if you remember this, but there was one time where Morris-Lina scared the shit out of Carmen, and Carmen got so mad, she yelled at Moe."

Christopher's eyes widen, and his mouth is agape. "Seriously?"

I snicker, nodding my head. "Yeah. It was around the time we all really met each other, and Morris-Lina was trying to do some kind of prank, and it totally backfired." I feel my smile widen.

The memory remains fresh in my mind as I tell Christopher the story. It feels like it all happened yesterday, but like I said, it was around the time we all really met each other. So, sophomore year. It was cutting close to Halloween, and Morris-Lina had planned the perfect prank on Carmen, but it was supposed to be something funny, not something to scare Carmen shitless.

Morris-Lina had purchased a fake spider from the Halloween shop in Cedarville Mall, which isn't too far from where we live, and she was going to put the spider in Carmen's locker for a sick giggle. But, somehow, Morris-Lina ended up putting an actual spider in Carmen's locker instead of the fake one. And it was dead. Morris-Lina said that she must've mixed the two of them up since she had her science class right before doing the prank, and she dropped the fake spider in the cage that the real spider was in. And they were the exact same kind of spider, so she was confused with trying to determine which one was which.

But, regardless, it wasn't a thrilling sight when Carmen opened her locker and found a real, dead spider sitting on top of her books. Carmen freaked out. The girl was screaming her head off. Meanwhile, Morris-Lina was laughing. At least, until Carmen realized what was going on. Carmen marched over to Morris-Lina with the spider in hand.

She was about to tell Morris-Lina off, but then the science teacher walked up to them and pointed out that Carmen was holding a real, dead spider. Not a fake. The teacher had the decoy.

Carmen's face was so pale, and Morris-Lina looked so shocked. Carmen threw the spider on the ground and scolded Morris-Lina so bad. But Morris-Lina didn't take anything Carmen said to heart. She felt terrible but seeing Carmen's face so red like a fire hydrant was funny as hell.

It still makes me laugh. The rage from Carmen. The look of shock and humiliation on Morris-Lina's face. The prank went terribly wrong, but it's honestly one of the best things that made my sophomore year unforgettable. At that moment, I knew Carmen was going to end up being Morris-Lina's closest friend. And boy, it was a riot.

As I tell the story to Christopher, he's wheezing in laughter, and I am too. The thought of Carmen being so mad over a prank is funny, but the way she looked was ten times better and is why it's such a funny story. I honestly thought the girl was going to piss her pants.

And then there's Morris-Lina.

Of course, she'd find humor in all of this. Her mind…her way of thinking is…I can't say. My God, what thoughts had gone through her mind?

It's hard for me to stop laughing as I hold my head in my hand. My ribs feel like they are burning as my chest heaves and my laughter continues to spill from my mouth, quivering.

Looking back, I should've told Morris-Lina that it was a bad idea. Maybe things would've turned out differently, and Carmen wouldn't have seemed so ridiculous. But Morris-Lina never really listens. Why would she? She's free to make her own choices. But some of her choices weren't always the most brilliant routes to take.

Then again, it doesn't matter what I'd think. Morris-Lina would still do her own thing anyway. But at least she would've considered what I thought. That's all I wanted from her. Just some consideration. She didn't have to be so rash. She didn't have to do things for the sake of the moment, like taking those pills.

She wasn't thinking clearly.

She didn't even leave an explanation as to why! That's just how she is—never being clear on why she had to do some of the things she did. First, she hated taking them friggin' pills, and then, she uses them to…!

My chest feels tight, and my breathing starts to thin. My lip trembles. My face feels warm as I keep my head in my hands, and soreness starts to explode within my cheeks. I don't know if it's from all the laughing or is just something that randomly happens.

All I know is that I wish she had at least come to me first before doing something so…!

Why couldn't she have talked to me?! I'm her twin brother, for crying out loud! I get why she wouldn't want to trouble mom and dad. They're not the best people to come to when problems occur. It was our mom who pushed the idea of sending Morris-Lina away to that rehabilitation center in Baltimore. And I get why. Morris-Lina wasn't doing what the doctor suggested for her to get better, but at the same time, she could've explained why.

Morris-Lina could've just talked to me more.

I would've listened. I know I would've without question.

Yes, I was tough on her too. But I didn't want this to happen! I loved her. She was part of me in more ways than she could've ever imagined. Like my God! What the hell?!

I don't think I was too tough on her, though. Was I?

I thought I did everything right. Why didn't she just come to me? She needed me but didn't come to me in the end.

Did I not love her enough?

She probably needed me more than I thought, but I didn't love her enough. That's why. That's precisely why she did what she did. Because I wasn't there. I wasn't friggin' there!

A sharpness bursts inside my chest, and a rush of tears spills from my eyes. I try closing my eyes to hold them in, but I can't stop. I just can't stop. The tightness in my chest gets the best of me, and I can hardly control my breathing. A bunch of weird sounds come out of my mouth—like pants and gasps—that I can't hold in. I lose all sense of where I am as an excruciating weight hammers down on me, and I feel like I'm falling into a bottomless pit. No matter how much I try to settle down my breathing, it can't be settled. No matter how much I try to open my eyes, the tears just keep on running down my face.

And as much as I hate this feeling, I let it swallow me whole. I just give up and give in. What else can I do?

My thoughts get louder as I lose all sense of control over myself. It's like whispers swimming around me—suffocating me until I drop.

She needed you. Your own sister needed you, and you weren't there.

Talk about the love of a sibling.

What the hell, Donald?

This is your fault, you hear me? It's your fault!

She needed you! Only you! And look what you made her do!

"I'm sorry!" I cry out, unable to hold in my sobs. "I'm sorry!"

The voices get louder and louder. I feel my nails sinking into my forehead as I try to block them out, but the thoughts still linger.

They don't poof away like in the movies.

It all hurts so *friggin'* much!

Your fault. It's on you!

Yeah, all on—!

Strong arms wrap around me, pulling me back. My body shakes, and unsteady pants and gasps escape from my mouth. My head settles against a hard chest, and the arms remain wrapped in my torso, holding me close as I shake.

Christopher whispers to me, "It's alright, mate. You're fine."

I shake my head. Taking one last heavy and shaky breath, I sit up and turn my head to look up at Christopher. I try to steady my breathing so I can speak clearly.

"No, it's not," I muster up. "She needed me. I always needed her, but she needed me more. And I wasn't there." I grit my teeth, shutting my eyes to prevent another flood of tears from escaping my ears. "I wasn't there."

Christopher tightens his hold on me. "Donald," he says my name softly. "Mate, look at me."

I do what he says.

The tightness in my chest starts to ease up as I give Christopher my attention. His eyes glisten from the sunlight that peaks through the rear car window. His chest slowly rises and falls, and encouraging my heart to go back to its calming pace. He opens his mouth to speak, but he suddenly hesitates. So, he closes it and exhales through his nose.

I swallow down the ball in my throat when he gently wipes away the tears on my cheeks with his finger. I realize that this is probably the only time Christopher's seen me like this. A mess. An actual crying mess. Usually, I'm able to hold myself together, especially around him. He's seen me upset before, but not like this. It's not only weird, but it's unsettling. But it doesn't surprise me that he's so calm about it. He always responds well to things.

Christopher keeps his eyes on me, and his arms start to relax while remaining locked around me.

A sigh. "You have nothing to apologize for, Donald."

Of course, he thinks that. He's just looking on the surface.

I try to oppose. "Chris, I wasn't—"

"You weren't what?" he sharply cuts me off. "Perfect? Because believe it or not, anyone who thinks they are perfect at loving someone is more fucked than you'd think. They don't know a thing about love because love isn't perfect. If it were, we would all be living the dream, and divorces and heartbreak wouldn't be a thing."

I nod. *He does have a point.*

Christopher goes on, adding, "You'll never be the perfect brother or the perfect friend. But you sure as hell let us know how you bloody feel about us. And that's the best thing about you. That's how we know you love us." A pause. He softens his eyes. "That's how she knew you loved her. There's nothing wrong with you. And I damn well know she'd attest to that."

I let his words sink in. All the loud voices in my head go away, and I feel my lungs start to open up as the tightness in my chest leaves my body.

I chuckle to myself. "I doubt Carmen stays mad at you long, huh?" I joke, hardly looking Christopher in the eye. "You're a real sweet talker."

He jabs me in the side with his finger, making my body tense up from the feeling. Christopher groans, sitting up. I lift myself up off him and wipe my tear-stained cheeks with the back of my hand.

"So, what's the plan?" Christopher asks, slipping his arms through the straps to his bookbag. "We bang on the door for her to let us out and tell her that we kissed and made up?"

I don't get a chance to respond since someone is knocking at the car door, making Christopher jump. He lets out a sigh of relief once we realize it's Carmen. She unlocks the car doors with her remote control, and Christopher and I jump out without a second thought. I close the car door behind me, and when I look up, Christopher has Carmen pulled up against him with his arms wrapped around her waist.

Peter and Benton stand close by, snickering.

"Damn, Chris," Peter smirks. "You would've thought you just been let out of the hole."

Christopher shoots a glare at Peter, flipping him off. Peter sticks his tongue out mockingly. But he stops the second Benton nudges him.

"Y'all good?"

I turn around, and my eyes lock on Meagan. She puts her hand to my shoulder, and the corners of her mouth slightly pull upward. "The two of you were in there for quite some time."

"Yeah!" Peter chimes in, agitated. "Quite some time that I'm no longer craving food since my stomach ate itself!"

I suck my teeth, slowly dragging my attention to Peter. "Quit whining, you big baby." I lift my arm up to wrap around Meagan's shoulders. I feel her ease against me as she gently rests her head on my shoulder.

I shift my attention to Benton as he stands beside Peter with his arms folded across his chest. A tiny smirk plays across his lips.

I smirk. "You see how he is, Benny? Good luck when prom time comes around. You're gonna need it."

Meagan snaps her head up off of me, and her eyebrows wrinkle in utter confusion. "Wait." She snaps her attention straight at Benton. "What?! You're going to prom?!"

Benton's face becomes as red as a cherry. He just nods his head.

Meagan's eyes widen, and her mouth is agape. "Since when?!" It's like she's been stabbed in the back. But just because she didn't want to go to prom didn't necessarily mean Benton couldn't go. Though, I'm sure she knows that.

Peter raises his hand, calling for Meagan's attention. "It's me! That's why!" He throws his arm over Benton's shoulder. A wide smirk stretches across his lips. "Jen Li kicked me to the curb, and I didn't want to waste an extra ticket. So, Benny-boy signed himself up to go to prom with me. Kind of like my wingman."

Benton's face flushes again as he shrugs his shoulders, unable to look at anyone. The poor guy hates having the spotlight, but Peter just tells Benton to lighten up and gives him a genuine smile.

Meagan settles back against me, still in disbelief.

I poke my lip out teasingly. "Aww," I coo, "you okay, dearest?"

Meagan nudges me in the chest with her elbow. "Shut up," she murmurs, folding her arms like a child. It's kind of cute. "Let's just get out of here."

I wink at her. "With pleasure."

Week 4, Thursday

I got a text from Alejandro last night, asking to meet up after school. I honestly didn't want to respond, but I knew he would be on my tail if I said nothing. I talked to Christopher about it, and of course, he didn't want me to speak to Alejandro again. But after what happened on Saturday, whatever Alejandro wants from me, I have to be upfront with him. I have to be. No way out of it.—D.G.

I stare blankly at the dashboard as I keep my head against the headrest. My heart pounds in my chest, rattling my eardrums. I keep the windows slightly cracked open to get air circulation going, but it still feels unreasonably humid. I checked the weather before I left the house this morning, and it's only sixty-seven degrees out. And it's cloudy.

So, it's not like the sun is making me hotter because there is no sunshine. It's just gray skies, and I like it that way. At least, when it's not raining.

I keep the sound to my radio low as I try to gather my thoughts. I know that as much as I want to go home, I can't. I already messaged Alejandro early this morning that I'd be over to see him and hear whatever he has to tell me. Though, I'd rather be at home, for once. But I'd probably stay up in my room to avoid the chances of running into my mom after our conversation last night when I came home.

Instead of going straight home after hanging out with my friends, I stayed over at Christopher's place for a bit. His dad was home, so I couldn't stay long. But the two of us just talked. I forget all the stuff we talked about since most of it was random, but college did come up during our conversation. Christopher told me that he had submitted his deposit two weeks ago to attend Strawson University in Atlanta, Georgia. For a moment, it slipped my mind that he was planning on remaining in the United States for college, but I guess for the sake of keeping his father sound, it was his best bet.

Plus, Strawson did have a solid engineering program, and they did offer him the best scholarships. Hell, he hardly has to pay anything out of pocket. I remember asking Christopher how Carmen felt about him going to school in a different state since she's planning on attending West Solomon College in Washington D.C. for biomedical sciences or something like that.

Christopher said that Carmen was okay with it, but the expression on his face contradicted his words. I believed that Carmen would've been okay with it—but I don't know how Christopher feels about being that far from her. We didn't talk about it much, though. Mostly because Christopher refused to dwell on it.

Anyway, when I came home last night, the lights were dimmed, and mom was sitting on the living room couch, waiting for me. She's never done that before, but I tried paying her no mind. Of course, I addressed her when I walked through the door, but I wasn't in the mood for conversation. But, like always, my mom just wouldn't let things go.

· · · · · · · · · ·

"It's late, hijo," I heard mom say as I hung my jacket up in the closet near the front door. "You could've called." Her voice was hardly quiet, but she didn't sound annoyed either.

I snorted, shutting the closet door.

I tried to cover the smirk that crept on my face with my hand since I didn't want to give her the satisfaction that her concern actually intrigued me. Any other time I rolled in home late, mom wouldn't care. She would be either in bed or just tell me to make sure the door was locked behind me. She's never shown any actual concern for me when it came to my whereabouts. Not unless Morris-Lina was with me, but it wasn't like she really gave a damn about her either.

If anything, mom was just concerned about Morris-Lina doing something out of line, and I had to be the babysitter.

I rolled my eyes.

I kept my eyes forward in an attempt to block my mother from my vision. I made it to the steps, ignoring mom's gaze on me. She didn't even open her mouth to stop me. That's how I knew she really didn't care.

It's all an act as usual.

I made up the first couple of steps when mom sprung off the couch and sharply said my name, calling for my attention. "Donald!" she snapped, and I looked at her.

I stopped moving the second she said my name, and my eyes found their way in her direction. In a way, I was looking down at her, even though I was only up to four steps. My mom remained where she stood, staring right at me. From the way her lips parted, I could tell that she was trying to get her thoughts together before speaking. I knew she had something to say because she wouldn't have said my name for no reason.

Something was obviously on her mind.

I quirked an eyebrow. "Yeah?" I kept my voice down since I knew that dad was probably upstairs in bed, and the last thing I needed was for him to come downstairs, asking all sorts of questions.

Mom took a sharp inhale and cleared her throat. She looked at me with a stern gaze, but I wasn't at all moved by it. Still, I listened to whatever it was she had to say.

"Listen," mom started off, taking a small step forward. "I know that you're mad at me. And you have every right to be." The look on her face grew soft, matching the timid tone of her words. "It's just…" She paused and averted her eyes from me.

Right away, I could tell where this was going. This was her attempt at an apology, but I wasn't in the mood to hear it. To be frank, even though I should've been angry at my mom for all of eternity for what she had done, I wasn't. I managed to convince myself to get over it, and it's nothing but a distant memory. Somewhat. I'd be lying if I didn't admit that I often want to yell at my mom for what she did. But that'll never happen. She's my mom. Plus, dad will make sure I'm dead first before I even think of yelling at my mom ever again.

I interrupted my mom's words, but I wasn't abrupt when I did so.

I shook my head. "Mom," I got out. "It's fine. Just forge—"

Mom cut me off. "It's not fine, Donald." Her words had a bit more force behind them this time, as if she was pointing out a state of fact. "You and your father never want to hear me out on things. You're going to listen to me this time, got it?"

I nodded and turned my body so I could give her my full attention.

Mom fiddled with her fingers as she spoke to me. Obviously, she was nervous, but if she was being honest, she had nothing to be nervous about. Not unless she was pulling out of her ass.

Regardless, I listened to what she had to say. "I'm gonna be honest," she sighed as if a weight was coming off of her. "I don't know why I did what I did. I was so proud to see your acceptance letter, but part of me was worried about losing you. I was already losing you, and the thought of you not being around for a whole four years terrified me."

I swallowed thickly. "It wouldn't be a whole four years," I reminded her. "I would still come home for Christmas and then at the end of the year."

Mom huffed. "But what would be the chances of you wanting to come back? You'd be open to so much, and you're so smart and talented." Her eyes started to water, and her voice croaked. "I was scared. After your sister…" Mom closed her eyes and paused. I could tell she was contemplating what to say next. She cleared her throat and lifted her gaze back up to me. "I was selfish. I know that now. And I'm sorry."

I knew she meant every word she said. Whenever mom gets choked up while talking, she feels guilty. I sighed and told my mom, "It's fine," before proceeding up the steps.

She just watched me go up the steps, not saying a word. I didn't expect her to anyway. But then, something crossed my mind, and I stopped halfway up the steps. I looked back, and I asked my mom, "Did Moe's psychiatrist recommend for her to go to the facility in Baltimore, or was that all you?"

Mom looked up at me with her lips parted as if she was lost for words. Even though I knew it wouldn't change things, part of me wanted to know if what my mom said about Morris-Lina's psychiatrist wanting her to be admitted into the rehabilitation center in Baltimore was true. For all I know, mom could've just said that to get dad and me on her side and have Morris-Lina sent away. It wouldn't surprise me if she did.

Mom just looked at me, baffled by my question. I had a right to know. Even if the truth wouldn't bring Morris-Lina back, I wanted to know because the truth mattered to me. If Morris-Lina didn't need to be sent away, then maybe things would've played out differently. Perhaps I wouldn't have been as harsh with her. Perhaps she'd still be here.

Mom took a step forward. "Donald—"

"Mom," I said, never letting my eyes leave her. "Just tell me." I felt my throat tighten. "Please?" I croaked.

Mom's eyes became glossy, but she was able to hold back her tears. She put her hands to her hips and let out a quivered breath. I watched as she swerved around on her heels and slowly guided herself back to the couch. Every quiet second felt like a prison sentence. Dread sort of washed over me as I anticipated whatever my mom had to say. As much as I wanted to know whether or not sending Morris-Lina away to Baltimore was actually mom's idea, another part of me was pleading that my mom would just encourage me to drop it.

Yet, she was honest with me. More frank with me than I had anticipated. Once she sat back down on the couch and finally got herself to relax, she looked up at me as I remained on the steps.

"Your abuela hit me once when I was little. Real hard, too. I don't remember what I said or did to deserve it. But your tía Yoselin almost took me to the hospital. I just remember being terrified of your

abuela. The rage she had was unlike anything I had ever seen. But as time went on, I saw more and more of it. Occasionally. She would have really high highs and really low lows. It was a mess, but it wasn't something people often talked about at the time. So, I just endured it, and I did not…always know how to accept it."

Mom leaned back into the couch as she crossed her arms over her stomach. "When I was pregnant with you and your sister, I did lots of reading and learned that conditions like your abuela's were possibly hereditary. So, once the two of you were around five or six years old, I had you both examined, and the doctors said that they couldn't find anything. But, then, your sister, she started acting out. She had really high highs and really low lows. Her anger was out of control sometimes. A lot like your abuela."

The words continued to spill out of her effortlessly. Meanwhile, my throat was getting insanely dry with each word she said, and I felt my palms start to sweat. For a moment, I actually thought I was going to hurl, but the sickening feeling that I was all too familiar with had suppressed itself. I kept blinking to clear up my vision as mom's words started to swirl around my head.

Then, while looking at me, mom said, "You were always easier. I didn't have to worry about you doing something irrational or being difficult. And I would try to be patient when it came to dealing with Morris-Lina's mental state. But I saw how it ate up your grandmother. And I tried to love your sister as much as I could and be as patient as I could. But I know it wasn't good enough. And I tried to do better each time. I really did." Her words broke towards the end, and her bottom lip was trembling as she spoke.

I know that she probably wanted me to feel sorry for her, but after listening to every word that came out of my mom's mouth, that was impossible. I knew she meant every word she said about thinking I was "easier" to handle, but that didn't make me better. I never thought I was better. And for my mom to confess that—my blood boiled.

I could hardly look my mom in the eye at first, but then, I took a sharp inhale. I drew my eyes to her, and she still looked at me for sympathy. I clenched my jaw.

"That's the thing, mom," I told her, trying to keep my voice calm and clear. "You shouldn't have to try."

I tightened my hold on the banister as I noticed mom open her mouth to speak. But nothing came out. She struggled to even find anything to say. Even if she did have something to say, I'm sure it would all be in her defense, rather than admitting her mistakes. She always got defensive when it came to Morris-Lina, and I didn't want to hear another word.

Without a second thought, I walked the rest of the way up the steps and went straight into my room.

....

My phone vibrates in my pants pocket, and I sigh. I take a quick peek to read the notification, and I roll my eyes when I see that it's a text message from my mom. I don't bother reading the message. I tuck the phone back into my pants pocket, and I push back my jacket sleeve to check the time on my watch.

Quit stalling, I think to myself as I throw my head back into the headrest. *You've been sitting in here for about twenty minutes. Just go and see what Alejandro wants. In and out, that's all!*

I suck my teeth. "Riveting," I mumble to myself.

I get out of my car and close the door shut behind me, locking it up. The cold breeze attacks the back of my neck, sending a fit of shivers down my spine, awakening an army of goosebumps along my arms.

I walk up to the front door of Alejandro's house and ring the doorbell. The neighborhood is quiet, surprisingly. I look over my shoulder, rocking on my heels, and I notice only one or two older people sitting outside on the porch of their homes. The one older lady scowls at me from across the street, and I avert my eyes from her. Just then, the front door swings open, and a woman stands in my presence.

"Can I help you?" she asks with annoyance ringing through her words.

It's the same woman from the last time I was over.

Constance, I think is her name?

She looks pretty much the same, wearing a tube top that pushes up her cleavage and jeans that shape her hips and legs. The only difference is that she has her bleached blonde hair in a messy updo, and her face actually looks human since it's not caked with globs of makeup and feather-duster eyelashes.

I let out a faint breath. "Hi," I force a slight grin. "My name is Donald. Is Alejandro here?"

Constance raises an eyebrow, and her lips shape into an 'O' as the realization hits her. "I remember you," she points to me with one of her long, brightly colored fingernails, which I notice is also coated with glitter. "You're a friend of Alejandro's or something?"

I snort, shrugging my shoulders. "Something like that. Yeah."

Constance steps aside to let me enter the house. I feel my throat close up the second I do with how stuffy it feels inside. The blinds are slightly open, allowing sunlight to enter for natural light. The smell of mothballs and storage fills the house, and specks of dust fly in the air.

"This way." I look in the direction of Constance's voice as she stands at the bottom of the steps. She crooks her finger, gesturing for me to follow her upstairs.

The sly smirk on her face makes me choke on my own breath.

I keep a reasonable distance between us as I follow Constance up the steps, and she leads me to a room. She knocks on the closed scratched-up wooden door.

"Alejandro," she says his name nasally, and I cringe. "You have a visitor." She looks at me. "Donald."

The doorknob starts to jiggle as a clicking sound follows, unlocking the door. The door swings open, and Alejandro stands at the doorway. His arms cross over his bare chest, and he keeps his shirt draped over his shoulder. I clench my jaw as I stare at him. He has more tattoos than I would've thought. It's not like his entire upper body is covered in tattoos, but he has a few small tribal designs along his sides and a large one of a solid colored dragon inked on the right side of his chest and collarbone.

"Like what you see?" Alejandro says smugly. He opens up his arm, giving me a full view of his bare torso while somewhat flexing his toned muscles.

I roll my eyes and scoff. "Piss off," I mumble under my breath.

Alejandro lets out a small chuckle, crossing his arms over his chest. Meanwhile, Constance continues to admire Alejandro, failing to be discreet about it. It starts to bug the hell out of me. I don't even know why she's still here. Thankfully, she leaves once Alejandro tells her to do so. She rolls her eyes with a sly smirk on her face before walking away. I watch as she goes down the steps and then looks back to Alejandro.

He snickers. "You good?"

I arch a brow. "Yeah," I say. "Why wouldn't I be?"

"You were giving her the stink eye." A sinister smirk tugs on his lips. "You jealous?"

I roll my eyes, feeling my face grow warm. *He's got some nerve.*

"Bullshit," I retort. Alejandro's smile remains on his face, no matter how much I glare at him. "Get your head up out of your ass, why don't you?"

Alejandro snorts a chuckle. "Relax, shot glass."

He takes a step aside, letting me enter his room. I shield my eyes when the sunlight strikes my vision, blinding me. I hear the door close behind me before Alejandro rushes over to the window, adjusting the blinds. I lower my hand once the sunlight thins and my eyes adjust to the new lighting of the room. He has his bed up against the wall with one fitted sheet with spotted bleach stains to cover the mattress, an oversized gray comforter practically hanging off the foot of the bed, and two thick pillows up against the wooden headboard the bed. He has his dresser beside his closet, and when I turn around, I notice his desk, which is near a tall bookcase filled with all sorts of books, and it looks mounted to the wall.

"Make yourself comfortable," Alejandro smirks as he removes the shirt from over his shoulder and fumbles with the buttons to open it up.

I give him a slight nod before turning my attention to the bookcase.

I take down a book from the highest shelf that is within my reach. The cover is rugged, and it looks old as hell, but the book is surprisingly intact. When I flip through the pages, it has that old book smell that someone could love or hate, depending on what they are into. Even though I don't read as much as I probably should, I prefer books that smell new since old books have a bit of a sewage stench.

The book is thick, and when I flip through the pages, I stop on the last page, numbered 712. I notice one of the letters is faded, and no matter how much I squint, trying to figure out what it says, I can't make it out. I closed the book and read the title on the cover.

The Espionage of Che Twan by *Lukas M. Hermas.*

I quirk an eyebrow. I honestly had no idea Alejandro was into classic books like this. I mean, when we were kids, he would sometimes sneak into his father's room and pick out books to read to me if we were bored. A lot of his dad's books were— what I considered at the time—"for old people," but Alejandro didn't mind reading them.

I hear Alejandro moving around behind me, but I pay him no mind as I put the book back and take another book from the bookcase. This time, I take one from a lower shelf. It's a hardcover with a smooth sleeve. The words on the sleeve cover feel nice against my fingers as I trace them.

Caesar's Renegade: Armageddon of GODS *by Lucille Deveron & Manuel Joseph Jr.*

A faint chuckle. "I had no idea you were such a sucker for old-timer works like this," I say, turning on my heels to face Alejandro.

Alejandro lifts his head and looks at me as he slips his arms through his dark red button-up shirt. He rolls the sleeves up to his elbows, and the hem of the shirt drapes over his pants, which he keeps secured up around his waist with a brown leather belt.

He smirks while buttoning up his shirt. "Really?" he asks, slightly tilting his head while scrunching his brows. "All the stories I'd read to your slow ass, and you didn't pick that up?"

I roll my eyes. "I wasn't slow," I affirm as I put the book back on the shelf. "I got better grades than you."

"Oh, *pfft!* By like what? Two points?" Alejandro titters. "Please."

I roll my eyes and quickly poke my tongue out at him.

Still better than you, I think as I lean back against his bedroom door with my arms folded over my chest.

Alejandro fixes the collar to his shirt and leaves the top two buttons undone, revealing his chest. He tucks the bottom of his shirt into his pants and smooths out his shirt. He sets one foot back and slightly extends his arms out to show off his look.

"Thoughts?" He arches an eyebrow.

I let my eyes wander, examining Alejandro from head to toe. The gray highlights in his hair stand out, and he has his hair styled with the front of his fringe draping over his eyebrow. I can tell that he probably got a shape-up since his undercut looks fresh. His dark red button-up shirt is smooth and crisp, and he wears black slacks with dark brown dress shoes.

I slightly nod my head. "Nice," I say. "But if you invited me over here to be your fashion examiner for some hot date you got, I'm punching you in the balls." I was joking, of course.

Alejandro sucks his teeth, dropping his arms to his sides.

"First off, that's harsh." Alejandro walks over to his bed and sits down on edge. "Second, that's not it at all." The expression on his face changes as he pats the open space beside him on the bed, calling for me to sit beside him.

I sigh and drag myself over to sit beside him on his bed. I ask Alejandro what it was that he wanted to talk about, and I hear his breath hitch. He rubs his hands together, barely looking me in the eye.

I try to get a good read on him, but I can't. Although, it's evident that something is on his mind, judging by how he keeps his eyes narrowed to the floor while slouching forward a bit. I can't tell if it's something wrong or something good. Ever since the night at the warehouse, Alejandro has hardly spoken a word to me. Even on the ride home when he took me home that night, the car ride was silent. Any time I tried to talk to him, he kept his mouth shut and ignored me. It was annoying, but I also knew that he was probably still shocked by how things went down. From Álvaro showing up out of the blue and being scolded, Alejandro had a lot of crap thrown at him that night. And Lord knows how things probably went between him and Álvaro once Alejandro came home after dropping me off.

I clear my throat. "Alejandro," I force the words out as I try to suppress my memories of that night. I gently nudge my elbow against his arm to get his attention. "Hey, what is it?"

Alejandro lets out a quivering sigh, clasping his hands together. "Álvaro wants me to meet up with him tonight. He says that it's nothing serious, but after what happened…*that* night, I don't think so." I hear Alejandro gulp as his words start to break.

I scoot closer to him. "What do you mean?"

Alejandro tightens his jaw. "After I took you home that night, Álvaro and I had a talk. He said that I had failed him and that in this family, failure is not an option."

His words fall apart towards the end, and he lowers his head while clenching his eyes shut. He takes a deep breath and turns his head to face me.

My stomach churns oddly when I meet his eyes. His eyes glisten as they are on the brink of tears, but I can tell that Alejandro is doing all he can to hold them in. His breathing quivers as he grits his teeth. I can't help but feel scared for the guy.

I put my hand on his shoulder. "Alejandro, just ta—"

"I need you to help me," he blurts, sitting up.

I furrow my eyebrows. "What?" I slip my hand off his shoulder.

Alejandro turns his body to face me. He practically grips onto my shoulders, looking at me with his eyes big and desperate. "Álvaro is going to kill me, Donald. I know it."

I shake my head and blink rapidly to process his words. "W-W-W, Wait a minute," I stammer. "Alejandro, come—"

"You don't get it, do you?" Alejandro's grip tightens, and I feel the bones in my shoulders crush together. "You've seen what he's capable of, Donald. And he said failure is not an option in our family. Last I checked, that's a death threat."

"Alejandro, please—"

"You saw what he did to Diego, Donald! You were there! You were with me, weren't you?! Even though Álvaro never told me what he does, I'm sure it involves making people disappear, and I don't want to do that!"

I wince as his nails pierce through the fabric of my jacket and shirt and make contact with my skin. I try to get him off of me, but he's too strong. It's like he's on drugs all of a sudden and is unmovable.

I grit my teeth. "Let me go—"

"I need you to do this for me, Donald," he abruptly demands. "You and me, we-we-we, we'll take him on tonight and make a run for it. Just like we always said we would. We'll get out of here, and it'll all be good."

My heart catapults up my throat as Alejandro's words grow louder and louder. The air suddenly becomes humid, and the walls seem to close in around me. Alejandro continues to ramble on and on, but my heartbeat conquers my eardrums.

It gets louder.

And louder.

And louder.

Alejandro's words start to cut through again, and I hear him go, "I'll cue you in or something. That way, we have an advantage over him." He goes to say something else, but I roughly put my hands to his chest, shoving him off of me. Alejandro uses his elbows to catch himself from falling back onto his bed.

I spring up to my feet as my heart thumps heavily in my chest. Alejandro looks at me with his eyes wide and lips parted open, but he falls silent. My bones shake, and I keep my fists tight by my sides to settle my nerves.

Get out of here, I tell myself. *Go! Leave!*

I have to get out of here. I ignore the sound of Alejandro saying my name as I swing the bedroom door open to get out. I go down the steps as fast as possible, setting my eyes for the front door to the house.

"Donald!" Alejandro calls for me again, but I don't look back.

I manage to unlock the front door, ready to get out when a hand comes out from behind me and pushes the door shut. Alejandro grips onto my arm, forcing me to turn around. I feel the doorknob jab into my lower back as Alejandro holds me hostage.

"Donald, just hear me out," he pleads. "You have to hel—"

"Shut up!"

I roughly shove him back, using every ounce of my strength. Alejandro stumbles back but manages to stand tall with a look of dismay.

My mind flashes back to the night at the warehouse. Christopher and I going at each other's throats. The way Diego's face looked after being beaten senseless. The way Álvaro looked at me. The way Diego laid on the ground so still, I couldn't tell whether or not he was breathing. It all comes rushing back to me, and I hate it. I hate it so goddamn much!

And the thing is, I didn't ask for any of it. The only reason why I was there was that Alejandro asked for my help. That one time, I let him get to me, just like when we were kids. I let him get to me. But I never had any blood on my hands.

At least, until now!

I shake my head. "I'm not doing this, Alejandro," I force out through my teeth. I glare at him. "Not this time. This is your shit, and I want no part of it!"

Alejandro scoffs, looking at me as if I have lost my mind. "Don, don't be like that. If we don't do something, then—"

"Stop saying *'we'* all the fucking time!" My hands are practically shaking as I fire back at him. "There is no *'we,'* and there never was a *'we'!* This all fucking you! It was your idea to play some vigilante and lure Diego out that night! It was you who fucked up and got your brother involved!" A burning sensation erupts through my chest as I manage to finally take a breath.

Alejandro just looks at me. His eyes are like daggers, and he clenches his jaw, his nostrils flaring. He really expects me to help him come up with some bizarre plan to get rid of his brother as if we're professional psychopathic mafia men who do this shit without breaking a sweat?!

"You owe me this, Don," he firmly retorts through his teeth as he takes a step forward. "Think of all the times I helped you out, huh? If it weren't for me, those guys who jumped you would've beaten you to a pulp!"

"I didn't ask for your help!" I remind him. "I never asked for you to get involved in my shit! Never!" A massive ball forms in my throat, and I shoot a glare at Alejandro. "Get your shit together, man," is all I'm able to say to him as I feel my words start to break.

Alejandro's eyes soften, and knots twist in the pit of my stomach. As I open the door, I feel Alejandro's hand touch my shoulder. My body quickly reacts, and my elbow jabs into his chest, backing him up off me. I hear Alejandro grunt as I briskly walk out of the house.

The second I step outside, my throat opens up, and I'm able to breathe. My heart beats loudly, pulsing through my eardrums. My teeth start to chatter, and I know that it is probably my nerves.

I push Alejandro out of my mind as I retrieve my car keys from my pocket. I am quick with unlocking my car and getting in. I pull the door shut and lock all the doors.

I put my key in the ignition as I strap myself into the driver's seat. The thumping of my heart gets louder and louder, and a sudden ache on the side of my head surfaces. I squeeze my eyes shut, tightening my grip on the steering wheel.

I curse under my breath.

Get yourself together. Just let it go!

I try listening to that demanding voice in my head as I lift my head up from the steering wheel. I rest my head back against the headrest, letting out a deep breath. My grip on the steering wheel starts to loosen as my heart settles down.

I take another breath, softly exhaling through my mouth.

Count to three, I tell myself. *Just count to three.*

And that's what I do.

I take another breath, keeping my eyes closed.

One.

Exhale.

Another breath.

Two.

Exhale.

One more.

Three.

A deep exhale, and I open my eyes. I use the back of my hand to wipe away the tears that rest on my lashes. The pain in my head vanishes into thin air. I clear my throat, getting rid of the lump stuck in there. I tell myself to relax as I switch gears, putting the car in drive. I keep my eyes forward as I drive down the street while taking small breaths.

June.

Week 1, Monday

"Make sure you all pay attention to the beat and watch your feet!" Mr. Aziz reiterates for the fortieth time after cutting off the music on the stereo. "It's step-step-pause! Step-step-pause! Move to the right, move to the left!" His words boom with frustration as he glowers at all of us as we stand in a single file line down the middle aisle of the auditorium.

We have been on our feet rehearsing for graduation since fifth period. The only benefit of having a graduation rehearsal is that seniors get excused from the sixth period. But having Mr. Aziz as the choreographer is a death wish itself. Initially, it was supposed to be Mr. Yuen from Global Science, but he is on paternity leave to help his partner care for their newborn child.

I honestly wish they had their baby *after* our graduation. And with the amount of groaning and huffing that comes from the other students, I'm not the only one who feels that way. Mr. Aziz has always been a pain in the ass, but he's really pushing it this time.

Fortunately, the bell sounds off, signaling the end of classes and the end of rehearsal. As everyone rushes to gather their things, Mr. Aziz reminds us that we have rehearsal again on Wednesday and Friday, which everyone dreads.

"Don't give me any lip!" he barks at us one last time. "This is *your* graduation, and the last thing I want to see is all of you look like a couple of jackasses because you can't keep rhythm."

I sigh, stretching my arms over my hand while keeping my fingers laced together. I feel my shoulder bone pop, releasing all the tension that's been building up inside me since the start of rehearsal. I let out a sigh of relief as I ease my arms down.

"You alright, mate?"

I turn around, meeting Christopher's tired green eyes. He forces a smirk across his face to bury how obviously tired he looks, but I don't fall for it. I chuckle.

"I'm certainly better than you," I remark, slipping on my leather jacket. "Seems like you're the one fighting sleep, huh?"

Christopher rolls his eyes. "Ha-ha," he feigns his smile out of spite. "Very funny, Captain Obvious."

I put my hand to my chest, shrinking back a little bit. "Why, such hostility I sense," I gasp dramatically. "I do declare, someone woke up on the wrong side of the bed." My attempt at a southern accent makes Christopher cringe, and I snicker.

"Don't ever do that," he says, shaking his head.

"Oh, come on," I throw my arm around the back of his neck, letting my hand drape over his shoulder. "It's not like I'm signing up for voice acting or something for my future."

Christopher snorts under his breath. "Thank God for that."

I use my free hand to jab him in his side, making Christopher practically yelp. I press my lips together tightly to hold in the laughter ready to burst out of me. Christopher smacks his hand over his mouth, looking around with wide eyes. His face is red as a cherry, and I can't help but let a tiny little giggle slip out of my mouth. The look of embarrassment on Christopher's face is hard to come by, and seeing him all nervous like this is priceless.

Still, he scowls at me, calling me, "Pian san asal."

"Sorry," I manage to say through the soft laughter that spits from my mouth.

With a huff, Christopher shoves me away while shaking his head in annoyance. He knows I'm only teasing, and I know that he doesn't take my teasing personally. The slight smirk that cracks onto his face is proof of that. He just insists on looking away from me to hide the amusement.

As we make our way out of the auditorium after I slip on my book bag, Christopher asks me how things went with Alejandro the other day. My mouth goes dry as the memory resurfaces in my mind. I haven't heard anything from Alejandro since the last time I saw him. It was only a couple days ago, but it feels longer than that. I was expecting him to blow up my phone, asking to talk or something, but nothing like that happened. It's not that I want that to happen. It's just—Alejandro can be relentless, and for him to back off…

It's unlike him.

Don't feel bad about it, the voice in my head demands. *He saw this coming, just like you did. It was only a matter of time.*

I nod, realizing that it's true. This was bound to happen. Even if I didn't know it, it's for the best. Besides, I don't need any more blood on my hands than I do now.

"Don?" Christopher nudges my arm with his elbow, pulling me out of my thoughts. He raises his eyebrows with curiosity. "Well? How did things go?"

I stop in my tracks to gather my thoughts, and Christopher stays where he stands beside me. Christopher's green eyes practically pierce into my soul, pleading for me to be honest with him about what happened. I can't lie. As much as I want to make something up from off the top of my head, I can't think of anything. It's as if the creative side of my brain no longer wishes to function and just throws in the towel.

I sigh, looking Christopher right in the eye.

"You were right," I tell him, trying to keep my voice straight. "I've always worn special goggles when it came to Alejandro, and I blocked out all the warning signs people told me about. But I don't know. I told him how I really felt once the goggles came off. And…" I swallow down the lump forming in my throat. My mind goes back to Alejandro's words—him saying that I owed him. After all this time, he felt that I owed him something. Even though I've never asked anything of him. I clear my throat. "…well, he told me how he really felt. So. That's that."

Christopher puts his hand on my shoulder. He presses his lips together in a faint smile, and the look in his eyes softens. He doesn't have to open his mouth for me to know that he wishes I had come to my senses early on. Even though Christopher wasn't there with me this time, I know part of him feels terrible. He probably wishes that circumstances were different. Or maybe that's just me.

Christopher pats my shoulder. "You alright?" he asks softly.

He gives me a look, and I look away from him, knowing that I'll laugh. I see that face. That's his *"I'm sorry, but I was so right"* face.

"What?" I can tell he's smiling as he questions me.

I shake my head. "Your face," I point out.

"What?" he chuckles. "I'm not making a face."

My lips part open, and I stare at him in disbelief. "Are you kidding me?" I cross my arms over my chest, trying to suppress my laughter. *He's got to be kidding me.* "I already admitted you were right. Don't rub it in with that smug look you got on your face."

Christopher lightly pushes me, going, "*Pfft!* Please."

We continue walking, making our way out of the school through the front entrance. I notice some people huddling together, pointing to something across the street. Some people look on while walking down the sidewalk to get to wherever they have to go. I wrinkle my eyebrows.

I nudge Christopher, catching his attention. "What's going on?" I ask him, keeping my voice low.

Suddenly, I hear a familiar voice shouting out, "The fuck happened to my car?!"

I whip my attention towards the direction of the voice. In the parking lot stands Austin Brown, gripping his hair, pacing back and forth. He shouts all sorts of curse words that run together as he rambles on about the shape of his car.

My eyes widen when I realize the monstrosity Austin's referring to actually *is* his car. The windshield is completely shattered and practically caves into the car. The side mirrors are on the ground, the one front tire has been slashed—and I'm assuming so are the other three tires—and the window to the driver's seat has been bashed in. All that's missing are some bullet holes or graffiti, and it's a classic hit on a car as some kind of trademark.

But Austin's car isn't the only one that's in a wreck. Two other guys are crying out about their cars being totaled. Their cars are also in the parking lot. I realize that the other guys are part of Austin's goon group as they stare at their cars with their eyeballs practically popping out of their heads. One of the two guys looks as though he's on the brink of having a massive breakdown as tears spill from his eyes, but he doesn't make a sound. He just paces back-and-forth, keeping his distraught eyes on his own car with his mouth wide open.

"Holy shit," I slip out, trying to cover my hand to hold in the inevitable laughter bubbling inside of me.

The sight is way too rich. Some of the other students looking can hardly believe it either. They are either trying to hide their smirks or look in shock. Meanwhile, I don't know whether to continue walking or stick around to wait and see what happens next. I mean, a guy like Austin Brown getting his car completely pulverized is hard to miss out on. Even though the damage was obviously done while we were all still inside the school, the thought of someone actually having the balls to bash his windows in, bang up his car, and slash his tires—it's a godsend.

I lightly tap Christopher's chest with the back of my hand, unable to look away from Austin as he freaks out while dialing on his phone. I lean in, asking Christopher, "I'm not the only one thinking it's Christmas morning, right?"

Christopher smirks, going, "Hm," under his breath. I notice him looking on as well, but his smirk widens more than I expected. "I say he had it coming," he says nonchalantly.

His eyebrow arches as he twists his lips, unable to look away from the scene. It's like he's in a trance that no one could pull him out of, even if they tried. It's as though he's in deep thought about something while also looking on in admiration. The only times I've ever seen Christopher like this is when he's proud of himself about something. Something he did—

I think for a moment.

"Dude." I grab Christopher by his arm, forcing him to look at me. He wrinkles his eyebrows in puzzlement. I come out with it. "You didn't—you couldn't have— but you—do you know who…?" I can hardly get my thoughts together as the idea of Christopher having something to do with this battles with my brain.

There's no way Chris would even have the gall to do something like this! No effing way!

But the look he gives me begs me to differ. He rocks on his heels, crossing his arms over his chest as he tightly presses his lips together in a straight line. His arm comes around my neck, pulling me closer to him as his hand drapes over my shoulder.

My bones stiffen as I look up at him.

Mierda!

I don't even have to say anything further for Christopher to give me an explanation. I guess the expression on my face is enough for him.

"I heard about what happened in the locker room a few weeks ago. You know, with the doll," he confesses.

My lips are slightly part open. Honestly, I did all I could to push that memory in the far back of my mind. Seeing that rag doll fall out of my locker with the words ALIEN stitched on it—I wish I had punched Austin's balls deep inside of him and punched him in the throat. Ugh.

I stuff my hands into the pockets of my jacket. "How did you hear about that? Common gossip?" I mutter under my breath.

The one side of Christopher's mouth perks up. "Actually, Erik and I have econ together, and we're partners for our in-class project. We were talking, and you sort of came up, and that's how I found out. So. Call me nosy, but I have a very low tolerance for people like Austin Brown." Christopher wrinkles his nose when he looks back to Austin, who is now cussing up a storm while on the phone, rambling out the damages to his car. Christopher snorts, spitting out the word "Wanker," under his breath.

I just look at him. I really can't believe Christopher would do something so bold. I know he means it when he says he'll be there for me, but Goddamn.

"But…" I think for a second. "…you were in school all day. They don't let anyone out."

Christopher shrugs, feigning innocence. "I mean. I did text you during homeroom to let Mister Hua know that I got caught up in traffic and would be late, aye?"

Oh shit.

He did text me this morning during homeroom that he'd be late showing up. It wasn't like him to be late. And it wasn't like he had a late start to the day because, on my way to school, Christopher sent me a text, asking if I wanted to come over after school for movie night—like a squad hangout. So, it was a little weird when he rolled into homeroom twenty minutes late. Although, he didn't seem like he was in a rush either.

I guess he did do it.

Of course, he did. He just said so.

"So," Christopher chirps up as we start walking down the steps to the school's entrance, "with Carmen having to go home early for a doctor's appointment, Meagan being stuck with theater, and Pete and Benton going home…." He takes a breath. "Still up for that movie oooorrr…?"

I lightly jab my elbow into his side, making Christopher squirm. "Prick," he hisses, removing his arm off me as he rubs the spot where I elbowed him.

I snort, smirking. "Please." I throw my arm on his shoulder, rocking into him. "Your life would be lame without me."

"Hmph!" Christopher raises his eyebrows, twisting his lips. "That's what you think." He shakes his head, rolling his eyes.

Week 1, Wednesday

I slip off my jacket, throwing it over my shoulder as the warm sun beams down on me. I cross my arms over my chest as I lean back against the gate, waiting for Yago and Gabriel to be dismissed from class for the day. Yoselin messaged me this morning during homeroom, asking me to pick the boys up from school since she would be working late. Like always, I couldn't say "no."

Plus, the last time I was on the phone with Yoselin, I could hear Yago begging her to lend him her phone, so he could talk to me. But as she was getting ready to give him the phone, I guess the boys' father came to pick them up for the weekend. I felt kind of bad, but at the same time, it was out of my control.

So, I had no problem getting the boys today, and I clarified that to tía Yoselin. She was grateful, of course.

I just wish it wasn't so warm out. There is hardly a breeze, which makes me even more irritated. But I stand off to the side, keeping to myself since I don't want to be around people. I just want to get the boys and take them home, so we're out of the sun.

This is probably the warmest Spring day I've ever experienced so far.

78 degrees, my ass. I suck my teeth. The weather app lied.

I pull out my phone from my back pocket to check the time since it feels like I've waited an eternity for the boys.

I roll my eyes when the time shows up on my lock screen. It's five minutes past their regular dismissal time. I can only imagine what's the holdup.

I shove my phone back into my pants pocket and let out a frustrated sigh.

"Don't worry," a familiar voice comes up from behind me. "They'll be out in the next three minutes tops. It's been like this for the past couple of days now."

I turn around, letting out a deep breath. Aitana approaches me with her hands in the pockets of her baggy gray camouflage pants. She wears a black deep V-neck tank top and black-and-white high-tops to go with her pants, and honestly, it doesn't look bad. She keeps her hair loose, curls falling down her back and over her shoulders while shining in the sun. She's more radiant than I remember. It probably has something to do with her makeup. The little blotches of highlights along her cheekbones shimmer in the sunlight.

She moves to stand beside me, looking straight ahead to the other side of the gate with a slight smirk on her lips. I feel a tug in my throat as I look at her.

I wonder if she knows about everything that went down at the warehouse, considering that she had talked to Álvaro before that night, which is why he even showed up. And now, Alejandro thinks it's him against the world since Aitana told Álvaro about Diego, which is equal to the biggest sibling betrayal in anime history.

I shake my head.

Why do I think about this? Why do I even care?

Looking down, I kick the front of the sneaker into the ground, scraping up some dirt onto the bottom of my shoe.

As I stand there, waiting for the boys, Aitana suddenly asks me, "Are you going to do it? Go to Europe?"

I forgot about our conversation on me determining which college I'd attend. It was hardly a conversation since I did most of the talking, and she gave occasional feedback.

I chuckle. "I had no idea you're still so fascinated in my personal life."

Aitana twists her lips in a grin. "And I had no idea you were so invested in mine," she responds, crossing her arms over her chest.

She looks me up and down as if she's trying to get a read on me. I gulp. She obviously knows about everything that went down at the warehouse. I mean, maybe not *everything* if she doesn't know about Álvaro showing up. But she probably knows about the plan Alejandro and I had with handling Diego. Unless she's just trying to make me sweat. Regardless, I have to play dumb.

I look away from her

"I don't recall that," I hastily remark.

Before Aitana can say anything, the side doors finally open and little kids come bursting through the door with their teachers. Parents who were waiting came up to the gate with great anticipation. The lady with the clipboard who usually stands at the gate blows her whistle as she steps outside. All the kids stand against the wall without being told, waiting for their names to be called for dismissal.

The lady wobbles over to the door of the gate, huffing with each step she takes.

I roll my eyes.

The lady scowls at me as she unlocks the gate as her stubby fingers fumbling with the lock. It's no secret that she doesn't like me. And I don't even know her. Even when she speaks to me, asking me for my name—there's such disdain in her voice.

Ruggedly, she goes, "Name?"

I answer, "Donald Gonzalez for Yago and Gabriel Ortega-Howard."

She goes down the list, checking off their names. "Ooooh," she drags out, pushing her glasses up onto the bridge of her nose. "I remember you." The pleasure in her voice is *so* convincing.

I tightly press my lips together in a forceful grin, squinting my eyes. But as soon as she looks away, my lips fall into a flat line, and a blank expression washes over my face. She blows her whistle, calling for the boys.

"Ortega-Howard!" she calls out to them as if they're inmates. "You're free to go!"

The boys snap their heads up, and they beam from ear to ear. Yago gains incredible speed, dashing over to me while Gabriel barely keeps up but still keeps his arms extended out to me.

I manage to catch myself from stumbling backward when Yago throws himself at me, latching his arms around my waist. A small laugh slips out of his mouth as he rests his head against my side. I can't remember the last time I've seen the boys, but I know it hasn't been too long. Has it?

I run my hand through Yago's unruly hair, smirking.

"Chill out," I laugh, ruffling his hair.

Yago finally lets me go as Gabriel finally manages to catch up. I crouch down to their level, letting Gabriel's arm come around my neck as he pulls himself up against me. I let out a soft chuckle as my arms circle around his little body, and his head nuzzles into the crook of my neck.

I move my head, making Gabriel lift his head up from my neck. I push the front of his hair out of his eyes.

I smile. "Hey, bug," I softly call him by his nickname, which I hardly ever use.

Gabriel shows his toothy smile, clasping his hands together.

I put Gabriel down to stand up, and I noticed Yago run out of the gate from the corner of my eye. I call out to him, but I see him chasing after Ricardo up and down the walkway, laughing.

I sigh.

My mind goes back to when I had picked the boys up from school and learned that Alejandro was Ricardo's uncle. I didn't want to believe it at first, but I slowly started to see a sinister glint in Ricardo's eye. It must be a Reyes family trait, I guess. But at the same time, there was always something about Alejandro that made me want to be around him. Similar to how Yago always wants to be around Ricardo. As much as I hate to admit it, I liked being around Alejandro when we were kids. Even as I try to suppress the memories I've shared with Alejandro—the good and the bad—I can't help but see the two of us in Yago and Ricardo as they stand next to each other, giggling as if they're sharing juicy secrets with each other.

I look down at Gabriel as he puts his fingers in his mouth. I gently squeeze his hand to get his attention, and he looks up at me with his big puppy-like eyes.

"Keep your hands out your mouth," I warn him, trying to keep a straight face.

Gabriel rolls his eyes at me and yanks his hand out of my grasp. He folds his arms with much annoyance, turning his head away from me.

I shake my head, snorting a chuckle.

I reach down and scoop Gabriel up in my arms. He kicks his feet in an attempt to make me put him down, but I refuse. When I finally get a good hold on him, managing to carry him with one arm, he settles down but keeps a stern scowl on his face.

"Hey," I try to be stern with him. "Fix your face or no dino nuggets, huh?"

Gabriel shakes his head, still frowning up his face.

I roll my eyes. "You're impossible."

I look over my shoulder, and I notice Aitana looking at me with a slight grin on her face. I feel Gabriel starting to slip in my arms, so I lift him up, securing him in place with both of my arms.

Aitana keeps her eyes on me as I ask her, "Everything good?"

She nods. "Yeah." A haste grin flashes on her face before her lips return to a flat line.

I press my lips together in a faint smirk and slightly nod.

This feels awkward.

I decide to go get Yago so we can head home, but Aitana abruptly blurts, "Wait!" and I freeze. I look back as she slips off her shoulder bag and starts rummaging through the bag while muttering to herself.

I quirk an eyebrow as I watch her. "Um," I start off, trying to figure out what she could possibly need from me, "are you ok—?"

"Here," she cuts me off, holding a small white sealed envelope in my face. "I almost forgot to give this to you."

I tighten my hold on Gabriel with one arm as I use my other hand to take the envelope from Aitana. She looks at me with soft eyes, and my eyebrows wrinkle in confusion. I flip over the envelope, reading the words on the front side.

Donald, please read me.

I recognize that handwriting.

"He left it for you on his dresser," Aitana blurts. "It's the only thing that was left in his room when I checked in the other day. I guess he just never had the chance to give it to you face-to-face."

A ball forms in my throat, and I pull my gaze up to Aitana.

I struggle to keep my words straight as I choke out, "What?"

Aitana looks down at the ground, smirking to herself. A soft chuckle slips out her mouth, but it sounds so shaky, I thought she was crying. But when she looks back up at me with dry eyes and a faint but genuine smile.

"Don't read into anything too much," Aitana says, taking a small step forward, resting her hand on my shoulder. She lets out a deep sigh. "Just read it when you get a chance, okay?" Her smile fades as she walks past me.

I look over my shoulder as Aitana calls for Ricardo, extending her hand for him to take. Ricardo runs up to Aitana, waving goodbye to Yago.

Aitana holds onto Ricardo's hand as the two of them walk across the street, her eyes never leaving him as they make their way to her car. The smile on her face never fades as she looks down at Ricardo, listening to him babble about whatever it is that he's talking about.

I shift my gaze to the envelope in my hand, and I eye the handwriting on the front. I run my finger across the ink, letting out a quivering breath. I can only imagine what Alejandro could've possibly written to me. And I know Alejandro is behind this because—hell—who else would it be?

Yago runs up to me and tugs on the hem of my shirt.

"Can we go now?" he whines, poking his bottom lip out.

I sigh. I stuff the envelope into my back pocket before running my hand through Yago's hair. I nudge my head over to the side.

"C'mon, let's go," I say, smiling down at him.

. . . .

I gently close the book, ensuring I don't wake Yago as he keeps his head on my shoulder. I reach over, gently placing the book I read to him on the dresser beside his bed. My movements are slower than a tortoise as I try not to make a sound since this was the fourth book he had me read to him before finally drifting off to sleep. Gabriel was easier to put to bed since he usually falls fast asleep after one bedtime story.

Yago, on the other hand, is impossible to please.

I felt myself dozing off as I read him *Courageous Gini*—a book about a lemur who is adopted by a zoologist from New York City—twice in a row. Yago loves that book, and I don't understand why. The illustrations are weird, and the book is incredibly long for a children's book.

I slip out of bed without bothering Yago. His eyes remain closed as little snores come from him. I tightly press my lips together as I tuck him into bed. He looks much younger when he sleeps. But I guess that's common whenever people sleep, including kids. I reach for one of his stuffed animals from off the shelf drilled into the wall above his dresser, and I fluff it out for him. I gently settle the green plush fish, though bigger than his head, beside him and immediately throws his arm around the fish. He nuzzles his face against it, letting out a soft breath as he sleeps.

The one side of my mouth curls upward as I take in Yago's peaceful state. Usually, I'm at home by now, so I'll hardly get the chance to see the boys all tucked in and asleep. I'll help them get ready for bed, but Yoselin usually comes home before it reaches their bedtime. But today, I had to be the one to get them to bed. And it was not easy.

I make sure to lightly walk on my toes as I head out of Yago's bedroom. I click off the bedroom lights, only allowing for his nightlight to shine as it remains plugged to the wall across from his bed. I quietly shut the door before letting out a sigh of relief. A rush of exhaustion suddenly hits me like a freight train as I press my back up against the door, ready to collapse to the ground. Yet, I drag myself to the steps, rubbing my eyes to wake myself up as I start to walk down the steps.

Once I'm downstairs, I go straight to the kitchen and wash my hands. I try splashing some water on my face in an attempt to wake myself up. I still have to drive myself home once Yoselin comes home, and I don't want to end up falling asleep behind the wheel. And what's crazy is that it's only fifteen minutes after seven, so it's not even late.

But I guess with getting the boys home, making their dinner, helping them with homework, and getting them to bed—it took more out of me than usual. I don't mind helping mi tía with the boys, but my God, they're a handful. Thank God I don't have any assignments to do tonight and no tests until the following Monday. With prom being around the corner, teachers are pretty lenient with giving us a break from tests.

I get myself a glass cup from the cabinet and fill it with water. I sit down at the dining room table and prop my elbows up on the table, rubbing my eyes. As I remain in the chair, I feel something jabbing me, and I reach between my back pants pocket and the cushion. I realize that I still have the envelope Aitana gave me, and I pull it out.

I swallow thickly as I hold the envelop in my hands. I feel goosebumps awaken on my arms as I read the words on the front of the envelope. I can hear Alejandro's voice as if he's begging me to read whatever message he wrote for me.

I still can't wrap my mind around Alejandro just leaving. From the way Aitana described her realization, he didn't leave her a note or anything. He just grabbed what he could and dipped. The only person he left a note for was me. Me! Of all people?!

I take another sip of water to get rid of the scratchy feeling in my throat. I place the cup back down on the coaster, taking a sharp breath.

I poke my finger through the crease of the envelope, making a slit. I tear at the top, carefully going across to open up the envelope. I slip out the folded piece of paper that is small enough to fit in my palm. As I open up the letter, I realize how ridiculous Alejandro must've felt when he folded it more times than necessary. It's just a regular size sheet of paper that was folded eight times, maybe.

I scan over the words, taking in his handwriting. He's always had neat penmanship. Better than me. That's for sure. I sit back in the chair, holding the paper near my face as I read every written line. I clench my jaw, taking in Alejandro's words as if they are the last he'll ever say to me. Perhaps, they are.

Donald,

I know this is the last thing you'd expect from me. By the time you get this, I'll be catching a plane to God knows where. I can't really say where because I don't know where "where" is yet. Aitana always had this strange belief that I wasn't cut out for this life, and I thought she was just messing with me. But now, I get it. But I'm not quitting on anything here, either. I always wanted to watch a sunset go down along the horizon. A nice one. No buildings or cop cars in the background. Just complete silence and maybe with some trees or an ocean or something. That probably sounds like some fucking bullshit, but it's something I've always dreamt about. And then, maybe, go live off somewhere and meet someone, you know? Anyway, you really do owe me something, though. I heard that you're going to Europe for college. Fancy. Enjoy yourself there for me, will you? Get the hell up outta here and go somewhere far as much as possible and do what I could never do. What I now want to do. And if you're not chicken enough, take that cute girl I saw you with the other day with you. You owe me that, at least. And also, try carrying around some kind of knife, will you? I don't know what Europe is like, though, compared to Philly.

Take care of yourself, shot glass.-

AR

The sound of the front door opening so suddenly makes me jump, and I fold the paper before slipping it under the table. Yoselin lets out a grunt as she comes in through the door, closing it behind her with her foot. She slips off the heels that make her look much taller than she actually is and look insanely uncomfortable.

I spring up from the seat, stuffing the letter into my pants pocket as I check the time on the digital clock on the stove. It flashes *7:44 PM*, and my eyes widen.

Yoselin places down her bags by the front door and smiles at me.

"Hola, mi sobrino favorito." She keeps her voice down, knowing that the boys are asleep.

I chuckle. "I'm your only nephew," I remind her.

Yoselin rolls her eyes, approaching me. "Oh, hush," she retorts. She plants a kiss on my forehead before taking a step back to look at me. "You should go home. Your mother and I were just talking about you."

I swallow hard.

"Oh," I manage to get out. "Thanks."

Before I grab my stuff, Yoselin gently grabs my arm, forcing me to look at her. She keeps her lips pressed together in a straight line while furrowing her dark brows. She doesn't even have to say anything for me to know that she's well aware of the situation between my mother and me. For all I know, she's probably given mom some advice on what to say the next time she sees me. That's not all too surprising.

Before I go, I check to make sure I have all my things packed up, and I wish Yoselin a goodnight. Yoselin thanks me again for taking care of the boys, and like always, I tell her it was no problem.

I feel Yoselin watch me as I leave her house and head to my car, which is parked right in front of her pathway. Exhaustion consumes me, but I blink rapidly to fight it.

As soon as I get into my car, I throw my head against the headrest. I sigh as I narrow my eyes forward on the road ahead. I think about all the places Alejandro could be right now. I know he doesn't know where he'll end up, but I still can't help but wonder where he'd be.

I snort a chuckle, shaking my head as I lean forward to start the engine. I lean back and shift the gear, putting the car in drive.

"Damn you, Reyes," I sigh as I pull off.

Week 1, Friday

I had my last counseling session with Counselor Malik yesterday. It honestly went better than expected, considering that he usually likes to have the last word, and deep down, I was anticipating for him to have some harsh words for me. I mean, he's been harsh enough, in my opinion. He'll read whatever I write in this Godforsaken journal and then judge me—or as he likes to say, "perform an interpretative analysis of the situation." Regardless, even though he does it all the time, I can never get used to hearing him read my stuff aloud. It always bothers me, and I'm pretty sure he knows that, but he continues to do it anyway. But, I guess with it being our last session together, he cut me a break. And I'd be lying if I didn't say that I was kind of jubilant about it. Although, part of me knows that I'll miss him. Hell, I'll miss Mr. Hua too. Mr. Enrique, Principal Vickins…even the Hell Spawn himself, Mr. Aziz.

Ugh. Listen to me getting all sappy. My crew is rubbing off on me since they always talk like this—getting all emotional. I don't know. It's slowly starting to sink in that graduation is next Wednesday. Mr. Aziz has been bugging us with getting the steps just right for when we walk, but I have it down packed. I'd say at least 70% of students walking have it down. It's not that hard. Ha! I can only imagine how Moe would look trying to walk down the aisle. She can't march to save her life. Crazy. Speaking of Moe, Counselor Malik brought up this ridiculous idea that the only reason why I want to go to school in Europe is that I have some unsettling desire to please her and everyone else rather than do what's best for me. I mean, yeah, I want to go to Europe for Moe because she's my sister and that was her dream for me, but that doesn't mean that's the only reason I want to go. I mean, the truth is, I didn't really think I'd get into either one of those schools. I'm okay with staying in the States. The only reason I'm going is that everyone says it's the best. But I also think it's the best move too.—D.G.

"Well, Donald," Counselor Malik sighed as he leaned forward in his chair to slip on his burgundy blazer. "I have to say, I didn't expect you to go through with me as long as you did. Especially since you never fail to point out how you feel about my methods of counseling."

I snorted, grinning as I kept my eyes on him.

"Well," I leaned back in my seat, crossing my right leg over my left as I laced my fingers together on my lap, "even if I did want to leave, what are the chances Principal Vickins would be on my team." I tightly pressed my lips together, forcing a smile as I squinted my eyes.

Counselor Malik shook his head, smirking. He knew that I was right. There was no way Principal Vickins would allow me to drop counseling altogether. She felt it was necessary for me, and so did my folks. I wasn't acting out when Morris-Lina had died, and my grades weren't slipping either. So I never really understood why it was so necessary for me to be in counseling when I was actually pretty okay. I mean, yeah, I got in a few fights, but I was fighting long before Morris-Lina had died. So, that can't be a reason either.

I guess I'll just never really know.

Counselor Malik adjusted his glasses as they sat perfectly on the bridge of his nose as he looked down at the stack of papers settled against his lap. I had given my journal to read through, but he placed it on the table and hasn't paid it much attention, which is pretty shocking. Usually, he'll be all over my journal entries, reading through them and then figuring out what to nip-pick me about. So, for him to not do that is strange.

Maybe because it's our last session together. I don't know.

But I'm not going to point it out to him either. The less talking about whatever I wrote in that damn journal, the better.

"So," Counselor Malik said, still looking through the papers on his lap, "are you still in need of my stress ball, or...?" He narrowed his eyes up to me, smirking.

I gulped. I honestly forgot that I had taken the stress ball from his office a while ago. I meant to give it back to him, but I thought if I held onto it a little longer, I'd find the right time to sneak it back into his office. The only reason why I took it was because of what he said about me wanting to stay "broken" that one time. It was stupid of me to just take the ball, thinking it would've mattered to him whether or not it was still in his office. But I wasn't thinking clearly. I was just so...angry? Hurt? I don't know. I was doing a lot of things that day.

I sighed and reached for my bookbag. As I unzipped the front pouch to my bookbag, Counselor Malik let out a low chuckle. I quivered my eyebrows, narrowing my eyes up to him.

He looked at me with great satisfaction as he twisted his lips into a grin and leaned back, propping his elbow upon the arm of the chair while pushing up his brow with his finger.

I lifted my head up, giving him my full attention while I mindlessly reached my hand inside my bookbag in search of the foam ball. Then, I asked him, "What?"

Counselor Malik pressed his lips together, shaking his head with a smile. He told me, "You can keep the ball, Donald. Consider it a parting gift."

I drew my hand out of my bookbag. "But, it's yours."

He nodded. "It is." He sat up. "But, clearly, you'll need it more than I will."

I quirked an eyebrow. "What do you mean?"

Counselor Malik flashed that unsettling smirk of his, which I'll never grow into liking since it always led to us talking about some deep, emotional shit that I never wanted to discuss. Still, I always ended up engaging in the conversation with him—not that I had a choice. If I never said anything, he'd probably hold me hostage until I finally caved in and cooperated. It wouldn't surprise me if he did attempt to do something like that. Counselor Malik was relentless.

I set my bookbag off to the side, and Counselor Malik set the papers in his laps on the table beside him. He laced his fingers together as if he was some kind of mastermind about to have his fun on toying with his test subject. He reminded me of some cartoon villain from the old shows I watched with Morris-Lina when we were kids on Saturday mornings. Geez.

I slumped back in my chair, ready to take whatever questions or "observations" he had about me since he thought I needed the stress ball more than I believed. But then, while looking me in the eye with a faint smirk stretched across his face, he asked me, "Why do you want to go to Europe for college?"

I furrowed my brows. "Hm?" It wasn't that I didn't understand the question. I just didn't know why he'd ask me something like that.

It's our last session together, and he now wants to know why I want to go to college in Europe? He could've asked me about anything else, but that's the direction he goes? Weird.

Counselor Malik sighed. "I was there with you when you sent out your college applications. Welmur's and Charleston were the only schools you applied to that were out of the country. You also applied to some good schools here. But you chose to attend school in Europe, not that I'm against it. I congratulate you."

"Thanks?" I get out, shrugging my shoulders.

"But I've read your journal entries, and quite often, you mention how your sister pushed you to go to school out of the States. So did your friends and other people who hold a lot of influence over you."

I don't get where he's going with this.

Yes, I did apply to some good schools in the US that offer programs specializing in what I want to do, but Welmur's and Charleston were the better options, and I ended up going with Welmur's. Anyone with half a gnat's brain would know that it's best to go somewhere that offers the best. Plus, the scholarship from Welmur's was better too, which was a sweet bonus.

I cleared my throat. "I mean," I started off, shrugging my shoulders, "yeah. Some people did have some input on where I should go for school, but isn't it like that with everyone when figuring out where to go for college?"

Counselor Malik shifted around his seat, trying to get comfortable. "Yes, but you often mention how everyone thought it would be best for you to go to school out of the US." A long pause as he clicked his pin, staring right at me with a deadpan face. "You never talked about what you wanted. And if you did, it was always about wanting to do what everyone else wanted you to do. Mainly your sister."

I swallowed hard.

I wish he'd stop mentioning her. I get that I'd often write about Morris-Lina in my journal, but he didn't have to bring her up whenever he had some kind of point to make. Although, there was no point needing to be made here.

I shook my head. "You're not making any sense," I mumbled, averting my eyes away from him. I pressed my lips together as I looked out the window.

Counselor Malik scoffed. "Donald, don't be like that."

I whipped my head around, clenching my jaw. "Like what?" I made sure to keep my voice low as I felt my blood starting to boil. I didn't want to blow up at him and give him the satisfaction of something being wrong.

"You know what I'm talking about," Counselor Malik said calmly.

I watched as he reached forward, picking up my journal from off the table. He sat back in his chair, adjusting his glasses as he flipped through the book with one hand. He was like a man on a mission, trying to find something to use against me. I could feel my heart pounding harder and harder in my chest as he flipped through the pages.

And finally, he stopped once he locked his sights on something I wrote.

"Here," he said, tapping his finger on the page. "You said, 'Moe always thought it was best for me to get out of here. I can't say I blame her. Maybe getting out of here would be best. It's what she would've wanted anyway. So how can I deny her of that.'"

Counselor Malik slowly drew his eyes up from the page to look at me. His gaze sent a shiver down my spine. My heart sank as he closed the journal, still keeping it settled on his lap. I remember the day I wrote that journal entry too. I was skeptical about going to school so far away from everything I knew here. I remember feeling anxious for the longest time since I didn't know whether or not it'd be a good idea. I would toss and turn at night, unable to sleep. It was a real pain in my ass. But then, I got over it. Once I realized that the idea of me going to Community College was ridiculous, I had pushed aside my doubts and decided to go big. That's all I knew how to think, anyway. I never knew how to think any less than that.

Besides, even if I went to Community College, I'd get bored. That's a fact.

But Morris-Lina did think going to school away would be good for me. And she was right. Once I got used to the idea, I was okay with it. Not because she had some hold over me. It's just…just…I don't know.

I couldn't look Counselor Malik in the eyes as I slumped back into my chair. Sure, I'd miss everyone here. Chris. Carmen. Pete. Benton. Meagan. My folks. But I was all taken care of. Once Christopher heard about me applying to schools in Europe, he was kind enough to hit up some of his folks overseas and convince them to let me stay with them, although I thought about living on campus. But I guess commuting wasn't a bad idea.

Christopher was all for it.

Everyone was all for it. I didn't want to…let them down.

I groaned to myself. Shit.

Counselor Malik cleared his throat to get my attention, which I gave him. He took off his glasses and settled them down on the table. He looked at me with a slight curl to the corners of his mouth. He said, "There's nothing wrong with wanting the best opportunities. But it has to be what you want, Donald. Because I'll tell you this, no matter how much you try to do or say all the right things, not everyone is going to be happy with you. And you can't determine the satisfaction of the dead because they're already at peace with things. As for living, we don't know how to be happy because we want to please others. That's why some people end up dying before they really get to live."

I felt my bones stiffen as a giant ball formed in my throat. I tried clearing my throat, hoping that would help eliminate the feeling, but it didn't. I just looked down at the ground.

Then, he added, "You're not superhuman, Donald. You can't satisfy everyone, even if you think so. If you want to go to Europe, go because you want to. Not because everyone is telling you. Because then, you won't enjoy it as much as you think."

I swallowed thickly.

As much as I wanted to dismiss Counselor Malik's words, my brain kept them on replay like a record player. I knew he was making some valid points, but the thing is, I don't mind going to school away from home. I don't mind the idea of being out of the States. I know it's not going to be easy, but it sure as hell beats trying to carry on here.

I sighed and nodded my head, not knowing what to say.

....

BEEP! BEEP! BEEP!

The timer on the stove rings rattles my eardrums, and I squint, trying to block out the sound. I snatch up the oven mitts lying on the kitchen counter and slip them on before opening the oven door. A massive blow of heat hits my face as I reach inside to retrieve the tray of freshly baked cookies, and I sigh.

I stand up straight and use my free hand to turn off the timer.

As I settle the tray of cookies down on the countertop, I hear footsteps coming towards the kitchen from the garage. I look up as I slip my hands out of the oven mitts.

Meagan lets out a huff, using her finger to push aside the loose strand of her hair that dangles over her eye.

I snicker. "You good, kid?"

She furrows her dark brows as she drags her feet into the kitchen.

"You could've told me that you kept the baking soda in the box by the garage door," she grumbles, making her way beside me. "I was searching all over, trying to find it. I thought you were messing with me."

I roll my eyes, turning my attention to the tray of sugar cookies I just finished baking. I carefully start to separate them on the tray.

"Honest to God, I only knew that it was in the garage," I admit. "If I knew where in the garage, I would've been more specific."

Meagan slams down the bag of baking soda, groaning. She presses her palms into the edge of the counter, hanging her head. "Well, as much cooking as you do, I don't see how you don't know where you keep your baking ingredients."

"Technically," I correct her, "I cook. Baking is a rarity for me." I smirk. "I'm only doing this upon personal request." I wink at her.

The corners of Meagan's mouth slightly curve upwards, and her eyes trail down to the tray of cookies. "Well, I appreciate you helping me out with this," she says softly. "You're sure you don't mind?"

I suck my teeth, shaking my head. "If I minded, I wouldn't have agreed, am I right?"

Meagan shrugs her shoulders, looking at the tray of cookies.

Today, it was only Meagan and me during lunch since everyone else was preparing for prom tonight. Meagan thought I was a fool for missing out on my senior prom, but I told her that I knew I wouldn't be missing out on much. Besides, I didn't have anyone to go to prom with. Although, Carmen and Christopher had been on my head constantly about asking Meagan to prom. But the girl simply didn't want to go. I wasn't going to pressure her. I respected her wishes, unlike them.

But, while we were at lunch, Meagan told me about Preston and someone named "Jordan Q." I think, coming up with an idea for a bake sale as an End of the Year Fundraiser for theater. Meagan was tasked with making cookies. Not bringing, actually making them since Preston believed that when it came down to fundraisers, *"homemade products sell faster than things from the stores unless they are condoms."*

Of course, Meagan was freaking out because she wasn't sure if she could make many cookies by herself. So, I offered her my help. And while I hate baking, I'd do it if it meant getting her to calm the hell down by taking some pressure off of her.

Plus, the idea of baking alongside Meagan didn't seem too bad.

My heart thumps loudly in my chest, and I gulp.

With how close Meagan is standing beside me, I wonder if she can hear my heartbeat. As much as I try to calm down the pace of my heart by taking slow breaths, nothing really helps.

I shake my head, letting out a sharp breath.

I turn my attention back down to the cookies on the tray as Meagan walks behind me. I make sure that I'm careful as I separate the cookies since they're fresh out of the oven, and I don't want to break them. The smell lingers along my nostrils, and I'm honestly tempted to eat at least one. But I resist. It's one thing if it's for me, but this is for Meagan. God forbid Preston is on her head for missing a single cookie with how insane he is about everything being precise.

I clear my throat, dusting my fingers together to get the sugar off my fingertips. I slip on an oven mitt before moving the tray into the dining room to rest on the wide metal plate at the center of the table under the fan. Once I place the tray down, I flick on the fan and adjust the setting, ensuring it isn't too high so the cookies can cool down properly.

"Donny," I hear Meagan say, and I look over my shoulder. "Can you tie me up?"

Meagan turns around, holding out the strings to the apron.

I nod, slipping off the mitt before making my way over to her. I feel my heart climb up my throat with each step I take.

Chill out, man. You don't want to seem like a weirdo.

I take a deep breath. I grab the strings to the apron from Meagan, and she keeps her arms across her chest as I loop the strings around her waist. I make the first knot and pull it.

"That's not too tight, is it?" I ask her.

Meagan slightly turns her head, hardly looking back at me. "It could be a little tighter," she replies.

I undo the first knot and try at it again. I take a small step forward to be closer to Meagan and make sure that the knot is a bit tighter than before. As I make a loop, I hear Meagan let out a shaky breath. I ask her if she's alright, and she nods.

I go back to tying her apron, and I tightly pull the knot in.

I hear her grunt.

"That's too tight?" I ask, concern surging through me, but I try to keep my voice relaxed.

Meagan nods. "Yeah, a bit."

I start to undo the knot again. "How about this?"

I take another step closer as my fingers lightly brush against her back as I undo the knot. I can feel Meagan's body stiffen as I stand behind her. The distance between us is thin as I concentrate on tying her apron. Meagan tries to straighten her posture, and my fingers make contact against her back from when she moves.

I lean in, letting my lips practically hover over her ear as I tell her in a low voice, "Hold still."

Meagan's body stiffens again as I draw my face back.

I finally manage to make a decent knot, and I slowly pull at it.

"How 'bout that one?" I ask, keeping my hands on the strings.

Meagan slightly lowers her head, taking a shaky breath. "Better."

I nod. "Alright." I draw my eyes back to the strings. "I'll do another one. Try to hold still this time."

"No promises." I can hear the smile in Meagan's words this time.

I smirk. "Don't be cute."

My fingers brush against her back as I make another knot, and I feel my throat tighten. I clench my jaw as I softly exhale through my nose, trying to concentrate.

I pull at the second knot, tightly securing it around Meagan's waist.

"Not too tight, is it?" I ask her.

She shakes her head. "All good."

Meagan drops her arms down to her sides and swiftly turns around. I feel my body stiffen when she practically presses up against me, but she doesn't do it intentionally. All she did was turn around, and I guess with how close we were, she slightly tripped forward. I look down at her. Her eyes look lighter than usual, and her lashes look longer, but I know that they're her natural lashes. Even though Meagan wears makeup, she's not the type to wear feather dusters for eyelashes. She has naturally long eyelashes. But maybe her mascara is making them look longer today. And she has her glossy lips slightly parted open as she lets out a sharp breath.

My heart feels like it's ready to burst as a newfound warmth shoots through me. My face feels warms, and I can only imagine how I probably look at her right now. I feel my chest tighten as I draw my hands back around her, bringing them to my sides.

I take a small step back and shift my eyes away from her.

Meagan also takes a small step back, and from the corner of my eye, I see her fold her arms over her stomach while looking down. For all I know, I probably made things weird for her. I didn't mean for us to end up being so close. If abuelo was here right now, he'd smack me upside the head with his bota. And maybe, just maybe, abuela would've hit me with her chancla.

Damn, damn, damn.

Meagan then mutters, "Thanks."

I draw my attention back to her, and she gently rocks on her heels, pressing her lips together in a faint smile while looking at me with soft eyes.

I clear my throat, folding my arms over my chest. "No problem, kid." I flash her a smile before I walk over to the sink.

I run the warm water over my hands, trying to get my nerves to settle down. It feels like I just gulped down twelve butterflies, and they're all fluttering around in the depths of my stomach. Honestly, if I could turn back the clock and smack some sense into myself, I would.

Get a grip, Donald. You're overthinking. Nothing happened.

If that were the case, then why is your heart still beating like a rabbit, jackass?

I swallow hard.

"Donny?" I hear Meagan say my name, and I turn around to face her. The sunlight that peers through the blinds shines on her brown eyes, making them glisten like diamonds. She asks me, "You alright?"

My heart pounds heavily in my chest as I take a sharp breath.

Say something, you friggin' weirdo, I demand myself.

A smirk tugs on the one side of my mouth.

"Yeah," I chuckle out. "Why wouldn't I be?"

Meagan twists her lips, shrugging her shoulders. "Just wanted to make sure." Her eyes look past me. "Um, the water," she points.

I quirk an eyebrow and follow the direction of her finger. When I turn around, I realize that water is still running, and the sink is nearly full since I have the drain plugged up. Quickly, I shut the water off and reached my hand into the sink to pull out the plug to the drain down the water.

Shit, I huffed to myself.

A deep gargle comes from the bowels of the sink as the water spins like a twister down the drain. Meagan steps up to the sink, looking down as the water slowly vanishes down the drain. I can't resist the urge to look at her as she stands there beside me.

Meagan keeps her lips in a straight line as she practically stands on her toes, looking down into the sink. She keeps her lips twisted to the one side of her mouth as if she's in full concentration mode. Kind of like how she gets when studying for a test or doing her assignments.

A low chuckle slips out from under my breath, and I press my lips together. But by the time I try to hide the sound, Meagan draws her eyes over to me, furrowing her eyebrows.

"What's so funny?" A small smile starts to tug at her lips.

I try loosening up my shoulders as I reach over for a paper towel to dry my hands. I honestly don't know why I laughed. I mean, I know why—she looked adorable, seeming so focused on watching the water go down the drain. It'd make anyone laugh.

I shake my head as I dry my hands with the paper towel. "Nothing."

I walk over to the trashcan and toss away the paper towel. I clap my hands together, swerving on my heels until I'm facing Meagan.

"Ready to whip up the next batch?" I arch an eyebrow, slightly tilting my head forward as I point to her.

Meagan rolls her eyes, leaning back against the counter while keeping her palms pressed into the edge of the countertop.

"You're way too excited about this, don't you think?" she asks me, trying to suppress the smile just itching to curl on her lips.

I shrug. "Someone has to keep the mood light, am I right?" I wink at her, clicking my tongue as I reach for a baking tray from the drawer underneath the stove.

. . . .

I keep my arm behind my head as a cushion between me and the soft arm of the couch as I lie back. Meanwhile, Meagan keeps her head rested on my chest while lying on top of me, barely on her side. She rests one of her hands under her head as a divider between her face and my chest. I let my free arm drape over her waist, and she doesn't move or make any indication that she minds, which brings me at ease.

We baked about three more batches of cookies until Meagan finally threw in the towel, insisting that we had more than enough. I honestly couldn't agree more. As we bagged the cookies up in threes in sandwich bags to put them in the fridge, Meagan was counting the cookies one-by-one. I think we ended up making like a hundred cookies.

She was satisfied, and so was I.

We cleaned the dishes, wiped down the counter, and put everything away before we decided to chill out for a bit. The idea of watching old episodes of *Allegiance Society* on my computer came to my mind as we sat quietly on the couch, not knowing what to do next. Meagan wasn't ready to go home, and honestly, I didn't really want to take her home just yet.

The rest of our friends are at prom, probably having the time of their lives, while the two of us are tired from baking and being on our feet. And my parents still weren't home—even though it is kind of early still. So, I suggested that we'd watch *Allegiance Society*. And now, here we are, stretched out on the couch, eyes glued to the computer screen as we watch episodes as if we've never seen them before. Although, Meagan is the one who's really into the show right now than I am.

I hardly get a thrill from re-watching shows or movies, especially if I've watched them about a dozen times because someone else wanted to. But, I was fine with re-watching a few episodes of *Allegiance Society*. It's the best show right now, and it's something Meagan and I love talking about whenever we have the chance.

It's also an excellent way to settle my anticipation for the new season premiering this summer. I haven't watched the official trailer yet, even though it's been out since January. Many things have been on my mind lately, and my urge to jump on the bandwagon in seeing the official trailer for the third season slipped my mind.

Sigh.

I hear my phone vibrate against the wood of the small square table near the side of the couch's arm, above my head. I lift my arm from under my head and reach for my phone. At the same time, Meagan reaches into her back pocket, pulling out her phone while keeping her head on my chest.

I click my phone screen awake and tap on the notification.

It's a message from Carmen in our squad group chat.

I unlock my phone and open up the message. As I'm scrolling down, Meagan lets out a chuckle while eyeing her phone and nuzzling her face against my chest.

I smirk, drawing my phone down so I can look at her. "What?"

Meagan looks up at me while keeping her head against my chest. "Carmen sent pictures of them at prom in the group chat."

I turn back to my phone and scroll down until I finally find the pictures Carmen sent. A smile tugs on the corners of my mouth as I look at all four pictures Carmen sent. The first two pictures are nice and formal.

The first one is of Carmen and Christopher doing a couples picture with a black and purple gradient sequin backdrop. Carmen wears a sleeveless turquoise gown that shapes her figure well, and the hem stretches down to the ground like a small tail at her feet. The front of her dress has a small slit, revealing her legs and her bedazzled open-toed heels. Her makeup makes her look like a princess with her light blue glittery smoky eyeshadow, her glossy lips in a perfect smile, and whatever she uses to make her cheekbones look so defined. Meanwhile, Christopher keeps his arms wrapped around her waist from behind while smiling at the camera. His hair is slicked back, and he wears a teal fitted suit with a black tie that he keeps tucked into the vest under his blazer and also wears black dress shoes.

In the second picture are Peter and Benton. Peter has his hair in long dreadlocks, but he keeps them pulled back in a ponytail, showing his fresh cut along the sides. He wears a burgundy blazer to match with his slacks and silky tie. He wears a black dress shirt tucked into his matching dress slacks. He also wears burgundy-colored dress shoes. I notice the thin gold watch he wears on his wrist, and he has his arm draped over Benton's shoulder with an eager smile. Benton wears his hair loose as it falls over his shoulders in slight waves. He wears a red suit with a white dress shirt underneath his buttoned blazer and a black tie with matching black dress shoes. He stretches his arm behind Peter, resting his hand on Peter's shoulder while smiling wide with crinkles by his eyes.

I check out the other two pictures, chuckling to myself at the ridiculous poses all four of them do together while using props.

"Looks like they're having a good time," I hear Meagan say against my chest.

I put my phone back in sleep mode and settled it back down on the table above my head. "They sure are." I go back to using my arm as a cushion as I settle my head back down on the arm of the chair.

I stare at the computer screen as the third episode of the second season of *Allegiance Society* plays, but I'm hardly focused on what's going on. My gaze lowers to

Meagan as she remains lying on top of me. She presses her lips together in a straight and settles her head back down on my chest. I notice the glossiness of her eyes and how her lips turn downward. I can tell by how she exhales through her nose that something is on her mind, but she keeps her eyes on the computer screen.

I tilt my head a bit, quirking an eyebrow. "You okay?"

Meagan just nods her head. "Mn."

I roll my eyes. "Don't lie to me. I know you all too well. If I gotta deck someone, then you know I'll do it."

"It's not that," Meagan mumbles, still facing the computer. Suddenly, I feel her fingers curl from under her head, clutching my shirt. Her body stiffens, and a quivering breath escapes her lips. "Call me a sap all you want, but I am going to miss you while you're away at college." She shifts around a bit while staying on top of me.

The way her words come out of her mouth, I'd expect her to be crying. But she stays strong. She tightens her grip on my shirt, still facing the computer. My heart sinks. I move my arm from behind my head and settle my hand on her back. I lift up my head to get a better look at her, but she refuses to look at me.

As I look at her, the fluttering in my stomach becomes unstoppable. I'd be a fool if I didn't finally accept that there are things about her that are impossible for me to resist liking. Like how childish she'll get when she runs out of things to say, and I get the last word. She'll even get real snappy one second but then be a softie the next. Or when she overthinks about something so simple, but then she'll immediately calm down once I assure her that everything is going to be okay. The way her eyes light up when she's talking about something she really likes, whether it's *Allegiance Society* or theater—it always makes my chest feel like it's caving in. But I don't mind the feeling. At least, not anymore.

Even now, as we lie on the couch, just chilling, my stomach starts to feel kind of funny, and my chest tightens. And as much as everyone insists on me doing something about it, I remember that I'm graduating and that I'll be attending college in Europe. Maybe in another universe, I would have done something about it because there would be a chance for something to come out of it in another universe. But it's something I've come to accept long before I submitted my deposit to attend Welmur's University.

I sigh.

"C'mon, kid," I say, still looking down at Meagan, even though she keeps her eyes glued to the computer screen. "You have nothing to—"

Before I can finish my sentence, Meagan pops her head up and whips it around, so she's looking me right in the eye. Sharply, she demands, "You better write to me. At least once." For a second, she seems taken aback by the way she spoke, and she cowers her head back down to my chest while poking her bottom lip out like a pitiful child. "Just once. Promise?"

I try biting down on my lip to prevent myself from laughing, but a giggle still manages to sip through. It's hard to not find humor in how childish she looks right now. From her big brown eyes to the way her bottom lip pokes out, and her face frowns up—of course, I'm going to laugh.

I lift my hand from off her back and gently pat her head. "One won't be enough for you," I grin. "We write to each other every other week and call it even. A'ight?" I move my hand off her head and hold up my pinkie for her to take.

Meagan chuckles softly. She lifts up her head, moving her hand so she can lock her pinkie with mine. "Bet."

A smile tugs on my lips.

Just then, the front door swings open, pulling my and Meagan's attention away from each other and to the direction of the door. My mom lets out a huff, coming in through the door first while my dad stays behind her. As soon as dad closes the door behind him, mom kicks off heels, groaning.

"Donald! Estamos en—!" As soon as my mom turns around, she freezes when she spots us. Dad turns around after hanging up his coat in the closet and doesn't move. He just stares right at Meagan and me.

I remain still while Meagan pushes herself up off of me. She tries to laugh everything off as she sits up, keeping her eyes on my parents, who continue to stare at us as if they just walked in something inexcusable. Knowing them, they're probably assuming that Meagan and I were in the middle of something, which is far from the truth. I sit up, swinging my legs over the edge of the couch cushion.

I clear my throat, covering my mouth with the back of my hand.

"Mom. Dad," I say, looking between the both of them as I remain seated on the couch.

With much hesitation, Meagan chimes in, "Mister Gonzalez. Missus Gonzalez." I narrow my eyes to her hands as she starts picking at her the skin of her fingertips.

I gently nudge my knee against hers to get her to stop. She does.

My mom clears her throat and straightens her posture. "Meagan," she greets with a warm smile. "Nice to see you again."

Dad nods. "Yes, very nice to see you again."

A slight head nod from Meagan.

I swallow thickly. *This is weird.*

Though it is brief, the silence becomes unbearable. I feel my skin starting to crawl the longer I sit on the couch, trying to dodge making any form of eye contact with my parents. My mom opens her mouth to say something, but Meagan uses the silence as her cue to get up and suggest for her to head home.

"It is getting pretty late, and I have to keep the cookies cool for Monday," she says, keeping her hands clasped together. As I stand up from the couch, Meagan playfully nudges her arm against mine. "Thanks again for helping me out with the cookies."

I smirk. "It was no problem at all. Besides, you would've been tired out by the second batch," I joke.

Meagan rolls her eyes, holding a slight grin on her lips. "I've come to terms that it's okay to be tired sometimes. It's part of living and being human." I then hear her mumble under her breath, "Unfortunately," before walking past me to get the bags of cookies from the fridge.

I call out to her, "I'll be outside for you," and I walk over to the closet to put on my jacket. As I'm opening the closet door, my mom creeps up on me from behind and taps my shoulder. I look at her. She has a ridiculous smile on her face that sends a wave of confusion and terror rushing through my body.

"What?" I quirk an eyebrow.

Mom leans in, pressing her lips tightly together in a smirk. *"Soooo?"* mom coos with way too much enthusiasm as she keeps her voice low, "When did all this start between the two of you? I always thought she was a nice girl."

I groan, throwing my head back and shutting my eyes.

Oh, God.

"Mom," I sigh.

Mom shakes her head and grabs my shoulders. "Wait," she goes, eyes wide, "it's not anything like…." She looks to my dad as if she's begging for assistance. "…what is it called? 'F-W-B'? Is that what's going on with you two? It's not, is it?"

I can hardly wrap my head around anything she's saying as she throws a million questions my way over something that is a misunderstanding. I can't even believe she'd consider Meagan and me being Friends With Benefits. No way in hell would I let that happen. I don't do that shit, and I know damn well that Meagan doesn't either. But I can't get a word in to shut down mom's ridiculous theories because she rambles on faster than an ongoing freight train.

Then, finally, dad steps in and starts pulling mom away from me.

"Luciana, please," he urges her, keeping his tone relaxed and low. "Let the boy breathe. I'm sure if something was happening between him and his friend, he'd tell us."

Thank you!

"Plus, our son is a gentleman. If he knows what's good for him," dad cheekily grins, looking at me. He leans in close to my ear. "You've been using protection, right, son?"

WHAT THE FU—?!

I grit my teeth and widen my eyes. "For the love of all that is Holy, stop!" I hiss at them while keeping my voice low enough for only them to hear me. "Please, just stop, alright! Nothing is happening between the two of us! She's just a friend!"

Mom crosses her arms over her chest, slightly tilting her head to the side. "But you're blushing," she points out. "And friends don't lie on the couch together like that, honey."

I feel my cheeks burn as I shake my head.

It's the twenty-first century. Friends cuddle all the time.

"Just forget it," I grumble as I snatch my jacket off the hanger.

Meagan walks in with two plastic shopping bags full of the cookies we baked in sandwich bags. I waste no time and take a bag from her. Meagan opens her mouth to protest, but I shake my head, telling her that I got it.

I quickly open the door and check my jacket pocket to make sure I have my car keys....

And I do.

I guide Meagan out of the house as she wishes my parents goodnight. And, of course, they wish her the same. But I hastily slam the door shut just to make sure that is all they have a chance to say to her.

Week 2, Sunday

I sit at my desk, tapping the end of my pencil to the blank page of my journal. The evening sunlight pierces into my room from behind me, aiding the dim light from the lamp on my desk. Silence fills my room, and I lean back in my seat, still tapping away at the blank page.

I know there's no point in writing in this thing anymore. I had my last counseling session with Counselor Malik the previous week. But before I left, he suggested that I'd write one final letter to myself as a reflection of my progress this year and I what I want out of my future—whatever that means. Even though I told him that I'd consider it, I didn't actually want to follow through with it. The only reason why I ever wrote in this damn journal was that he would always read whatever I wrote. Our counseling sessions are over, and I'm set to graduate on Wednesday, so there's no need for me to worry about some kind of self-reflection and my future expectations.

I already have that stuff sorted out, and I know it's not going to be easy. Hell, nothing in this life is, but that doesn't mean I'm going to lower the bar for myself. I made this far anyway, and not a lot of people expected that out of me.

I drop my pencil on the desk and run my hands down my face, groaning. I don't even know why I considered doing this. Counselor Malik will never know if I've actually done it or not, so what's the point?

I sigh.

I lean forward, sitting up at my desk with my arms folded on top. My eyes shift over to the folded piece of paper sticking out from under my textbooks, and I swallow thickly. I lift up my textbooks and pick up the paper, unfolding it. An odd feeling of knots starts to twist in the pit of my stomach as I skim down Alejandro's letter. I've thought about tossing it away a few times, but I still hold onto it. I don't know why. I guess, maybe, I just can't let go of the fact that I'll never see him again.

I doubt I'll see him again. And I'm fine with that.

Still, I can only imagine where he'll end up going. It was a spontaneous move, him leaving without having a clear plan on where to go.

A chuckle comes up in my throat.

Only Alejandro, I think to myself as I fold up the paper, setting it back down on my desk and under my textbooks.

I whip my attention over to my phone as a familiar ringtone comes from it all of a sudden. I don't even bother checking the name because I already know who is calling.

I answer the phone, putting it to my ear. "Yo."

"Hey," Christopher says on the other line. "You busy right now?"

I shake my head. "Just fiddling with my fingers, wasting energy."

Christopher snorts. "Sounds lame. Even for you, Gonzalez."

"Touché, Duncan."

As I lean back in my seat, Christopher asks me if I'd be down meeting him at the sandlot in about a half-hour.

I smirk, sitting up. "I'm guessing I should bring that pitching machine you gave me, huh?"

I can tell Christopher is smirking through his words. "Why not?"

I tell him that I'll meet him in about a half-hour, and we end the call. Honestly, going to the sandlot for a couple swings doesn't sound like such a bad idea. It certainly beats being stuck at home, contemplating on whether or not I should actually attempt to do a self-reflection. If anything, I've reflected on myself enough during my sessions with Counselor Malik. Hearing him critique every little thing I wrote in that damn journal was enough for me to realize that I need more days on the sandlot than off.

It's the perfect stress reliever.

I throw on a pair of jeans and a white tee-shirt, tucking the shirt in. Even though it's a bit warm outside, I know it will get cool as the sun goes down, and Lord knows how long Christopher and I will spend out there. So, I throw on a gray flannel, cuffing the sleeves up to my elbows, and I leave the shirt open. I sit down on my bed to put on my black and white converse when there's a knock at my bedroom door.

I lift my head as I reach for my sneakers. "Yeah?"

The door opens, and dad takes a small step inside, leaning against the doorway with his arms crossed over his chest.

"Hey," he sighs, looking down at me.

I sit up while slipping on my sneakers. "Hey."

Dad clears his throat. "Your mom is going to cook chicken over rice for dinner, so I'm going to the store now. Is there anything you need?"

I shake my head. "No, I'm good."

I can barely look him in the eye. Dad never comes to my room. For anything. It's always been that way. If there's ever anything he needs from me, he'll just call me from downstairs and tell me to come to him for something. Even if it's for something small, he'll just call out for me. He never comes to me.

I can already feel my pulse soaring as I tie my shoelaces, and dad has his eyes on me. He asks me where I'm going, and I tell him about my plans to meet up with Christopher at the sandlot, but I assure dad that I'll be home by dinner time. The last thing I need is for mom to get fussy about me missing out on dinner since we always try to have dinner together on Sundays.

I stand up from my bed and retrieve my car keys from my desk. I check to make sure I have my phone…

And I do.

Dad flashes a half-smile and steps aside so I can walk by.

I nod my head. "See you, dad."

Just as I'm walking out of my room, dad gently grabs my arm, stopping me in my tracks. I look at him, furrowing my eyebrows. His eyes are soft when he looks at me, and I can tell he's in deep thought on whatever it is he has to say. He opens his mouth to speak but then shuts it.

"Dad, what is it?" I ask, giving him my full attention.

Dad shakes his head, slipping his hand off of me. "Nothing," he clears his throat. "It's just…." He averts his eyes from me, looking down. A sigh. "I know that you hear your mother and I fight sometimes." He looks right at me this time. "And I know that it kind of makes you feel a certain way, as it should."

I take a sharp inhale. I have no idea where he is going with this, and part of me does not want to find out. As much as I can't stand them fighting, I try not to make it super apparent how much it frustrates me. Especially during the week when I have tests coming up and sleep is a necessity to focus.

"Dad—"

"No," dad cuts me off. "Just listen to me. Okay, son?" There is much demand in his words, but he tries to keep his voice low as if he's trying to speak to me softly.

I stuff my hands into the pockets of my jeans and nod.

He assures me that every fight between him and mom has nothing to do with me or what happened to Morris-Lina. I feel a tug in my throat at the sound of her name coming from his mouth. It doesn't bother me, but it hits differently hearing my dad say her name. It's as if he feels awful bringing her up, but he's okay with mentioning her.

As much as I want to cut dad off and tell him that there's no need for him to explain things between him and mom, I keep my mouth shut as he talks. If I even dared myself to interrupt him again, I know that he'll raise his voice. Even if he has good intentions, he'll get stern, and I do not want to face that wrath right now.

Then, after taking a deep breath, dad tells me, "Recently, your mother and I started going to counseling."

I wrinkle my eyebrows. "What?"

Dad nods, standing up straight. "Honestly, your mother wanted us to have this talk with you while sitting down at dinner tonight, but I didn't want it to seem like an ambush on you with that kind of setup."

I feel a ball start to form in my throat.

I mean, I know my parents have been fighting a lot, but I always thought they would've worked things out on their own. Like they used to. Plus, abuelo never believed in marriage counseling. Abuelo would always share his thoughts on marriage counselors, calling them *"manipuladores maestros"* since he felt that all they ever did was make couples feel like shit for having arguments while creating more problems in the marriage.

"Couples should sort stuff out on their own," abuelo would say. *"And anyone who charges an arm and a leg for something that is meant to be between partners is a thief! Malditos sean esos ladrones! Todos son animales! Oyes!"*

Abuelo is probably turning in his grave now that his own son is seeing a marriage counselor. I tightly press my lips together in a straight line. The irony.

Dad starts to talk about how good their therapist is for him and mom, and they started seeing the guy two weeks ago.

My eyes widen.

TWO WEEKS?!

This has been going on for two weeks, and *now* is the time they want to tell me?!

What a way to keep me in the loop of things. But still, as shocked as I may be, I'm not upset about it. In fact, I'm actually kind of…proud? I guess? For them to actually go see someone about their problems rather than let their problems continue to build takes a lot of balls and guts.

I mean, it took me how long to finally sit down have a civil conversation with Counselor Malik? Even though that wasn't under my free will, it took a lot of guts to talk to him sometimes. So, I can imagine how much time and willpower it took for my parents to go see someone about their marriage. But knowing them, my parents probably didn't know how to tell me about it, which is why they kept it from me. Although, two weeks is a long time.

I sigh. "Dad, please," I finally manage to butt in. I put my hand on his shoulder and looked him in the eye. "It's okay." I keep my voice straight as dad looks at me with his eyes getting glossy, but not a single tear sheds. I assure him, "We'll be okay."

He tightly presses his lips together, smiling.

"I know, son."

He gently grabs the back of my neck, stroking his thumb against my hair. I swallow thickly as I press my lips together, letting the corners of my mouth slightly curve upward.

Dad slips his hand off of me and steps aside. "Well, I won't hold you. I know how antsy you and Christopher get when one of you isn't somewhere as planned," dad says. He walks past me and heads to the steps, but before he goes downstairs, he reminds me, "Don't be late for dinner, understand? And this stays between us."

I nod my head. "Yes, sir."

I wait for dad to be downstairs before I head down. I hear dad leave the house as I make my way to the garage. A million thoughts start running through my mind. It isn't like dad to act so…soft…around me. And it's unlike him to go against mom's wishes and spill things to me without her being present. But he does have a point. Mom telling me about them going to marriage counseling during dinner would've felt like an ambush. It's like the worse move to make and such a typical way of breaking any sort of news to someone—especially when it is bad news. Although, I don't really consider this bad news.

At least they're not fighting as much as before.

I'm not saying that every night has been a blissful sleep, but at least I can sleep and not be an insomniac because of their arguing.

Once I'm in the garage, I unlock my car and open the backdoor. I already know that it's going to be a pain in the ass getting this pitching machine in the car as I push forward the front passenger's seat to make more room for the machine. I use my strength to pick up the machine and get it into my car. Once I manage to fit it in the back of my car, I strap it in place, so it's not moving around as I drive, but with how tight the space is, there's no chance of that happening. But I still strap it in place to be on the safe side.

I shut the back door before getting into the driver's seat. I let out a sigh as I start the engine, and I feel my phone vibrate in my pants pocket. I check the notification and arch my eyebrow when I see it's a message from Yoselin. I think. Today is her day off, so she should be home with the boys. I doubt she'll want me to come over to babysit them unless she got called into work last minute, which I doubt since her work hours are often in her favor.

I unlock my phone and click on the message. It's a video, and the face I see on the thumbnail is a blurred-out Yago.

I press the PLAY button.

In the video, Yago wears an apron that hangs low on him since he's so tiny. Gabriel is beside him, and he too wears an apron that hardly protects his clothes since he's so tiny. I don't know why Yoselin didn't get them aprons that fit, but whatever.

Yago stirs up a giant bowl of what looks to be flour, milk, and eggs while Gabriel watches with a giant, toothy grin on his face. Yoselin asks the boys what they are making, and Yago eagerly responds, "Conchas!" while stirring.

"How do you know how to make conchas?" Yoselin smiles through her words as she films Yago stirring up ingredients.

"Cousin Don-O taught us," Yago says, not lifting his eyes from the bowl.

Yoselin focuses the camera on Gabriel and asks him, "Do you guys like it when cousin Donald comes over? He takes care of you and shows you how to make things?"

A nod from Gabriel with a smile.

The video ends the boys laughing as Yago hands the wooden spoon to Gabriel to get a crack at stirring.

A faint chuckle gets past my lips. I remember the day I showed the boys how to make conchas, even though I didn't intend to conduct a baking tutorial. I was babysitting the boys, and they just waltzed into the kitchen as I was getting the stuff prepared to make them some kind of dessert. Of course, Yago was all over me, going, *"What are you making? What are you making? What are you making?"*

I told him, *"Conchas."*

"Can we see? Can we see?" Yago bounced on the balls of his feet with much enthusiasm.

I didn't want to risk the boys being in the way and getting hurt, but I couldn't say "no" to them. They pulled the classic *"kiddy-pup eyes"* on me. I hated that. But I ended up letting them watch me bake anyway.

The conchas I made didn't come out as rich as when abuela would make them, which is why I can't stand baking. But the boys liked them, and that was all that mattered to me.

I shake my head, snorting a chuckle as I think back to that day.

I slip my phone back into my pants pocket before starting the engine and backing out of the garage. Once I make it out to the driveway, I pull down the garage door from the outside and lock it. I get back into my car, turn on the radio to some random music station, and drive out into the street. I crank up the radio a bit and roll down my window, letting the spring breeze circulate through my car as I drive to the sandlot.

....

Christopher beats me there, which doesn't surprise me. Whenever he makes plans for anything, he's always the first one to show up. Plus, it's the sandlot. It's not that far from my house, which is why he always clowns me whenever I show up after him.

One of these days, I'll beat him in getting to the sandlot first.

One day, I swear to myself.

As I park my car, Christopher stands up off of his and takes a few steps forward towards mine. I turn off the engine and get out of the car. Christopher doesn't even give me the chance to shut the door before he clowns me.

"Oi, I was getting scared that yeh got lost," he snickers.

I roll my eyes. "Put a sock in it, Chrissy." I wink, and immediately, the look on Christopher drops as he scolds me while flipping me off. I snicker, raising my hands up defensively. "Hey, you started it."

Christopher scoffs. "Oh, don't pull that card." He opens the back passenger's door to my car while I remain on the driver's side. "Quit being a prick, and let's get this thing out here, yeah?"

I snort. "Sure, *I'm* the prick," I mutter as I open the back door on the driver's side.

Christopher unstraps the machine, and we manage to wiggle and lift the machine out of the car without making a dent or a ding. Christopher lets out a grueling breath and slams my car door shut.

I whip my head to him. "Yo! Watch my door!" I snap at him as I *gently* shut the back door on my end. Meanwhile, Christopher just settles his hands on his lips, taking another breather while giving me a deadpan look. I roll my eyes.

Christopher helps me carry the machine to center field before running back to his car to retrieve the baseball bat and the bag of baseballs in his car's trunk. I start setting up the machine as Christopher makes his way over to me.

I smirk. "You know, even though this is technically mine now, we could switch off, and this bad boy can always go home with you."

Christopher snorts. "The whole point of you having it so my old man can stop complaining about it taking up space." He puts down the bag of baseballs and hands me the bat once I'm done setting up the machine on the pitcher's mound.

I watch as Christopher loads up some baseballs into the machine, and while he does, my mind goes back to the night at the warehouse. Even though we've kissed and made up and everything is in the past, I know some of the things we said to each other still lingers in Christopher's head. It does in mine. And I know that whatever thoughts Christopher had about Alejandro still remain, even though he has no clue about Alejandro leaving.

There were a few times when I wanted to tell Christopher about Alejandro leaving for good. He would probably sing songs of sweet relief. But I also know that he would've been worried about how I felt about everything. But I was fine. Sure, I was stunned at first, but I'm all good now. I really am.

Christopher suddenly asks me if I'm ready for the first pitch. His eyes lock on me as he raises his eyebrows.

I clear my throat. "Yeah," I tell him. "Good to go."

I turn on my heels to head to the home plate when Christopher grabs my wrist, and I freeze. I look over my shoulder, meeting Christopher's eyes as they suddenly glisten from the evening light. He gives me a look while arching an eyebrow and slightly tilting his head forward.

I roll my eyes. God, I hate that look.

"Would you stop looking at me like that?" I groan, yanking my wrist free from his grasp.

Christopher folds his arms, arching an eyebrow. "Could you stop looking like that, then?"

"Like what?"

"Like you have something on your mind but are too much of a dunce to come out with it."

I snort. "Sure, I'm the dunce. Says the guy who looked like a washed-out blue troll," I tease, referring to one of the photos Carmen sent in the group chat of when they were at prom, doing ridiculous poses. Benton, Peter, and Carmen used props like glasses and posters, while Christopher threw on a blue wig that practically covered his face, and he was crouched down like some kind of deformed creature.

Even Christopher has to admit that it was a ridiculous photo of him. Instead, he rolls his eyes, shaking his head. I chuckle and lightly punch his arm. "Lighten up. You know I'm just teasing," I grin as I keep the baseball bat down by my side. "At least you guys had quite a time, huh?"

Christopher nods, poking his lips out. "Yeah." He stands on his toes and rocks back down on his heels while taking a sharp inhale through his gritted teeth. "It would've been even more of a delight if you and Meagan had been there." *Here we go.* "You could've asked her, you know? It's not like Donald Gonzalez to not take a chance."

I sigh, crossing my arms over my chest. I shift my gaze down to the ground as I rock on my heels. I know he's just saying all this and giving me ideas as a way of looking out for me. And it's not like I'm running away from how I feel if that's what he thinks. I've accepted my feelings, and I'm sure that if things were a bit different— if I wasn't going to college overseas, or if I was a sophomore like Meagan—I would've taken my shot with Meagan. But who knows what the end result would've been down the line. Especially once we graduated.

Although, I'm sure she and I will keep in touch. It's what she wants, and I'm more than happy to deliver.

The memory of when I was picking out her bracelet for her birthday resurfaces in my mind, and the woman's words echo in my head.

"Is she your soulmate?"

A low chuckle.

If I wasn't so flustered back then, I probably would've said, *"Yes."* Even if it wasn't as a lover.

I sigh and respond to Christopher, "No, he isn't. But believe it or not, he at least knows when to draw the line and think realistically to prevent some kind of fallout in the end." I shrug.

Christopher arches an eyebrow and presses his lips into a thin straight line. "It really doesn't sound good hearing you talk about yourself in third-person, mate."

A shiver runs down my spine. "Ugh, I know." I sound like a politician.

Christopher snickers and looks down, scraping the front of his sneaker into the dirt. "But seriously," he says before lifting his gaze, "what's on your mind? I know you."

I arch my eyebrow and pull the one side of my mouth into a smirk. I lean close to him, "Or so you think."

Christopher sucks his teeth. "Come on, Don. I'm serious."

I sigh.

I try to think of something off the top of my head just to get Christopher off my back, but all I think about it is Alejandro, which does no one anyone good. He's ultimately out of the picture, so why should I even bring him up? Scratch that completely.

I keep on thinking.

"Is it Alejandro?" Christopher abruptly asks.

Are you friggin' kidding me?!

Peter has always suspected that Christopher had some type of power to read minds, but I never took him seriously. Turns out, the son of a bitch was right. Still, even though he was right on the nose, Christopher shouldn't have to worry about Alejandro anymore. And neither should I. In a way, though I wish him well, I'm free from Alejandro Reyes. And the best thing about it is that Alejandro gave me that freedom himself.

I walk around Christopher, throwing my arm around his neck while pulling him in closer to me. He looks at me with eyebrows wrinkling in confusion, and I grin.

"We're good," I tell him. "Trust me."

Christopher sharply breathes. "Does that mean——?"

"It's all in the past," I assure him, letting both corners of my mouth slightly curve upward. "Besides, certain things are more important than others." I raise my eyebrows, pointing to him as if I just had an 'aha!' moment. "Like graduation."

Christopher clicks his tongue while pointing to me in agreement. "Yeah, that's a big deal." He jokingly gasps. "Oh, and college!"

"Pfft! Oh, yeah," I nod, smirking as I go along with him. "That's *huge*. We can't be getting distracted from that."

"I couldn't agree more," Christopher winks.

I chuckle lightly while looking down at the ground. The fact that graduation is finally coming our way starts to sink in, and the idea of us attending different schools makes my heart skip a beat. I swallow down the lump forming in my throat as I envision the three of us--me, Christopher, and Carmen--walking up on stage to receive our diplomas. In a way, it's like poetic justice because I'm basically giving everyone the finger without actually doing it. But at the same time, it's like...*damn*. But at the same time, nothing can keep us completely apart. Especially not forever.

"We did it," I softly breathe, lifting my head up.

I feel Christopher's arm come around me as he rests his hand on my shoulder, pulling me into him a bit. He pats my shoulder.

"Yeah," he sighs out, looking forward at the open space before us. "Yeah, we did. Kind of crazy, don't you think?"

I shrug. "Eh. We're not hopeless, you know?"

Christopher tilts his head. "Perhaps. Maybe it's just luck."

"You did always say we were lucky."

Christopher shakes his head, wagging his finger at me. "Nooo, I said *you* were lucky." He draws his arm off of me, and I roll my eyes.

He always said I was lucky, but he has to admit that he's fortunate to have made it through the hellhole for four years. I'm not saying that high school was all bad things and nothing more. It does have its good parts, like all things. But my God, it's not something I'd ever want to boast about.

I check the time on my phone when I realize the sky is getting dark. I groan when I know I have to be home in about an hour, which doesn't give us much time to get a few swings in. Well, it doesn't give *me* much time to get a few swings in. Christopher is still reluctant to give himself a shot at home plate with the bat. But I have all summer to convince him to grow some balls and have a crack at the bat. At least until I have to fly off to Europe and give myself time to settle in Wales before school starts.

But until then, I have nothing to worry about since we'll make it possible for us to have all the time in the world.

I stand at the home plate and get into position. I tell myself to relax as Christopher starts up the machine, and I exhale. I can see the smile forming on his face as the first ball comes flying at me. I swing, and we both watch as the ball goes flying to the far end of the field.

I smirk. *Nailed it.*

THE END.

ACKNOWLDGEMENTS

I am going to be upfront and admit that I did not think this book would be possible. Many nights, I debated whether or not to go through with it and move on from *We, pEOPLE*. And yet, the love that was received from the first book encouraged me to take the characters' stories to the next level! And for that, I am truly grateful and am so glad that I went through with this story.

First and foremost, I would like to thank God for blessing me with the love and support I have received after publishing the first book, *We, pEOPLE*. And also, for laying the idea of *Depend on Me* on my heart. Without trusting in Him, I am honestly not sure if I would have pushed myself to write this book in the first place.

Next, I would like to thank my family for always supporting me in all of my endeavors. There would be times where I would be up late hours, still writing, and my family would get on me about getting proper sleep. But still, they knew that it would lead to something great in the end. I would also like to thank my friends who were by my side during this journey and kept me inspired and encouraged.

And finally, I would like to thank *you* most of all for being the incredible person you have always been. It probably seems typical to say, "you have no idea how much your support means to me," but it is true. Words cannot describe how grateful I am for the encouragement and love I have received from various readers. I may sound like a sap, but believe me when I say that if it weren't for you guys, I would have no motivation to produce the content that I do. And from the bottom of my heart, I thank you, and I encourage you to never turn away from your dreams—no matter how odd, complex, or impossible they may seem. God bless, and in the words of Donald Gonzalez: I'd bet my car on you, kid.

ABOUT THE AUTHOR

Born and raised in Philadelphia, Pennsylvania, Amaris I. Manning has lived with a cardiac condition called Prolong QT Syndrome since she was born. She spends most of her days listening to a variety of music and writing stories while taking on the world's craziness. As a teenager, she was a fanfiction enthusiast and even wrote some of her own and received an extensive range of followers on multiple writing platforms. Amaris always craved sharing stories for all types of people. The romantics, the adventurous, the weird, the mysterious, and even those who enjoy a variety. Amaris also enjoys storytelling by creating her short films, both live-action and animated, aside from writing. She is also an artist and sells her artwork on her website, www.amarisimanning.com.

*If you enjoyed reading this story, please consider reviewing it
and recommending it to other readers. Thank you!*